The Wanderer's Notebook Volume III

By Christopher Emrys

Cover Design & Artwork by YoyoDeng

Contents

The Wanderer's Notebook Volume III

I

Discovery
Niwltir, +197 ER

The wood elf crouched on a tree branch high over the snow, examining the wide, flat footprints with long claw marks below. The air stood cold and still. He scanned the details of the tracks and their path through the forest. This far north in the new elvish homeland, the forest was beginning to thin as it approached the foot of the mountains. The trees in this new land tended to be several feet thick and very tall, like the forests in which he had grown up. Nearer the mountains, they began to diminish in size and became more spread out. He would not be able to stay in the trees for much longer and would need to track on foot. This was not the preferred method of the wood elves who favored traveling branch to branch to stay above their prey and to avoid leaving tracks that predators could follow.

Ymladdwr stood and gazed into the distance with his mist-grey eyes that had whisp-like traces of yellow-brown in them. His hair was brown and tied back, exposing his pointed ears to the cold air. His clothes were mostly leather dyed in shades of green and brown. He carried several knives and pouches on his belt, a large quiver on his back, some rope, and a bow in his hand.

The elf followed the trail as best he could through the tops of the trees until they became too thinly dispersed. With a sigh, he stepped off the branch and dropped to the ground, knees bending as he landed in a crouch.

After walking for several minutes, the wood elf could begin to detect unusual animal noises. They sounded like snorts and grunts interspersed with occasional loud cracks. His eyes scanned ahead until he found the source of the sounds. Silently he moved between the trunks, using the now more common bushes and large rocks for cover as the forest faded away.

Up ahead, on a long flat area of stone and rocks lounged several large horned bears. These lean animals had small, stub-like horns protruding from their foreheads. A few yards away, two larger ones with long, curling horns were backing away from each other. After some instinctive distance was achieved, the two males lowered their heads and rushed straight at each other. Their horns slammed together with a loud crack, and they pulled apart with snorts and grunts. This continued for several minutes before one of the horned bears decided he had lost the contest and turned away, trudging up into the mountains. At this, the triumphant male returned to his pack.

Ymladdwr had not seen such creatures before in their previous homeland. He waited and watched as the animals continued to lounge around on the rock-strewn ground. The wood elf wondered what such animals ate and was eager to continue deeper into the mountains to see what else he might find.

Sensing unseen danger, Ymladdwr turned in time to see another, smaller, male horned bear stalking up on him from behind and to the side. Turning quickly, he drew an arrow, nocked it, and aimed at the creature.

The horned bear paused, then decided it did not care that it had been seen by its prey. The beast lunged at the wood elf and Ymladdwr released his arrow before diving to his right. The arrow went straight down the horned bear's throat, tearing through its internal organs. It landed with a thud where the elf had been crouching.

Much to the elf's surprise, it was not actually dead yet, though blood gushed from its mouth and rage filled its eyes. The creature staggered to its feet and turned its head toward Ymladdwr. In quick succession, Ymladdwr put two more arrows into its neck. The beast let out a mournful howl, tried to rush him, but crashed into the ground.

Growls and snorts answered the howl, and Ymladdwr looked to see the rest of the pack moving in his direction. They had seen him.

The wood elf spun on the spot and ran back toward the trees. He could hear the pursing paws on the ground as they ran after him. As soon as he reached a larger tree, he ran up the side a couple steps, grabbed the lowest branch, and pulled himself up. It was more difficult to climb back up with his bow still in his right hand, but he managed to do it with his free left hand and a couple fingers of his right. Ymladdwr put his arm through his bow, so that the string lay across his chest with the bow around his back, and climbed higher.

The elf turned and watched the horned bears approach. The lead male did not stop when he came to the base of the large tree. Instead, he began to climb toward the elf.

Ymladdwr turned and began climbing to the next branch. When he found one going in the direction of a nearby tree, he ran along the branch and jumped to another on the neighboring tree.

There was an angry annoyed snort, and the horned bear dropped back to the ground, catching up quickly with the others who had followed the elf to his new tree.

Ymladdwr began to run from tree to tree, the horned bears keeping pace with him below. The forest was getting denser, but was still thin at this point, so he was forced to take the first path available, leading him more west than south, roughly parallel with the mountains. Suddenly the trees ended, and Ymladdwr found himself facing a clearing with a large stone structure in the middle. A raised stone dais with four outward facing gryphons and three inward facing sphinxes stood before him.

The wood elf looked to his right, then to his left. The horned bears were climbing all the trees to either side of his on the edge of the clearing. The scraping of claws below made him consider turning back altogether, but even the trees behind him were now occupied.

The horned bear beneath him was almost to his level. Ymladdwr ran out and launched himself toward the stone statues below. He landed on the head of a stone gryphon, scrambling to pull his bow free as he ran down its back and toward the structure's center. He could hear the creatures dropping back to the ground behind him. He would not be able to outrun the bears, and he was not sure he could kill them fast enough to survive.

Arrow nocked, the wood elf faced the pack and prepared himself for the attack. Much to his surprise, the horned bears stopped just outside the ring of gryphons. The lead male eyed the gryphons, then glared at the elf. It let out a loud bellow, stared at the elf balefully, then turned and sauntered away into the forest. The others waited a few seconds, then followed. Slowly, the elf lowered his bow.

*　　　*　　　*

4

Gwyddoniaeth awoke to the gentle caress of the breeze as it drifted through her window. She opened her eyes to reveal mist-grey irises that had whisp-like traces of red-orange. Her long black hair was spread out around her on the pillow. Closing her eyes, she took a deep breath of the cool, moist fresh air and stretched. The sensations were pleasant to her relaxed and well-rested mind and body.

The high elf sat up and went about washing and dressing herself. The room was mostly baren, with a simple bed on one side and a table covered in pens, ink, books, and paper on the other. She clothed herself in her typical attire of a tabard over her tunic and trousers. Returning to the table, she sorted through the papers and books, gathering what she needed for the day's tasks.

Gwyddoniaeth's room was in a tower in the midst of an elaborate elvish city that was currently being constructed in the heart of the continent's main forest. The high elves had desired to craft new structures to replace their lost mountain citadel. The heart of the forest lacked any mountains, but it did possess the intersection of two rivers and was roughly centrally located in the new elvish homeland.

The towers, carved from the outside to resemble trees with vines wrapped around them, were several hundred feet tall, but still not as tall as the trees surrounding the fledgling city. The buildings extended deep underground where they were connected by a network of tunnels. On the surface, these were replaced by paths lined with trees and covered by their foliage. High overhead, stone walkways arched between the towers, lined with pillars to support their vaulted roofs. The open-sided designs allowed the elves to enjoy the movements of the wind as they walked along the pathways.

Similar to the pattern of their old mountain citadel, stone structures had been built along the walls of the towers and sides of the paths for smaller plants to grow. These allowed for various fruits, vegetables, herbs, and vines to be grown throughout their city. The vines would eventually wrap around and cover the towers and the arched walkways that connected them high above the ground.

Gwyddoniaeth wound her way through the stairs and corridors until she came to a stone clearing just outside the city's main area. Here, there were several circular stone platforms, each surrounded by a ring of smaller trees. Inside, some of the platforms were strewn with broken rocks. Others were empty. One contained a class.

She stood just inside the ring of trees and observed the seated elves on the stone platform. Most were high elves, but there were a few sea elves and wood elves among them. Each sat cross legged on the ground with a large block of stone hovering over their heads. There had been some disagreement at first, but the necessity of being able to face danger had convinced the council to allow more dangerous and possibly lethal training. Not all of the elves had wanted to learn, but it was satisfying for Gwyddoniaeth to see her teacher's lessons being passed down through the generations of students. She nodded at Gwarchod as he stood to one side, observing his students. He nodded back. The younger high elf had been her first and most devoted pupil. She was proud of his accomplishments and certain that she had chosen wisely when naming him as her successor as teacher of the meddwlgrym training program.

Her rounds took her next to the new library near the city's center. She walked among the many scribe tables set up, watching as elves either re-recorded their own knowledge and lives or diligently copied other books or scrolls. They were rebuilding the library lost in the dragon fires that had destroyed their original homeland. It would take many years to rewrite what had been lost. This time they would also be sure to make extra copies and keep them in various locations, to lessen the risk of permanent loss in the future. This initiative most thrilled her yet always saddened her that she could not spend more time with it. As she left the library, she looked back with a sigh before continuing her rounds.

Gwyddoniaeth continued through the city before making her way to an underground chamber. Here, she raised her hand, reached out with her mind, and a section of the chamber wall moved aside to reveal a smooth, carved tunnel. Once inside, she returned the stone slab to its original place.

She followed the tunnel as it gently sloped downward and wove its way back and forth. Eventually she came to a complex of tunnels. These were carved elaborately with images of nature, like the tunnels of the mountain citadel that had been destroyed. The halls were lit periodically by lanterns containing bioluminescent insects casting off a soft blue-green glow. The previous realm had been dominated by different bioluminescent insects whose glow was yellow-green. Gwyddoniaeth preferred the new blue-green variety.

She followed the labyrinthine passages until she reached a large chamber with a set of three arcing tables arranged to form a circle. The outer perimeter of the room featured a series of pillars, and more of the insect-filled lamps lit the space. Gwyddoniaeth took her place at the center of one of the tables and reviewed her documents and notes while she waited for the rest of the council.

*   *   *

Gwarchod paced around the perimeter of the dais, watching the students hold the large stone blocks over their heads. He had taken over teaching Gwyddoniaeth's meddwlgrym classes several years prior. Being chosen to take on his mentor's previous responsibilities had been a joyous moment for him. His keen eyes scanned the faces of the students and the stability of their tasks. He was looking for signs that anyone's concentration was wavering. He preferred not to touch their minds directly, as it might disturb or surprise them, and then their concentration would shatter. A smile crept across his mind and face with the pleasure of seeing his students succeed. Their success was his joy.

"Gently place the blocks on the ground in front of you," he instructed from behind them.

The class did as directed. He walked around to stand in front of them.

Practice on your own tomorrow if you prefer or allow your subconscious to process what you have practiced today. Two days from now, we will increase the difficulty, and you will be responsible for holding a block over someone else's head.

There were nods from most of the students, with some shifting uncomfortably and looking around.

"Why do we have to risk our lives and the lives of others for this training?" asked one of the young high elves. "It has been almost two centuries since we came here, and nothing has attacked us."

This was a complaint more common among the high elves than the sea or wood elves. Gwarchod reasoned that the sea and wood elves more frequently faced the dangers of predators and nature and thus understood the value of learning to handle such life-threatening situations.

"And it had been many more centuries before that attack came. We need to be prepared. We do not know what other threats exist in the other realms. You may very well be required to use your skills to protect yourself and others. This class is a relatively safe training environment, but the real world outside is not. We may never face a threat as great as the dragons, but there are always dangers in the forests, mountains, and seas. These lessons provide an environment in which to ingrain these skills so that they become natural while gradually increasing the stress and danger so that you learn how to overcome such obstacles. Here we have a certain level of safety and protection, but should the need arise, you must be able to use what you have learned instantly without your mind being impeded by stress or fear."

The young elf tilted her head down slightly, pondering what Gwarchod had just said. Such questions did not stir anger within him, as he understood her concerns.

"If that is all for today, you are dismissed."

The elves stood and dispersed.

Gwarchod made his way through the mostly completed city to a structure near the forest on the outer edge. It connected to a small set of docks on the river that the sea elves used to travel between the city and the ocean.

Inside, Gwarchod checked in with the elves who were busy receiving written reports and maps from visiting wood and sea elves. On one wall, a large map of this new realm was being constructed. Parts of the map where exploration had been completed were filled in with great detail. Regions that had yet to be explored or more thoroughly mapped were blank or only faintly outlined.

The western coastline was highly detailed, but the eastern one only lightly sketched. Details and features of the landscape between the western coastline and the city were drawn in with great care. A large forest seemed to roughly span across the continent. To the north, the forest eventually faded at the foot of a mountain range, apparently forming the land mass's northern edge. No one had yet explored beyond it, and the waters that far north were impassable via ship. To the south, the forest faded into a patchwork of swamps and rainforests until it reached the southern end, broken sporadically by mountains. The southern tip was also very cold, but not quite cold enough to be surrounded by impassible ice. Sea elves had managed to sail around it, but most preferred to crisscross the central landmass by way of the rivers.

"Has anything of particular interest been reported?" Gwarchod asked the elf working on the map.

"Nothing out of the ordinary has been reported yet," she replied. "The most interesting reports do not affect the maps. Scouts have found new plants and animals, but most of the samples have been taken elsewhere for study."

Gwarchod nodded and continued his rounds.

His next stop took him to the city's central tower. From there he could view a series of eight towers along the perimeter, each with their own observation posts at the top. He closed his eyes and reached out with his mind.

His mind touched the occupant of the first tower he faced. An elf stood, watching the sky, stretching forth his mind to sense anything that might be approaching.

Is there anything to report, he thought at the sentinel.

Nothing. The skies are clear. I have not seen or sensed anything other than birds for the last several days.

The council appreciates your vigilance. Your replacement should be arriving tomorrow, then you can relax and pursue other endeavors.

Thank you.

He had similar conversations with the other sentinels. Gwarchod was pleased with their vigilance. The sentinels and their towers had been his suggestion. As Gwyddoniaeth's first student, he had been inclined to think of ways to put her training to use.

Eventually, the high elf made his way to the council chamber and took his seat next to Gwyddoniaeth. When they had first landed in the sea cave, he had asked her to teach the things she had learned from the Elders and asked if she had any guidance for the survivors. She had responded that she was merely a teacher, not a leader, but over the years since, she had become both. He was proud of her accomplishments and honored that he got to sit on the council with her. After a while, the rest of the elves arrived, and the council began its meeting.

The council consisted of three high elves, three sea elves, and three wood elves. Everyone had separate duties to keep track of as they endeavored to build a new life for their people in this new realm.

Gwyddoniaeth gave her progress reports on the city's construction projects. She moved on to describe updates at the library and began to touch on the state of meddwlgrym training programs.

Gwarchod politely interrupted her, as this was now his responsibility. She smiled in embarrassment and nodded. He reported that the class sizes were beginning to dwindle, which made sense as those elves who wanted to learn had already started, and there had not been major population growth since coming to this new realm. He also reported on the state of the sentinels and the scouts. The sentinels did not have infinite range either in sight or in mind but had not found signs of any threats.

The rest of the council presented their various reports. The emergency supplies being stored in the deep caves were monitored and replaced routinely to prevent any spoilage. The sea elves had been continuing their expeditions around the continent and the surrounding islands, mapping as they went. Undersea caves were always of interest, possibly providing locations in which they could hide submersibles in case they needed to evacuate the realm. The original sea cave in which they had landed was being maintained should the need arise, and more ships, submersibles, and harbors were being constructed.

Some of the elves had even begun their own explorations of the mist wall. Since Cyfeiriad had disappeared mysteriously, they had been forced to reinvent skills that he otherwise might have been able to teach. Fortunately, the original pilots had felt a taste of his ability when they had escaped the destruction of their old homeland, which had made it easier for them to replicate his skills. Following their success, many had begun teaching their newfound skills to any elf interested in learning.

The various elf subgroups shared hunting and survival skills training. The sea elves were comfortable with the lifeforms and tactics of the sea, but not of the forests. The opposite was true of the wood elves. The high elves had a more academic understanding of nature with little practical experience surviving in it, but they possessed great and well-practiced skills in analysis, planning, and the crafting of metal and stone. Since arriving in this new realm, precautionary measures had been taken to make sure these skills were available to everyone.

*   *   *

Ymladdwr exited the forest and blinked slightly. The area around the city was more open, and there were less clouds in this region. The excess sunlight was not immediately pleasant to him.

He made his way along the paved paths of the city, noting to himself how nicely the various trees, vines, and other plants had grown in, covering the stonework with life. It had been years since he was last here, and much had changed. The wood elf made his way to the river docks, growing less pleased the more he could sense the increasing number of elves around him, even if they were not all immediately visible. The solitude of the forest was blissful by comparison. Ahead he could see that the stone building of the map keepers was now completely covered in vines and plants.

Once inside, he approached the main table cluttered with books and maps.

"I have new maps and diagrams to turn in," he said.

Ymladdwr made a point to be as pleasant as possible. He had spent the last several days whispering to himself as he walked through the trees to ease his voice back into existence.

"Thank you. Let me get you some blank pages and a blank book," replied the elf.

She turned away from Ymladdwr and retrieved the items.

"Where were you scouting?" she asked as she traded his old book and map for the blank ones.

"I was mostly hunting in the northern mountains. I found an artifact that the council may want to investigate," he said.

The other elf paused; "Do you mean an artificial

construct indicative of another sentient species?"

"Yes."

"Would you be willing to wait around for a while? One of the council members should be here soon."

"Yes."

Ymladdwr stood and waited off to the side. Though he would have preferred to return to the forest as soon as possible, the wood elf was accustomed to the traditional exchange of information and supplies with the high elves. He watched as several of the elves gathered around his notebook and map, excitedly pointing to the diagrams within. One of the elves took the map and began adding to the large one on the wall.

After some time, another high elf entered the room and greeted the others. He was shown the book and turned to approach Ymladdwr.

"Thank you for bringing this to our attention. My name is Gwarchod. Would you be willing to come to the council meeting with me?"

Ymladdwr agreed and followed the high elf through the city and down into the caves beneath to the council chamber. The feeling of being surrounded by others diminished noticeably in the caves, relaxing him slightly.

The wood elf looked around those sitting at the tables. A female sitting next to Gwarchod directed him to relate how he found the artifact. He explained his experiences with the horned bears, which, in and of themselves, sparked some interest in other members of the council.

"Would you be willing to lead us to the artifact?" asked the female high elf eagerly. Despite himself, he found her youthful excitement pleasant.

"Yes. When would you like to leave?"

*   *   *

Gwyddoniaeth followed Ymladdwr through the northern woods. It had taken several months to get this far, but they were finally nearing the northern mountains. Gwarchod followed close behind. It had taken the two high elves several days to get used to moving through the tree branches instead of along the ground. The elves moved in silence, though sometimes she would initiate mind to mind conversations. Ymladdwr was not talkative, but Gwarchod would more readily discuss their shared academic interests. This was the most time she had spent with a wood elf. She reasoned that his silence was probably a naturally occurring habit in a solitary hunter.

Ymladdwr turned and began heading more parallel to the mountains. He gestured in the wood elf sign language to beware of the horned bears in the area. Gwyddoniaeth took note and scanned the area with her physical and mental senses. She could not sense, see, or hear anything nearby.

Soon they reached the clearing. Gwyddoniaeth stood in awe of the impressive craftsmanship of the artifact. The stone figures' eyes looked like they were closed, but there was the tiniest hint of a crack between the lids, and she could almost see the glint of gemstones beneath. She wondered how such a thing could be constructed.

"Do either of you recognize these symbols?" asked Gwarchod from the center of the dais.

Gwyddoniaeth turned to look at the metal rings in the center of the stone platform, which were inscribed with strange symbols. Beneath the metallic lattice at the center, she could see hints of gears, cables, and gemstones.

"I have not seen them before. This looks like the

15

diagrams of the sphinx gate that the Elders said the Enemy destroyed in the first days," she responded, crouching and reaching out to touch the inscribed symbols.

Ymladdwr looked at her; "The wood elf Elders did not speak of those times, and I never spent much time in the high elf library. Do you know how it works?"

She shook her head; "The Elders never got to learn how it worked. The Enemy destroyed it in a rage very early in their history."

Gwyddoniaeth stood, held up her hand, and reached out with her mind. She began to push and pull on the various parts of the device. The rings began to rotate. They moved almost too easily. She stopped.

"Ymladdwr, would you try to think about moving the outermost ring by two symbols," she asked.

Ymladdwr gave her a puzzled look but turned to face the device. A moment later, the outer ring moved two positions to the right. The wood elf looked stunned.

"I never underwent the meddwlgrym training with the high elves; how did it move just now? Was that one of you?" he asked, looking between them.

Gwarchod shook his head.

"Perhaps it is designed to respond to our thoughts directly," she suggested. "The Elders called it a gate. I wonder how it opens."

She began to move the outer ring one unit at a time. Gwarchod retrieved his notebook and began documenting the symbols. Ymladdwr wandered away out of sight, though she thought she heard him sharpening a knife somewhere high in a tree behind her.

Several hours of systematically rotating through various combinations began to tire Gwyddoniaeth. She had not seen Ymladdwr in quite some time, and Gwarchod had started to set up camp after finishing his diagrams. Suddenly there was a click.

Something inside the device began to turn and whir.

Something is happening. Come here quickly, she mentally called out to her companions.

The others returned promptly, and they watched a swirling sphere of multicolored energy grow over the metal rings. They walked around it slowly, confirming that it was spherical and not a mere circular disc.

"What is it?" asked Gwarchod.

"Do not touch it, we do not know if it is dangerous," cautioned Gwyddoniaeth.

Ymladdwr walked off the platform and returned with a small rock. He tossed it into the sphere.

They looked on the other side, but the rock did not land on the platform.

"I have an idea. May I borrow some rope?" she asked Ymladdwr.

The wood elf handed her his rope, and she walked over to a tree to find a fallen branch. She tied the branch to the rope and tossed it into the sphere. They waited a minute, then she pulled it back. The stick was still intact.

Ymladdwr started to move but Gwarchod stepped into the sphere immediately. The two remaining elves stopped in their tracks, unsure of what would happen next.

Gwyddoniaeth tried to reach her mind into the sphere but could not sense anything.

"I cannot sense his mind through the sphere. I am not sure what that means," she stated.

Ymladdwr took a step forward, but Gwarchod stepped back out of the sphere.

"It is another land, a rainforest. I do not think it is part of this continent or even this realm," he reported.

The others followed him back into the sphere.

Gwyddoniaeth stepped out onto the stone dais of another identical construct. The stone sphinxes and gryphons looked the same as the ones they had just left. Her gaze drifted past them to the environment beyond.

A dense tangle of trees, vines, and bushes surrounded the artifact.

"Have you seen any place like this in your travels?" Gwarchod asked the wood elf.

Ymladdwr looked around; "No. I have not spent much time in the jungles to the south, but this does not look familiar."

Gwyddoniaeth walked off the stone dais and began examining the plants.

"These do not match any of the specimens I have seen from the wandering wood elves," she reported.

Ymladdwr moved past her and began climbing into a tree. She watched him move from branch to branch and tree to tree.

What do you see?

It looks like this rainforest has multiple canopy levels. There is a river nearby.

We will meet you there.

Gwarchod was watching her, unable to hear her communication with the wood elf.

He found a river, let us meet him there.

He nodded, and they began to make their way through the dense rainforest along the ground. They stopped when they reached the running stream.

Below them, a steep bank led to a wide waterway. Above them the trees were covered in vines and large flowers the size of her head. She watched in awe as an insect, the size of a large bird, flew through the gap between the trees. A bright, multicolored bird with a wingspan wider than her height swooped out of a tree and snatched the insect away to its new perch.

A splash caught her attention and she saw a large moss and bark colored jaguar climbing out of the water with a reptilian creature in its jaws. The prey appeared to be a reptile with large powerful jaws, a snake-like body, and two front legs, with fins on the top and bottom of its tail.

They followed the river for a while until they found a group of large, armor-plated otters swimming and playing in the water. One was lying on a log eating a large, shining, almost metallic fish.

This is amazing, commented Gwarchod.

She replied with her sense of agreement. Gwyddoniaeth was captivated by the beauty of and her curiosity for the plants and animals. She wanted to stare and to study.

She sensed movement behind her and turned, but it was only Ymladdwr landing silently on a large root next to them.

"We should head back to the gate," he signaled to them in wood elf sign language. "We do not know how long it will stay open."

Gwyddoniaeth scolded herself slightly for not thinking of that sooner. She nodded her agreement and the three of them made their way back.

Once back in their own realm, she made quick notes of the alignment of the symbols.

Ymladdwr turned to the gate; "Off."

The sphere collapsed in on itself and vanished.

"We should take precautions when we next explore," suggested Gwarchod. "One of you should stay behind to reopen the gate should there be a time limit."

Gwyddoniaeth agreed; "We should also send word back to the council. If we are ever threatened, this could be another escape route."

"Or a potential source of danger," suggested Ymladdwr.

"Either way, I am eager to explore further," she replied with a smile.

* * *

Ymladdwr stepped out of the gate carrying a large animal carcass. He mentally commanded the portal to deactivate, and it closed behind him. He nodded to a high elf standing nearby, who checked off his arrival on the portal schedule.

The gate was surrounded by a series of tents and the beginnings of some stone structures. The clearing was now slightly wider than when he had originally found it, and a team of about a dozen elves moved around, documenting and examining specimens brought back by the various scouting teams. While he much preferred his solitary sojourns into unknown realms, he had grown accustomed to the presence of the other elves in the camp around the gate.

He brought the new creature over to Gwyddoniaeth's table and set it down. The animal had a large, amorphous body with two legs ending in webbed feet. Its toes seemed to spread and curve upward slightly like shallow bowls. Several tongues seemed to lull out of its wide, gaping mouth.

"Fascinating, where did you find this creature?" she asked, leaning over to examine it more closely.

"It was living near a pond; it burrows into the mud, then spreads its toes, using the wide, webbed feet to anchor itself, then it shoots out six retractable tentacles to grab its prey. Those it cannot consume immediately it holds under the water to drown."

"Thank you for bringing back such a fascinating specimen," she said, not looking up.

Gwyddoniaeth continued to examine the creature, her attention now consumed by it.

Ymladdwr found her enthusiasm contagious.

"You should join us on the next expedition," he offered.

Gwyddoniaeth straightened and looked around at the scattered contents of her table; "I need to be here to help coordinate the portal schedule, the testing of the iterations, and the cataloging of maps and specimens. Not to mention that I want to remain available if Gwarchod needs my advice on running the council."

"There are plenty of elves here who can handle things for a few days. The council is months away at best, and you have already taught Gwarchod what he needs to know. You obviously enjoy the exploration of this project; why not take full advantage of it?" he argued.

She paused as if considering. "Agreed. I will join the next expedition."

Ymladdwr smiled.

A couple days later, Ymladdwr and Gwyddoniaeth walked through the portal to explore the newest destination together.

They stepped out of the portal onto the dais in the new realm. Before them lay a vast swamp on all sides. The air was still, and tall trees grew out of the mud and water. Vines adorned the sides of some of the trees and hung down from their branches. Large arthropods could be seen flitting about. A ten-legged parasitic arthropod flew too close, and

Ymladdwr snatched it out of the air. He examined it closely, then held it out to Gwyddoniaeth.

"These parasites are quite large. I have seen similar things in other swamps. They tend to be quite numerous. When they are this big, they can drain a dangerous amount of blood, because their bodies expand," he explained.

Ymladdwr could see excitement and curiosity in her gaze as Gwyddoniaeth took the bug and examined it. Involuntarily, a smile twitched at the corner of his lips. In his previous wanderings, he had been content, neither joyous nor sorrowful, but in recent years, this internal peace had been disturbed.

"This expedition's schedule involves the base team reopening the gate in one week's time. We can explore outward for three and half days, then head back." She looked up from the bug; "Let us see what else we can find."

"We will need to walk on the ground and wade through the mud," he said looking up at the trees. "The branches are too high to reach easily and too small to hold our weight."

Ymladdwr stepped off the dais on to the nearest patch of solid ground near the base of a tree. They moved from one patch to the other, using fallen sticks and reeds to make bridges where the ground was too soft. His mind slipped into a state of quiet, peaceful enjoyment as they walked through the swamp. He did not exude excitement or elation, yet he was filled with a deep satisfaction from the activity and the surroundings. It did not even occur to him that this included the present lack of solitude.

A sound caught their attention. Ymladdwr's head snapped to one side, and his eyes scanned their surroundings. He caught sight of movement and focused in on it. There were large, muscular animals rooting around on all fours in the mud a hundred yards away. He drew an arrow and nocked it to his bow as a precaution. The creatures' backs were just above the muddy water, and they would periodically lower their long heads into the swamp. Their heads contained two protruding tusks that pointed upward and at least one of the creatures kept its head out of the water to scan their surroundings. When they raised their heads out of the water, their tusks were usually covered in dirt.

One of the creatures' bodies began to thrash back and forth violently, as if shaking its head back and forth under the water. The head lurched up to reveal a large animal grasped tightly between large canines, which were now revealed since it could not fully close its mouth. The successful creature took its kill over to the others, and they began to tear into it.

Ymladdwr turned to see his companion make notes in her book. He admired her diligence but was unsure about the wisdom of doing this now while still within sight of these creatures.

Ymladdwr gently tapped her shoulder and signed to her, "We should keep moving. It will be dark soon, and we need to find a safe place to sleep."

Agreed.

Ymladdwr had grown used to the high elf's tendency to project her thoughts straight into his mind. It was a useful skill but not something he was particularly motivated to learn. Outside of the gate expeditions, he spent most of his time in solitude.

He led the way through the swamp until they found a group of smaller trees set close together. Ymladdwr set up two hammocks between the trees, tying them to several branches to spread out the weight. When it was finished, it resembled a makeshift spiderweb of ropes.

Night fell and they stayed awake to observe the darkened swamp. Nothing happened after several hours, so each of them climbed into their hammocks. The fabric of the hammocks closed around them, hopefully blocking out any bugs that would be drawn to their sleeping forms.

Ymladdwr lay there, listening to the swamp's night sounds. His eyes closed and he drifted off to sleep.

The wood elf's eyes snapped open. He had felt air move past his hammock. Silently, he opened the hammock and slipped out onto the ground. His eyes were already adjusted to the darkness and scanned the air as he picked up his bow and nocked an arrow.

Movement caught his attention on a nearby tree. A large bug fluttered its wings and took off. A moment later, a large, long-tailed bat swooped down and grabbed the bug in midair with its hind feet. As its massive wings pulled it back up into the sky, the tail arced down and stabbed the insect with a bulbous spike. The bug stopped moving. From this distance, Ymladdwr was not sure if the bat had impaled or poisoned it.

Ymladdwr turned to see Gwyddoniaeth half out of her hammock, watching the bat fly away. She looked at him and he signed that it seemed safe, but he would keep watch.

When you are ready, I will take the next watch so that you can sleep.

He nodded in agreement, and she went back inside her hammock.

Several hours later, Gwyddoniaeth emerged, and he climbed back into his hammock and fell asleep.

The next day was fairly uneventful.

On the third day, they found another pack of the creatures that had been rooting around in the muck. The elves watched these six creatures from a distance while

Ymladdwr kept his bow at the ready. This time one of them noticed the elves. It snorted and the others raised their heads to look at them.

Ymladdwr raised his bow and whispered, "Be prepared to run. I do not know how fast they move or how easy they will fall."

Understood.

The pack began to spread out and move closer. Ymladdwr knew that fighting back or fleeing would be harder if surrounded. Twisting his torso, he turned to face the outermost flank of the approaching pack and released his arrow. As the arrow sank into the creature's thick neck, it bellowed and thrashed. The others growled in response and began to run toward them. Ymladdwr nocked another arrow and released it at the second creature, but it ducked at the last second, so the arrow only grazed its back.

"Run!"

He turned and both elves began leaping from one patch of mostly solid ground to the next. The creatures splashed through the muck and water behind them, following a straighter path than their own. Ymladdwr glanced over his shoulder and realized that this was not going to work as distance from their pursuers began to shrink. He looked at his companion and made his decision.

Without warning, he stopped and turned, nocking an arrow and releasing it at the nearest creature. This one went straight through the side of the mouth and into the skull.

He fired another arrow, blinding one eye of the next creature. It shrieked and stumbled away, futilely trying to shake the arrow out.

The remaining three were almost upon him. Not wanting to get caught mid draw, he dropped his bow and drew his daggers, his knees flexing, awaiting the fight.

The nearest creature leaped out of the water, revealing powerful limbs and wide feet with long hooked claws.

A dead tree slammed into the creature and knocked it out of the air, the rotten wood crumbling with the impact.

The other creatures came to an abrupt halt, apparently as shocked by the sight as Ymladdwr was. He turned to see Gwyddoniaeth standing next to a tree several yards away, her hand stretched out in his general direction.

That was the only one I found within reach, she warned.

Sensing movement he did not see, he spun back around in time to see the creatures had regained their senses. Both leaped out of the water at him. The one on his right smashed into the other and they went flying to one side. Ymladdwr rushed forward, daggers in hand and leaped at the closest creature. His blades sank into its flesh, piercing ribs with one while the other was thrust up under the jaw and into the skull.

The next creature staggered to its feet and turned toward the wood elf, but not fast enough. A metal blade slammed through the side of its neck near the base of the skull, separating head from spine. Ymladdwr pulled his dagger free. The creature dropped.

Ymladdwr turned and retrieved his bow. He looked around for the ones he had shot to retrieve his arrows, but they had already sunk beneath the water or limped away. Deciding it was not worth the effort, he made his way back toward Gwyddoniaeth.

"Thank you," he said as he approached.

"You are welcome," she replied. "Are you injured?"

Ymladdwr glanced down at himself; "I do not think

so."

They began to make their way back to the gate. Gwyddoniaeth took the lead and Ymladdwr followed her.

He was grateful that she had been able to use her abilities to stop the creatures. Perhaps he should consider learning them as well.

The path they took back toward the gate was different, arching around so that they could explore as much as possible before returning.

The next day, they came to one of the trees that had vines hanging from its branches. Gwyddoniaeth paused by the tree and walked around to examine the vines along its trunk.

"They do not look like normal vines. There is something different about the texture. It is colored like rough bark, but when you get close, you can tell that the surface is actually very smooth."

He took a step closer and looked at the vines. Something felt wrong. She reached out her hand toward the vine, but Ymladdwr grabbed her wrist.

"I do not think we should touch it," he said sternly.

"Why?"

Ymladdwr's eyes followed the vines down into the water, then up into the tree. He was not sure what was wrong, but he intuitively knew there was something dangerous here. He turned to look at the other trees; they were all the same. Multiple vines had grown up along the sides of each tree with their ends dangling from the branches in roughly a thirty-yard radius around the water.

"I cannot quite place it," he began.

His mind emptied, waiting for an intuitive epiphany, then realization sparked within him. Ymladdwr could see now that the vines all came out of the water, forming a rough circle, only climbing up the sides of the trees facing the center and forming a curtain of hanging vines around an empty pool.

"They are not vines," he said. "They are tentacles. There is something in the center of the water."

Gwyddoniaeth took a step forward next to him. "I can see why you would think that, but how can you know?"

Ymladdwr looked around for some way to prove his hypothesis. A few yards away on a tree he spotted a large bug.

"Can you grab that bug and bring it over?"

Gwyddoniaeth reached out, and the bug was pulled away from the tree and through the air until it was close enough for Ymladdwr to grab it. It was roughly four inches in diameter and seven inches long with ten wriggling legs.

Grasping the bug so that it could not flap its wings, he turned to face the hanging vines in front of him. He threw the bug at the nearest vines. As soon as it touched the vines, they lashed around the bug. The vines were then yanked over the branches and down underwater with a loud splash. The water rippled as something surged just below the surface toward its center, then went still. After several minutes, the tip of the vines could be seen slowly creeping out of the water and back up the tree.

"Excellent instincts and observational skills," she commented.

He nodded, not sure how to respond. Ymladdwr turned and led them around the apparent vine trap.

The remainder of their journey was without incident, and they made it back to the gate early. Ymladdwr sharpened his knives and Gwyddoniaeth documented their discoveries in her notebook while they waited for the appointed time. Even in this quiet, seemingly mundane time, he felt a pleasant satisfaction. When the time came, the gate opened, and they returned to the facility.

*   *   *

Gwyddoniaeth finished reviewing the maps from the latest expeditions and cataloged them with the records from that specific realm. By now the facility around that gate had grown to include several vine-covered stone buildings. The one she was in was a miniature library where all the notes and maps were sorted and ordered based on the realm from which they came.

She quickly placed the books and map scrolls in their proper places and moved onto the next building, glancing quickly at the specimens that had been collected from the other realms.

There were indeed some fascinating and colorful new plants that had been discovered. These were stored alongside strange animals that were not native to this realm or their homeland. The unknown organisms and the detailed analyses required to understand them would normally have consumed her concentration. However, despite her love of research, she found herself giving short replies and hurrying through the facility. When she came to an exit that faced the forest instead of the gate, she quickly slipped through, eager to be somewhere else.

A few footpaths surrounded the facility, but they did not extend into the forest. Her steps were quick and silent as she walked swiftly between the trees, heading south away from the mountains. The air was pleasantly cool with a soft, gentle breeze that only heightened her excitement.

A sound drifted along the breeze, and she slowed her pace. A smile crept across her face as she began to sneak up on her prey.

Just ahead, in a small clearing, she heard excited, happy sounds. In a couple more steps, she could see a young elf child standing with her back to Gwyddoniaeth. Next to the child crouched an adult male elf. He whispered to the child and watched her pull back her miniature, child-sized bow. Gwyddoniaeth's eyes followed the point of the arrow as it aimed at a large target roughly ten yards away. She saw the adult's head jerk upward slightly and turn almost imperceptibly in her direction, before turning back and whispering to the child. The child released her bow and the arrow hit the target in the center.

Gwyddoniaeth stopped and smiled at the happy squeals from the child. The sounds filled her with a joy that surpassed anything she had yet experienced. The adult whispered something to the child, and the child quieted, then spun around suddenly and pointed her empty bow at Gwyddoniaeth.

"Gotcha!" she cried.

Gwyddoniaeth laughed and the little child rushed over and leaped into her arms.

"Are you having fun with your father?" she asked as she smiled and carried her daughter toward her husband.

The little girl nodded and hugged her neck.

Gwyddoniaeth leaned her cheek against the top of her daughter's head and turned to face Ymladdwr.

He gathered the bow and the small arrows, then greeted her with a hug.

"She is learning quickly."

"But father still says I am not allowed to go hunting," sulked the child.

Gwyddoniaeth chuckled softly and replied, "Yes, and when you are older you can hunt with him to your heart's content."

"But why cannot I hunt now?" the child whined.

"It is neither wise nor loving to allow one's children to enter danger before they are ready," replied Gwyddoniaeth.

Llyfryn rolled her eyes but did not argue.

She smiled at her daughter's reaction.

Gwyddoniaeth and her family walked a while through the trees before coming to a spiral staircase that wound around a tree. They climbed the stairs leading to an elaborate treehouse that rested in the branches between two close and sturdy trees.

They ate supper and Gwyddoniaeth put Llyfryn to bed, gently singing her to sleep. She paused and looked at her sleeping child. These past few hours spent with her family were the things that she appreciated most in life. When she was younger, her joy was found in study with her brother, but that had ended in the sorrow surrounding the attack by the dragons. In the years since, the pain of his loss had faded as she buried herself in teaching and later organizing their new life on this continent. Finding the gate had given her a rush of youthful curiosity and excitement, but now she found that such things almost did not matter to her. The love she felt for her child was much more important.

Silently, Gwyddoniaeth crept back into her bedroom and curled up next to Ymladdwr. Without opening his eyes, he wrapped an arm around her and held her close. The tactile sensation and nearness to her husband filled her with a sense of love and safety. Here she could be happy, relaxed, and at peace. Her eyes gently closed as a subtle smile played across her lips.

Gwarchod reached the research facility surrounding the gate. He had not been here in several years. Wandering through the many buildings, he finally found his old mentor bent over a new map. The facility had grown much in that time, and he had spent most of it in the city, working on the council.

He waited patiently for her to sense his presence so as not to disturb her concentration. Despite the familiarity of her activity, something seemed different about her, though he could not name it.

Eventually she perked up, turned toward him, and greeted him with an especially warm smile, which somewhat surprised him. In all the years he had known her, he had not seen her quite so outwardly happy.

"It is good to see you again," she said.

"You as well. How has the research gone?"

"We have found the coordinates for around three hundred realms at this point, but there are millions of combinations, and it will take many more years before we try them all. So far, we have cataloged over a thousand new species of plants and animals. I even have a list of potential refuges, should we need to flee again, though the portal will slow our escape."

"That is amazing. I am glad to hear you have been so successful," he said with a smile.

"But none of that matters; I have something to show you," she said abruptly.

Gwarchod tilted his head slightly in confusion. Gwyddoniaeth had always been fond of research and often lamented not being able to spend more time doing it during the rebuilding projects. She gestured for him to follow, and she led him quickly through the buildings and out into the forest. They headed south and he kept pace. He was not sure why she was so excited, though he was happy for her regardless of the cause.

They approached an elaborate tree house and began climbing the spiral stairs. Once inside, he was greeted by an unexpected sight. In front of him stood a table with a little girl next to it.

"This is my daughter, Llyfryn," said Gwyddoniaeth.

Gwarchod was surprised. He had had no idea that any of this had happened.

"Who—" he began but stopped when he saw Ymladdwr carrying trays of freshly cooked deer meat.

"Welcome back, Gwarchod," greeted Ymladdwr.

"I am surprised yet happy to meet your family," Gwarchod said to Gwyddoniaeth.

The four of them ate supper, and Gwyddoniaeth put her daughter to bed. Afterward, the three adults sat around the table.

"I see now why you were so excited when I arrived, but why did you invite me out here anyway?" Gwarchod inquired.

Gwyddoniaeth and Ymladdwr looked at each other, then back at him.

"Our people did not truly know death until the dragons destroyed our homeland. We have had more than two centuries of peace since then, but there are no guarantees that it will last. We are regularly exploring new realms, and they frequently are inhabited by unknown creatures. Should something happen to us, whether another cataclysm or a tragedy on an expedition, we want you to watch over our daughter," explained Ymladdwr.

Gwarchod was stunned. "I have no experience with

children," he began.

"But you have trained many students, and you have been my student, so I know I can trust you," replied Gwyddoniaeth.

"But none of my students were children; they were all adults," he protested.

"We know this is new for you, so we asked you to come out here to spend some time with us and Llyfryn. This way you will both be acclimated to each other, and it will not be an added shock should something befall us," answered Ymladdwr.

Gwarchod thought about it for a while. His eyes mindlessly scanned the empty table while he waited for an epiphany. None came. Their argument was sound, and there was no reason to refuse.

He looked up; "Very well, I accept."

Gwarchod spent the next several days with the family, observing the child's daily lessons and the family's shared meals.

"We are going away for a few days to examine some recent discoveries in realm fifty-seven. We want you to watch over Llyfryn for us while we are gone," said Gwyddoniaeth.

Gwarchod felt unsure but agreed.

When the day came, he stood with Llyfryn as she said goodbye to her parents. It was the first time they had both been away at the same time, but she did not cry as much as he had feared.

After the portal closed and she had composed herself, she looked up at him and asked, "So what do we do now?"

"We continue with your training and your studies," he replied. Despite spending several days with the family, he still felt awkward around the child. Continuing with what he had seen of her usual tasks seemed like the best approach.

They returned to the treehouse, where Gwarchod watched over her as she read the next section of the book she was studying. Afterward, he quizzed her on its contents.

Next, they went out to the practice range that had been set up in the clearing near the research facility. He watched her shoot arrows at the target and move away slightly farther each time. She even practiced shooting by switching her bow to either hand and used both sides as her draw arm.

In the afternoon, he led her to the base of the mountains just north of the facility. Llyfryn sat quietly and lifted a rock in front of her.

"How would you like to try something new?"

"Like what?" she asked, looking up at him and dropping her rock.

He looked around and found a wide but thin flat rock.

"Can you lift that one?" he asked, pointing.

"Of course."

She held out her hand, and the flat piece of rock floated into the air.

"Let us play a game," he said and walked away from her. When he reached a reasonable distance, he faced her and held out his hand to one side. Several small rocks flew up to his hand and he caught them. He pointed with his other hand to the rock she had levitated; "I want you to use that wide flat rock to block these small ones. Do you think you can do that?"

Llyfryn looked between the slab she held with her mind and the stones in his hand and said, "I think so."

"I will not throw them too hard, so just do your best."

Llyfryn nodded as she rotated the wide flat sheet of rock into a vertical position to act as a shield. Her eyes focused on him, and she gained a more serious expression.

He tossed a rock in her general direction, and she swung her arm through the air, moving the thin slab to block it. He made sure to toss them next to her but not directly at her. The more they practiced, the better she got, eagerly swinging the blocking stone around to stop the pebbles. Her focus and demeanor became more playful as the game progressed. As a teacher, he was pleased to see her progress but also found himself smiling at her enjoyment of the game. He ended the game when she showed signs of fatigue, and they returned to her treehouse home for supper.

When it was sufficiently dark, he put her to bed.

"Mother always sings me to sleep," she said as he got up to leave.

Gwarchod paused. This was not something he usually practiced, and he was not sure what sorts of songs children enjoyed. He searched his memory and found a song from his own childhood. He sat down on the floor next to the small bed and began to sing to her. Before long, she fell asleep.

He looked down at her, realizing he felt a protective affection for her already. He reasoned that this must be a fraction of what Gwyddoniaeth and Ymladdwr felt for the child. It now made a little more sense to him why his mentor was so excited about her daughter.

The next several days passed quickly and uneventfully. When Gwyddoniaeth and Ymladdwr returned, Llyfryn eagerly greeted her parents, flinging herself into their arms and saying how much she missed them. Gwarchod felt a small pang of hurt at the realization that his time as a temporary parental figure was ending, but he suppressed it quickly.

*　　*　　*

Llyfryn rushed out of the gate, ignoring the greetings of the elf in charge of the gate schedule. She dropped her pack and walked swiftly through the research facility. She was dressed like a wood elf and, now that she was fully grown, it was clear she had her father's eyes and her mother's hair. Excitement lit her eyes and propelled her steps.

Her body twisted and turned as she swiftly slipped between the working researchers until she found her mother.

"Mother, come with me quickly, I have something to show you," she said, grabbing Gwyddoniaeth's wrist.

Gwyddoniaeth dragged her gaze away from a book and looked at her daughter; "What is it?"

"I cannot tell you; you need to see for yourself," she replied with a smile, enjoying creating a mystery to conceal the surprise.

Her mother stood, and Llyfryn immediately pulled her along.

"Where is Father?" she asked excitedly as she paused just outside the building and looked back and forth.

"If you were calm and patient, you could search mentally for him," her mother suggested gently from behind.

Llyfryn rolled her eyes, then closed them and reached out with her mind, scanning across the area until she found him. She yanked on her mother's wrist and dragged her through the facility until they reached the room where her father was.

Stay quiet and let him finish, admonished her mother as they slipped into the back of the room. Llyfryn's father was standing at the front, speaking to a group of elves, preparing them for some of the new animals they might encounter in the other realms. Many of the realms were fairly unique, but there were similarities between some. It was still unclear if some of these were different realms with similar ecosystems or if some realms had multiple sphinx gates.

She waited somewhat impatiently, eager to reveal her surprise to her parents. Her father acknowledged her presence with a nod and finished his lesson. The elves asked some questions and then dispersed.

"What has you so excited?" he asked as he approached and gave her a hug.

"I have something I have to show you," she said, grabbing his wrist as well.

Llyfryn barely noticed the glance between her parents and their bemused smiles as they followed her.

Quickly they were back at the gate. Llyfryn checked her notes and commanded the gate to reopen. Her expedition had come back safely, so it had been closed behind them.

They stepped out into a darkened, snow-covered forest of tall pine trees. She led them through the trees out to the shores of a wide lake. As they walked past the tree line, they could see that snow was falling gently through the night sky.

"It is a very lovely lake," said her mother.

"Wait for it... there!"

Llyfryn pointed off to the right as a large bird with shimmering bioluminescent wings took flight from a tree. The bird glowed in shades of purples and pinks as it sailed over the lake, watching things they could not see. Suddenly it dived, its talons breaking the water's dark surface and causing it to ripple in intense bright waves of blue and green light. The bird beat its wings, pulling away from the rippling lights with a large iridescent fish in its claws. It then flew to their left, and they saw a brightly colored aurora in the sky over the trees.

Llyfryn spun around to see her parents' faces. They were staring in awe at the glowing bird, brilliant aurora, and falling white snow amidst the black night. The young elf was elated to see their reaction. Of all the realms she had explored, this was one of the most beautiful and unique. She smiled and twirled around in the snow, not seeing the smiles on her parents' faces as they watched her.

*   *   *

Ymladdwr directed the elves around the gate to be ready. Gwyddoniaeth reiterated the very tight schedule for opening and closing the gate on this expedition. Extra precautions needed to be made this time.

The world they were about to enter had signs of sentient life. So far, all of the one thousand plus realms they had visited had been inhabited only by plants and animals, at least within the gate's vicinity. She knew that not every inch of each realm had been explored fully yet, which meant there could be other sentient species they had merely not yet discovered in their eagerness to test every gate combination. The last time the elves had seen something other than an elf was when they received the Warning before the dragons attacked.

Ymladdwr and Gwyddoniaeth finished passing out their assignments and approached the gate. The elves had been instructed to close it immediately after them and only open it for an hour at a time every three hours. Usually, gates were kept open all day to allow the expedition teams plenty of time to return. They did not know if they would find enemies or allies on the other side but wanted to minimize the risk of an incursion.

The precautions and protocols were now much more personal for Ymladdwr, and he sensed something similar in his wife. His mind reached out reflexively and gently touched her and their daughter, as if to reassure himself that they were both safe.

When the protocols were first set up, they were an almost academic exercise in preparing for a contingency that had no certainty of happening. There had been a logical sense of responsibility at the time, but now that the moment had come, he felt a deeper instinct and desire to protect everyone on this side of the gate. It started with his family and extended to the other elves out of empathy for their own connections to each other. This was another reason why he and Gwyddoniaeth were going alone. They were the ones most responsible for the expeditions through the gate, imbuing them with a quasi-parental sense of responsibility for everyone involved. This sensibility combined with the realization of the potential to bring about another cataclysm, should the sentient life on the other side be hostile. They did not want to be responsible for another horror like that of the dragons befalling their people.

The portal hummed to life. Ymladdwr and Gwyddoniaeth stepped through.

On the other side, they found that the sphinx gate was in a large, circular stone chamber. The gate closed behind them. The air was still. They stepped off the dais and walked around, examining the walls. Round openings about three feet in diameter were dispersed around the room. Each opening appeared to lead upward at a curving angle. A doorway with a large metal door loomed on one side of the chamber.

They approached and examined the door. There were

no signs of a handle or latch on this side.

I have a bad feeling about this place, but I cannot identify anything to justify it, Gwyddoniaeth thought to him.

I cannot either. Do you sense anyone on the other side?

I have not. Should I break the door?

If we do and there are sentient creatures on the other side, they may take it as hostility. But if we do not, then we will not know for sure what is going on here.

I will pull it open gently.

Gwyddoniaeth raised her hand and slowly pulled back. The metal door creaked in response, and the stone wall next to it cracked slightly. She stopped, relaxing her mind and dropping her hand.

I guess we wait, he thought.

Ymladdwr returned to the dais and sat down. Gwyddoniaeth joined him. Patiently and silently, they waited. He sat with his elbows resting on his knees while she sat next to him, back straight, gazing at the door. He allowed his mind and senses to fill the room, merely observing rather than pondering the possible explanations. If they waited more than a day and nothing happened, he would suggest breaking it open.

About an hour later, Gwyddoniaeth's head perked up; *I sense someone coming.*

They both stood and Ymladdwr reached instinctively for an arrow. He paused, watching to see what happened.

Loud clinks and thuds resounded within the door and it slowly creaked open. In the doorway stood a figure that was only slightly shorter than them. It had green skin, black hair, and long pointed ears. Dressed in plain clothing, it wore a strange medallion hanging from a chain around its neck.

The creature spread its hands to either side and said

something they did not understand, but that they sensed was a greeting.

I can skim its mind... I sense no malicious intent, Gwyddoniaeth informed him.

The figure turned to face down a corridor and gestured for them to follow.

Be ready if he becomes hostile, he warned.

Ymladdwr moved toward the figure, and Gwyddoniaeth followed him.

The figure led them through the stone passageways until they reached a large room with a long table. Three more creatures had been sitting at the table but rose when the elves and their escort entered. The escort gestured for the elves to take a seat on one side of the table.

Ymladdwr looked over the chairs and nodded to Gwyddoniaeth. They sat down. The other creatures all sat on the other side facing them.

Should we delve into their minds? Gwyddoniaeth asked.

Unsolicited mental intrusion would not be in keeping with the Narrow Path, as it violates their privacy and their inner minds. Let us keep with skimming their surface thoughts to understand what they are saying. We also don't want to reveal our full capabilities yet, in case these creatures truly are an enemy.

Agreed.

The first creature said something.

"I am Gwyddoniaeth, and this is Ymladdwr."

The creatures looked at her.

They tried saying something in a noticeably different language, but Ymladdwr still did not recognize it.

The creatures tried what sounded like a third language.

Gwyddoniaeth held up an empty hand, palm out, and slowly reached for something at her waist. She pulled out a piece of paper, ink, and quill. She drew the sphinx gate and figures on either side. She gestured to herself and Ymladdwr, then at two of the figures. Next, she made a motion with her fingers to indicate them passing through the portal and pointed to the figures on the other side, then at the creatures. They nodded as if understanding. One hurried off and returned a minute later with their own paper and ink.

Ymladdwr closely observed the creatures before him while his wife attempted to communicate via drawings and hand gestures. Their eyes were focused and attentive, watching her drawings, hand gestures, and facial expressions. When she finished a thought, they would either smile and nod or look confused. There were no obvious weapons in the room other than those carried by Gwyddoniaeth and himself. The creatures' eyes never strayed to his weapons. Their postures and gestures were relaxed. He could see no signs in their movements that indicated hostility, nor could he sense any when he grazed their minds.

Despite this, something felt wrong. He could not explain the feeling and his eyes began scanning the room, looking for anything to verify it. The walls were plain and barren, as was the furniture. The creatures' clothes were simple but well made. The only thing of any significant detail were the medallion devices they wore.

Give me two arrows.

Ymladdwr looked back to his wife and handed her two arrows. She gestured between them and the creatures, then broke the arrows in half and laid the broken pieces on the table. The creatures seemed to understand and nodded.

Everyone stood up and their escort led them back to

the gate. He stood and waited with them until the gate opened. They bowed slightly and left.

Back in their own realm, the two elves looked at each other.

"I sense something is wrong, but I could not find anything to confirm it," he said.

"I agree, but their surface level thoughts were entirely benign," she replied.

"Did you recognize any of the languages they tried?"

"No," she said looking down as if searching her memory.

"If they knew three different languages, it is possible that either their species has three distinct languages, or that they already know of two other species other than themselves."

"True..." Gwyddoniaeth seemed to ponder the possibility. "We should inform the council."

"It would be irresponsible to introduce a potential threat without notifying anyone else," he agreed. "Outside of that, what is your conclusion?"

She looked up at him with hesitant optimism; "I am cautiously curious, as these are the first sentient beings we have encountered. It would be interesting to learn more."

*   *   *

Gwarchod stood in the trees overlooking the research facility around the gate. Ymladdwr and Gwyddoniaeth were nearby. He watched the elves move back and forth between the buildings. He took special note of the green-skinned creatures as they moved about as well. They had allowed a small group of the newly acquainted goblins to enter their realm as a sign of friendship, but there were still misgivings.

44

It has been almost a year. The council wants to know if they have shown any signs of hostility, he asked. He had a duty to the rest of their people, and they needed to be certain about their safety.

So far, they have not. The goblins have learned our language and vice versa, replied Gwyddoniaeth.

We have not shared the map of the continent with them nor allowed them to leave the research facility, added Ymladdwr.

At this point, I am beginning to fear that we are unjust in our suspicions. They have done nothing wrong, but we have treated them like enemies, noted Gwyddoniaeth.

Perhaps you are right. Has anyone delved into their minds? asked Gwarchod.

No. The prohibition on violating someone's inner mind still stands. We still believe it to be a violation of the Narrow Path, replied Ymladdwr.

That is reasonable, commented Gwarchod.

Perhaps we should bring them to the city, let them meet the council. If they are truly peaceful, then we may have found an ally, suggested Gwyddoniaeth.

Gwarchod weighed the possibilities in his mind. How long should they wait to test the trustworthiness of the goblins? Was it fair to continue to view them with suspicion when they had done nothing wrong?

*   *   *

The goblin trudged along as he followed the elf through the temperate rainforest. He marveled at how easily she bounded along the ground. Llyfryn would stop periodically and wait for him. He was grateful but also somewhat ashamed of his own lack of ability. He should be more used to this terrain by now.

"We are almost back to the gate. When we get there, you can rest," she said pleasantly.

He nodded and smiled. While he knew that the elf was older than himself, everything about her movements and personality seemed to be imbued with a boundless youthful energy. All of the elves he had met seemed to possess a similar seemingly limitless energy, though many of them had a sense of maturity as well. In some ways, he wanted to call them quieter by comparison. When he had asked about the relative ages of some of the elves, he had realized that this quality of quiet maturity was greater in those who were older.

They eventually arrived at the gate and set down their packs. He was relieved to be able to ease the tension on his shoulders.

"How long until the gate is scheduled to be opened?" he asked in the elves' language.

"About an hour or so."

He leaned back against one of the stone structures and closed his eyes, enjoying the coolness of the stone against his body.

The goblin winced and rubbed his head. He had had strange pains the last few days and they were getting worse.

"Have the headaches returned?"

"Yes. When we get back, I will retire to bed early. That should help," he said.

Llyfryn nodded.

The gate opened on time, and they returned to the elves' realm. The goblin made his way through the facility to the barracks that had been built for the goblin guests. He entered his room and shut the door.

He leaned over the water basin and a slight

annoyance flitted across his mind as the pain in his head spiked again. The elves never seemed to feel ill, tired, or weak, so why must he?

For a moment he was surprised at himself. Why was he feeling so jealous and bitter?

The medallion hanging from his neck began to twitch and whir.

The pain spiked again, and his expression momentarily twisted into one of extreme resentment and rage. Why should those blasted elves have such good fortune? Why must he only go where they allow? Who were they to make such decisions for him? He was after all, a—

What was he?

The whirring and humming peaked before a loud crack snapped in the air.

Memories rushed back and he straightened up.

He was a high goblin. He was not accustomed to following the commands of the lesser creatures who lived outside their realm. Only the Ascended were allowed to command him.

The high goblin paused, calming his mind; it would not be wise to inadvertently alert the mentally perceptive elves to his reawakening. He looked down at the device around his neck, which had been designed to limit his memories and personality to only the most gentle, innocent, and docile version of himself. It had originally been developed to thwart the gate guardians, but there had been mixed results and other methods had been developed. When the jinn rebellion had been realized, they had used the devices to try to hide their intentions, produce false memories, and send spies that might be trusted as refugees or defectors. The plan had not worked, as the technologically curious jinn had quickly dissected the devices and realized their purpose. When the guards alerted them to elves, of all things, exiting the gate, they decided to give it another try. This way they would have agents in the elf realm who could reopen the gate when necessary. The goblins knew their own coordinates, but not those of the elves.

The high goblin sat down and pondered his next move. The elves were active at almost all hours of the day and night, though they tended to be slightly less so in the middle of the day and the middle of the night. The leaders of the facility had left to explore another realm only a few days prior. They were not scheduled to return for a couple more days.

He waited, quieting and calming his mind to mask his intensions.

Night fell and the sounds of the facility grew quiet.

Silently, the high goblin snuck through the facility. No one was near the gate when he arrived. He mentally commanded it to dial the coordinates and opened the gate to his home realm. He tossed his medallion into the gate and ran.

"Why is the gate open?" he heard someone call out behind him.

The high goblin did not turn or wait to see what happened next. The sound of something large and hard rolling across the stone followed him as he slipped between the buildings and ran toward the forest to wait out the initial attack.

*   *   *

The wood elf sat in his room, carving a piece of wood. A familiar sound and shifting multi-colored lights flickered through the window. He walked down into the courtyard around the gate and saw that it had been activated.

"Why is the gate open?" he said out loud to no one.

Movement in the corner of his eye drew his attention and he turned, reaching for an arrow.

The sound of something large and hard hitting the stone made him turn back in time to see a large egg, about three feet in diameter, roll out followed by about two dozen more. Confused, he took a step forward. He commanded the gate to close and watched the egg.

The eggshell cracked, and a reptilian head broke through. The elf stepped back and aimed his bow.

A second later, two large wings pushed their way out. What looked like a small dragon clawed its way free. It had two wings, two hind legs, and a tail. The creature turned in the elf's direction and screamed at him. The sight of something so similar to the creatures that had destroyed the Elders elicited an instinctively hostile response.

Without hesitation, the elf released the arrow into the creature. He was not going to let these things destroy their new home. He turned to shout a warning and heard several eggs crack at once.

He turned back, reaching for another arrow. The sounds of elves running to his aid could be heard behind him. He aimed at the nearest hatchling.

A rushing sound to his left made him turn, but not fast enough. Sharp teeth tore him open.

*   *   *

Gwarchod awoke with a sense of impending doom. He looked out the window of Ymladdwr and Gwyddoniaeth's treehouse and saw the research facility on fire.

49

Rushing down the stairs, he could hear Llyfryn running through the trees above him.

Do you know what happened? she asked.

No.

Gwarchod was unsure if he should allow her to rush into danger, but she was fully grown and had survived expeditions alone for years. Her assistance would be helpful, so he set aside his momentary trepidation.

When he got closer, he could see a dragon-like creature climb on top of one of the buildings. It only had four limbs; two wings and two legs, unlike the dragons that had destroyed his homeland, which had four legs. Gwarchod skidded to a halt in shock. How could dragons have found them? How did they get here?

That did not matter right now. His eyes scanning the flaming facility, he knew that if anyone was still alive in there, they needed to get them out.

Get down here, we need to move as one, he ordered.

Llyfryn landed on the ground next to him, and they silently crept through the shadows toward the facility. They slipped inside the first building. There were signs that the creatures had torn through the rooms. Tables and objects were strewn about. He reached out with his mind but only found the creatures.

If anyone survived, they fled, he observed.

My parents are not scheduled to be back until the day after tomorrow. We need to reopen the gate for them.

They crept to a window and watched the creatures moving about the sphinx gate. He reached out again and scanned for the creatures themselves.

There are only about half a dozen in the facility's general vicinity. Most are near the edges, he thought to her.

I think I see the remains of at least a couple dozen

eggs on or around the platform.

He could see that she was right. From their vantage point, he saw four dragon-like corpses near the gate, but it was obvious that they were smaller than the ones moving around.

A strange sound rang out and he turned to see one of the creatures on the far side of the gate eating a corpse. As it ate, it seemed to grow, grunting and whining with its growing pains. The sight gave him a sinking feeling. Now he knew why the dragon-like creatures that were still alive seemed larger than would have fit in the shattered eggs. There was no way to know if these creatures would get as big as the dragons that had destroyed the Elders, but if they grew this fast each time they ate, then they might become too large to stop.

We are not going to get reinforcements in time, and those things are growing already, he thought.

He weighed their options in his mind. There were six of the creatures still near the facility, but most were slowly moving away. Working together, they might be able to kill them one at a time, but it would be dangerous. While focusing on one, the other five could still attack from multiple angles, and if they died or were delayed, Gwyddoniaeth and Ymladdwr would not make it back. Gwarchod glanced at Llyfryn. He remembered her as the bright young child she had been when they first met and was not eager to risk her life. Perhaps they should wait until the dragon-like creatures had dispersed?

What is that?

Gwarchod looked down and saw a figure carefully approaching the gate. It was a goblin.

The gate reactivated and more eggs rolled through. The goblin slipped back into the shadows.

Now we know if the goblins can be trusted, he mused bitterly.

Should we hunt them down?

We can deal with the goblins later. That one has already disappeared back into the forest. I would guess that they cannot control these creatures, at least not newly hatched, considering how quickly he ran away. We need to close the gate and get rid of those eggs before they hatch. The creatures that are on the outskirts can wait until your parents return. This way we ensure their safety and increase our chances of success in killing these things.

Llyfryn nodded.

Stay here and keep guard. I will sneak closer to the gate to get within range, so I can close it properly. I do not want to risk damaging it by forcing the rings out of alignment from this distance, and it only reacts to mental commands from a short distance away. If that creature on the other side notices, shoot it.

She nodded again, drew an arrow, and nocked it.

Gwarchod silently slipped out of the building and moved toward the gate. He kept in line with one of the gryphons in case the glowing swirling portal was not enough to block the sight of him. By the time he reached the dais, one of the eggs began to hatch.

Quickly, he stretched out his hand and reached out with his mind and threw the egg back into the gate.

A crack caught his attention, and he turned to see another hatching. As quickly as he could, he began hurling the hatching eggs into the portal, but he was not fast enough. The last egg had already hatched and the creature let out a cry as it flew through the air toward the portal.

The dragon-like creature on the other side of the gate turned in his direction and began to move around the gate to see what had caused the noise.

One of the smaller hatchlings stepped back out of the gate. Gwarchod flung it back in and closed the portal with a mental command.

The creature's head snapped to look straight over the now empty dais. It charged over the dais and Gwarchod held out his hands, his mind halting the creature mid stride. An arrow shot out of one of the buildings and pierced the side of its throat. The creature screeched, raising its head and twisting its neck. The next arrow entered where the jaw met the throat on the underneath side of its head. It went limp and he dropped it.

The sounds of flapping wings and scraping claws drew nearer, and Gwarchod rushed back to the building to hide before the other creatures returned.

Thank you, he thought to Llyfryn as he rejoined her.

You are welcome.

Hopefully these will disperse soon, he commented as three of the creatures began examining the remains of their comrade and exploring the gate area again.

Day and night passed; by the time the sun rose on the day that Ymladdwr and Gwyddoniaeth were scheduled to return, three dead creatures lay slain in the room with them, while one dead goblin remained slumped near the gate. The rest of the creatures who had been near the facility had wandered away by this point, and no other goblins had returned.

In the early morning hours, before it was fully light, Gwarchod and Llyfryn left their hiding place.

Silently, they crept out of the building to the dais.

Gwarchod mentally commanded the gate to open, and Llyfryn rushed through. He turned to watch the surrounding area while he waited.

Gwyddoniaeth and Ymladdwr followed Llyfryn back out of the gate a few seconds later. They made their way quickly into the forest and up into the branches.

Do we know how the dragon-like creatures got here? asked Gwyddoniaeth.

It appears the goblins let them through, replied Gwarchod.

He could sense the disappointment and guilt mixed with anger in Gwyddoniaeth and Ymladdwr. He felt sorry for them as they were the ones to make first contact and advocate for allowing the goblins into their realm.

Do you know how many goblins are left? asked Ymladdwr.

We only killed one goblin while we waited. We do not know if the other three survived the creatures or not, replied Gwarchod.

And as for the dragon-like creatures, how many are there? inquired Gwyddoniaeth.

There were remains of approximately twenty-four eggs when we arrived with four creatures already dead. We killed four, so there are most likely at least sixteen remaining, calculated Llyfryn.

We need to hunt these creatures down before they cause more damage, or even breed. If we are fortunate, we may be able to rescue survivors, though by now that seems unlikely, stated Ymladdwr.

The creatures seem to grow in proportion to when they eat. We do not know if they have a maximum size yet, added Gwarchod.

Based on what I saw when we came through the gate, these might not be "real" dragons. They do not have separate front legs, observed Gwyddoniaeth.

What about the goblins? asked Llyfryn.

We can deal with them if we find them. We can sweep the area around the facility in ever-widening circles to find both the creatures and the traitors, replied Gwyddoniaeth with a hint of anger.

Most of the creatures were gone when we got there, which means they might have been chasing fleeing elves. Since the first goblin ran away immediately after opening the gate for the second batch of eggs, they might stay away until they think the creatures have dispersed again, commented Gwarchod.

The four elves moved deeper into the forest.

There; I sense one of the creatures about a hundred yards to the right, thought Llyfryn, projecting her inner sense of the relative location.

The four elves snuck up on one of the creatures and looked down at it. At nearly six feet high at the shoulder, it was now much larger than the four-foot-tall ones that he and Llyfryn had killed near the gate. This one was currently eating a horned bear. It did not seem to be growing as rapidly as before.

Llyfryn moved to a branch positioning herself to one side of the creature, drew an arrow, and nocked it while Gwarchod raised his hand and reached out with his mind. He was vaguely aware of a subtle sense of surprise from Gwyddoniaeth as his mind slammed the creature into the ground and restrained it. Llyfryn released her arrow into the creature's ribs. It struggled against the invisible restraint but was not dead. Most likely its larger size was going to make it harder to kill.

Ymladdwr dropped from the trees and walked over to the creature. He drew his daggers and rammed them down through the top of the skull. It died instantly.

Gwarchod released his grip and glanced at

Gwyddoniaeth. He projected the images of his memories of him and Llyfryn learning to attack the creatures that entered the building they were hiding in. He would restrain the creature, while she killed it with her bow. They were smaller than the one below and died more easily. Gwyddoniaeth nodded in understanding.

"We need to find the rest," she said.

*　　*　　*

The high goblin returned to the research facility after several days. The wyverns should have dispersed by now. These freshly hatched wyverns were nearly feral and would not obey commands, so he proceeded cautiously.

When he arrived at the devastated facility, he quickly reactivated the gate, his head swiveling around repeatedly. After a few minutes, five lesser goblins came through. They were slightly shorter than him, and their skin was green mottled with purple.

He motioned for silence then gestured for them to follow him. The high goblin led them into one of the buildings and showed them a room where several elvish bows and quivers full of arrows were stored.

"Search the rest of the buildings and the corpses. Gather what weapons you can. When the batch comes through, we will begin the next phase. Until then, I want guards in every outward facing room of this facility. If you even think an elf might be approaching, sound the alarm."

The lesser goblins nodded their understanding, and moved to obey.

*　　*　　*

56

Several days later, Gwyddoniaeth stood over the corpse of the thirteenth dragon-like creature they had tracked and slain. Part of her felt a twinge of guilt every time she held one down for it to be killed, but she was not about to let any kind of dragon destroy their new home. Seeing the dead elves at the gate facility had resurrected the sorrow she felt immediately after they had fled their previous homeland. When she had looked at the remnants of the corpses, her mind had immediately overlaid them with images of Cariadllyfr and Ymchwil. The sorrow was compounded by a sense of guilt for having allowed the goblins into their realm in the first place. It had taken a few days for the reflexive emotions to pass as she focused her efforts on ensuring that no one else shared that fate.

"Do you smell smoke?" asked Llyfryn.

She turned and looked at Llyfryn, then at Ymladdwr.

"Could it be a forest fire?"

"I doubt it; the weather has been fairly damp these past several weeks," Ymladdwr said.

"Something has happened near the gate," said Gwarchod, his gaze focused on the distance, as if trying to see through the trees and miles separating them from the facility.

Gwyddoniaeth and the other elves began running through the trees.

*   *   *

The trees were on fire. Gwarchod followed Ymladdwr and Gwyddoniaeth as they ran east, around the fire to get a better look at the area surrounding the gate. The winds were coming down from the mountains and pushing the fire away from the gate. It had not spread far at this point and was mostly on the facility's south side.

When the gate facility came into view, they stopped.

The research facility was swarming with creatures that looked similar to the goblins they had met previously, but with noticeable differences. These were slightly shorter, about chest height, with green and purple mottled skin. Their faces seemed etched in expressions of resentment, hatred, and rage. Some of them carried elvish weapons. Others carried crudely and quickly fashioned spears, knives, and arrows with stone blades.

He must have let more of them through, commented Gwarchod.

It will take months to reach the council and warn them, thought Gwyddoniaeth.

The gate is open, but I do not see any coming through at the moment, observed Gwarchod.

Father and I still have plenty of arrows, added Llyfryn.

We need to kill the goblins and secure the gate. Then we can consider whether to warn the council first or pursue the remaining dragon-like creatures, decided Ymladdwr.

We should move around to the north side of the facility, trap them between us and the fire, advised Gwyddoniaeth.

Agreed, everyone replied.

They maneuvered their way into position. Gwarchod and Gwyddoniaeth stepped back. He began to scan the area mentally as Ymladdwr and Llyfryn moved forward and took aim. By now the four of them had much practice working together. Ymladdwr and Llyfryn would act as the main offensive force, while Gwyddoniaeth and Gwarchod would serve as surveillance and defense. While their minds could sweep the area and sense other minds at a great distance beyond their physical senses, the range of the direct physical effects of their abilities was noticeably less than the range of the archers' arrows. Llyfryn and Ymladdwr were much more well practiced with their bows, while Gwyddoniaeth and Gwarchod were the first and second generation of teachers who had taught all of the other elves in the meddwlgrym training program.

When the elves mutually sensed each other's readiness, Ymladdwr and Llyfryn released their arrows. Two goblins on top of one of the buildings fell with arrows protruding from them.

I can sense about a hundred goblins dispersed throughout the facility, stated Gwyddoniaeth.

Two more goblins fell.

The four elves stepped out from behind the sparse trees and moved closer. The next goblin to fall was followed by a shout.

They know we are here, warned Gwarchod.

More shouts rang out among the goblins, and Gwarchod could sense them running through the buildings.

An arrow shot down out of a window, and Gwarchod raised his hand to knock it from the sky. Llyfryn's own arrow replaced it in the opposite direction, and the goblin fell to the ground.

They are gathering together, warned Gwyddoniaeth.

The elves rushed between the buildings in time to see the goblins running out of the buildings on the south, east, and west and moving quickly toward the ones on the north side of the gate. Many seemed surprised to see the intruders and skidded to a halt.

Gwyddoniaeth stretched forth her hand and several of the goblins went flying into a wall.

Gwarchod did the same.

Ymladdwr and Llyfryn put arrows in them as quickly as they could.

Despite the quick arrows and mental assaults, there were too many goblins. Arrows quickly began to pelt them from windows as goblins who survived impact recovered and crawled inside for cover. The more the two high elves had to block arrows, the less they were able to attack.

Unwilling to abandon the gate, the group backed into the nearest doorway, hoping to find cover.

This building is mostly stone, so they cannot burn us out, thought Gwarchod.

Stay back from the windows except when firing, Ymladdwr instructed Llyfryn.

Move to the second floor. We will have a better vantage point there, directed Gwyddoniaeth.

The elves ran up the stairs to the second floor. Gwyddoniaeth and Gwarchod reached out with their minds and moved shelves and tables to cover the windows and the hole in the floor at the top of the stairs. Gwarchod and Gwyddoniaeth positioned themselves at one window and Llyfryn and Ymladdwr positioned themselves at the other, both facing the gate. The pairs were split on either side of their respective windows, everyone peering through the gaps between the walls and the repositioned shelves.

There may be too many of them for us to handle, noted Gwyddoniaeth.

What happens when we run out of arrows? asked Llyfryn.

We can use ones that they have shot at us, but that will not last if they realize what we are doing and just try to starve us out instead, replied Ymladdwr.

Look! alerted Gwarchod.

A group of goblins walked out of the gate. Another

began shouting to them to go back and warn the others.

Ymladdwr and Llyfryn shot two of the goblins, but the others turned to flee. They froze just before the gate, unable to move as the two high elves held them in place. The elvish archers finished them off.

We need to shut the gate, thought Ymladdwr.

Gwyddoniaeth stepped forward and reached out. The metal rings resisted but popped out of alignment and the portal collapsed.

We could probably kill more if you did it mentally, noted Ymladdwr.

Gwarchod paused. This idea had occurred to him, but even when he exerted force directly onto the creatures to push or hold them, his mind touched theirs and he could feel their pain. It was easy to ignore when striking, but during a prolonged contact, it became more unnerving as it persisted. He was not sure how bad it would be if he ended a life directly with his mind. He looked at Gwyddoniaeth who was gazing at the floor, obviously pondering the same thing.

Let us see if we can find some debris to use as projectiles, she suggested, looking back up.

Gwarchod and his mentor turned and began tearing the furniture apart, placing the pieces in a stack on the floor. They then removed the shelf blocking their window and broke it down.

We need to clear the area around the gate first, then we can clear the buildings, instructed Gwyddoniaeth.

The two high elves stepped up to the window. They each raised a hand, pointing to the debris and lifting a piece into the air. Once they had selected their targets, they began sending the pieces of wood flying into the goblins below. They released them before they hit the targets, and the goblins were crushed or impaled. As they stepped back and turned to acquire more projectiles from the pile, the archers stepped up and fired their arrows.

Goblins scurried into the buildings to escape. Gwyddoniaeth picked up wreckage and held it near the outside of the windows to block the goblins' arrows as the others continued the assault. The elves aimed their respective projectiles as best they could at the goblins who fired at them from windows of the other buildings. Gwarchod was able to steer his around corners.

Some of the goblins managed to sneak around the base of the building out of line of sight while the elves were focused on other targets. Whenever footsteps sounded on the stairs below, Ymladdwr would spin around, his arrow impaling the skull of the intruder as soon as it peaked above the floor. If a goblin carried any arrows, Ymladdwr would retrieve them and toss them over to the windows, so he and his daughter could use them. Then he would return to firing arrows out of the windows.

I doubt they intend to keep sneaking in and dying. If we do not find a way to break out of here and directly into another building, then we will be at stalemate, since whoever leaves through a doorway will be shot by the other, commented Ymladdwr.

A thud on the roof above broke the concentration of the two high elves and distracted the archers. A moment later, the roof's plates were being torn apart to reveal the dragon-like creatures they had been hunting. These were not as big as the ones they had most recently killed, implying they were younger. Shouted commands in the goblin language could be heard from outside, and the creatures reacted accordingly. In the back of his mind, Gwarchod took note of this; the goblins could command this new batch of creatures.

The high elves held the first creature still while the archers filled its throat with arrows. The corpse was soon replaced by two more creatures as different parts of the roof were torn open. Footsteps below warned of more goblins. Ymladdwr turned his attention to the opening in the floor, firing repeatedly as the goblins peeked over the edge. He rushed onto the stairs, trading his bow for his daggers in the tight space. Llyfryn began putting arrows into the dragon-like creatures' throats, while the high elves held them in place. The barrier over her window exploded behind her, and another reptilian head rammed into her back, sending her to the floor.

Gwyddoniaeth shifted her focus immediately and gripped the creature's head with her mind. Her fingers closed into a fist, and she crushed its skull. Gwarchod saw her expression wince in pain, but she recovered quickly.

Noise from above drew his attention back to the creatures tearing through the roof. He reached out and crushed the skull of the first one he saw. His mind could feel the anger, followed by pain, then fear just before it died. It was disturbing to feel it so directly, but circumstances required that he endure the creature's suffering. He needed to protect his mentor and her family. Gwyddoniaeth killed the next one.

Crashing and growls from below caught their attention. Ymladdwr leaped back up into the room, quickly followed by one of the creatures. Just before it bit Ymladdwr, Gwyddoniaeth smashed it against a wall, breaking the floor and stairs in the process. Gwarchod could hear the bones shatter with the impact.

Get Llyfryn out of here, commanded Gwyddoniaeth.

Right away replied Gwarchod.

He turned to the far wall and stretched forth his hand;

the wall exploded outward. Across a small gap was the sloped roof of the next building.

Onto the rooftops, he instructed.

He leaped onto the next rooftop, spinning around, hand outstretched, scanning for threats behind him. It was clear for now.

Go, he ordered.

Llyfryn joined him and then ran past him along the edge of the roof that sloped up to her right, bow in hand, looking back and forth. He watched as two more of the creatures burst out of the hole in the floor and Gwyddoniaeth and Ymladdwr turned to deal with the new threat.

A moment later, an arrow whizzed past his head. He looked up to see goblins mounting the rooftops nearby, on the other side of the building they were fleeing from, and aiming their bows. His mind slammed into them, knocking them from their perches.

A mental shout made him turn in time to see three more coming over the edge of the roof they were on, very close to Llyfryn's right side. At point blank range, they aimed their bows at Llyfryn, but she could only hit one with her bow in time.

Gwarchod reached out with both hands and crushed the other two goblins. In the process, his mind touched theirs and he felt their anger and hatred followed by pain, then fear and despair as they realized they were going to die. Since their minds were more like his than the dragon-like creatures, their mental distress hit him even harder. The sensation made him stumble for a second, but it was one second too long.

*　　*　　*

From a distance, Gwyddoniaeth saw Gwarchod kill the goblin archers and stumble. As his concentration broke, an arrow hit him in the shoulder as another goblin peaked over the ridge. A second goblin appeared behind Llyfryn, who was still turned toward the one she had just shot. Gwyddoniaeth started to stretch out her hand, but it was too late. The goblin instantly stabbed Llyfryn with its spear, the tip bursting out of her chest. Her eyes went wide in a pained gasp.

Pain and rage filled Gwyddoniaeth, and the goblin with the spear exploded, ripped apart limb from limb. She rushed to her daughter's side. She tried to stop the bleeding while Ymladdwr stood over her shooting anything that moved. Gwarchod joined him.

Gwyddoniaeth touched her daughter's mind, trying to comfort her, even as she realized that the spear had pierced her heart. Despair and panic washed over her as she clutched at the wound. Her daughter's pain and fear as the life flowed out of her consumed Gwyddoniaeth's awareness. As the seconds ticked by, she could do nothing but experience directly the fading of Llyfryn's mind until she was dead.

A pain unlike anything she had ever experienced erupted inside her; rage and hatred at those who killed her daughter and her own lack of ability to save her. The inner turmoil boiled over. She spun around to face the facility. She reached out and clenched her fingers in fists of rage and grief. Buildings imploded. Rubble went flying. Her vision became a tunnel. Nothing else existed except her immediate target. She crushed and tore goblins limb from limb. The dragon-like creatures were pulled out of the air screaming in pain as they were ripped to pieces before being crushed or broken. Everything needed to die, but none of it was enough to quench her sorrow.

It was not until the building she was on began to crumble that she came back to the world. She hit the ground hard.

Ymladdwr grabbed her arm.

We need to leave, he stated firmly.

Her anger spent, she was numb and empty. She allowed Ymladdwr to lift, then guide and almost carry her out and away from the facility.

"Llyfryn..." she muttered, looking back for her daughter's corpse.

"Gwarchod has her. We must keep moving." Ymladdwr's voice was stern but not harsh. She had nothing left inside of her to even consider arguing.

Glancing back, she saw her former student carrying her dead daughter and then cried as she ran through the forest.

*　　*　　*

The high elf walked through the forest, staring at the ground, his mind preoccupied by the hand held in his. Telynor's companion was Ystyriaeth, to him the most beautiful elf on the content. He looked over at her, an unstoppable smile on his face.

She smiled back and they continued their walk in silence, enjoying the forest and each other's presence. Ystyriaeth began to hum a song under her breath as they approached a stream that ran swiftly toward a waterfall to their right. She knelt down to touch the water. Telynor stretched and looked around, enjoying the cool wet breeze that drifted over the water.

The humming stopped. They both sensed something was wrong.

Telynor heard several strange sounds at once. He turned in time to see arrows flying out of the forest. He stepped in front of Ystyriaeth and tried to stop them, but there were too many. His mind could not concentrate on them fast enough. Even if he made sweeping gestures, there were more and each time they seemed to originate closer and closer. Eventually, he could see strange green and purple mottled creatures approaching between the trees.

A cry rang out behind him. He turned in time to see an arrow protruding from Ystyriaeth's shoulder. Desperate, he spun back and tried to directly kill one of the creatures with his mind. The horrible sensation of feeling a sentient creature die overwhelmed him.

His shock was replaced by pain as arrows pierced his left shoulder and right thigh.

He stepped back and Ystyriaeth reached out to support him. Telynor glanced to his left in time to see an arrow pierce her throat and she fell away. He turned and reached out to catch her. Grief devasted his mind, blinding him to all but her as the waters carried her downstream.

Another arrow pierced his right side. Instinctively, he clutched at the wound and gazed at the blood. He turned to face his enemies, eyes drifting up to see the creatures approaching between the trees and readying more arrows. The elf took a couple steps back, fell into the river, and was carried off by the rushing water.

*   *   *

Caredig and her younger brother were crouched in a tree overlooking a herd of deer a few yards away. She whispered instructions to him as he raised his bow. He was young and had been practicing since he could walk, but this was the first time he had gone hunting.

The moment before he released the arrow, the deer's heads perked up and they ran.

Both elves stood and looked around curiously. Caredig noticed a strange sound in the air above.

Before she could identify it, a large creature crashed down through the trees.

Caredig and her brother were knocked off their perch by a falling branch. They landed on their feet in crouching positions.

She looked around to see a large, dragon-like creature stalking toward them.

Quickly, she was on her feet, bow in hand, arrow nocked.

The first arrow hit the creature in the side of the neck close to the shoulder.

She called for her brother.

He responded from a few feet to her left.

"Run!" she yelled.

The creature rushed them.

She fired an arrow down its throat, which caused it to stop and writhe in pain, yet it did not die. She nocked another arrow and fired into its upturned throat.

There was a crash and a scream behind her. She turned in time to see another of the creatures lunge at her brother.

Her arrows came too late.

*   *   *

Ymladdwr followed Gwyddoniaeth and Gwarchod as they moved slowly through the forest. His senses continually scanned the surrounding vegetation, waiting for inevitable signs of goblin pursuit. It had been about a week since they had fled the gate facility and, so far, they had not seen any signs of the invaders. He reasoned that the goblins must be fortifying their position around gate.

He glanced in irritation at the two elves in front of him. Gwyddoniaeth was still moving slowly, lost in a grief-induced stupor. Gwarchod alternated between using his mental abilities to carry Llyfryn's corpse and his own physical strength.

Once they had slowed from their initial flight from the gate, Ymladdwr had switched to the rear position in the group. They had only been able to maintain a running pace for a short period of time until physical and mental limitations began to set in. Gwyddoniaeth was too consumed with grief and inwardly focused to even care to move quickly. Gwarchod was obviously draining himself mentally and physically by carrying Llyfryn the whole time. This left Ymladdwr as the only one physically and mentally capable of dealing immediately with any new threats. The rear position allowed him to watch the others and guard without risking leaving them behind accidentally.

When the sun set, they made camp. Gwyddoniaeth sat staring off into space until Gwarchod moved away from where he had set Llyfryn's corpse. She then moved to sit with her dead daughter, refusing to ever even glimpse Gwarchod. Ymladdwr watched her eyes tracing along the ground and looking into the forest, making sweeping arcs to avoid catching sight of her former pupil.

Ymladdwr moved up into the trees to keep watch while the others slept. Eventually, sleep overtook him as well.

A small sound, the breaking of a twig, caused Ymladdwr's eyes to snap open. He scanned the dark forest and moved silently through the branches until he spotted the goblin patrol. There were about a dozen goblins, and they were following the trail the elves had left.

For the past week, he had felt neither joy nor sorrow, but looking at the goblins below filled him with a lethal rage. He drew his dagger and dropped from the tree to land behind the last goblin in the group. Swiftly and silently his hand shot out, the dagger's blade piercing the skull of the goblin. As the corpse fell, he moved forward. Before the sound of the body hitting the ground could register in their minds, the next goblin was dead. They turned, shocked and terrified by his sudden appearance and rushing attacks. Those who tried to fight were quickly cut down. Those who fled dropped with arrows in their backs.

Ymladdwr looked at the goblin corpses. Part of him wanted to turn back, to return to the gate and kill every last one of them, follow them through the portal and eradicate their entire species. But another part of him knew that he should not. Justice would not allow for killing an entire species. Compassion for the other elves would not allow for them to not be warned of the impending threat. He was still responsible for his wife and her former student. There were things that needed to be done, and his emotions were only a hindrance.

The dead calm returned and Ymladdwr made his way back to his sleeping companions. He watched them for a moment before his eyes drifted to his daughter. They needed to bury her, both physically and mentally, so they could move faster. He wandered through the surrounding forest, searching for a suitable spot until he found a large tree whose massive roots protruded above the ground in such a way as to form a small hollow. He cleared out the space, removed some of the soil, and gathered various sticks, leaves, and small bushes. He then returned to the camp and retrieved his daughter's corpse. He placed her in the hollow and spent several long moments staring blankly before returning to his companions.

When the sun was beginning to rise, Gwyddoniaeth and Gwarchod began to stir. Gwyddoniaeth's hand reached out instinctively for her daughter but found only empty ground. She immediately sat up and looked around in concern.

"Where is Llyfryn?" she asked hastily as she began to walk around, scanning the forest.

"Do not worry, I just moved her body," Ymladdwr said.

"Where?" she asked harshly.

By now Gwarchod was awake and watching them.

"I will show you."

Ymladdwr led the two elves to the burial site he had prepared and pointed at her body lying in the dugout hollow under the tree's roots. "We need to bury her so that we can move on."

"Move on? What do you mean move on? I'm not abandoning my daughter out here," Gwyddoniaeth shot back angrily.

"Last night a goblin patrol came within a hundred yards of us. Carrying the body is slowing Gwarchod, and your grief is slowing you."

Gwyddoniaeth glared at him; "Well at least I am grieving. I haven't seen you shed a single tear this whole time. Do you even care that your daughter is dead?"

Ymladdwr's eyes narrowed, and he suppressed his instinctive rage. "We do not have time grieve now; we need to warn the council."

"Carrying the body means we can't move through the

trees, which slows us down and makes us easy to track. We still need to reach the city and alert the council. The longer we take, the greater the risk that other elves' sons and daughters may die," said Gwarchod quietly from behind her.

Gwyddoniaeth refused to turn, but her glare lessened slightly. She looked down at her daughter's body for a while before kneeling down beside her. She gently stroked her face and whispered, "I love you. I will come back for you."

With that, she stood up and walked a few paces from the tree. Gwyddoniaeth raised her hands, and large clumps of soil were lifted. She spent the next several minutes covering Llyfryn, then positioning the sticks, leaves, and small plants so as to best disguise the grave's location.

About two and half months later, the three elves met with the council as soon as they arrived. Gwarchod took his seat with the other eight. Gwyddoniaeth and Ymladdwr delivered their testimony. He noticed that Gwyddoniaeth faced any elf but Gwarchod when she spoke. The council ended the meeting with the decision to send out warnings immediately and to discuss strategies the next day. In the meantime, the three travelers were advised to rest for the night.

That night, Ymladdwr sat alone in an empty room. The tasks were done. There was nothing left to distract him. The grief poured in, and he collapsed in the darkness. All of the emotions that had been held in check by necessity were now free to flow. Agony and grief flooded his mind. He just wanted his daughter back.

The next morning, Ymladdwr found himself involuntarily wandering into the council chamber to listen to what they had planned. He felt calm and empty after the catharsis of the previous night. He leaned against the wall, back between two of the pillars, and listened.

"We should abandon the city and this realm as soon as possible. We can use the caves to gather everyone in the city and then use the submersibles to leave this realm," he heard one of the council members say. There were some murmurs of agreement.

Anger stirred within Ymladdwr, deepening the more he thought about what they were saying. The council members were considering leaving and letting his daughter's killers go unpunished. They would abandon the wandering elves to lose their own children to these monsters. How could that be in accordance with the Narrow Path? This was not right; it was not just. Betrayers and murderers deserved justice. The goblins had earned their reward; they had earned death.

Rage blazed in his eyes as he ceased leaning against the wall and began to focus more intently on the council's debate.

*   *   *

Gwarchod hung his head as he listened to the council discussing options. The messengers had left the previous night with warnings for everyone they could find. Gwyddoniaeth stood in the center of the ring of tables. She would not even look at him now. She had not said it, but he knew why. If he had not frozen, he might have been able to save Llyfryn. It was his fault she was dead. Knowing that Gwyddoniaeth likely blamed him validated his own sense of failed responsibility, guilt, and self-hatred. He deserved it.

Someone suggested fleeing the realm.

Gwarchod lifted his head, about to point out the logistical issues with such a suggestion, when an angry voice rang out from the shadows. Ymladdwr had been calm the

73

entire trip back, but now he was responding vehemently. The calmer part of Gwarchod wondered if the death of Llyfryn had only just settled in or if the grieving father had finally reached his breaking point.

Ymladdwr stepped forward into the light of the lamps, objecting to the plan to flee. "The goblins killed my daughter; they killed our friends. The Narrow Path demands justice, and abandoning this realm will bring neither justice to their killers nor protection for those we leave behind. They will die while we run, and the murderers will never be stopped."

The hostility in his voice was palpable. Gwarchod glanced around, confirming with his eyes the discomfort and shame he sensed around him.

Gwyddoniaeth spoke up, "I agree. We should not flee. We know there are other realms and that there are existing passages between them. If we run, it only prolongs the inevitable. One day we will be forced to stand and face those that wish to kill us or we ourselves will be destroyed."

Gwarchod could not help noticing that she was extremely calm now. The barely restrained tears and the cracking voice she had possessed during their trip back were gone. She had barely spoken during the trip back, and when she gave her testimony the previous day, she had been quieter and more subdued. Her voice was stronger and clearer now, though she had not quite returned to her former disposition. There was something almost too calm, or perhaps, something cold about her now.

*   *   *

Gwyddoniaeth was at peace now. The long months of walking back to the city had allowed her to work through her

74

grief. She regretted her harshness when they buried Llyfryn. The time for grieving was over. Now was the time for action.

"I propose we fortify the city. It will stand as a beacon for our people, a place where we can offer refuge and training. We can prepare behind our high walls. If everything fails, we can always retreat to the caves and flee the realm, but such a course of action should be our last resort," she proposed.

"Why waste our time building our own tomb? We need to go back to the gate and kill them," said Ymladdwr, now standing beside her.

She could feel his anger. How could he allow his emotions to control him in this moment? Making decisions based on emotion was not wise in these circumstances.

"We do not have trained armies or enough weapons to launch an assault. By the time we reach the gate again, they will have fortified their position, and our people will die needlessly. Fortifying the city gives us a safe place to prepare. The sentinels will alert us should the dragon-like creatures approach, and by then we will have more arrows or other projectiles to hurl at them," she countered, turning to look at Ymladdwr.

"If we wait to attack, the goblins will be too strong to dislodge. They have an entire realm's worth of resources behind them. You and your students have been training for a couple centuries now. Surely there are high elves who are useful for something at this point," he said in irritation, returning her stare.

"Most have never hunted, and none have killed with their powers. You saw the effect it had at the gate. Your own daughter died because of the hesitation. If you throw the students at the goblins now, unprepared, most of them will likely die. The only ones who survive will do so only because their friends are being killed instead. Do you really want to waste more elvish lives?" she stated coldly.

"I have no desire to waste anyone's life, but I also have no intention to stand by idly while the goblins build their strength and raid our people. While you hide behind your gates, what will stop the goblins from spreading out and killing more of our kind?" Ymladdwr responded, the furrow in his brow and tone deepening with his anger.

Gwyddoniaeth glared at Ymladdwr. Why could he not see the wisdom of her plan. Why could he not see her reasoning?

A voice cut through them, but she looked away from its source, while Ymladdwr turned to face the speaker.

"You both have valid points. We need a defensive position in which to prepare, but we also need to weaken the goblins and protect the wandering elves. I propose that Gwyddoniaeth lead the project to fortify the city. Ymladdwr can form a warband with whoever is able and willing to fight right now to patrol the northern forests. I will organize with the existing scouts to arrange reconnaissance, warnings, and escorts to bring everyone back to safety. The others here in the council will coordinate supplies, so we can arm the city and move resources north so that the warband does not need to make the complete trip back to restock."

Gwyddoniaeth looked at a random elf on the council; "I agree."

Ymladdwr snorted, looked off to the side, then back toward the speaker; "Agreed."

The sentiment was repeated with increasing enthusiasm around the tables.

*   *   *

Ymladdwr crouched in the trees in the northern forest. The land in front of him was a wide swathe of destruction. In the months since he had left, the goblins had cut or burned most of the trees around the broken research facility. They had created a clear area around the facility of over five hundred yards, too far for the arrows to reach the goblins and enough space for them to see any attack before it arrived.

More of the four limbed dragon-like creatures could be seen wandering about. These beasts seemed to respond to orders from the goblins.

Ymladdwr's anger had diminished in the long trek back here from the city. Perhaps he had been too harsh on Gwyddoniaeth and the council. There was a benefit to their less aggressive plans, but he still believed that they needed to harrow the goblins to prevent them from becoming too powerful.

The few elves he had managed to gather before leaving the city waited in the branches nearby. Most were wood elves who had volunteered to help, but two of them had already seen what the goblins had wrought. One was a high elf whose betrothed had been killed by goblin raiders. He had been very quiet on the journey north, but the anger in his voice was unmistakable whenever he spoke about the goblins. The one time he spoke of his dead love, his voice cracked, and he never mentioned her again. The other was a wood elf whose younger brother had been killed by one of the dragon-like creatures. She would talk about him frequently, her eyes gaining a faraway look. She would then suddenly stop talking and her wistful expression would vanish before being replaced by one of hatred.

Ymladdwr considered his options. They could wait until dark and sneak in, but they would be outnumbered, and if arrows came from too many directions, they would not be able to escape unscathed. He did not want to lose any of his elves unnecessarily.

The empty fields also meant that the goblins' movements were easy to observe. He could look for patterns in their movements and would know if and when they left the safety of the facility.

Ymladdwr watched them moving back and forth, as if patrolling. The dragon-like creatures wandered around as well. A few flew around the perimeter of the clearing. The elves hid whenever the creatures came near.

That night, a band of goblins left the facility. They ran close to the ground, moving as quickly and as quietly as they could into the forest.

Ymladdwr smiled. In the darkness, they would not know what killed them.

*   *   *

Gwyddoniaeth stood in the war room of the city's central tower. In the years since the initial goblin attack at the gate, the elves had successfully constructed the walls around their city. Messengers came and went from the room, bringing her reports of the progress in their war against the goblins.

Standing on a balcony, she surveyed the city. She could see the high walls and the eight sentinel towers that each housed guards capable of extending their minds to scan the surrounding area to warn of an impending attack. Though they were not always visible, she knew that there were ballistae in each tower and spare bows and arrows at various stations along the walls. At the northern gate, couriers left with supplies to restock the caches that had been set up throughout the forest for the warbands.

Though she had not seen the wisdom of it at the time, she was now glad that Ymladdwr had begun the warbands. Without them patrolling the northern forests and picking off goblin raiding parties, she would not have had time to prepare the city; it would have been unprotected and likely would have fallen easily.

She moved to a different balcony, observing messengers and scouts returning. To the south, she could see hunting parties returning from the southern forests. Her experiences of the goblins' despair when she killed them with her mind had prompted preparatory hunting expeditions. These were the first steps in their new, more aggressive training program. The majority of the meddwlgrym trainees were high elves or sea elves. Most of the wood elves had opted to take more direct and immediate action by aiding the warbands with their archery skills.

The majority of all three factions had opted for archery training, which was much quicker and easier for them to learn, especially considering that few elves had never touched a bow, even in play. The archers' range was also greater than that of the mind.

The results of the new meddwlgrym training program were that the trainees fared better at handling the sensations of killing with their minds. The high elves, compared to the wood elves and sea elves, tended to be more sensitive to the animals' deaths. She had also noticed that many of the older elves who had lived before the destruction of the dragons had the hardest time killing the goblins, whether by bow or mind. Their lives had mostly been ones of peace, untouched by destruction and death. Ultimately, this still worked in favor of Gwyddoniaeth's plans; those who could not fight could build.

The Elvish Alliance was quite organized now. She smiled with satisfaction. They were almost ready to drive the goblins back from the gate.

*   *   *

Ymladdwr led his warband through the high branches of the trees. They moved silently, avoiding a direct line of sight as they tracked the goblin patrol below. The goblins traveled in a very spread out, haphazard formation so that it would be harder for them to be picked off in quick succession should they be spotted.

The goblins had learned long ago that a lone patrol was likely to never return if it left by itself, but if several patrols left in different directions, they had a better chance at survival. This patrol had managed to reach deeper into the forest than most. It was headed roughly south, yet still fairly close to the mountains. Based on how far east they were relative to the facility, Ymladdwr was beginning to suspect that the goblins had found a way from the gate into the mountains and were using unseen passages to avoid the warbands. If they became entrenched in the mountains, it would not be good for the elves.

This time the warband included a couple new recruits from the city. They had completed Gwyddoniaeth's new training system, and it was time for them to gain real experience while surrounded by more seasoned elves.

The warband came into position, surrounding an area just ahead of where the goblins were walking.

Ymladdwr turned to the nearest newcomer. He was a high elf named Bwriad, who was almost as old as Ymladdwr. He carried a long knife and a bow but had the bow set aside. He was here to test his new skills.

80

The goblins entered the trap.

Bwriad made eye contact and Ymladdwr nodded. The newcomer reached out his hand toward the last goblin in the group and began to curl his fingers. The goblin stopped and grabbed its head. The newcomer's fingers closed into a fist and the goblin's head caved in. His arm dropped as his eyes went wide. The corpse fell limply to the ground.

Now was the moment of truth. The goblins had not noticed the loss of one of their own yet.

Bwriad closed his eyes, took a deep breath, and reached out again. His hand began to clench, but it wavered. The goblin was pulled back but managed to gurgle out a sound.

The other goblins turned and realized what was happening. Shouts went up and the goblins began to run.

Ymladdwr was not surprised. He did not blame anyone for not having the stomach to kill. In his calmer moments, he understood it. In the heat of battle, he did not care; only the death of his daughter's killers mattered.

Ymladdwr raised his bow and released his arrow. It bent slightly around a tree and tore a gaping hole through a fleeing goblin.

*   *   *

Telynor watched Bwriad fail. Most of them did, and it irritated him each time. He was older than their arrival in this new land, but he had learned to deal with the mental backlash from directly killing a sentient creature. Why could the newcomer not do the same?

Once the goblins realized what was happening, they began to scatter. Telynor reached out with his mind and began crushing and tearing goblins. Each time his mind touched one, he felt their fear and panic at the realization of their inevitable death. None of it stopped him. Each time, he focused instead on the pain of Ystyriaeth's death. The rage of that moment was enough to drown out any sorrow or sympathy that he might have had.

Two goblins turned and fired arrows at his position. With a sweep of his hand, he knocked them from the air. Simultaneously, his other hand shot out and both goblins were flung back.

A moment later, both his fists were clenched before him, and the goblins were dead.

*   *   *

Caredig knew the newcomer would fail. She had met few high elves who were useful in battle up to this point, especially the older ones. The warbands were much smaller than the goblin patrols, and she knew they needed as many capable fighters as possible, but sometimes she wondered if it was really worth the effort.

When the goblins began to scatter, she was quick to attack. Killing sentient things was different than killing an animal, but that no longer mattered to her. These little monsters had brought the dragon-like creatures, the wyverns, and she would never forget her brother's last screams.

She almost took joy each time an arrow buried itself in the chest or head of a goblin.

She caught movement out of the corner of her eye. One had strayed farther than the others and was running. With a predatory smile, she raced through the trees. It would not escape. It would not live.

*   *   *

Gwarchod stood on the deck of a sea elf ship as it sailed down the continent's eastern coast. The wind whipped through his hair, and he gazed ahead at the sea and the shoreline. He enjoyed these quiet moments, closing his eyes and sighing as the wind moved over him; a pleasant peace amid the horrors of the last several years.

A shout broke his reverie and he turned, sensing where the sea elf lookout was indicating. Ten wyverns had broken out past the tree line and were soaring in their direction.

He ran to the back of the ship and faced the oncoming threat. On the main deck below, sea elves rushed to aim ballistae.

The creatures came closer, and he could see the irregular mass of goblins clinging to their legs.

The closest ones came within ballista range. Giant wooden bolts with huge, barbed metal spikes shot into the air. The first creature was impaled through the chest, but the second, which was slightly behind, managed to avoid the bolt.

The elves below hurried to reload before the creatures came too close. There was a limit to how high the ballistae could aim. They could only angle upward so much, meaning that if the creatures got too close, they would not be able to use the ballistae against them.

More bolts launched. Two more creatures fell from the sky.

The creatures came within arrow range, and a couple elves began firing to pick off the goblin passengers. At this height, the arrows were not likely to do much damage to the flying creatures, but the goblins were softer targets.

The first of the seven remaining creatures came

within the range of his mind. Mentally bracing himself, Gwarchod reached out and crushed its skull.

He killed two more and the ballistae got their fourth kill before one of the others made it over the ship.

Goblins rained down onto the deck, and the sea elves below turned to fight. With so many goblins spread across the deck, the elves switched to knives and daggers, as they were too close for their bows.

Knowing that the wyverns would remain circling the ship for now, Gwarchod reached out and began crushing the goblins below. Each time his mind touched one, he felt their pain, fear, and panic just before death. It hurt, but he hardened himself with calm resolve. He would not let anyone else die under his watch.

The goblins were quickly dispatched. The last one screamed some command to the flying creatures who had been circling during the battle.

Gwarchod suspected these attacks were meant to capture the ships, because the goblins never attempted structural damage until they knew they had lost.

But the elves were prepared. As soon as the creatures began to dive toward the ship, the elves below raced for their bows. When the creatures were low enough, they shot arrows upward until the first creature's neck bristled with their wooden shafts. It hit the side of the ship and slid into the water. The ship swayed, but the elves held their ground.

Gwarchod reached out with his mind and crushed the second creature's skull. He had to push it away before it lifelessly hit the ship. The third made it to the deck at the front of the ship, began biting, and rushed toward the elves.

Just before it reached them, Gwarchod's hand thrust forward, and his mind instinctively pushed the creature's head back. Before he could shatter the wyvern's skull, the elves pelted the exposed flesh with arrows, piercing its throat and the underside of its jaw. Gwarchod threw the corpse overboard.

*   *   *

       Gwarchod entered the war room in the central tower. Gwyddoniaeth stood with her back to him. He stood behind and slightly to one side of her while she looked down at the reports on the table in front of her.
       When he sensed her focus shift away from what was in front of her, despite not turning at all, he said, "Various scouts and warbands report the goblin raiding parties being discovered far from the gate yet close to the mountains. There is a concern that the goblins have tunneled into the mountains and are using them to avoid the warbands."
       Gwyddoniaeth turned to another elf; "Send messengers to Ymladdwr's warband. We need to formulate plans to retake the gate."

*   *   *

       Ymladdwr stood with the council around a table upon which lay a large map of the continent. Gwyddoniaeth stood across from him. Telynor and Caredig stood behind him, and Gwarchod stood behind Gwyddoniaeth.
       "What can you tell us of the current situation near the gate?" someone asked.
       Gesturing at the map, Ymladdwr responded, "The goblins have cleared an area around the gate roughly one thousand yards out from the facility's outer perimeter. The facility has been transformed into a stone fortress. We have never seen a supply raid by the goblins, so we think they are

85

gaining resources through the gate.

"During the day, goblin patrols are on the walls, and wyverns are flying around the clearing's perimeter. Before sunset, they send out a team to light torches stuck in the ground about 500 yards from the walls. We usually do not see the wyverns flying at night, but some walk around near the walls.

"The goblins themselves are mostly armed with bows. Many also carry knives, daggers, and axes. There is minimal use of armor. We suspect they have decided not to waste time and resources on it since the patrols never return."

"How do we destroy their fortress?" someone else asked.

"From what I have seen, the best division of skills is for the meddwlgrym practitioners to tear down the walls and kill the wyverns. Archers can kill the goblins. We could try to bring ballistae to help with the walls and wyverns," said Ymladdwr.

"Transporting ballistae either whole or in parts will slow down the army. Do we want to take the time, or do we need to eliminate them now before they solidify their foothold in the mountains?" a council member asked.

"It may be too late to prevent them from infesting the mountains, but if we can cut off their access to the gate, then we can cripple their ability to resupply themselves and decrease or eliminate their ability to acquire more troops," commented Gwyddoniaeth.

"The warbands are not perfect at stopping all goblin patrols. Many still make it through and will need to be avoided. A swift force that can get to the gate and enact a strategy without being seen or a warning being raised would be best," suggested Ymladdwr.

"We cannot attack directly, even at night. The torches will reveal our approach," a council member warned.

"We need to find a way to remove them simultaneously. They will know that we are there, but they will not know exactly what we are planning," suggested another.

"We should use a decoy to lure their attention away from the main attack," suggested Ymladdwr.

"Archers can kill goblins and the myfyrwyr can break walls, but how do we defend against the goblins' arrows? Too many targets from too many directions will still be a problem for the myfyrwyr," noted another council member.

"We need a shield," answered Gwyddoniaeth.

*   *   *

After the war council, Ymladdwr and Gwyddoniaeth retreated to their room. Thoughts passed quickly between them, some in words, but many in the underlying images and feelings those words described. They lived each other's memories, sensed their feelings, and expressed their understanding, all without uttering a sound. Time had worn away the frustrations and irritations that had made communication difficult. Events had transpired to bring them together in the same room for the first time in years. Finally, they were able to understand and forgive each other.

Gwyddoniaeth understood his need to suppress his grief immediately after their daughter's death and how once the tasks were done, it had all come rushing back. His desire for revenge and to protect everyone else from the same fate had led him to pursue a more aggressive response to the incursion. Over the years since, she had seen the wisdom in this and was now finally able to convey that to him.

Ymladdwr could feel her overwhelming grief at feeling their daughter's death through direct mental contact and how it had taken the long walk back for her to sort through those emotions. Her failed desires to protect her child had inclined her toward a more defensive strategy. Those precautions had been of great service to the warbands in the years since. Now, he was able to transmit his understanding to her.

It had been many years since they had seen each other face to face. For the first time in a long while, they looked at each other with sympathy and understanding.

They stepped toward each other and embraced.

*   *   *

Gwyddoniaeth and Ymladdwr stood in the darkness at the edge of the forest on the south side of the gate fortress. A cool, gentle breeze moved around them. Their forces were moving into position around the fortress that was now surrounded by a thin ring of torches. Gwyddoniaeth was linking the minds of the elves. When she had confirmation that everyone was in place, she gave the commands.

*   *   *

The goblin stood on the fortress wall staring out at the darkness that was broken only by the evenly spaced torches. The elves had never bothered to attack the fort directly the entire time he had been here. Staring at the torches was mind numbingly boring.

The flame twitched.

Was that the wind? He dismissed the thought; it was

always the wind.

The goblin yawned.

All the torches suddenly sprung away from the fort.

He stood up, more alert now. This was not normal. The spacing was different. He had not imagined it.

The torches went dark.

The goblin turned and shouted an alarm.

*   *   *

Caredig crouched in the darkness about a hundred yards past the tree line on the north side of the fortress and fired her arrow at the assigned torch when the mental command came.

Pull!

She yanked on the thin rope tied to her arrow and pulled the torch swiftly to her.

Out!

She smashed the torch into the ground, putting out the fire. Goblins cried in the distance.

As soon as the fires were out, she ran across the open field, followed by several other archers and a few specially trained high elves who carried a large shield on each arm. When they got within range, they stopped.

Fire!

She sparked a flame and lit her first arrow. She released it to sail high over the fortress walls. The elves around her did the same. They filled the air in rapid succession with a cloud of fiery bolts. There were no specific targets. The goal was to strike fear in the goblins and draw their attention.

The goblins' own arrows whistled out into the night, and the high elf next to her raised her arms. The shields rose

89

into the air above the archer. Arrows thudded against the wooden planks.

*   *   *

Telynor crouched in the darkness at the edge of the forest on the south side of the fortress next to the high elf Bwriad and several elf archers.

Attack!

At the signal, Telynor's group and several others raced out from the trees across the field. Each elf carried a tall wooden shield on each arm. The fire arrows from the north were doing their job and keeping the goblins distracted.

They passed the torches without incident. When the group got within arrow range, Telynor dropped his shield.

Bwriad, next to him, raised his arms, and Telynor's shield flew to join Bwriad's overhead, forming a protective canopy over the moving elves.

They came within range of the walls and Telynor stepped forward. He raised his hands and reached out with his mind, gripping the earth beneath as an anchor, while he grasped the top of the wall and began to pull. The stone began to crack and break. A few moments later, it started to fall.

*   *   *

When the walls were broken, Ymladdwr rushed in first. The breaking of the walls had drawn attention, and the goblins must have realized the fire arrows were a distraction. They swarmed along the remaining walls and out of the buildings. Many had bows and began firing arrows. Out of

90

the corner of his eye, he could see the shields being mentally maneuvered over the archers.

Arrow after arrow he released into the goblins. Each time it hit with such force that it tore through their bodies. Even when they tried to hide, he could find them. His focus was such that his arrows would bend around corners or smash through obstacles.

As the chaos grew around him, he made his way toward the gate. A strange rumbling caught his attention. It came from a large hole in the ground. A moment later, a large, monstrous creature emerged.

The creature was approximately ten feet tall, its body hideous but powerful. Its baleful gaze fell upon the elves.

Ymladdwr raised his bow and fired at the creature. The arrow became lodged in the thick muscles of the creature's chest, but its body was tougher than the goblins' and it did not stop. It raised a fist and prepared to charge Ymladdwr, but a shout rang out. Ymladdwr caught sight of one of the high goblins standing behind the creature. The monster turned and walked over to a shed with a pile of large round, irregular stones. It picked one up and hurled it at Ymladdwr.

The elf dodged the rock and turned to fire another arrow at the creature. Surely it had a weak point, even if it was just the eyes.

A loud crack sounded behind him. Ymladdwr turned in time to see the rock explode and a small, mishappen creature emerge. It turned first to another elf that was close by. The elf looked down at it curiously. The creature leaped with startling speed and clamped its jaws over the elf's leg. The elf screamed in pain as the creature's teeth completely severed it.

Ymladdwr launched an arrow into the little creature.

He turned to see that the pile of stone eggs was greatly diminished. Spinning around, he saw more of the creatures hatching and attacking the elves.

*   *   *

Gwarchod followed Gwyddoniaeth as they walked behind the southern attack force. He mentally held shields ready above them while she communicated with the other elves' minds.

Diversion unit, move to the breach in the wall.

He could sense her concern as Ymladdwr and those nearest him ran into the gap.

A minute later, something went wrong. He sensed her mental connection break and a terrible scream escape her throat as she fell to her knees.

He tore his eyes from her and focused ahead to see the problem.

The courtyard was scattered with fragmented stone eggs. Monsters were tearing chunks out of elves and consuming them. Those who were not injured rushed to kill the creatures or treat the wounds. The ones who chose treatment first, chose wrong.

With each bite of consumed flesh, the monsters grew bigger.

One of the monsters, now as tall as an elf, ran in their direction. Gwarchod stepped forward swiftly, attempting to block the creature with the shields. It smashed the wooden panels to pieces and kept coming. He reached out with his mind, dragged its head into the ground, and crushed its skull.

*   *   *

Gwyddoniaeth looked around at the battlefield through her own eyes. The direct sensation of death from so many within a matter of seconds had been too much for her, and she had broken her connection to the others. Ahead of her, the elvish shields were either shattered or tossed aside. Elves screamed in pain, clutching their gaping wounds. Others hurried to render aid. Survivors turned to kill the swiftly growing creatures. Arrows still came from the remaining goblins, piercing the dying, killing the merciful, and wounding the fighters.

She staggered to her feet, her mind desperately racing against her fear as she sought to reconnect with her husband. Her daughter was dead, but she would not lose him too. As her mind scanned the area, she was vaguely aware of Gwarchod moving beside her, wielding a shield that someone had discarded with one hand and mentally killing goblins with the other.

Gwyddoniaeth found Ymladdwr's mind. Relief flooded hers.

We need to evacuate the wounded, he thought.

Agreed. These creatures were unexpected, she replied, borrowing his calm to help her refocus on that task at hand.

The decoy unit rushed through the breach behind her, pausing at the sight of the carnage before moving to aid and attack. There was a lull in the chaos. For a brief moment, she thought they had pushed the goblins back enough that they might be safe.

She felt the reactions of Gwarchod and Ymladdwr before she sensed the impending danger herself. She looked up in time to see the wyverns flying back over the fortress from the north. More of the stone eggs fell from their claws.

Gwyddoniaeth and Gwarchod reached out and

stopped as many as they could. Once she had them, she crushed them in the air completely. Stone pieces, dust, and gore rained down around her.

Retreat! Gather the wounded, leave no one behind, her thoughts rang out to all around her.

*   *   *

Telynor and Caredig regrouped beside Ymladdwr. They kept a rear guard as the others prepared to retreat. Telynor's clothes were torn and bloodied. He had an arrowhead lodged in his left shoulder, but he had no intention of letting it stop him.

The retreat was not long lived.

Screeches and shouts rose from the breach.

The wyverns had landed.

The cry of the dragon-like creatures was answered by the roar of more of the large monsters coming out of the tunnel.

Blind the monsters. Bury or collapse that tunnel! commanded Ymladdwr.

Telynor ran to the side as Ymladdwr and Caredig buried arrows in the monsters' eyes. He reached out, lifted rubble with his mind, and began piling it into the tunnel.

One of the blinded creatures stumbled in his direction and he had to duck out of the way. As it passed, he turned and reached out, pulling the creature back by the head. He smiled as he closed his fist and the skull caved in.

*   *   *

Gwyddoniaeth's heart sank as she saw the wyverns land in the field just outside the breach. There were too

94

many to kill individually, and the monsters' roars behind her meant that her people had no time to spare.

She might not be able to crush the wyverns all at once, but she could push them back.

Both of her palms pushed forward, and the wyverns were thrown back from the breach.

Go!

The elves began to drag and limp through the gap, those strong enough to stand on their own carrying those who were not.

*   *   *

With the tunnel blocked and the monsters finally dead, Caredig was able to turn her attention to her retreating comrades. They were moving slowly, many having injuries much worse than her own. She was mostly just cut and bruised from arrows and rocks she had failed to avoid completely.

She scanned the fortress around her. The remaining goblins that she could detect seemed less inclined to leave the safety of their hiding spots than their dead comrades had been.

Turning back to the retreat, she looked ahead and saw the wyverns. Some of the elves were pushing them back with their minds so that everyone else could escape. They seemed exhausted, and she guessed that several of them were of the weaker variety, unwilling to kill with their abilities. Only a few were fulfilling their duty properly.

A smile crept on her face; she enjoyed killing the wyverns the most. She ran through the gap and fired arrows into the wyverns' eyes.

95

*   *   *

Gwyddoniaeth and Ymladdwr took their seats in the central tower's council chamber. Like its counterpart in the caves, this one was ringed by pillars, and a three-piece circular table sat in the center. In the shadows between the pillars stood Gwarchod, Telynor, and Caredig. The former stood behind Gwyddoniaeth and the latter two stood behind Ymladdwr.

The journey back from the battle had been a somber one. Many of the survivors had been gripped by a deep sorrow that did not dissipate even when they returned to the city. Years ago, they had lost the Elders, friends, and family when the dragons attacked. Most of those had been unseen, but now they had personally witnessed the death and dismemberment of their people.

The husband and wife looked at each other, then around the room. Of the nine chairs, only seven were filled. In the center of the ring stood two elves.

"It is with deep regret that we inform the council of our departure. We understand and respect the sacrifices of those present and those who returned from the battlefield. However, those whom we represent are united in agreement that we do not wish to see our friends and families slaughtered, nor do we wish to visit such horrors upon others."

Ymladdwr glanced at Gwyddoniaeth, and she squeezed his hand. He felt the reassurance of her mind's touch. His gaze shifted forward again.

"We understand your sentiments and will not force you to stay," he said to the two former council members.

"We do not wish to completely abandon you either. We will be moving to the southern rainforests where we

96

hope to rebuild and from where we can aid you with any supplies you need. The wildlife there is more voracious and plentiful. Hopefully, this will provide an extra layer of deterrent to the goblins.”

“Thank you. We appreciate your generosity and wish you the best,” replied Gwyddoniaeth.

The two elves bowed and left the room. When they had gone, Gwyddoniaeth and Ymladdwr each released a single deep sigh.

II

The Long Dark Road
Dynoltir, +2018 TR

The headlights of Cassie's car carved out a patch of reality in the void of the night. Fields and forests bounded the highway on either side, only gently grazed by the light. Beside her, curled up in the warm interior of the vehicle on a reclined seat, lay her best friend, Harriet. They were on their way back from a vacation before their next year of college. They had wanted one final adventure before their senior year and the real world immediately following it.

Cassie glanced at the gas gauge again. The gauge was at the halfway mark, and she never liked it going any lower than that.

"Hey, wake up," she said, glancing at her sleeping friend.

Harriet didn't respond.

She grabbed an empty bottle from the cup holder and, with a quick flick, smacked her friend.

"Wake up, I need your help."

"Wha—?"

Harriet turned and stretched. She yawned, pulled the blanket away from her face, and sat up.

"What's happening?"

"I need your help to navigate and find a gas station. Check your phone."

Harriet glanced at the gas gauge and sat up straighter.

"Do you remember any cities we've passed or mile markers?"

"Umm, I think we passed Isra a while back. I don't remember what the exit number was though."

Harriet looked at her phone and began scrolling through the map.

"It looks like there should be a gas station off of exit 210."

Cassie switched to the outside lane and started looking more intently for the exit. The gauge dipped slightly below half, and she felt a nervous twinge.

Another fifteen minutes passed, and Harriet pointed; "There, I think that's it."

Cassie looked at the sign. It matched what her friend had said, so she pulled off on the exit. They were still out in the middle of nowhere when they pulled up to the exit's stop sign.

"Which way?"

Harriet looked down at her phone and twisted her head slightly; "Go right."

"Are you sure?"

"Yes."

Cassie turned right and drove down the unlit country road. "What street are we looking for?"

"Um, it's called County Road 47."

Cassie leaned over the steering wheel and swiveled her head back and forth, trying to see the signs for the cross streets. The country road wound back and forth in wide arcs, following the contours of geographical features she could only imagine while driving at night.

The road made a couple hard turns where it met some cross streets, and each time Cassie took the wider of the two paths, assuming it was the road's continuation and not a cross street. "What was the street again?"

"County Road 47," Harriet repeated.

"Have you seen it?"

"No, but I think we should have found it by now."

"Have you seen any street signs?"

"No, but this area is really overgrown; maybe we just missed them," Harriet answered.

Miles of dark woods swept passed as Cassie grew more anxious. "I'm worried that we're lost," she said.

"We can turn around and backtrack to the highway," suggested Harriet.

"That's probably the best idea."

"Oh wait, what's that ahead?" interjected her friend.

Cassie could see two red lights in the distant darkness.

"Surely we can see street signs at the stop light, and the intersection will be an easier place to turn around," her friend suggested.

"Ok."

As they approached, something seemed off. It took a second, but then it clicked; "Why are there two red lights when this is only a two-lane road in the middle of nowhere?"

Harriet shrugged, "I don't know; maybe they're just weird here."

Cassie smiled faintly but felt uneasy.

She slowed the car as they approached the stoplight. The darkness ahead seemed just as impenetrable as it had been when they were farther away. It was like the headlights could not illuminate anything under the stop lights.

Confused, she looked out of the side windows. She could see dark trees on either side, while straight ahead was pitch black.

"What?" she muttered.

The car slowed to a crawl and stopped at what she hoped was the appropriate distance from the stop lights.

"Do you see signs... or the intersection... or even the street?" Cassie asked.

Harriet kept shifting her position to find a better angle but shook her head.

"This doesn't seem right; I think we should leave," said Cassie.

She put the vehicle in reverse and looked behind them.

A great rushing and scraping sound swept past them. The car bounced and the girls screamed.

"What's happening?" cried Harriet.

The area behind the car went black. The girls turned, but there was nothing behind, ahead, or beside them. Everything was solid darkness.

"What happened to the road?" asked Harriet.

"Where did the trees go?" questioned Cassie.

The car rocked slightly back and forth. The girls looked around, confused and afraid. Metal groaned above as the shape of the car deformed. They looked at the top of the car, and then the ceiling and sides collapsed inward toward them.

*   *   *

A man held a firework close to a campfire.

"You can use my lighter," said another from a safe distance.

"Nah, I got this," Lenny replied confidently.

He reached in closer, and the flames caught the fuse closer than he expected. With a yelp, he dropped the firecracker in the campfire and fell back, but not fast enough. He clutched his singed fingers and stood up.

Derek laughed and took another drink of his beer as he sat on his truck's tailgate. Off to his right, Cooper stood by the fire, laughing as Lenny ran to dunk his hand in the nearby lake.

"Are you sure you don't want to use the lighter this time?" called Derek.

"Shut up," came the reply from the water's edge.

"Hey, remember that time he thought it was a good idea to flip off that stray dog?" laughed Cooper.

Lenny walked up and held up his closed fist with his stub of a middle finger sticking up.

All three laughed.

Derek tossed his lighter to Lenny, who then went about lighting fireworks and throwing them out over the lake.

The three friends continued to chat about random topics while drinking and entertaining themselves with the small explosions.

Cooper's phone rang, and he walked away to answer it.

"Probably his master telling him to come home," Lenny sneered to Derek.

Derek did not say anything and took a sip of his beer.

Cooper returned; "I've got to head out. My wife has an early doctor's appointment tomorrow that I forgot about. I have to get up early to go with her."

Lenny playfully slapped Derek's shoulder with the back of his hand; "See, I told you. The boy is whipped."

Cooper rolled his eyes and opened the door of his truck; "It's called being responsible. You should try it some time."

Cooper got in his truck and left.

Derek smiled, but Lenny turned to him with a scowl. He looked back at Lenny and then took a drink of his beer to hide his own expression and shrugged.

After a while Derek sighed, "It's getting late, and I'd

rather sleep in my bed than the truck. I'll see you tomorrow."

"Fine. See ya."

Derek hopped down, tossed his can in the fire, and slammed up the tailgate. When he climbed into his truck, he paused for a moment and sighed, then turned the ignition.

*   *   *

Alice sat in the bathroom staring at the positive pregnancy test. She was not sure what to think at this point. Part of her knew she should be happy, but she also dreaded the impending strife. Her subconscious solution for the moment was simply a stunned numbness, so she could avoid the greater pain of going from one extreme to the other.

The sound of the front door opening snapped her back to reality. She mumbled curses under her breath and wrapped the test in toilet paper before stuffing it in the trash. She flushed, washed her hands, and walked out.

Derek startled when he saw her.

"What are you doing up so late?" he asked.

"Where have you been?" she countered.

"I was just hanging out with Cooper."

Alice took a step closer and sniffed his breath.

"Drinking? You've been out half the night drinking in the middle of the week?" Her annoyance at his irresponsible behavior was heightened by her recent revelation.

"It wasn't that much; I can still get a couple hours of sleep before work. Don't worry about it," he said dismissively.

"Being hungover and sleep deprived at work isn't safe, let alone driving back here drunk. You need to act more responsibly." Her irritation was now compounded by her natural concern for his safety and the impending well-being of their child.

"Why are you getting on my case about this? You used to be fun; you used to like hanging out with the guys and drinking every night. What happened to you?" His tone was annoyed and defensive, which only served to rile her even more.

"I grew up," she said sharply.

Derek scoffed, "Grew into a self-righteous—"

"I'm pregnant."

That shut him up. Smug accomplishment replaced her anger.

Derek just stared at her for several seconds. Her moment of satisfaction faltered in the long pause that followed. Doubts about how he would react began to replace the triumph of her rage.

"You're joking," he voiced quietly.

"No, I'm not. I've suspected it for a while now, but I just took a test to confirm," she replied.

"Why are you doing this?" There was a sharpness to his tone now.

"What?!" She focused on her anger to hold back her tears. Was he accusing her?

"You never said you wanted kids. I don't want kids. Is this a trap? Are you trying to control me?"

"You have got to be kidding me. I didn't do this on my own, and you know it." How could he turn this around on her like this? Now he was trying to paint her as the villain?

Derek just shook his head, eyes darting around the room. He turned abruptly and walked out the door, pulling it shut hard behind him.

Alice just stared at the door. She knew his reaction would be bad, but it still hurt to see it for real. Some part of her had hoped that it would sober him up and inspire responsibility or maybe even make him happy, but deep down she had known better. Her hands instinctively rubbed her belly. She took a step back and collapsed onto the couch. Tears began to well up in the corners of her eyes. She cupped her face in her hands and cried.

*   *   *

Farmer Jones drove his riding lawnmower around the large pond on his property. He liked to keep the area clean, so it was easier for him and his grandchildren to go fishing close to the water. The sun was just beginning to peak over the horizon. Birds were singing in the trees.

When he reached the far side of the pond, he stopped. Ahead of him was a wide patch of torn up earth and grass. It led from the pond, across a field, and all the way out to the road. He got off his mower and walked over to inspect it. Walking along its edge, he looked for tire tracks but did not see any.

Jones snorted. He did not know what had happened, but he definitely did not want anyone messing around on his property without his permission.

The old man drove his mower back to the house, then took his truck to the local diner.

Entering the diner, Jones was greeted by the waitress, Crystal.

"Good morning, Jones."

He nodded to her, walked to the end of the counter, and sat down next to the sheriff. The sheriff was younger than him but still middle aged, and they had known each other for years.

The sheriff looked up from his breakfast and smiled;

"How can I help you this morning?"

"Someone has been messing around on my property. They've torn up the ground between the pond and the road."

"That's a pretty good stretch of dirt to tear up. Were there any tracks?"

"No, not that I could see. Have those Welch brothers been stirring up trouble lately?"

The Welch brothers were three teenage siblings who been caught multiple times on his property trying to grow drugs, poach deer, and who knows what else. Jones had nearly shot them on more than one occasion. They were the only locals he had ever had any issues with.

"No, they've been keeping their noses clean since they spent three months in jail this winter. I think the lesson finally stuck this time."

"Hmm." His gaze drifted down, pondering what else might have created the torn-up path. He did not like the idea of anyone out there without his knowledge in general, and he especially did not want any trespassers hanging around where his grandchildren might be.

"Listen, I'll send a deputy out later to take a look. I can't make any promises, but we'll see what we can do," the sheriff offered.

Jones looked up and nodded; "Thank you sheriff." He was honestly grateful.

The sheriff went back to eating his breakfast and Jones left.

*   *   *

Derek slumped onto the bar stool and gestured to the bartender. He had spent enough time there that no words were necessary, and an open bottle was set in front of him a

106

moment later. He downed its contents and stared at the empty bottle. So far it was not enough to stop the swirl of thoughts and feelings inside him.

First Cooper got pulled away by some woman and turned his back on his friends. Then Alice stopped being fun. She changed; not him. He had always been this way. Neither of them had wanted kids when they first met. They both liked to have a good time, but now he was the bad guy for doing what they had always done? Who was Alice to try to change him? And now she was claiming to be pregnant? Was this a trap? Was she trying to force him to change by tricking him into this? Was it even real?

He sat there and thought about his options. He could leave. Why should he bother with someone who did not accept him as he was? Why should he waste his time with someone who looked down on him? Why stay with someone who would manipulate him?

But they had had so much fun in the past. He loved being around her, even when they were sober. Part of him knew it would hurt to leave.

He gestured to the bartender and his empty bottle was replaced with a full one.

The second bottle hit the bar empty.

He gestured for another.

His hand reached for the third, but another snatched it away before he could grab it. Angrily he turned to see who had stolen his one consolation in life.

A woman he had never seen before stood next to him draining the bottle. She was remarkably attractive, especially compared to the women in town. She slammed it down on the bar and smiled at him.

"Thanks for the drink."

Derek had spoken with beautiful women in the past,

felt the distracting mental fog of attraction before, but this was different; stronger. In this moment he was convinced that she was the most beautiful, desirable thing he had ever seen.

The woman leaned against the bar and looked him up and down.

"You look stressed. It's always such a shame to see a wild creature in a cage."

This woman was right. Of course, she was right; how could she ever be wrong?

"No one will ever cage me," he said, straightening up.

Derek gestured for the bartender to bring two beers this time.

They each raised their bottles in a toast.

"To freedom," he said.

"To a life without restraint"; she smiled back.

*   *   *

Alice was driving down the country road as the sun set to where she and Derek lived together. When she arrived at their trailer in the woods, she did not see his truck. She searched inside and did not see any signs of him there either.

She had had the whole day to think about the situation. She was not sad anymore, but she was determined. She knew what it was like to grow up without a father, and she was not going to let that happen to her child. Derek would grow up, even if she had to break him to do it.

Walking back out to her car, she called Cooper as she got in.

"Hey, Alice."

"Hey Cooper. Is Derek hanging out with you?"

"No. He never showed up for work today. Is everything ok?"

"Yeah, everything is fine."

She hung up the call. She turned and headed toward the bar. Most likely she would find his sorry ass passed out in a corner somewhere. Annoyedly, she shook her head at the thought.

By the time she got to the bar, the sky was already dark. Inside, there were only a handful of customers. She approached the bartender.

"Hey, have you seen Derek?"

The bartender looked up at her; "He was here earlier."

"Do you know when he left or where he went?"

The bartender paused. Alice sensed something was not right.

"What is it?"

The bartender sighed; "He left with some out of towner, some woman I haven't seen before. They left when the sun started to set."

Anger flashed across Alice's face.

"Thank you," she said sternly, spun around, and walked out of the bar.

Disgust and rage boiled inside her, and she slammed the door as she got back into the car. She turned the key, switched gears, and slammed the accelerator. The car angrily sped off down the street.

There were hotels a few miles up off the highway, and she had no intention of letting him escape.

*   *   *

Derek awoke in the bed of his truck, mostly naked.

His head hurt and he was confused. Memories of his argument with Alice began to trickle in. His anger and frustration had subsided, replaced by hesitant resignation to face the unpleasant conversation that would inevitably follow.

He looked around. It was dark and the truck was surrounded by a field. He did not remember getting undressed or how he got here. He stood up and put his clothes on. Partially turned toward the cab, he thought he saw something sinister crouching on the roof. Startled, he turned quickly to see what it was.

The girl from the bar lay stretched out on top of the cab, gazing at the stars. She turned and gave him a smile.

Derek's heart fluttered slightly at the sight of her gorgeous form illuminated by the moonlight.

The beautiful woman sat up, her long legs swinging into the truck bed. "That was amazing, but the night is young. I know another bar up the highway where we can have more fun."

Derek wanted to go. He wanted to go wherever she suggested.

But he needed to get home. There was something he needed to—

The woman stood next to him. Her beauty filled his gaze, her scent infiltrated his nostrils, and his heart yearned to be free and to possess her.

"Our desires are nature, restraint is unnatural. No one should be caged," she whispered to him, a hand gently touching his chest.

She was right. Nothing would hold him back. No one would tell him what to do. He bent down and kissed her hard, then jumped out of the truck.

"Get in the cab."

The woman laughed, slid through the window at the back of the cab, and fell into the passenger seat.

They took off through the field, tearing up the ground and crops as they went. Once on the road, he made his way to the highway.

Several minutes later, they turned onto the exit and skidded into the parking lot of a bar. It was across the street from a couple hotels and a large truck stop.

He followed the woman's laughing and dancing form into the bar. His head spun with the intoxication of her presence mixed with the alcohol they had consumed.

She pulled him onto the dance floor.

Time and surroundings began to spin out of existence as he orbited around the woman.

Suddenly, he was shocked back to the hazy bar by something shoving his shoulder.

Derek looked up to see an angry man glaring at him, attempting to yell something over the loudness of the crowd and the music.

Derek raised his hands; "Sorry man, it was mistake."

The man angrily pointed a finger at him. Derek had no idea why he was so angry.

"Are you going to let him talk to you like that?" whispered the woman in his ear. He was not sure how he could hear her voice, so clear, yet so soft over the loud din of the bar, but he immediately forgot this strangeness as she continued. "Who is he to tell you what to do? Why should you listen to him? Why should you listen to anyone who wants to control you? He's just like Alice, so convinced of his own righteousness, that his rage is holy and yours isn't. Be angry. Be free."

She was right. This man was just as bad as Alice. They expected him to yield, to bow, to restrain his anger. No more. Now his anger would be felt. They would yield. They would bow.

Before he knew what was happening, the man was down on the floor. Derek's knuckles slammed into the other man's skull over and over. His fists came away bloodied, and he could feel things starting to break beneath him.

A sweet laughter filled the space around him, supporting, encouraging, delighting.

The laughter broke slightly as rough hands grabbed his arms. He tried to struggle, but he was dragged out of the bar and tossed onto the pavement.

Angrily he took a step forward. How dare they interfere.

The woman was in front of him. She pulled his head down and kissed him. He forgot about the bar, the men, and everything else.

*   *   *

Deputy Young sat in his patrol car staring mindlessly out into the dark at a large pond. He was parked close to some trees on one side in the hopes that any intruders would not immediately notice him.

He hit the contact on his phone. It was better to question orders where only one person could hear you as opposed to everyone on the radios.

"Sargent?"

"Yes?"

"I'm out by the pond, but nothing is happening. Do I really need to be here? This seems like a waste of time."

"Look, farmer Jones is an old friend of the sheriff's. It'll be worse if you leave and some dumb kids come by and tear the place up or, worse, get hurt. Just be thankful you got the easy shift tonight and stop whining.”

Deputy Young sighed; “Fine.”

He hung up and waited.

Young watched videos on his phone, stared at nothing; played a game on his phone, stared at nothing some more. Eventually, the boredom got the better of him and he dozed off.

A loud noise of rushing water and scraping surfaces woke him. He sat up straight and looked around. He turned on the headlights.

The chaotic ripples were just beginning to subside on the surface of the pond. His eyes followed them to what looked like their source. There was a new patch of torn up ground by the pond.

Cursing under his breath, he started the vehicle and drove around the pond. He followed the torn-up path back to the road and followed the direction it seemed to be pointing.

Adrenaline shot through him as he raced down the road, looking back and forth for any clue as to where the culprit may have gone. He knew he could get in big trouble for falling asleep on the job, so he needed to catch these guys first.

The road curved through a stand of trees, and up ahead he could see two red lights. The deputy kept looking left and right as he approached the intersection.

Intersection? There should not be a lighted intersection around here.

The deputy stared ahead, confused. He slowed down and leaned forward to look for street signs as he reached the stop lights, but there were none. There was nothing in front of him, only darkness.

He looked left and right, trees visible on either side. He looked forward again. Why was there nothing ahead?

There was a massive rushing sound, the car lurched, and everything around him went black.

*   *   *

Alice blinked awake in a parking lot next to a hotel. She groggily looked around. She remembered where she was and why she was there with irritation and disappointment.

The sun was just beginning to peak over the horizon. A few minutes later, she saw a familiar truck pull up and two figures get out. They stumbled to a nearby door and into one of the rooms.

Angrily, Alice stormed over to the hotel and banged on the door.

A woman opened the door and squinted at the growing light; "What do you want?

Her clothes and hair were disheveled, and she reeked of alcohol. Alice's eyes moved past the woman to see Derek passed out on the one bed in the room.

The woman repeated, "What do you want?"

Alice glared at the sleeping form of Derek. She was too infuriated to speak, and she could feel a deep sadness threatening to show itself.

The woman followed her gaze, then looked back at Alice with a smirk. She looked Alice up and down; "Well, I can see why he wanted to get away from you."

Alice angrily turned to the woman; "You can have him. If he ever bothers to ask you, tell him I said I'll kill him myself if he ever steps foot in my house again."

The woman laughed and Alice stormed off to her car. She was not sure why she had even bothered coming here. Had she expected to see something other than evidence of his infidelity or for her to feel anything other than the pain and rage she now felt?

Maybe it was better this way. Maybe her child would be better off without such a pathetic influence in their life.

*   *   *

The stranger got out of his car and placed an earpiece in one ear. He checked that the police scanner was picking up the local dispatch and stuffed the device in his pocket. This early in the morning, there was usually nothing interesting to hear, but he did not want to miss anything.

He entered the diner. There was a waitress behind the counter, an old man at one end, and an elderly couple in a booth.

"Welcome to Canon's Diner," the waitress called out pleasantly.

"Good morning," he replied in like fashion.

The other occupants glanced in his direction, then turned back to their meals.

The stranger sat down and looked at the menu.

"I would like two eggs and three servings of bacon, please and thank you," he said.

"Do you want anything to drink with that?" the waitress asked.

"Oh, do you have sweet iced tea?"

"Of course, we do. What kind of crazy people would we be if we didn't," she said with a smile.

The stranger laughed; "I'll take sweet tea then."

"Coming right up."

The waitress called his order back to the cook, then went to fill his drink. She returned a moment later.

"So, what brings you to our small town?"

"Oh, I'm just passing through. I'm working on a

115

book about myths and legends. Do you happen to have any local legends around here?"

The waitress thought for a moment; "Well, I can't think of any, but Farmer Jones down there, his family has been here for several generations. If anyone will know anything, he might."

"Thank you."

"Hey, Jones, do you know any local legends?" the waitress called down without waiting for the stranger to act.

The old man turned; "Why do you ask?"

"This young man is working on a book."

The stranger turned to the old farmer, slightly embarrassed by the brashness of the waitress; "I was just curious. If you don't want to talk, that's fine."

The old farmer stared off into space for a moment. "You know, my grandfather used to tell stories back in the day that there was a monster that ate horses and cars at night. He used to tell us that story just before bed and say we should never leave the house after dark."

"Psh, sounds like just a story to scare kids," said the waitress as she handed the stranger his food.

"Or an excuse for people who ran out on their spouses," chimed in the woman sitting at the booth.

"You know, Deputy Young's wife was in here earlier asking for him; maybe your monster got him," said the waitress.

"More likely he ran off with some hussy," said the old woman.

"Now, now, we don't need any gossip," cautioned her husband.

"Psh, you know it happens. Just the other day, Derek was seen leaving the bar with a strange woman. Kids these days have no morals," replied the old woman with a scowl.

The old farmer snorted, and the old woman's husband sighed. The waitress laughed.

The stranger finished his meal and set down the money; "Keep the change." He turned to the rest; "Thank you for the stories. I hope you all have a nice day."

He turned and left as the conversation continued on into more town gossip between the old woman and the waitress.

*   *   *

Derek opened his eyes to the darkness of the hotel room. He could feel the familiar unpleasant texture of a hotel comforter beneath his fingers. A searing pain stabbed through his head. He could not remember how he got to the hotel room. He started to sit up. His head snapped to one side, sure he had seen something lurking in the shadows watching him.

The woman from the bar sat on a small table, legs crossed in front of her, leaning forward so that her elbows rested on her knees. She smiled playfully; "Last night was incredible."

Derek tried to remember what happened the previous night. All he could remember was the woman, excitement, exhilaration... Flashes of drinks, dancing, and the thrill of released rage flew past his mind. He was not entirely sure what it all meant, but he felt much less intoxicated now.

Something scratched at the back of his mind, something he was forgetting…

The woman was beside him. His heart beat slightly faster as a thrill flooded through him.

"This place holds nothing for you. Free yourself from its shackles. Take what you rightfully deserve and embrace the wider world," she whispered to him, her face inches from his.

Excitement and rage rose within him. She was right.

The next thing he knew, he and the woman were sitting in his truck, in the dark, outside the truck stop. They pulled masks over their faces and stepped out. A smile crept over his unseen lips as they burst through the doors.

Inside the truck stop there was a cashier and three truckers. Derek brandished a gun and shouted, "You three, on the ground! You, give me everything inside the drawer! Is there a safe here?"

The cashier stammered and nervously tried to open the drawer. The three men slowly knelt down onto the floor. The woman threw her head back and laughed.

"I don't have a key for the safe. I can't open it," stammered the cashier.

"Are you lying to me?" Derek roared, shoving the gun in the guy's face.

"No, no, I'm not," the cashier stammered back.

"Look out!" the woman shouted.

Derek turned just in time to see one of the truckers rising to one knee and reaching for something at his waist. Derek swung the gun around and fired, hitting the man in the shoulder.

The woman raced over to the now prone man, stomped onto his wounded shoulder, and grabbed his gun.

"Don't try anything stupid," she said in a pleasantly threatening manner to the three truckers.

Derek turned back to the cashier, who was stuffing all the money into a bag. He grabbed the bag as he heard three strange cracking sounds. He turned to see the woman standing over the three truckers. Their heads were turned at unnatural angles, and none of them were moving.

A sobering sense of panic rushed through him.

The woman laughed and walked over. She touched his shoulder and turned him toward the door.

The panic dissipated.

"Look!" she whispered excitedly.

In the distance, he could see flashing lights on the highway.

"Quick!" she shouted.

He ran back out to his truck, followed closely by the woman, and they jumped in. He turned it on and sped out of the parking lot. Derek and the woman pulled off their masks and tossed them onto the floor of the cab.

Within minutes, the cops were behind him. Adrenaline rushed through him as he tore along the dark country roads. No one would catch him.

The woman beside him threw her head back and laughed.

Derek slammed the accelerator to the floor. He took turns sharper and faster than he had ever done, reveling in the rush each time. The woman next to him squealed in delight, gripping the door's arm rest to keep from being thrown around as they went back and forth through the woods. The flashing lights behind them would disappear and reappear as they were being chased.

Maybe the cops would not be able to follow him off road. It was worth a shot at least. Derek turned the wheel hard, and they drove through a field. He instinctively knew he needed to get somewhere safe, to hide and wait until the cops gave up. He burst out of the field and onto another street.

Several twists and turns later, Derek's truck came skidding into the grass in front of his trailer. He drove the truck around to the back and killed the engine.

The woman kept laughing and smiling beside him, her excitement infecting and intoxicating him.

They got out, he went around the truck, and he grabbed her hand to lead her inside the trailer.

*   *   *

The stranger leaned back in the driver's seat of his car, eyes closed, listening to the police scanner. His mind was just drifting on the edge of unconsciousness when a report came in about someone robbing a truck stop gas station, leaving three dead. The cops were in pursuit.

His eyes snapped open, and he raised the seat. He started the car and took off down the dark road.

*   *   *

Alice moved through the trailer with purpose, grabbing anything she thought useful and tossing it on her bed. Tears ran down her face as she failed to keep her focus on her anger. She was not going to stay here. She had made other arrangements and would move in with her mother tomorrow. At least this way, her child would be raised with some stability.

Too many items in the trailer reminded her of Derek. They reminded her of happy times, which made his most recent betrayal all the more painful. Anything that reminded her of him was tossed in the trash or in a corner, somewhere out of sight, so she would not have to deal with it anymore.

She returned to the pile on her bed and began stuffing things in suitcases and backpacks.

A bright light slashed across the trailer and a loud noise moved around it from the front to the back.

120

Confused, she looked out the back window.

Derek's truck skidded to a halt behind the trailer, and its engine and lights died instantly. The woman from the hotel hopped out of the cab, looked at the trailer, and laughed. Derek ran around and grabbed her wrist, pulling her toward the trailer.

Rage filled Alice. How dare he bring that filthy woman here. She wiped away the last of her tears and grabbed a baseball bat as she headed to meet him at the door.

*　　*　　*

Derek pulled the woman with him around the trailer, eager to reach the door before anyone else arrived. He stopped short when Alice burst out, wielding a baseball bat.

"Get out of here! I don't want to see you or your whore anywhere near me!"

Alice's rage and pain shocked Derek partially back to a sober mind. Such anger from her being directed at him hurt, and for a moment, he was not sure why she was angry.

A laugh from his right drew his attention back to the woman from the bar. He looked back to Alice, bat raised, ready to bash someone in the side of the head.

Lights exploded around them.

All three of them turned and shielded their eyes as headlights and flashing red and blue lights blinded them. Shouts rang out.

"On the ground now!"

"Drop the bat!"

"Everyone, on the ground now!"

Suddenly, the woman rushed past him, tears streaming down her face, anguish thick in her voice as she screamed, "Help me! He's crazy, he kidnapped me and killed

121

those people!”

Derek looked at Alice. She was stunned, staring at him, and the bat slowly dropped to her side, then slid out of her hand.

He turned back to the pleading woman from the bar. Her accusations rang out in the cold night air. The intoxicating excitement he had felt around her shattered. In an instant he stopped seeing her as irresistibly beautiful. He remembered all the things she had been whispering in his ear, encouraging him to do. Now those words were no longer sweet or enticing, but sickening. Rage filled him.

This was all her fault. He tackled her to the ground; “Liar! You did this!”

The woman screamed and writhed, pleading for help.

Two men grabbed him from behind, pulling his hands away from the woman’s throat. His arms were pulled hard behind his back. Metal slammed into his wrists, and his face was shoved into the dirt.

“Wait, why are you cuffing me? I had nothing to do with this. They just got here,” he could hear Alice cry out behind him.

From where he lay, he could see the woman also being cuffed.

Through tears, she said, “Why are you cuffing me? I’m a victim here. He kidnapped me and threatened me. I don’t know what’s going on.”

“We’ll sort this all out at the station,” said one of the officers.

“Make sure they’re in separate vehicles,” said another.

Derek was yanked up off the ground and pushed toward the cars. The blinding light lessoned as he moved past the front of the car toward the back doors. The door was opened, then one of the cops guided him in and shut the door.

As the cops walked away, he looked out the window to see the woman in the back seat of the car next to his. She looked over at him with a scared, tear-filled face. A smile flashed across her face, and she winked at him, then went back to sobbing.

Angrily Derek struggled against the cuffs and tried to shout through the window, "She's faking it! She can't be trusted!"

*   *   *

Alice sat in the back of a squad car, stunned by what had just happened. She had never seen Derek act like that. Such rage seemed insane. Yet that woman had not seemed scared or intimidated when she had confronted her at the hotel or when they had arrived at the trailer. Was he right? Was she lying? Or did things get out of hand after she left? Was he really this unstable? Had he killed people?

One of the cops got in the car and vehicles around them began to leave, forming a long convoy of half a dozen squad cars.

Alice looked up. She could see at least a couple cars in front of the one she was in. She turned, leaned her head on the window, and stared out at the dark scenery as it passed by.

Voices crackled over the radio; "Why are we slowing down?"

"There's a stop light."

"There are no stop lights out here. What are you talking about?"

"Did you get lost already?"

Alice repositioned herself. She could faintly see two red lights in the distance as the car slowed to a stop.

Suddenly the red lights shot forward, and the lead car vanished. Curses burst out over the radios.

"What the—"

"Where did he go?"

"What just happened?"

This time she could hear a loud rushing sound as the red lights surged forward again and the car in front of them was swallowed by impenetrable darkness.

The cop looked back, cursing as he tried to back up.

"We need to get out of here," he shouted.

Alice turned back to watch as the car swerved past the others and began racing backward down the opposite lane.

"What are you doing? Are you crazy?" came the remarks over the radio.

"What is that—" exclaimed someone else.

She turned forward again in time to see the red lights rise up over the road. A wall of nothingness rose beneath them, blocking out the trees and stars.

Suddenly, the red lights shifted to the side and began speeding past the line of cars. More shouts and exclamations exploded over the radios. As the red lights moved, the trees on the side of the road vanished. Empty darkness began to engulf the vehicles.

The car she was in skidded to a stop just as the red lights came to stand behind them. She was now next to the space between the car with the girl and the car with Derek.

A crashing sound made her turn and look forward again. One of the cars had tried driving forward and crashed into some unseen object in the darkness.

The red lights continued to move around the convoy,

spreading nothingness around them.

There was the sound of an unseen car rushing toward them, and bits of light could be seen high overhead, outlining the uppermost edge of an impenetrably black object behind them on the road. The red lights shifted position, almost as if looking down the road over its unseen body.

Bright light like daylight exploded from behind the wall of darkness. A loud screaming hiss erupted overhead. Alice squinted to see a giant, perfectly black snakehead silhouetted against the now illuminated trees on the side of the road.

The head rose up over the road, drawing its body into a coil underneath. The massive coil formed in the center of the road in front of the squad cars, pushing one of them off into the ditch on the side. The darkness that had been behind them on the road vanished to reveal the source of the daylight. Alice squinted and barely made out a car and a figure next to it, but it was too bright to look for long. The creature's mouth opened wide, and the bright light narrowed instantly to a tight beam.

The creature screeched and tried to lurch backward, but the beam followed its head. A moment later, the beam of light burst through the back of the creature's skull. The light vanished, and the creature hit the ground with a thud.

Alice watched the cop get out of the car slowly. The sudden light changes had stunned everyone, making it difficult to see clearly as their eyes tried to adjust. The cop held up his own flashlight toward the unknown car, which illuminated a figure standing there.

"Who are you?" shouted the cop, placing his hand on his gun.

The figure raised his hands; "I'm not a threat. I just

saved your lives. Please don't shoot me."

The other cops started converging on the figure, some with guns drawn.

"Who are you?"

"Where did you come from?"

"How did you do that?"

"Do you know what that was?"

"I wasn't here for that creature. It was more of a happy accident," the figure replied. "One of the cars was knocked into the ditch. We should check on everyone," he suggested, looking around at the cars.

One of the cops patted the man down; "He doesn't have any weapons."

The sound of shattering glass erupted from the car next to and slightly ahead of Alice's. Everyone turned toward the sound, then the cops and the stranger ran toward it.

When they reached the other cars, the stranger held out his hand, and the area lit up like daylight again. One of the back windows was broken.

"Where's the girl?" asked one of the cops.

The stranger swept his hand over the forest's edge, illuminating every detail. Something moved. It was the woman who had claimed to have been kidnapped. She turned to face the light. The broad daylight instantly tightened and narrowed into a beam which burned a hole through her body. The cops shouted at the man, and some turned, drawing their weapons. As she dropped, the light expanded again to illuminate the scene.

The woman's body transformed into a pale, hideous monster. Its hair was thin, and its fingers ended in long sharp points. Irregular, jagged teeth could be seen in its mouth.

The cops stood in stunned silence, guns lowering as

they stared at the dead creature.

"That was what I was looking for. Thank you for catching her," the stranger said.

The stranger turned and walked back toward his car. The cops looked from him to the two dead monsters. One started to protest but was cut off quickly. The stranger got in his car and drove away.

Alice looked over at Derek in the back seat of one of the cars. He stared ahead at the dead woman turned monster. Alice looked at the dead creature that had been the woman from the bar. Maybe Derek was right. Maybe she had been manipulating him. Yet even if she was responsible for his out-of-control behavior since they met at the bar, that did not change what had happened before then. Even if that woman had affected him, did it matter?

*   *   *

Derek looked out at the dead monster that had been the woman he had spent the last couple days with. Thinking back over the recent events, he could hardly believe it: The woman had been intoxicating to be around; every moment was an ecstatic lack of restraint.

He looked over at Alice. He knew he had hurt her. He did not know if the woman had planted the thoughts and impulses in him or just given him an excuse to set them free.

He sat, staring out the window, as hope died, and a dread future grew in its place.

III

The Sage
Dynoltir, + 2016 TR

Magara sat sideways in the front passenger seat of the car as her friends drove through the country, so that Brigette, who drove the car, was roughly in front of her. In the back seat, Sana sat behind Brigette, and Maylin sat behind Magara. The trees swept past them in the background.

Magara put her left arm behind the seat's head rest, hooking her hand around it; "So, what are everyone's plans for the fall when we get to college?" She smiled, hoping to revitalize the conversation that had died down during the long car ride.

"Parties, drinking, whatever I feel like doing whenever I feel like doing it," proclaimed Brigette with a laugh.

"For my first year, I'm going to take classes from several different subjects to get a feel for what I really want to pursue. Once I've tried a little of everything, then I'll decide what to focus on," said Magara.

"I don't know that I'll have much time for partying. I need stay focused and disciplined, so I can graduate on time." Sana nodded toward Magara; "My freshman year will have a little more flexibility as I narrow down whether I want to go to med school or law school. Other than that, I know that my parents are hoping I'll find a husband while I'm there too," she said with a nervous laugh.

Brigette's smile faded slightly, then she perked up and replied, "You should relax, enjoy life. A little partying

128

won't hurt you."

Sana fidgeted and glanced downward; "I don't know. I don't think..." she trailed off without finishing.

"What about you, Maylin, what are your plans?" asked Magara to keep things moving and avoid any awkwardness.

Maylin paused, then said, "I'm not really sure. There's so much to choose from. I don't have a set plan like Sana. I'm not sure what kind of career or family I want or when to have them."

"Don't worry about it," Brigette said to Maylin. "Stop talking about such serious things," she said, addressing the group as a whole. "This is our final vacation before we have to deal with that stuff. Just forget about it and relax. Have fun."

*   *   *

The girls continued chatting about random things for a couple hours. Magara mostly listened and watched her friends. Just being in their presence provided a certain sort of satisfied happiness. Sana was leaning forward, and Magara saw her look over Brigette's shoulder.

"Maybe we should stop for gas soon," she suggested.

Magara could hear a slight tension in her voice.

Brigette glanced down; "It's only half empty. Relax, don't be so uptight." Her tone was nonchalant and dismissive.

Magara looked down at her phone and scrolled through the map; "There's a gas station about five miles down the road. We can stop there, stretch our legs, and buy snacks. Someone else can drive, so you can relax in the back."

Brigette pondered that for a moment, then said, "Ok, we'll stop there."

Sana smiled at Magara, her lips silently forming the words, "Thank you."

The gas station was on a large patch of cement surrounded by thick forest. Magara rotated back to a normal position and got out of the car. She walked over to the pump and began refilling the tank.

"I've got the gas," she said as the other girls climbed out of the car.

Sana looked around at the gas station. Brigette stretched and walked toward the small convenience store.

"I'm going to take a leak. Sana, go find us some snacks," said Brigette.

Sana agreed and Maylin followed her.

When the tank was full, Magara meandered around the perimeter of the lot, looking at the trees and plants. The sound of an engine and tires on the pavement caught her attention. An old beat-up tow truck pulled into the gas station at the pump farthest from them. An old man got out and began filling his vehicle. While he waited, he seemed to stare blankly at the tops of the trees and the sky.

Magara came back and leaned against the car. Her friends returned a few minutes later. They were talking rather loudly, and she saw the old man turn in their direction. He was facing them, but he seemed to be staring through or past them. Magara turned, following the imaginary line of his gaze to see if there was something behind them, but there was nothing of interest. It struck her as odd but non-threatening.

Brigette seemed to notice what she was doing and looked over at the old man.

"Ignore that dirty old freak. The country always

breeds creeps like him," she said derisively.

Maylin looked over; "I don't know, he seems kind of sad."

"Get an eye full, old man?" Brigette shouted over at him and raised her middle finger with a laugh.

Sana looked between them and laughed nervously along with her.

"Brigette, let it go," said Magara, stepping up beside her friend. Turning to the old man, she said, "Are you ok?"

The old man's gaze shifted to Brigette, "Be careful on the road ahead."

"Is there something dangerous out there?" asked Maylin.

"He needs to mind his own business," muttered Sana.

"What's that supposed to mean?" asked Brigette, taking a step toward him, a hint of menace in her voice.

Magara looked at the man. There was something odd in the way he had said it, like he was resigned to something that could no longer make him sad.

"Come on Brigette, don't let him ruin our trip," suggested Magara. Brigette had a temper, and Magara did not want her starting a fight with a harmless old man for no reason.

Brigette glared for another second, then turned to her friends. "You're right, forget that old creep. Sana, it's your turn to drive. Maylin, you can sit up front."

Magara saw Brigette raise her middle finger to the old man one last time before they got in the car and drove off.

*　　*　　*

Magara let her mind drift as the others talked about

131

random things in the background. The road wound back and forth, bounded on both sides by a decline and then a thick wall of trees. She watched the trees move past, enjoying the happiness of her friends as they talked.

The car rounded a bend and Sana screamed.

Magara sat up and looked forward in time to see an old truck swerve into their lane. Sana jerked on the steering wheel to avoid it, but she over compensated and they went off the side of the road. The car slammed into a tree, and everyone was thrown forward.

Magara braced her hands against the back of the driver's seat, but the impact still threw her forward enough for the seat belt to cut into her painfully.

When the seatbelt's pressure eased, she sat back and looked around. Sana and Maylin were not moving. Beside her, Brigette was rubbing her head and muttering angrily.

Magara unbuckled her seat belt and stumbled out. She opened Sana's door and gently touched her neck. She had a pulse, but she was unconscious. Magara ran around to the other side and checked on Maylin. She was also alive. Magara sighed, relieved that her friends had survived, but still worried about their injuries.

Brigette stumbled out of the car and looked around. When she saw the other vehicle, she angrily stormed off in its direction.

"Wait, let me call an ambulance," Magara said and looked down at her phone. She barely had any reception, and the call did not go through. She started walking down the road, looking for a better signal.

The sound of a car door opening made her turn. An obviously drunk man stumbled out of the truck.

"What's wrong with you? What were you doing in our lane?" shouted Brigette at the man.

"What, I wasn't in the wrong lane, you were," he slurred back.

"Moron!" Brigette shoved him in the chest with both palms and the man toppled over, slamming the back of his head against the truck as he hit the ground.

He sat there, touching his head, while Brigette stood over him.

Magara ran over and pulled her friend away; "Don't start a fight."

"Serves him right."

A few moments later, an old tow truck drove up. It parked on the side of the road. The old man from the gas station got out.

"The sheriff will be here shortly," he said, looking directly at Magara.

Magara was not sure what to make of that. The old man could have stumbled across them by luck, but why would the sheriff be on his way?

"How does the sheriff know to get here?" asked Magara.

The old man did not answer.

"Your friends will be ok, the injuries are not mortal," he said, looking past her.

Magara took a step forward but was interrupted.

"Your friend is about to assault someone. It might not look good when the sheriff arrives," he was still gazing through her like he had at the gas station.

She turned to see Brigette had wandered off to rail at the drunkard again. She raised her foot and kicked the man.

Magara ran over and dragged her friend away by the arm, while Brigette struggled and threw curses at the drunkard. Irritation shot through her at her unruly companion. Their friends were unconscious with unknown injuries, and she was wasting time kicking a man too drunk to defend himself.

"Sana and Maylin are hurt, and a sheriff will be here soon. Behave yourself," she whispered harshly.

Brigette glared at her for a moment and pulled her arm from Magara's grasp, but she stayed where she was and did not return to attacking the man.

They did not have to wait long before the sheriff arrived.

Magara explained what happened and he radioed for an ambulance. She was relieved to see Brigette keeping to herself and not causing any more trouble.

The sheriff cuffed the drunk driver and put him in the back of the squad car. He told Magara and Briggette that once the ambulance crew got their friends out of the car safely, he would have the old man tow their wrecked vehicle.

While they waited, Magara pondered the various things the old man had said and the recent events. His warning at the gas station had turned out to be oddly accurate. How had he known where to find them or to have the sheriff already enroute? The sheriff had arrived too quickly to have only just been called when the old man arrived, and it seemed too unlikely that he had just happened to be in the area. The old man had made a couple more predictions, but it was hard to tell if they were mere observations or coincidence. Something felt off to Magara.

Eventually, the ambulance came, and the medics removed Sana and Maylin from the car. Once they were sitting in the back of the ambulance being examined, Magara walked over to the old man.

"How did you know we'd wind up in trouble?"

The old man stared past her at the trees.

"You told us to be careful at the gas station. When you got here, you said my friends would be ok, and you knew when Brigette was about to kick that drunkard without even looking. Explain yourself."

The old man shrugged; "Maybe lots of people have accidents out here who are not used to the roads. Maybe I was just trying to comfort you. Maybe I have excellent peripheral vision."

"No," she said, shaking her head, "that's not it. You called the sheriff before you even came out here. There's no way he'd get here in five minutes otherwise. It took us nearly half an hour to get here ourselves, and the sheriff wasn't at the gas station." She pointed a finger at him; "You knew this would happen. That's why you called him, and that's how you got here so soon after it happened."

The old man sighed and looked at her. He didn't look angry or annoyed, just sort of wearied and sorrowful.

"Tell me the truth. Did you plan this? How did you know this would happen?"

"Are you sure you want to know the truth? You might regret— ."

"What are you talking about, of course I want to know the truth."

The old man reached out and tapped her forehead with the tip of his finger. Magara's mind burst into agony, and she screamed as her knees hit the ground.

*　　　*　　　*

Magara woke up in a hospital bed and looked around. Her mother was asleep in a chair nearby. She squinted when she looked at the sleeping form. There was some kind of haze around her, various shades of teal, violet, and blue-white.

She shifted her eyes to scan the rest of the room and the haze vanished.

Magara felt exhausted and her head hurt slightly. She closed her eyes and tried to remember how she had gotten there. She remembered the accident and then talking to the old man but was not sure how she wound up in a hospital.

A sound caught her attention, and she turned to look as her father walked in.

"You're awake," he said and walked over. "How are you feeling?"

"My head hurts a bit, but otherwise I'm ok."

Her mother stirred and woke up. When she saw Magara, she came over and gave her a hug.

"I'm so happy you're ok," her mother said.

"What happened? How did I get here?" Magara asked.

"You collapsed in the road after the accident. Everyone else was sent home with concussions, cracked ribs, cuts, and bruises. The paramedics could not wake you at the scene, so you were brought to the hospital," explained her dad.

"How long have I been here?"

"You've been asleep for four days. I was so worried about you," said her mom.

"I'll get the nurse," said her dad.

He left and returned a few minutes later. The nurse examined Magara and went to fetch the doctor.

"How are you feeling?" he asked.

"Ok, just a headache. Oh, and sometimes, when I look at people, my vision seems a bit blurry."

The doctor made a note and checked her chart.

"When you were brought in, you were given an MRI,

and there was nothing wrong with your head and spine. We can take a look at your eyes and check your head again. After we check everything out, and as long as you are alright, you will be able to leave the hospital."

Over the next couple days, the doctors and nurses checked in on Magara and performed various tests and evaluations. They could not find anything wrong with her head; there was no internal bleeding or any other abnormalities. When they tested her vision, she was actually able to see better than normal.

After a while, it occurred to Magara that the fuzzy vision and headaches only happened when she looked at people. She was not sure why this would be but decided to keep it to herself, so she could get out of the hospital faster. Being cooped up in the room with her parents constantly hovering over her was beginning to gnaw at her patience. When the two days were up, she was able to leave and go home.

*   *   *

Magara sat on a public transportation bus. Until she figured out what exactly was going on with her vision, she did not feel like driving.

She casually scanned the passengers around her, looking up each time someone new boarded the bus. Every time she looked at someone, there was this strange haze around them, and her head would hurt slightly.

Tired of that, she sighed, leaned her head against the window, and stared out at the passing scenery. Objects moved past, shifting the light and shadows in and around the bus. In the right lighting, she caught a glimpse of her own reflection in the window. She shifted her focus and watched the shadows play across her face, then shifted again to watch the scenery. After a while, her eyes stopped focusing on anything in particular, her mind's focus expanded to nothing, and her mind drifted.

The bus came to a halt, and she glanced up. To her surprise, a large, growling dog and a small happy puppy outlined in blue-white were standing up and making their way toward the exit. Perplexed, she got up and followed them out of the bus and onto the sidewalk.

The glowing blue-white dogs walked down the sidewalk ahead of her. The larger one turned its head left and right, glaring at everything, and growling at anyone who got close. The little puppy frolicked and wagged its tail as it moved just ahead of the bigger one.

Suddenly the large dog turned on her. Its mouth opened, revealing large, sharp teeth, and it growled menacingly at her.

But the growl was not an animal sound. There were words she understood. Shocked, Magara blinked, and her eyes refocused to see a young teenage boy standing in front of her.

"I said, why are you following us?" the boy reiterated angrily.

"I, I wasn't. I'm sorry," she stammered.

Behind the young teenager was a little girl who had stopped and was looking around his legs and up at Magara. There were similarities in their appearance, and she reasoned they were siblings.

"Well, then why don't you find someplace else to be," he suggested aggressively and took another step toward her.

"I'm sorry, I'm sorry," Magara apologized again, holding up her hands, palms out, while backing away. The boy didn't approach any closer, and Magara spun around and walked away as fast as she could.

She felt embarrassed and confused. What had she seen? Why had she seen some weird glowing animal instead of a person? Was she hallucinating? Did the doctors miss something? Curiosity and confusion over the vision and its meaning clashed with her concern that she might have some kind of undiagnosed injury or condition.

*   *   *

Magara and her three friends sat in a booth toward the back of the restaurant. Brigette sat next to her on the outside, Sana sat across from Brigette, and Maylin sat across from Magara. Magara leaned back against the corner of the seat where it met the wall, so she could angle herself to see all of her friends at once.

"I'm glad everyone is finally healed up and out of the hospital, so we can go have some fun again," commented Brigette.

Magara wondered at this, if it was callous or merely a friend eager to spend time together again.

"Hey, this weekend, we can meet Marid at his uncle's cabin. He has a friend who can hook us up with something good, and his uncle always keeps the cabin stocked with alcohol. You can finally see what a real party is like," said Brigette with a smile.

Magara smiled and watched her friends' reactions.

Sana seemed slightly nervous but smiled, then glanced down. There was something in her mannerisms that seemed like hesitant eagerness. Magara shifted her gaze and saw Sana's hand replaced by a blue-white hand that reached over and scratched at Sana's other wrist. Sana said, "Yes, I

139

can't wait."

Magara blinked and the world returned to normal. Her mind began to focus inward, pondering what she had seen. She was only vaguely aware of the rest of the conversation as her friends continued.

Maylin said, "I'm sure it'll be lots of fun. I'm sorry that I wasn't able to do anything sooner." Her tone was eager and apologetic, and Magara glanced up when she heard it.

Brigette turned to Magara; "Well, what about you?"

Magara's gaze shifted back to Brigette and she smiled; "Sure, I'll be there."

*   *   *

Magara was in her room packing a bag for the weekend when her mom walked in.

"Are you going somewhere?"

"Yeah, Brigette, Sana, Maylin, and I are going away for the weekend. Our last attempt to take a vacation didn't succeed," she replied with a laugh.

"What about your vision and headaches?" Her mother's concern was obvious in her tone.

"Don't worry, someone else is driving," Magara attempted to reassure her.

"Who?"

"Maylin." Her mom was being a bit more forceful than usual, and it was beginning to annoy Magara.

"Maybe you should stay home anyway?" her mom suggested imploringly.

Magara sighed and faced her; "Mom, it's our last summer before college. We might not get to hang out for a very long time."

She tossed her full backpack onto a chair and went to

the kitchen, followed by her mother.

"Let me know when you get there. And text me in the morning."

"Mom, I'm legally an adult, and I'm leaving for college in the fall; you can't keep babying me," Magara snapped back in irritation.

Her mother paused.

"You're right," said her father from the other room, looking up from his chair.

Magara turned to look at him.

"You are an adult and can make your own choices with your own consequences, but your mother loves you, and you still need to respect her," he continued.

Magara shifted her vision and her slightly greying middle-aged father was replaced on the recliner by blue-white outline of a younger man holding a baby in his arms. He smiled down on it with the biggest smile she had ever seen. Her head snapped to her mother, and she saw a similar image.

She knew then what she was seeing. The vision was not a hallucination, it was a representation of how her parents saw her, how they felt. For them, eighteen years had not transpired. In their own minds, they were still young, gazing down with love at their newborn child. The understanding was followed by an indescribable emotion that tightened her throat and irritated her eyes. She shifted her gaze back and swallowed the new emotions.

"I'm sorry I snapped," she said in a gentler tone and gave her mom a hug. "I know you both love me. I'm not going to do anything foolish. You raised me to be responsible, and I'll be on my own eventually." She stepped into the next room and gave her dad a hug too.

*   *   *

Magara sat down in the coffee shop across from Sana. She had been pondering her new understanding of what she saw when she shifted her gaze. The haze around people was not an aberration, it was another layer to reality. It was like shifting one's gaze between one's reflection in a pane of glass and the world outside, except there seemed to be more than two layers here. These extra layers seemed to reveal the unseen truth of the world around her.

The growling dog and happy puppy were a protective older brother and his innocent little sister. Deep inside, her parents still saw her and loved her as if she was their newborn baby. Actually seeing this brought to life had given her a greater appreciation and empathy for how they reacted to things.

Now, sitting across from Sana, she wondered what the meaning was behind what she was seeing. Sana was surrounded by shimmering blue-white shields floating in the air. The shields were connected via chains at her wrists and Sana's ghostly hands kept scratching and fidgeting with the shackles.

"How are you doing?" she asked her friend, maintaining her new focus.

"I'm mostly healed since the accident, still a little sore in a few places, but overall, not bad. How are you doing? You were the one in the hospital for about a week."

"I'm fine."

"Did you ever find out what happened, why you collapsed and were unconscious for four days?"

Magara shook her head; "No, but I feel fine now." Curious what might happen, she asked, "So, do you think your parents will let you go with us this weekend?"

142

Sana paused and looked down for a second; "I think I've managed to find a way to convince them. They are such a pain though. They won't stop with the nagging and the rules."

The blue-white hands scratched hard at her wrists. They dug in around the shackles, pulling, and scratching as if trying to remove them without success.

"I'm sure they're just worried because they love you and want you to make wise decisions," Magara offered.

"Yeah, but it's smothering sometimes. There are just so many rules, and sometimes they only seem to make life less enjoyable. Sometimes, I just want to free, like you, or like Brigette." Sana's voice peaked slightly at the end, and her ghostly hands pulled hard at the shackles.

"Yeah, no one is freer than Brigette, but sometimes I think it's a bit much." Something bothered her about the eagerness in Sana when she spoke about being like Brigette. Brigette was a loyal friend, but Magara often wondered about the wisdom of her friend's behavior sometimes.

Sana responded somewhat defensively, "She's not held back by anything." She glanced down, "I wish I was like that."

*   *   *

Magara walked along beside Maylin as she perused the shelves of the library's fiction section, looking for something to read. Of the four of them, Maylin was the one most inclined toward reading for pleasure. Magara had been pondering the meaning of what she had seen with Sana and was curious to know what would be revealed about Maylin.

"Well, after the accident, my parents were concerned, but I pointed out how no one could have known there'd be a

143

drunk driver on the road. It wasn't really Sana's fault. And you and Brigette made sure the authorities came to help us," Maylin explained pleasantly as she scanned the shelves.

Maylin picked up a book and began reading the back cover. Magara shifted her gaze and saw a blue-white version of her friend as she had known her when they were in first grade, a wide-eyed and happy Maylin.

"I mean, you and Brigette have been watching out for us since we were kids, like when you stopped that girl from picking on me."

The wide-eyed child turned and looked at Magara. The expression shifted to one of concern.

"Are you ok? You look spaced out and sad all at once."

Magara blinked and shifted her vision back to Maylin's physical form. Now that she had seen both versions of her friend, she could see the childlike energy to Maylin's expressions and mannerisms in the real world. A protective affection flooded her, but she suppressed it so as not to reveal anything to her friend.

She shook her head as if shaking something off; "It's nothing, I'm fine."

*   *   *

Magara sat in the front passenger seat while Brigette drove to meet her boyfriend, Marid. She stared out the window, meditating on what she had seen in Sana and Maylin. She was not sure what the vision surrounding Sana meant, but the image around Maylin had her worried. After understanding the spectral forms overlaid on her parents, the idea that her friend might inwardly be childlike gave her pause. Did this mean she needed to be more responsible or careful around her? She glanced at Brigette and wondered what she would see when she looked.

A blue-white ghostly child sat in the driver's seat. Unlike the wide-eyed, happy child she had seen with Maylin, this one was angry, a bitter expression stamped on an already scarred face. Magara gasped involuntarily.

"What?" Brigette asked, glancing in her direction. "Is something wrong?"

"No, it's nothing," she said, looking away.

When they arrived at their destination, Brigette's boyfriend got out of his car to meet them. Brigette ran to him, wrapped her arms around his neck, and kissed him. Magara found the display quite surprising and unusual, because she was not sure she had ever seen her friend show any true affection to anyone. Marid held her and smiled pleasantly when they parted.

Magara did not pay close attention to what they said as she shifted her gaze and examined Brigette's boyfriend. The blue-white image before her was scarred with cold, cruel eyes.

"I got everyone to chip in. This should cover what your friend needs," Magara barely registered what Brigette was saying to her boyfriend.

Marid's alter image looked Magara up and down and mouthed something that looked like, "She doesn't need to know." She shifted her vision slightly and saw something dark flowing through what appeared to be his veins.

Magara shifted her gaze again and watched the two continue to talk, Brigette standing very close to him. She shifted her vision again and tried focusing on other layers.

She saw violet- and teal-tinged images of Brigette opening letter after letter. Each time she read the contents and tossed it in a trashcan, her expression darkened further.

Eventually, she raised her middle finger to the trashcan and tossed in a match. She threw her head back and guzzled the contents of a large glass bottle.

"Sorry, babe, I've got to go. I'll see you this weekend, ok?"

"Ok."

Magara shook her head and blinked. Brigette's boyfriend got in his car and drove off.

"What's with that look?" Brigette asked. "Are you staring at my boyfriend?" Her tone was joking, but with a hint of danger to it.

Magara laughed; "No, I just got lost in thought."

"Haha, sure," Brigette said with a wink.

Magara rolled her eyes and smiled.

They got in their car and headed back.

Magara stared at the dashboard, wondering what it all meant. Outwardly, Marid had seemed pleasant, but that layered image had implied the opposite. Was he deceiving Brigette, hiding his true nature?

And what about the images she saw with Brigette and the letters? Why were they tinged a different color? What did it mean? Was it symbolic? Was it her past or future?

Her mind drifted to what she had seen in their friends.

"Do you ever feel responsible for Sana or Maylin, like they are our little sisters, following us around?" Magara asked.

"What are you on about?"

"Ah, nothing. I'm sure I'm overthinking things... it's just, how well do you know Marid's friend? If he's a dealer, is that really safe?"

"Safe? What are you talking about? You should be grateful Marid is able to hook us up with something for this weekend," Brigette said with annoyance.

"Sorry, you're right. I didn't mean anything by it. I guess with the accident a few weeks ago and college looming closer, I've been thinking about things differently, worrying more, I guess. But you're right, I should just relax and enjoy this break before we go off to college."

"Yeah..."

Magara glanced at her friend. The ghostly figure stared down, a sad, hollow look in her eyes.

*   *   *

Magara sat in the cabin's kitchen area, staring across at the couches and recliner by the fireplace. Brigette stood with her boyfriend while Sana, Maylin, and two other guys, Marid's friends, stood talking with them. Magara could not remember their names but was not sure she cared.

The blue-white images of the boyfriend's friends were similar to his. They all smiled and laughed pleasantly in their physical forms, but their ghostly visages were scarred and predatory. Each of their ghostly forms seemed focused on a particular girl, facing her directly and staring more intently than their physical bodies did. From time to time, they would look at Brigette, but Marid's ghostly image would glare menacingly, and they would turn back to the others.

A voice interrupted her observations; "Hello, my name is Kevin. What's yours?"

Magara turned to see the ghostly image of the third stranger at the party. Up close it was easier to see the sludge in his veins and the scars on his face.

When she did not respond after a few seconds, the boy laughed; "Did you get a hit of the stash early? You look

147

out of it already."

Magara shook her head slightly and regained sight of the normal world. She smiled; "Sorry, I just zoned out there for a minute."

She grabbed some cups, the boy grabbed a couple bottles of alcohol, and they joined the rest of the group. She passed out the cups and each person filled their own.

Everyone sat down and continued chatting, though Magara was not paying attention to the conversation. Brigette sat on her boyfriend's lap in a chair. One of the boys sat by Sana on the couch across from the chair. Magara sat on the couch across from the fireplace. The boy who had tried talking to her in the kitchen sat next to her. Maylin, and then the last boy, sat on his other side. The boy from the kitchen seemed to give up getting Magara's attention and turned toward Maylin, who was smiling up at both of the boys on either side of her now.

Magara's vision shifted back and forth between the shimmering alter images and the normal world around her. Everyone was laughing and drinking. One of the boys brought out some pills and passed them around.

Sana hesitated and looked at Brigette. Her ghostly hands scratched at the shackles on her wrists.

Brigette made an excited noise and downed one of the pills.

"Try it," she said to Sana. "You'll love it."

Sana swallowed a pill, and one of the shackles cracked. The floating shields wavered in the air. Brigette laughed.

Maylin looked up at the two boys. One held out a pill.

"Are you sure?" she asked.

Magara could see the ghostly images of those who

had taken the pills grow gaunt. Teal and violet haze built up around them.

"Oh yes, there's nothing to worry about," said one of the boys

Maylin reached for the pill.

"I don't think you should take it," Magara said to Maylin.

"Oh, ok," she replied.

"Oh, stop being a wet blanket," chided Brigette. "You're not her mother; let her enjoy life." She laughed and fell back into Marid.

The ghostly images of the boys by Maylin glared at Magara in annoyance and anger.

Magara's vision shifted and the images around Brigette were tinged in teal and violet. She was older, her body worn, but she defiantly raised a bottle to her lips. The sludge in her veins was thick.

Magara looked at Sana, and the teal and violet images showed her walking away from her desk piled high with books. Her ghostly form moved through dark rooms tightly packed with people; cups, glasses, and bottles appeared in her hands, shifting and fading into one another as the crowds morphed around her from one group to the next. Sana sat up in various beds, each of them different. Images of her parents reaching out to her while her ghostly form drifted away faded into view. Eventually the vision evolved into Sana sitting alone in a fairly large apartment. The room was spotless and clean, every item exquisitely crafted and obviously expensive. But it was devoid of human life other than Sana. Her friend was older, dressed in expensive clothes, and leaning back in a chair, her head resting in one hand while the other held an empty glass. On the coffee table in front of her stood an almost empty wine bottle and small container of pills.

Magara's gaze came back to the normal world when Sana stopped kissing the boy, and they stood and headed for another room. Fear and concern made Magara shoot to her feet; "Wait, Sana. What are you doing?"

Sana turned to her in confusion and irritation; "None of your business?"

"Yeah, don't ruin her fun," chided Brigette.

"I'm not sure this is a good idea," Magara cautioned.

"You're not my parents, and neither of you can stop me anymore," Sana snapped back. She and the boy disappeared into the other room, but not before Magara saw the ghostly shackles break and the shields fall. Magara's eyes watched the ghostly objects hit the ground. Though she could not hear them, she could feel the weight of their impact. Her sense of foreboding intensified. Somehow, she felt disappointed in her friend's decision.

She looked down at Maylin, sitting between the two boys. They whispered in her ears, gently touching her. One offered her a pill again, saying it would make her feel better than she could possibly imagine.

The teal- and violet-tinged visions shifted Maylin's wide-eyed child form into an older adult, gaunt and wasted. Her body was almost skeletal, her clothes torn. The ghostly figure's eyes were sunken, and a deep dark sludge ran through her veins. She was on her hands and knees clawing through a puddle to pick up something while someone walked away down the alley, laughing. Magara blinked the real world back into existence, not wanting to see any further into this horrible vision. She could feel tears teasing the corners of her eyes.

Magara reached down and grabbed Maylin's hand; "We're leaving."

Maylin looked at her with a smile, not quite able to focus; "Ok," she said.

Magara glanced in the direction of the other room. It was too late for Sana. She started dragging Maylin toward the door.

"Hey, what are you doing?" yelled Brigette. "Why are you leaving?"

"Yeah, Magara, where are you going? Maylin was having a good time; she should stay," said one of the boys.

The other boy was now standing in front of her.

She moved to go around him, but he grabbed her arm. Magara instinctively twisted out of his grip. She saw a teal-tinged version of his ghostly hand reaching out for Maylin. Without hesitation, she pulled Maylin aside, and the real hand replaced the spectral one, missing its mark completely.

Before the boy could recover from his surprise, Magara and Maylin were out the door. She helped her friend into the car and got into the driver's seat.

"Why are we leaving, I was having fun," Maylin said pleasantly next to her as the car started.

"I'm sorry, I can't explain it right now. I just don't want anything bad to happen to you."

"Aww, thank you. That's why you're the best," Maylin said as her head rolled back, and her eyes roamed the vehicle's interior.

Magara stared into the darkness and drove away.

IV

Songs of the Deep
Niwltir, +253 ER

Josaja and three other mermaids swam through the great ocean, enjoying the thrill of the moment in the company of friends. The merfolk were covered in extremely fine scales that were lighter on what would be their front side if they were positioned vertically and darker on their back side. Josaja had dark black hair, but her friends had varying blends of dark blue and green that flowed behind them as they swam. Her irises were pale blue with misty grey ripples or wave-like patterns. One of her friends had eyes like hers, but the other two had red-orange ripples or wave-like patterns in their pale blue eyes. Their fingers were webbed, ending in short, sharp claws. Along the outer edge of each calf was a row of long spines that could be extended out and down so that the connecting membrane formed a long fin next to each webbed and clawed foot. When they swam, they kept their legs together and moved them as one powerful unit.

As they swam, they sang to each other. It was not a song of words, but of sounds that conveyed emotions and general ideas. The songs of the merfolk were a lesser imitation of the great songs of the deep that almost constantly permeated the seas around them. Here the music of the ocean was faint but pleasant.

The wind and the waves were favorable, and the friends found themselves moving great distances with ease. Slowly, the songs of the ocean around them began to change, but their attention was fixed on each other. They did not notice the rising discord until it had grown unavoidable.

The friends broke off from their revelry and looked around.

"We should leave, it is not safe," said Museoun.

"It is not that bad in this area. We will be fine," replied Yong-gi.

"I wonder what causes the discord," mused Josaja, focusing on the sounds.

Over several years, the normally pleasant and informative songs had begun to change. Patches of ocean now contained notes that seemed directly at odds with the usual flow of the music. No one knew what caused the change, and it was difficult to discern what, if anything, was supposed to be communicated by the new melodies. The merfolk had learned that where the discord was strongest, the ocean was least safe.

"Stop being so pessimistic. I can still sense in the songs that there is a school of fish nearby," chided Yong-gi.

"I am hungry," noted Gulmjulim.

Josaja followed her friends as they swam deeper, searching for the school. Ahead, she saw a large, shifting mass. It turned and twisted in a way that resembled a school, but there was something about the movements that seemed less fluid and agile than most schools she had seen.

"Something is not right," Josaja said, stopping her forward movement.

The others stopped a few yards away. As they watched, the school came closer and became larger. It was not fish, but sharks.

Josaja was puzzled. The sharks never swam in groups like this. These were only ten feet long and were not something that the mermaids would normally have reason to fear, but this behavior was abnormal.

"Well, we could eat shark today," commented Gulmjulim with a smile.

The friends turned toward each other in amusement and disappointment.

"They are coming this way," muttered Josaja.

The others looked. The sharks had turned and were heading straight for them.

The four mermaids turned and began swimming away, still not exceptionally concerned.

When the first shark took a bite at Gulmjulim, she turned and slashed with her claws, raking them through the shark's flesh. Normally such a cut would convince a wayward shark to retreat.

The other sharks moved in. The bites were not playful, curious, or accidental. They were harsh and direct. There was something in their movements that seemed almost antagonistic, as if the normally cold-eyed creatures were driven by some unseen hatred.

One of them came in on Josaja's left. She turned to face it and caught its nose with her palms. She pulled her body up and over it as it moved forward. While it was passing under her, she raked her claws hard down its back. Blood began to leak into the water.

Sensing movement in the water, Josaja twisted to face up and saw another shark diving down toward her. She was barely able to twist and move to its side as it passed. Her claws raked through its gills.

A severed mermaid hand floated past, a cloud of blood following in its wake.

Josaja turned and saw Gulmjulim being torn apart. Her blood attracted the other sharks, and they momentarily forgot Josaja and her other two friends. Horror and sorrow threatened to consume her, but she pushed them down. She could grieve later.

The three remaining mermaids turned and swam as fast as they could.

The sharks left their kill and pursued them.

Josaja sang out as she swam, hoping to catch the attention of something that could help them.

A massive dark shape appeared in front of and below her, rising quickly. Josaja felt a moment of fear that something else was coming for her friends. She was filled with relief a few seconds later when she realized it was heading past them.

A massive sea turtle rose behind them, mouth open, and bit into several sharks at once.

The mermaids kept swimming. Josaja was thankful that something had come to save them. She glanced back and saw the sharks swimming away. They would not be able to pierce the shell or the flesh of the turtle.

The sea turtle swam to join them, moving under them at first, then rising slowly. They grasped the ridged shell with their clawed hands, flattened their calf fins, and gripped with their toe claws as the turtle rose up below them so that they came to rest against it.

The three friends broke through the surface of the water and relaxed as they rode the turtle.

Josaja looked at her friends. They were relieved to be alive, but the sorrow was obvious in their expressions a moment later. She could feel her own throat constricting with grief the more she thought about it. She had known Gulmjulim for decades, and her death cut deeply. It was not unknown for sea life to kill merfolk, but it also was not something that one witnessed very often. The ocean was vast. Most who were eaten were just never seen again.

But this was different. This was not a chance

encounter with a predator too large to avoid or a wounded animal too aggressive to let you pass by. There was something wrong with these sharks. They were behaving abnormally.

She pondered the discord that she had heard in the songs. No one knew what caused it. It shifted through the ocean the way the songs normally did as their originators moved about in the depths. The Elders had been warning everyone to avoid the areas with the discord, but this was the first time she had seen the threat herself.

Josaja looked at her friends. She did not want to lose them too. She decided that she needed to find the source of the discord. Then, maybe, she could keep them from dying.

*   *   *

The sea elf Cyfeiriad sat in the pilot's chair of the jinn aircraft. His eyes were misty grey with wispy traces of pale blue, and his white hair was shoulder length. He swiftly manipulated the controls, turning and tilting the ship back and forth as it wove between the jagged peaks around them. Somewhere behind him, he knew that the jinn were likely tightly gripping their seats, but he was too focused on the task at hand to care.

The jinn airship threaded its way through the high mountains, twisting and turning as it was pursued by a large fiery bird. The ship itself appeared to be a large metal bird etched in red and grey where the aether crystals had been embedded. Traces of fire and air aether left thin traces of light in their wake. Their pursuer was at least as big as the craft, and its feathers were covered in actual flames. Ahead, a wall of mountains could be seen, and just above it, the mist wall.

Cyfeiriad pulled hard on the controls, and the ship angled up. He pushed the accelerator as far as it could go.

The ship just barely made it over the ridge line and plunged into the mist wall.

A moment later, they burst out over a vast ocean.

Cyfeiriad sighed and relaxed in the seat. He could hear the relieved sighs behind him. Looking ahead, the water seemed endless with no traces of land in sight.

The jinn crew began to get up and move around.

"Thank you for successfully bringing us to safety," said Libuat Alnaar as she approached the pilot's chair. She had long black hair and red-orange eyes with misty grey flame-like swirls around the edges of her irises.

"You are welcome," he replied.

"We were not able to map much of that realm," commented Muhandis as he pulled down a section of wall to reveal a map-making station.

"That bird was much more territorial than any of the other creatures we have encountered," added Nabat as she lowered another wall section and added to her notebook of sketches and observations about the flora and fauna they discovered.

"Make sure to note it on the map so that anyone who goes there is warned," instructed Libuat.

"Understood," responded Muhandis.

"This realm appears to be nothing but ocean," observed Libuat.

"Let us fly straight across. If we see signs of land, we can veer off to investigate. Otherwise, I think we should take this opportunity to relax," Cyfeiriad suggested.

"After this realm, we will return home. Muhandis and Nabat, you will stay behind and teach the mistwalkers how to reach this last batch of realms," said Libuat Alnaar, turning to face the others.

The other two jinn agreed and went about recording what they had seen in the previous realm. Cyfeiriad and Libuat had been leading these exploration missions for decades. After the defeat of the false queen, the jinn had arranged a ruse to convince the goblins that they were still being controlled. In secret, Cyfeiriad had helped train several jinn to mistwalk while others had completed the first airship. By the time they finished learning to fly, Cyfeiriad was eager to explore again. Based on practical considerations, Masidus, the king of the jinn, had been convinced to allow Libuat and him to begin exploration missions. The more they learned about the other realms, the better understanding they would have of what resources, havens, allies, or enemies lay beyond theirs.

As the sun moved through the sky, he could see that they were traveling roughly west. The next several days of flight were uneventful.

Cyfeiriad watched storm clouds gather ahead of them. He turned the ship, heading north to go around.

The storm clouds moved.

He tried heading south, but they moved again.

"Is that storm moving to intercept us?" asked Libuat, somewhat confused and surprised.

The other jinn turned to watch out the front windows.

The elf moved the controls and turned the ship back the way they had come.

"It is gaining on us," called one of the jinn from the back.

Cyfeiriad pushed the accelerator, but soon the dark clouds surrounded them.

"Everyone strap in," commanded Libuat as she sat down and secured her seat restraints. The other jinn complied.

The wind buffeted the ship. Rain pelted the windows. Lightning flashed around them.

The turbulence grew until the aircraft was being spun around. Cyfeiriad's mind reached out, attempting to steady the ship in the storm, but was unsuccessful. Lightning struck the ship. The aether crystals near where it hit immediately converted to fire and air. The explosive expansion of the elements further damaged the ship, sending it tumbling through the storm, making it impossible to steer.

"I cannot maintain control," Cyfeiraid warned.

"Everyone, brace for impact," Libuat shouted over the tempest.

The ship careened through the air. The elf thought he heard something tear on the outside. With a tremendous shudder, it hit the water. Something else broke on the outside of the ship. The waves surged over it, forcing it deep underwater.

For a brief moment, there was a dark peace. Cyfeiriad heard a strange, almost mournful sound as he looked out the window. Huge, dark shapes surged through the waters. A moment later, blue and green lights pulsed down the objects' sides. The windows began to crack from the water pressure. Water poured in through cracks in the ship.

The swirling waters began to ease, and the ship shuddered as if impacted from below. The remains of the craft broke the water's surface, and the elf looked out to see the storm slowly dissipating.

*   *   *

Libuat sat on top of the airship, looking out at the

wreckage. Her knees were drawn up close to her chest, her arms wrapped around them. Despite the brightness and expected warmth of the sun, she still felt a cold coming off the water. Pieces of the ship surrounded them. The wings had been torn off in the storm, and the lightning had damaged much of the aether arrays. The front window had cracked, so they had removed it to climb on top of the ship. Muhandis sat behind her while Nabat had elected to remain inside.

Her gaze drifted down to the seemingly endless dark depths, and she understood Nabat's sentiments. They came from a desert realm. In their homeland, the oasis was never that deep. In their travels, they had seen seas, rivers, and oceans, but there was always land nearby or the ship itself to which they could flee. Now, the ship was broken, there was no land, and the unnerving endless depths were only a few feet away. If she looked down, her imagination would begin to fill the blackness with a myriad of unknowable, inescapable horrors.

A splash off to her left, between her and the open window, drew her attention. Her head snapped to look in that direction in time to see the water ripple. A second later, Cyfeiriad's head broke the surface.

"I am not sure it is safe here," she cautioned, looking around again.

"It is the ocean. It is never truly safe," he said with a smile.

Libuat just looked at him. She knew that he was a sea elf, but his casual, almost flippant attitude about the dangers that could arrive unseen from any direction irritated her and did not comfort her. She made an effort to keep her face impassive to keep from burdening him or the crew with her fears and irritation.

"I am going to scout around," he said before taking a deep breath and diving underwater.

She extended her hand as if to stop him, but it was too late.

Libuat sighed. Part of her knew that scouting was wise and that she may need to enter the water herself at some point, but right now she was still not comfortable with the idea.

To ease her own worries, she reached out with her mind and gently grazed the elf's. She maintained the light contact until he reached the surface again.

"I went as deep as I could go, but I did not see anything down there," he reported. "You should come swim. It will be fun."

Libuat looked at him, then at the dark depths, then at the elf again. "I do not think so."

The elf followed her gaze and seemed to sense her trepidation. He switched the topic, "I could not find the sea floor or any fish. If I could dive deeper and find the bottom, I might find food for us."

"I will consult with Muhandis and Nabat to see if we can find a solution," she offered.

The elf spent the afternoon gathering bits of wreckage and bringing it to the ship. The jinn meanwhile made sure the rest of the water was removed and the cracks were sealed in the hull. They sat around in the debris-strewn craft and debated what to do.

"I believe we have enough aether crystals from the debris and the fuselage to create a propulsion system to drive us back to the mist wall," said Muhandis.

"I think I can make a breathing mask with some of the air crystals for Cyfeiriad. That will extend how far he can dive," offered Nabat.

Libuat paused; "Scouting and finding food will be useful, but," she turned to the elf, "I want you to maintain mental contact the whole time. We still do not know what those things were in the water when we went down. If you get lost or taken, I do not know that we could find or save you."

"Agreed," said Cyfeiriad.

"Meanwhile, I will scout from the air to see what is around us and estimate how far we have yet to go," said Libuat.

The jinn and the elf went about their tasks. Libuat climbed outside. The grey flames swirled around her, and she transformed into a bird.

High overhead, the wreckage seemed small. She flew and coasted in great arcs, but never so far as to lose sight of the ship completely. The ocean seemed endless, and the mist wall was so distant that it was hard to tell how far away they were. A sense of helplessness began to creep into the edges of her mind. She knew that giving in to such fears or passing them on to her team would not be wise, but that did not make them any easier to suppress. She sighed inwardly and turned back toward the ship.

*   *   *

Cyfeiriad finally reached the ocean floor. The mask that the jinn had made worked quite well. He held a lantern powered by a fire aether crystal in his left hand. It cast a reddish glow that was quickly consumed by the dark waters around him. Below, it lit the strange plants and animals that inhabited the depths.

The elf moved along the ground, searching for anything that was edible. Much of what he saw was unfamiliar to him. He was not sure if this was due to it being a different realm with different sea life or if he had just never dived this far before.

He came to a chasm in the ground and peered over the edge. The darkness below was impenetrable, and he could only barely make out the far side of the rocky fissure.

Continuing along, he eventually found a large fish several yards away, eating something. He tied the lantern to his belt and drew his knife. He reached out his hand and pulled with his mind. For a brief moment, the fish dragged him through the water before he reached down and mentally gripped the rocks below for support. He pulled his hand back again. The fish moved through the water toward him. When it came within range, he hooked it with the knife and hugged it to his body until it stopped moving. He put the fish in a net sack and slung it over his shoulder and across his chest. Then he retrieved the lantern from his belt.

Something large moved in the darkness, just out of range of the lantern's light. The elf's mind reached out and sensed the mind of a large predatory animal. Cyfeiriad looked up and pushed off the ground. His mind pushed down, and he propelled himself up even faster. He made sure to exhale as he rose.

Sensing a second large creature in the water, he looked down in time to see another long, dark shadow surge past beneath him, taking the first object with it.

The elf's head burst through the water, and he swam back to the ship and climbed out. He pulled the fish around to his front and fell onto his back, panting.

He felt Libuat's relief just before she broke the mental tether.

*   *   *

163

Josaja had been trying to track the discord, but its source had remained elusive. Its strength would shift and move, making it hard to pinpoint. She was beginning to fear that her search was hopeless when something unusual happened. A new melody, deeper and sadder than she had yet encountered, erupted in a distant storm. She had barely begun to swim toward it when it vanished. The sounds of the ocean returned to their now normal dissonant nature. Still curious, she swam in the direction of the storm until the songs around her became strange but close enough to drown out the discord.

Peaking her eyes and the top of her head above the water, she saw a strange object. It was beginning to move away from a patch of ocean that had lots of tiny bits of debris floating on it. She examined what appeared to be small bits of metal and even smaller fragments of aether crystal. She dove back under the water and trailed the object.

Over the next several days, she saw four different bipedal creatures. One of them would put something on its face and dive into the water. She would follow from a distance, guided by the strange red light that it carried. It was interesting, she noted, that larger predators seemed noticeably absent and the songs fairly pleasant and slightly protective. There were also hints of curiosity, strangeness, and even a deep respect mixed in, which confused her slightly.

Josaja dove deeper, past the swimming intruder, eventually moving out to track the songs. They were so close here. And then she found it. A large serpentine shadow swam in lazy circles in the deep ocean below the object that moved across the surface. This must be why the larger predators were so absent. An imugi was guarding the object. But why would one of the sea serpents do this? Who were the strangers, and why were they here? They definitely were not merfolk. The ocean might be vast, but her people had been here for millennia and there were no records or rumors of non-merfolk bipeds who used metal devices to move across the water.

She mused within herself; the discord was weakest here, and if she wanted to learn its source, she likely should look elsewhere. However, these strangers were the first anomalies she had encountered in her search. The discord was a perversion of the songs of the imugis, and if one was taking care to guard these strangers, then perhaps there was something worthwhile to be learned from them.

Returning to the surface, she continued her surveillance. The other three creatures seemed to prefer to stay out of the water, though they did get in for very short periods on a few occasions. This was extremely strange. There was nothing but ocean within the mist wall. How could someone from this realm not be comfortable in the water?

A couple days later, she noticed something strange. One of the creatures stood on the object, and blue flames leaped across its body. Josaja was shocked. At first, she thought that the creature had been incinerated by some unknown force, but then she saw a strange animal. It had long, weird fins; they moved up and down and were not like any she had seen on any sea animal before. The new creature moved up into the air, beating its fins to gain height. Josaja was beyond stunned and confused. How could it move through the air? Nothing could move through the air.

The strange thing circled high overhead. At times, it went so high, she could hardly see it. The creature began to make long, lazy spirals downward. Then, its path straightened.

It had spotted her.

Not waiting to see what happened, Josaja dove into the water. She went straight down until she was surrounded by darkness and sure that nothing had followed her.

*   *   *

Libuat turned as Muhandis transformed and landed inside the ship.

"Something is spying on us," he reported.

"Explain," she said.

"The creature looks like some kind of fish person. I saw it when flying overhead. I tried to fly closer, but it dove under the water."

She closed her eyes, reached out with her mind, and scanned the area. If it was still out there, it was too far away for her to sense. It was also possible that she had just missed it in the vastness of the area around them.

Opening her eyes, she continued, "Remain vigilant. We will continue on our path to the mist wall."

"Should we try to make contact?" asked Cyfeiriad.

"Our ship is damaged, and we are at a significant disadvantage in this ocean. We should avoid contact for now. We do not know if they will be hostile or not."

*   *   *

Deep beneath the strange object on the surface, Josaja approached the imugi in the darkness. Seeing one up close had been rare when she was growing up, and there was the possibility that she could learn something from it about the creatures above and why it was following them.

166

The closer she got, the stronger its individual song. It drowned out the collective songs that were the normal background hum of the ocean.

The imugis had long, snakelike bodies with eel-like heads. Along their necks, just behind their heads, they had three sets of spines that could either lay flat against their bodies or fan out to form wide fins on either side and on top of their bodies. Near the end of their tails were three similar, though smaller sets; one on either side and one on top. Though she had never seen it, she had been told that they had an inner set of jaws.

Josaja swam along beside the massive serpentine body. She knew from its notes that it was aware of her. Gently, she touched its side. She could feel the powerful muscles under its scales ripple as it swam through the water.

The imugi's individual song had several threads to it, woven together into something strange. One part indicated the sea serpent was relaxed, another was protective, part seemed like deep respect, and another part seemed to be recognition of her presence. She did not understand how these sentiments fit together. The imugi's actions implied that the protective notes were directed toward the strangers above, but did it also respect them? Why would it?

She tried singing to the creature in the merfolk's own wordless music. Josaja was not sure if the imugi would understand, but it seemed like a worthwhile effort.

The sea serpent's song indicated confusion, amusement, and then affection. Josaja sighed inwardly.

*   *   *

Cyfeiriad watched Libuat shift her neck into gills.

"It has been a long time since I studied a fish," she

167

said, opening her eyes. "It is also strange to just change one part of me and not everything."

She jumped into the water next to him. They were going to begin diving in pairs to both help the jinn grow accustomed to the ocean and to provide extra protection when he dove for food. They had not seen the fish person for several days, but Libuat had decided that it would be best for them to swim in pairs as a precaution.

He could tell that Libuat and the other jinn were very uncomfortable in the water. At first, he had thought this strange. They did have a lake at the oasis, after all. But it later occurred to him that no lake was as big as this ocean. He had spent most of his life in and around the seas surrounding the elvish homeland. He had learned to live with the dangers and the unknowns of the deep long ago. The jinn had not grown up in such an environment. Realizing this, he had chosen not to push them too hard and continued to volunteer to scout and dive for food, until Libuat had decided someone should go with him in case the fish person turned out to be hostile.

Libuat took a deep breath, most likely to steady her mind as opposed to gathering up air. "Ok, let us get this over with," the jinniya said.

She dove under the water. Cyfeiriad put on the mask and followed her. The dive was uneventful, though he could sense her mental reaction as the temperature of the water dropped the deeper they went. They eventually found the sea floor and a school of fish. He attached his red glowing lantern to his belt. Gripping the rocks below with his mind as an anchor, he pulled several of the fish to them. Libuat used a net sack and helped gather the fish.

He noticed that she kept looking around, holding her red aether lantern out ahead of her, and he could feel her mind sweep across the space around them from time to time. When the sack was full, he sinched it closed, and they rose to the surface.

When their faces touched air again, the elf removed his mask.

"So, how do you feel having completed your first deep dive?" he asked.

"The depths are extremely cold and still unsettling, but I feel much better about it now that I have been there and back again without incident," she replied, her expression and mind now more relaxed than before.

"I am glad. The more you and the others dive, the easier it will be," he said.

They climbed out of the water and prepared the fish.

Over the next several days, Cyfeiriad dove with each of the jinn. The trips were uneventful. Nothing attacked them, and the most they found were large four-foot-long fish. They were delicious.

Cyfeiriad observed that Libuat adjusted quickly to the deep. She still seemed to distrust the unending darkness, but she could mentally scan for threats and had more combat and survival experience than the others.

Muhandis was very tense when they dove. He was an engineer and not really an explorer. When they would resurface, he would often race Cyfeiriad to the top.

Nabat was fascinated by the sea life at the bottom, but she startled easily. She would get distracted by some new specimen but then would look around frantically if he moved out of her peripheral vision. She had joined the exploration missions to study the flora and fauna of Niwltir.

After several days of this, Muhandis and Cyfeiriad were diving when they discovered a deep undersea gorge. He was not sure if this was a new fissure or a continuation of the one he had seen on an earlier dive. The elf moved to investigate, but the jinni was hesitant.

We will take a quick look, then return to the surface. You can wait by the edge if you want, Cyfeiriad communicated with his mind.

The jinni moved reluctantly to join him by the gorge. Cyfeiriad swam down. There had been something odd about the rocks below. Now that he was closer, he could see what it was: About ten yards down into the gorge, the rocks on the side directly below them had been carved. Sea life had grown over much of it, but the shapes and smoothness that peeked through were obviously crafted. The elf kept searching and eventually found an opening. He held the lantern inside the opening and could tell that there was a tunnel big enough for him to swim through.

The elf paused and looked up. Cyfeiriad could sense the discomfort from Muhandis above as the jinni moved his lantern back and forth, scanning the waters around him. Cyfeiriad wanted to explore this new passage but knew that he could not just abandon the jinni to the darkness.

Swimming back to his companion, he communicated, *There is a carved passage down there. We need to explore it. It could be a civilization or the remnants of one.*

Muhandis made an unpleasant expression, shook his head, and pointed straight up emphatically.

Cyfeiriad sighed inwardly, nodded in response, and they made their way to the surface.

*   *   *

Josaja watched one of the strangers descend into the gorge from a distance. Their red light vanished over the edge and eventually seemed to disappear altogether. After a few

170

minutes it returned, and the two strangers swam to the surface. She waited until she was certain they were gone before approaching the gorge.

She descended into the fissure until she found overgrown carvings that surrounded the entrance to a cave merfolk city. They had not been seen in a very long time. If their city was overgrown, then either they had abandoned it or evil had befallen them.

She used the carved notches along the walls as handholds to propel herself inside through the zigzagging entrance. Once she was inside, she realized that the songs were different here. The music of the circling imugi above had drowned out other songs due to its proximity, but inside these tunnels, the stone blocked it. Here, she could hear the discord. It was quiet and far away, but it felt clearer. In the wider ocean it merely sounded like noise that was disrupting a beautiful melody, but here she could sense that it was its own music. She sensed resentment, anger, and hatred, all melding into an intense desire to kill.

*   *   *

Libuat listened to Cyfeiriad's description of the overgrown carvings. He projected his memories into her mind, and she examined them.

"We should explore," the elf said eagerly.

"I am not going in there. We have no idea where it leads or what might be inside. We have already seen one of these fish people. What if there are more waiting for us down there?" said Muhandis.

"We do not all have to go at once, and the carvings are overgrown. It is possible that no one has been there for a while." The elf turned to Nabat; "And imagine what new

171

creatures we might find inside to study.”

Nabat paused, obviously conflicted; “Well, that does sound appealing,” she admitted, looking down and pondering. Then she looked up; “But Muhandis is right, we do not know what is in there, and it might be hostile.”

“Cyfeiriad and I will investigate. You two can stay with the ship. If it turns out to be safe, we can bring back samples for Nabat or she can come down herself. If we are gone for more than a day, continue to the mist wall and do not look back,” Libuat said, looking around at everyone.

They nodded in agreement.

The next day, she and Cyfeiriad dove into the water and descended to the gorge. Though she was now accustomed to it, she was still cognizant of the change in temperature as they went. They each held out their lanterns and the red light illuminated the gorge as they entered it. When they came to the carvings, Libuat paused and examined them. They were simple and rounded, perhaps to resemble waves or ripples. The stone around the entrance looked like it had been carved in the shape of a large rectangle with rounded corners. On the inside surface of this rectangle, she could see indentations carved into the stone. They appeared at the midpoint of each side of the rectangle and seemed to continue in along the tunnel’s path.

She saw the elf watching her and she nodded. He tied his lantern to his belt and swam inside, instinctively reaching out and using the indentations to propel himself forward. Libuat followed suit.

The passage extended in past the entrance by about three feet before turning sharply at ninety degrees to the right. It then carried on for another six feet or so before making another sharp ninety degree turn to the left. This pattern continued a couple more times before the passage became a more straightforward path. It occurred to her that in the deep ocean, it would be nearly impossible to keep nature out of one's dwelling. Perhaps the zigzagging passageway was intended to keep out something large. Her mind conjured formless shapes too large to enter, lurking in the depths below. This was soon followed by the next logical question: What about smaller predators?

*   *   *

Josaja waited to see if the strangers would return to the cave merfolk city. The next day, two of them descended with their red lanterns and entered the gorge. She debated within herself if she should follow. The true nature of the discord was clearer in there, though she had not found its source the previous day. There was too much to explore in a day, and she had left early to avoid being caught by the strangers if they decided to explore it. There was no way to know how deep they would go or if they would take a different path and find what she had not.

The strangers might find death, either by nature, the source of the dissonance, or the cause of the cave merfolk's disappearance. If they found the source, would it be their enemy or their ally? Would they make it worse, better, or have no effect? If she followed them and she was caught, they might try to kill her, or they might welcome her. If they came across something hostile, she could be captured or killed as well. There was no way to know for certain what would happen. Josaja mulled it over.

They had seen her that one day but had not shown signs of looking for her afterward. There was an imugi guarding them. Most of them seemed unfamiliar with the water, and the fourth apparently needed the mask to breathe.

173

In the end, she decided that there was no evidence of their hostility, and it was more in keeping with the Narrow Path to risk death to protect someone rather than allow them to die. Following them would allow her to learn what they discovered and help them should dangers arise within the apparently abandoned city. She swam to the gorge and followed them into the underground city.

*   *   *

Libuat followed Cyfeiriad through the tunnels. In the time that she had known him, he had proven on countless occasions that his internal mapping abilities were invaluable. They used the handholds on the walls, ceilings, and floors to move about.

The tunnel angled down slightly until it opened into a large elliptical room. They untied their lanterns from their belts and held them out to better see their surroundings. Numerous passages branched off along the walls and down through the smoothly carved, but now overgrown floor. If this had been on dry ground, such vertical shafts would have seemed odd, but underwater movement in all three dimensions was easier. She also noted that as they had moved past the entrance and deeper inside the caves, that the ocean's background sounds had changed. She did not know what it meant, but somehow it felt different and more distinct.

They passed from the chamber into another tunnel. Several rooms later, they found carvings along a noticeably flat, elliptical wall. Part of the carving was defaced beyond recognition, but the rest appeared to depict various fish people and their cities. One part seemed to show fish people standing in caves underground. Another had them next to a

174

series of underwater volcanoes, and a third group stood on what appeared to be a giant flower on the surface of the water. Maybe they could return with a new airship and search for other people in this realm.

A few chambers later, she began to notice something different in the things growing along the walls. In the previous chambers, they had looked like amorphous masses of things that grew in colonies, imperfect cylinders, or other shapes. Here, there appeared to be dark red vines or roots, with tiny hairs all along their surfaces, that spread out across the walls, ceilings, and floors around them.

Libuat saw the elf pause and look at the root tendrils that snaked out of a tunnel. He turned to her.

I do not think we should touch them, he thought.

Agreed.

She turned to head back through the last tunnel they had left, but she noticed movement. The hairs on the roots behind them were twitching. She looked along the roots back toward the entrance where they seemed most concentrated. There was more movement in the hairs where they had passed than where they had not.

I think it senses us, commented Cyfeiriad.

She scanned in the direction of the tunnel from which the red vines seemed to originate.

I can faintly sense something predatory up ahead, Libuat agreed and hurried toward the exit.

The vines near her began to pull away from the walls and twist to reveal a double row of sharp hooks on their underside. The hooks pointed inward toward each other.

Instinctively, she pushed with her mind in an attempt to put distance between herself and the tentacles. Pain shot across her back and right shoulder as one of them latched onto her from behind. She dropped the lantern, reached up,

175

and pulled on the tentacle, even as she felt herself moving through the water toward the doorway they had tried to avoid.

Trying to rip the tentacle off her shoulder tore gashes in her upper back and shoulder on her right side. The agony shocked her mind, but she did not let go.

Another tentacle wrapped around her left calf. The claws tore into her skin and added to the force pulling her toward the darkness.

A third tentacle wrapped around her waist, tearing through her clothes and into her flesh.

Her mind was flooded by the pain as the claws dug into her. She saw the room with the fallen lantern diminish and move away as she was pulled through the doorway. The shadows grew as the light dimmed.

Libuat was surrounded by darkness in the ocean's cold depths, an environment unknown and unmastered. The fear and horror of the deep had come to life and was mixing with the agony of her wounds so that she was unable to concentrate her mind against her adversary. Seeking a skill that required less concentration, her mind flailed for an animal form to adopt, but she could think of none in that moment that would save her underwater.

All she could think was that she going to die here.

*   *   *

Cyfeiriad saw the tentacles grab Libuat a second before they grabbed him. The first one spiraled up his right leg. He did not wear boots when he swam, and the teeth on the tentacles tore through his trousers and into his flesh immediately. The pain ripped through him, and he dropped his lantern as he reached down instinctively and grabbed at the tentacle. It was wrapped around his leg and would not budge.

A second later, he was yanked through the entrance and into the dark chamber on the other side as another tentacle wrapped around his chest. He tried to focus through the physical torment and reached his hand and mind out toward the shrinking doorway. His body stopped, and immediately, the teeth began to pull on his flesh, increasing his agony. He released his mental hold and reached for his knife.

Cyfeiriad sank the blade into the tentacle on his thigh in an instinctive downward motion. The tentacle released his leg. With a surge of hope, he stabbed the one on his chest. It released him as well.

The elf focused past the pain, reached out with his mind, and pulled himself through the doorway and back into the red-lit chamber. His relief was short-lived when he realized that Libuat was not there. As he reached for the lantern, another tentacle wrapped around his right arm. Pain coursed through him as he was pulled toward the vine-covered passage again.

Something surged through the red glow of the room and the tentacle released him. He turned and saw a fish person in the water next to him. Her eyes were pale blue with ripples or waves of misty gray and her long hair was black. She grabbed his good arm and started to pull him back the way they had come. He shook his head and pointed at the opening through which more vines were now coming. She tugged on his arm in the direction of safety, so he projected an image of Libuat into her mind and pointed. The fish person looked surprised, released his arm, and backed away, but nodded a moment later.

Cyfeiriad grabbed the lantern and followed the stranger. They swam through the next room, following a trail of twitching tentacles. Whenever another tentacle broke from the wall in an attempt to grab them, the stranger would slash it with her claws. The cut tentacles then retreated down the path ahead of them.

They reached a massive open chamber. In the center of the chamber was a large, amorphous mass from which all the tentacles originated. In the center of the tentacles was a circular mouth ringed with multiple rows of teeth. It pulsated as if trying to swallow something that was not there yet. Libuat was steadily being dragged through the chamber and was about halfway to the mouth.

More tentacles flailed toward them, and the stranger swam around the elf, slashing the grasping tentacles with a speed and grace that he could not have matched in the water. He swam to Libuat and began stabbing the tentacles that held her. Once they had all released her, he turned and dragged her back toward the doorway. He reached out with his mind and attempted to project calm. He felt her fear and panic subside, but the emotions spiked again when the fish person grabbed them from behind and swam with them back the way they had come.

She is helping, he asserted.

Libuat calmed again as the stranger carried them faster than they could have swum themselves. Soon they were out of the caves and heading for the surface.

*   *   *

Libuat climbed out of the water and onto the ship, panting. Cyfeiriad crawled up next to her and removed his mask. They lay there catching their breath and wincing.

178

Muhandis and Nabat started to climb out onto the top but stopped.

"What is that?" asked Muhandis.

"Who is that?" asked Nabat.

"A friend," Libuat said between breaths.

Libuat closed her eyes and the gray flames rippled over her body. The pain subsided as she shifted herself whole.

She sat up and projected the concept of thankfulness toward the stranger.

The fish person's mind and face exuded surprise and confusion, both at the method of communication and the jinniya healing herself. The stranger surged backward in the water, putting distance between them but not leaving.

Cyfeiriad staggered to his feet, walked across the ship, and climbed inside. He sent a mental image of bandages back to her, and she remembered that he could not shift himself whole like she could.

Libuat turned to the stranger and projected the sense of questioning for a name. She skimmed the stranger's mind to pick up the meanings of the words as the stranger spoke them.

"Josaja," the stranger replied.

The jinniya projected the question of what Josaja was.

"I am one of the merfolk. What are you?" Libuat's mental connection translated.

Libuat projected memories of the distinctive features of her people, "jinn."

"And your companion?"

"Elf"; Libuat repeated the process for Cyfeiriad.

The conversation carried on like this for some time. Slowly, the mermaid relaxed and moved closer.

Over the next several days, the mermaid would visit them, and they would discuss themselves and the events that had led to their meeting. During that time, Libuat slowly gained an understanding of Josaja's language as she explained to the jinniya about the imugis, the discord in the songs, and the merfolk in general. Libuat also explained how they had come to be in this realm, how their ship had been knocked out of the sky by the storm, and the things they saw and heard when they hit the water. Josaja seemed surprised and intrigued by the description of the mournful sounds and the pulsing blue and green lights on the massive shadowy forms.

What sparked Libuat and Cyfeiriad's curiosity the most was when Josaja noted that following them had led to her discovering that the discord was clearer in the underwater caves. When both the elf and mermaid raised the question as to whether or not they would return with Josaja to continue the investigation, Libuat said that she would meditate on it and confer with her team.

*   *   *

Cyfeiriad sat removing his bandages in the ship as Libuat explained what they had learned from Josaja. She ended with the question of whether or not they would help the mermaid with the search for the source of the dissonance. The elf was eager to return to the cave city so that he could simultaneously satisfy his curiosity, aid the merfolk, and repay the mermaid who had saved their lives.

"Those tunnels are obviously not safe," said Muhandis.

"Yes, but she needs our help," argued Nabat.

"Are you going to go into those caves? Can you fight

180

off one of those strange tentacled creatures?" he countered.

The elf's eagerness to help and explore began to fade. While part of Cyfeiriad understood the jinni's hesitation, he found the almost aggressive resistance to helping the merfolk irritating.

Nabat hung her head, then looked up; "I do not want to go myself, but I will if I have to."

Muhandis snorted. "And what about the elf? He is still healing, and he did not fare much better down there."

"I have healed enough, and I have no problem returning to those tunnels, especially now that I have some idea what type of threats exist in them," responded Cyfeiriad, suppressing his irritation.

"It is not even our problem. It is theirs. Why should we risk our lives for them?" argued Muhandis again.

"Is it in keeping with the Narrow Path to turn a blind eye to their troubles? Josaja risked her life to help us. Even if she had not, we should be willing to risk our lives to help others"; Cyfeiriad glared at Muhandis.

The jinni seemed somewhat ashamed but did not relent.

"Cyfeiriad is right," said Libuat. "In addition, there is the possibility that this discord is caused by the Enemy. We already know that they attempted to infiltrate, manipulate, and control our people, and it is quite likely that they had something to do with the devastation of the elves. It is reasonable to suspect that they would also attack the merfolk. At the very least, strategically, it could gain us an ally. It may also gain us knowledge or a victory over the Enemy."

Cyfeiriad relaxed slightly. He was glad that Libuat seemed to agree with him.

Muhandis's shoulders sank.

Nabat asked hesitantly, "Are we all going down there?"

"No. Cyfeiriad and I will descend with Josaja," Libuat answered. "You two will take the ship and proceed to the mist wall. Return home and report what we have learned."

"How will you get back if you do not have the ship?" asked Nabat.

"Josaja has informed me that she can arrange for us to be carried to the mist wall on the back of a large sea turtle," Libuat explained. "Apparently, the merfolk and them are on very good terms, and they are one of the few species that has not shown any aggression toward them, either before or after the discord."

*   *   *

Libuat followed Josaja and Cyfeiriad through the frigid underground tunnels. The lanterns illuminated everything with their red light. They made sure to avoid the ones lined with the tentacles that had previously attacked them. Whenever they reached an intersection, Josaja would listen to the dissonant songs and then choose the direction in which they sounded clearest or loudest. The farther they went, the more obvious they became, even to the jinniya. Along the way, Libuat would scan with her mind. Now that she knew what dangers lurked in the tunnels and that they were possibly attempting to sneak up on the Enemy, she was taking extra precautions.

Deep in the tunnels, they came across a hole in the passage wall. This was not a carved intersection, but a rough break in the stone. Libuat extended her mind to search the unseen corridor ahead of them.

Nothing.

They carefully swam down the rough-cut passage. The sounds in the water grew more noticeable.

Wait, I sense something up ahead. We should hide the lights, she warned.

Libuat and Cyfeiriad deactivated the lanterns and tied them to their belts. A faint yellow light could be seen ahead. The three of them swam until the tunnel opened out over a large cavern. Inside, the cavern was lit with a sickly yellow light from something that was dispersed through the chamber, on the ceiling and the floor.

Below them, the bowl-shaped chamber was filled with large eggs that were taller than the jinniya. A strange, black, weblike substance covered everything, connecting all of the eggs to a mass in the center of the floor. The discordant song was noticeably clearer here, even to her non-merfolk senses. It sounded like one monstrous voice leading a chorus of smaller ones. She could sense rage, hatred, jealousy, and possibly pride in it. She scanned the chamber with her mind and sensed the minds inside the eggs, minds moving on the far side of the cavern, and something horrid and massive in the center.

Libuat looked down at the large eggs. She swam next to one and examined it closely. Something large and serpentine moved within.

What are these? she asked.

Those are imugi eggs, but something is wrong with them. The hatchlings are mimicking the dissonance exactly, replied Josaja.

They looked around the room.

Are those merfolk on the far side? asked Cyfeiriad.

They are the cave merfolk, replied Josaja in surprise. *They have not been seen in many years. It is concerning to see them here in the midst of the discord.*

Libuat looked across at the distant figures moving through the eggs. They seemed to be tending to them.

She turned her attention back to the imugi hatchling. She reached in with her mind to study its anatomy. If she could get a good sense of how it was put together, she might be able to shift into it. This would give her a better chance of survival should something attack them in the depths.

The way the hatchlings move reminds me of the way the creatures with the lights moved in the storm, commented Cyfeiriad as he examined another egg.

Josaja responded, *I have never seen an imugi create a storm, but I have seen them play in one. The Elders have told tales of the first imugis, Abeoji and Eomeoni, the ones who sired all others, that they were bigger and more powerful than the ones we grew up with. Such creatures have not been seen in centuries.*

The music around them suddenly stuttered. Libuat and the others looked up immediately. Across, in the center of the room, the large black mass stirred. A slit opened across its slimy, uneven surface, revealing a massive eye and a gold metallic iris streaked with red and green. The eye turned toward them, and the song began to change.

The cave merfolk turned in their direction and surged through the water.

The three immediately turned and swam back into the tunnel. Josaja surged ahead, her natural abilities propelling her faster than the jinniya or the elf. Cyfeiriad was behind the mermaid, his years of experience in the water and his mental abilities granting him speed. Despite the danger, Libuat was calmer this time and used her mind to grasp the rocky surfaces ahead of her to pull herself forward.

As the yellow light from the egg chamber dimmed,

they reactivated their lanterns but kept their hands free to aid in their escape. They reached the carved tunnel and began to retrace their path. After a couple chambers, Josaja paused, looking back and forth between the various passages leading out. Cyfeiriad swam past her and motioned for them to follow.

Soon they left the cave city and began swimming toward the surface. Libuat could hear Josaja calling out her own song into the water around them as she took the lead again.

*   *   *

Cyfeiriad followed Josaja toward the surface. He pushed down with his mind to gain speed. Below he sensed Libuat following close behind and the cave merfolk just exiting the city. He listened as Josaja continued her song.

A new sound washed over them. It was similar to the melody in the egg chamber, but it felt like it was coming toward them. The elf's eyes and mind scanned the area as best he could. Something large was rising from the depths toward them.

Above, the light suddenly disappeared. He looked up, momentarily worried that whatever pursued them had gotten ahead and was going to attack them. Then he realized that the shape above was a massive turtle.

Its front flippers were longer than he was tall, with long, sharp claws on the ends. The shell had a rough, almost serrated edge to it.

The turtle swam past them in the opposite direction they were traveling, turned, dove, then came up underneath them. It rose to meet their bodies and they all grabbed onto its rough shell.

185

The sea turtle broke through the water's surface, and they sped across the ocean. The wind tore over their bodies, causing the elf and jinniya to shiver slightly as they adjusted.

Cyfeiriad turned back and saw the cave merfolk's heads bobbing in the water. A massive shape rose out of the ocean and pursued them just beneath the surface.

"An imugi," declared Josaja with a look of concern on her face.

"Is it following us or chasing us?" asked Libuat.

"Chasing."

"I thought you said the imugi was guarding us," questioned Cyfeiriad.

"Its song was gone when we exited the city," Josaja replied.

The elf and jinniya looked around in concern. He could not see the ship or sense the other jinn when he scanned the area.

"Where is the ship?" Libuat asked, worry evident in her tone.

Josaja hung her head; "The best-case scenario is that the imugi guarding you took them to safety, but the worst case is that the imugi and your friends are dead."

The elf clung to the large shell, his head pressed against it and his eyes closed as he attempted to suppress his grief and guilt. He could sense mostly guilt and anger coming from the jinniya at the possibility that those for whom she was responsible were dead.

After some time, he looked up.

"Where are we going?" he asked.

"To safety," Josaja replied.

They rode the turtle for several days, but the imugi never gave up the chase. They slept in shifts to make sure no one fell off while asleep. The passage of time gave the elf the opportunity to let grief dissipate naturally. He could sense Libuat undergoing a similar experience.

One afternoon, Libuat pointed ahead, and Cyfeiriad turned to see something in the distance. As it grew, he realized he was looking at something that resembled a flower and leaves floating on the ocean, except this flower was the size of a hill.

Two large shadows surged toward them as they approached the flower. For a moment, Cyfeiriad feared that it was another threat, but they veered around the turtle and converged on their pursuer. The ocean behind them churned, but the imugi that had chased them came no closer.

Soon they reached one of the large leaves surrounding the flower. The turtle stopped next to it, and they stepped off onto the plant.

*   *   *

Libuat and Cyfeiriad followed Josaja across the giant leaf. She estimated the leaf had been at least three feet thick when the turtle had brought them to its edge. Ahead of them, there was a gap between the petals near where they met the leaves. Libuat looked around in amazement as they passed through.

There were several layers of overlapping petals arrayed in a massive ring. Where the bases of the petals converged at the center, there was a large coral structure surrounded by a forest of tall stalks. The coral city rose high overhead, shaped by some unknown art that allowed the merfolk to create gently curving mounds and towers.

Josaja led them between the petals, across the open space, and into the forest of stalks. Merfolk that they passed stopped what they were doing and stared at the jinniya and

187

the elf. Every so often, one would see them and run away. After a long while, they reached the coral structures in the center of the huge flower.

Libuat followed along as they made their way through passages inside the coral and spiraling stairs around the outsides. She noticed that the entrances here did not have the same tight zigzagging pattern that the cave city had had.

Eventually they reached a chamber at the peak of the highest tower. Inside the chamber were gathered several merfolk whose eyes were the same as Josaja's: pale blue with ripples or waves of misty grey. There were also a few others whose eyes were pale blue with ripples or waves of red-orange. They all turned to look at the intruders.

"Elders, I apologize for the interruption, but we have discovered a grave threat that cannot wait," Josaja said to them.

The Elders asked what she had to say, and she relayed the events that had transpired with Libuat, Cyfeiriad, and herself in the cave merfolk city. When prompted, Libuat and Cyfeiriad gave their input as well.

"The return of the Enemy and the corruption of some of the imugis and their offspring explains a lot," one of the Elders said gravely.

"Thank you for bringing us this news," said another.

"Abeoji and Eomeoni have not been seen in centuries, but perhaps they sensed the Enemy before us."

"How long before this city reaches the ring?" asked Josaja.

Libuat noticed the glances from the Elders in the direction of her and Cyfeiriad. Josaja had not mentioned a ring or even the existence of this city. She suspected the merfolk were disinclined to reveal unnecessary information to outsiders.

"It will be sealed within the week."

"Hopefully the eggs do not hatch before then."

"What about the Enemy? What if it comes here directly?" asked Josaja.

"We will confer with the other Elders. We have never fought the Enemy or the imugis, so there is much we do not know."

Libuat glanced at Cyfeiriad and met his gaze. Then she turned back to the Elders.

"Elders, one of the Enemy infiltrated the jinn and replaced my mother. My father, this elf, and I killed the imposter. I do not know what skills your people have cultivated, but the Enemy is not truly immortal."

The Elders looked at her, then at Cyfeiriad in surprise.

"How did you do it?"

"They held it down and I rammed a dagger through its skull," said Cyfeiriad.

The merfolk council looked at each other as if considering this new information.

"Thank you," said one of them, turning to face her and Cyfeiriad again.

"You may stay or leave as you wish," said another.

Libuat opened her mouth to respond, but Cyfeiriad answered before her, "I would be delighted to get a chance to explore your amazing city."

The Elders nodded.

Cyfeiraid and Libuat spent the rest of the day with Josaja, who led them on a tour of the city. They stood on one of the leaves and watched the growing mass of mountains rising from the ocean in the distance.

Libuat could feel the air beginning to cool as night approached. "This flower city is impressive," she commented. "I can tell that the city is moving. Where are we going?"

"The Elders have prepared a safe haven for the floating cities; a mountain ring to keep out anything that may seek to destroy us," she replied.

"Did your Elders receive a warning?" asked Cyfeiriad.

"A few centuries ago, yes. Nothing happened, so plans were made but never enacted. When the discord started, we put the plans into motion."

"How do your people raise mountains from the sea?" asked Libuat.

"It is a slow process. The ring we are approaching surrounds the undersea citadels and rises for several miles into the sky. All of the floating cities have been moved there. This one is the last."

Libuat marveled at the idea but was still very much aware that Josaja had avoided answering her question about how it was possible to raise mountains from the sea.

"Are the leaves curling up?" asked Cyfeiriad looking around.

Josaja seemed shocked, like she had just remembered something. "Oh, I am so sorry. I forgot to warn you. The flower city's leaves and petals fold up and it sinks beneath the surface when the sun sets. It is not an issue for us, so I completely forgot."

The elf laughed and put his mask on.

*   *   *

Deep in the caves under the ocean, the weblike mass of the Enemy began to pulsate. Its song grew in intensity and volume. The cave merfolk swam up around it, adding their

190

voices.

The song reached a climax, and the eggs began to hatch.

The corrupted young imugis tore free of the eggs and twisted and surged through the water of the cave. The hatchlings created their own music. Inspired by the song of the Enemy, it conveyed their own unique hatred, rage, and indignation.

As one, the hatchlings poured through the tunnels and out into the ocean. The teaming mass exploded and surrounded the massive adults that waited outside.

The songs of the corrupted adult sea serpents were elated with the arrival of their children. The discordant music of the adults and hatchlings fused together, and the imugis swam to destroy the merfolk.

*   *   *

Cyfeiriad stood with Josaja and Libuat on a cliff part way up the steep rock wall overlooking the gap in the mountain ring. The air was cool as it moved through the opening. Below, the flower cities were spread out across the artificial sea, with the most recent arrivals nearest the gap. The mountains themselves reminded him more of the mountains that the high elves and jinn had mined or carved than the volcanic rock he had seen on new islands.

The elf looked at the sea within the mountain ring. From this height, the floating cities made it look like a pond, despite how massive everything really was. He looked down at the water in the gap, at the first hints of rock that now protruded but had not when they first arrived. A strange yellow-brown glow could be seen below the surface. He still did not know how they could grow mountains. Now that the

191

last of the floating cities had been brought in, they were sealing the opening.

"What is that?" he heard Libuat ask.

He turned to look out over the ocean where she was pointing. In the far distance, the ocean was beginning to boil. Below them, the water around the mountain ring surged as the guardian imugis moved toward the boiling water.

"It is the corrupted imugis. They hatched," exclaimed Josaja.

A cry rang out below and horns blew around the mountains. The yellow-brown glow in the water became brighter, and the rocks in the gap began to rise faster, but they were thin and uneven.

"What do we do, how can we help?" asked Libuat.

Josaja pointed at the flower cities; "Everyone knows to evacuate. Even the citadels will be empty soon."

The elf looked and saw swarms of merfolk diving out of the cities and swimming to the rocky shores. Even more were rising out of the water to join them. The slope of the mountains rose until it was almost vertical. The escaping merfolk climbed the rocky inclines all along the mountain ring until they reached the paths that had been carved, leading them up to the cave shelters above.

Cyfeiriad looked back out at the ocean.

The boiling mass reached the imugis attempting to guard the gap. He could see that the hatchlings were accompanied by other adult imugis. The water turned red as the swirling mass tore through the guardians.

The attacking imugis churned the water in the partially sealed opening. The adults threw themselves at the protrusions, cracking the thin rock until the hatchlings were able to swarm through. The dark mass of sea serpents flowed into the mountain ring.

By now, most of the merfolk were out of the water and moving up the slopes. The imugis shot through the sea and began attacking and destroying the cities. The adults rose up out of the water, fanning the fins on the sides of their necks as they screeched at the sky.

At least two of the cities were fully destroyed before the sea serpents seemed to realize that most of the merfolk were gone. The adults began leading the hatchlings toward the mountain slopes. The merfolk closest to the water began to die. At various places around the mountain ring, the Elders stepped forward. Where they stood, the imugis were repelled, crushed, or torn by unseen forces while the merfolk fled to safety. When there were no longer any merfolk still in the waters nearest the Elders, a yellow-brown glow appeared, and a rock wall began to form along the shore. As their paths were cut off, the hatchlings began to maneuver toward the edge of the growing rock wall, moving in the general direction of the watching elf and jinniya.

Below, Cyfeiriad could see the merfolk trying to climb as quickly as possible, but it was not fast enough. One of the adult imugis left the water and began pursuing the merfolk.

Cyfeiriad and Libuat ran down the slope. Out of the corner of his eye he saw the gray flames ripple across her body, and she shifted into a bird. She dove past him, covering the distance much faster. When she neared the approaching imugi, the flames rippled again and Libuat hit the ground in the form of another sea serpent.

The imugi pulled up short and screeched at the sudden appearance of one of its own. Libuat's head shot forward, snapping at the sea serpent. Their bodies coiled and twisted, attempting to clamp their teeth over the other's neck.

Cyfeiriad ran past the merfolk. Some were shocked at the fight below them and others were just focused on escaping. Hatchlings were starting to make their way up the slope. There were hundreds of them in this one area alone. While the adults were several hundred feet long, the hatchlings were at least a dozen feet long.

One of the hatchlings reared up before him and attempted to strike. Cyfeiriad's hand and mind reached out and stopped it. He looked at it for a second, unsure what to do. If he threw it back into the water, it would either come back up or find new prey. The elf drew his knife, pulled the creature to him, and drove the blade through the top of the skull. He let the hatchling drop lifeless at his feet. This process was repeated several more times as the hatchlings advanced up the slope.

A loud screech drew his attention in time to see Libuat's teeth pull away from the throat of the most recent imugi she had been fighting. It fell back toward the water, hitting the rocks next to others who had suffered the same fate. Libuat then turned and continued attacking the rising hatchlings.

Cyfeiriad sensed impending danger and turned in time to see another hatchling about to strike. He caught it as before and raised his knife. A scream from higher up drew his attention. There were so many hatchlings that some had ignored him and moved past to attack the merfolk. The elf clenched his fist, crushing the neck of the hatchling. As he did, he felt its anger replaced by pain and fear right before it died. The sensation was horrifying, but he could see the other hatchlings beginning to tear into merfolk. Cyfeiriad reached out his hand and mind, gripping a creature before it struck. He crushed its skull and flung the corpse aside. He reached for the next one.

The clouds began to darken, and he glanced over in time to see a massive body, much bigger than the adult imugis, moving over the jagged rocks in the gap. A sound rose over the hateful song of the corrupted sea serpents. The attacking imugis stopped; their ire drawn to the two gigantic shadows that moved in the depths below.

The adults and hatchlings dove back into the water. Their song of rage clashed with the notes of sorrow that surrounded them. At first the twisted sea serpents swarmed over the mass of the progenitors, biting and tearing at their flesh. Abeoji and Eomeoni began swimming in great circles around the sea's perimeter. As they picked up speed, the others began to be swept along, carried by the rushing water.

Blue and green lights began to pulse along the sides of the ancient imugis. The clouds overhead turned black and lightning flashed in the sky above. The mournful song of the ancient sea serpents drowned out the rage and resentment of the younger ones. The speed of the pulsing lights increased.

Two giant imugis rose out of the tumult. Their neck fins flared out to the sides, and they roared up at the sky. They brought their heads back down, mouths opened, pharyngeal jaws reaching out toward the writhing mass beneath them.

Sparks crackled between their teeth and two massive bolts of blue lightning streaked down into the water. Water boiled, steam rose, and the song of the twisted imugis changed to one of pain and betrayal. The ancient creatures continued to pour their fury into the depths until the fog was thick and the song had died.

When they finally closed their mouths, they pointed their heads at the sky and let out long, low, painful notes. Even the elf could tell they were in agonizing grief.

Abeoji and Eomeoni returned to the water. Their

bodies swam in intertwining patterns as their sorrowful song continued. After a while, they left through the opening in the mountain ring.

*   *   *

When the fog finally cleared, they could see the aftermath. Libuat and Cyfeiriad stood above the shore, looking out over the floating corpses of the corrupted imugis.

The jinniya and elf spent the next several weeks helping the merfolk clear the sea. When life for the merfolk seemed to be returning to normal, Libuat approached the council of Elders.

"I grieve with you for your losses, but I am pleased that so many were saved, and you were able to rebuild," she said.

"We thank you and your companion for your aid in fighting off the corrupted imugis," one of them replied.

Libuat and Cyfeiriad nodded respectfully.

"Having seen what the Enemy was able to accomplish here and how successful you were at thwarting it, I wanted to propose that our peoples form an alliance for our mutual aid and defense against the Enemy," she suggested.

The Elders looked around the room at each other, then back at her.

"At this time, we are not inclined to accept your offer," stated one.

"While we appreciate your willingness to help, we do not want to become involved in additional conflicts whose origins did not directly involve us," said another.

Josaja spoke up, "But they helped protect our people,

196

and we might not have found out about the source of the discord if not for them."

"Abeoji and Eomeoni were obviously aware of it and were the ultimate source of our survival. Our responsibility is to our own children, not the children of the first elves or jinn," said one of the Elders.

Anger at the dismissive attitude of the Elders shot through Libuat. The Enemy started this fight long ago with all of them. The Enemy had sought out the merfolk on its own. There was no escaping this.

But she knew they could and should not be forced to participate if they did not want to, and their first responsibility was to their children. She exhaled her frustration, returning to a calmer state of mind.

"Perhaps, at the least, you would be interested in joining our explorations to improve our understanding of the other realms," she suggested, hoping to maintain their good standing and create a path to future cooperation.

"We have already lost much and do not wish to draw more attention to ourselves," replied an Elder.

"I understand," she said.

With a final respectful bow, she turned and left the merfolk council chamber, followed by Cyfeiriad.

Josaja looked at the Elders, then at the empty doorway before following.

V

Inside the Blizzard
Dynoltir, + 2008 TR

In a run-down old house in the woods near the mountains, Rue crouched behind a couch. On the other side, she could hear a man and a woman talking. A pair of jeans was tossed over the back of the couch, and Rue carefully reached up to check the pockets. She found the wallet and pulled it out. Quickly, she began searching through its contents. She ignored the man's ID's and went straight for the cash and credit card. Silently, she stuffed them in her pocket and reached up to put the wallet back.

The man said something indecipherable about needing something from his wallet, but the woman said he did not need it.

The sound of a door creaking open made Rue crawl to the edge of the hallway and the couch. Her little brother, Rhys, stepped out of the room. She put her finger to her lips and tried to gesture for him to go back.

Instead, he waved, held up a little bracelet, and said, "I figured it out." He held it forward, "I made it for you."

There was a confused noise and the man stood up and stepped around the couch. Rue turned her head to look up.

"You said you didn't have kids," he began, but stopped when he saw Rue's head peeking out from behind the couch. "What is going on?" he demanded.

The man turned on the woman, "What is this?" He gestured at Rue.

"It's nothing," said the woman as she stood and

198

walked around the couch. "Go back to your room," she yelled angrily down the hall to the child.

"I don't want this kind of hassle," the man said as he reached for his jeans. He started to put them back on in irritation.

"No, it's ok, please stay," the woman pleaded.

He tried shrugging her off and his wallet fell out of his pocket. He picked it up and looked at it. His eyes narrowed as he glanced at Rue, then at the woman, then back to his wallet. He opened it and cursed.

"Where's my money?" he roared.

"What are you talking about?" the woman feigned ignorance.

The man pushed past her and reached for Rue. She stood quickly and stepped back further behind the couch.

"If you know what's good for you…" he threatened.

Rue fumbled in her pocket and pulled out the cash and credit card. She handed it back to the man. He flipped through it and stuffed it in his pocket.

"Rue, how dare you try to rob my friend," the woman began in false indignation.

The man snorted and walked out, slamming the door behind him. The sound of an engine starting and angrily driving away could be heard through the door.

The woman turned and glared at Rue. She shook her head in disgust; "You couldn't even keep the money, you useless waste of space."

"Mommy?" Rhys said, now just inside the living room.

The woman turned on the child and back handed him across the face. He collapsed in tears.

"When I say 'stay in your room,' I mean it," she yelled at him.

Rue glanced at the woman and rushed to her brother.

The woman walked away grumbling, "Worthless kids, ruining my life and wasting my time."

She grabbed a bottle off the coffee table and walked off to her room on the other side of the house, drinking as she went.

Rue hugged Rhys; "Shh, it's ok. Here, let me see."

She turned his face to get a better look and saw a cut across his cheek.

"Come on, let's get you cleaned up."

She led him to the bathroom where she washed his face and put a little bandage on the cut. It would not really do much, but he always seemed to feel better once a cut or scrape was bandaged.

Her brother hugged her; "Thank you. Here, I figured out what you showed me and made this for you."

He held up a little bracelet she had tried to teach him to make the other day. He had been playing with bits of string and yarn, trying to replicate it.

"Thank you, it's wonderful," she said, accepting the gift and sliding it onto her wrist.

She led him back to their room and watched him play for a few minutes. Her eyes drifted to the small cut on his cheek. Her fingers reached up and touched a scar on her own cheek. His cut was not deep, this time. Anger hardened her eyes as her attention drifted inward.

After some thought, Rue turned and disappeared down the hall. She snuck up to her mother's room and peaked in to make sure she was asleep. The bottle was empty, and her mother was passed out.

Rue quickly returned to her room and grabbed her backpack. Quietly she went through the kitchen, gathering supplies. She made a point of grabbing a large, sharp kitchen knife while she was at it.

Returning to their room, she turned to her brother; "Would you like to go on an adventure?" she asked with a smile.

"What kind of adventure?" he asked with interest.

"An epic quest to an exciting new land."

"Like in the stories?"

"Yes, like in the stories."

"Yes, yes, let's go."

"Ok, go to the bathroom and then we'll go."

Her brother ran off down the hall. He returned a few minutes later, and she bundled him up in his snow boots and winter clothes.

As she was zipping him up and pulling up his hood, he asked her, "What about mommy? Will she come too?"

Rue shook her head; "This part's for siblings only."

"But I want Mommy to have an adventure too."

"We'll see Mommy later," she lied.

"Ok."

She put on her own jacket and grabbed her backpack. Quietly, they slipped out the front door.

*   *   *

Rue walked through the forest carrying Rhys as the snow fell in the night around them. Her brother was fast asleep, and she was enjoying the beauty of the falling snow at night. It was peaceful and still. Despite how late it was and that the snow was falling, it almost felt warmer than it had during the day. The white flakes drifted almost completely vertically to the ground, so the lack of wind might have been the cause.

Despite the beauty of the moment, she knew she

needed to find shelter soon. She might be able to tough it out in the cold, but she was not so sure about Rhys.

Rue looked around. She had chosen this direction from their house because she thought there was an old barn out here. She began to fear that she had missed it or misremembered, when she spotted it through the trees.

Grass and plants had grown up in front of the door, and she had to face her back to it and throw her whole weight into it to get it to move. Once inside, she set her brother down then went back to gather sticks and branches. Kneeling down next to her pile, she pulled out a lighter. It took a while, but she eventually succeeded in starting a fire.

Rhys woke up and moved closer; "I'm cold."

Rue pulled a blanket out of the backpack. She laid part of it on the ground for them to sit on, then wrapped it around them.

Rhys snuggled up next to her.

"This is part of the adventure," she said. "I like watching the snow fall in the night."

Rhys followed her gaze out the window on the far side of the barn. The snow fell faster now.

Rue readjusted and they leaned back against the wall.

The snow outside whipped past the window and the wind rushed around the barn. Things scraped the ground outside somewhere out of sight.

For a brief moment, she thought she saw a flash of light off to one side through some cracks in the walls. A surge of fear shot through her as she imagined someone walking through the snow with a flashlight. What would a stranger do if they were found?

A thick mist billowed up and seemed to surround the barn. No one came. There were no footsteps or shouts, no searching flashlight beams.

"I saw something outside," said Rhys.

"Shh, it's just wind and snow. There's nothing to worry about."

She pulled him closer, and he rested his head against her. She wrapped her arm around him and gently squeezed him.

Quietly, Rue's eyes darted around the barn, peering through any crack she found. All she could hear was wind and scraping, which she assumed was from tree branches or sticks against something outside. Worry and fear crept into her, gnawing at the back of her mind. What if this was a mistake? What if there was something or someone out there?

She looked down at her sleeping brother and saw the cut on his right cheek. She gently traced her finger along her matching scar. An irritation and anger grew within her, and she shook her head internally. No, this was for the best.

The mist began to creep into the barn. When it reached them, she was surprised that it felt slightly warmer than the cold night air had been up to this point.

Fatigue slithered into her mind as her eyes gazed blankly at the flames. The sound of the wind created white noise upon which her mind drifted. Eventually, she fell asleep.

*   *   *

Rue shivered in the early morning sun and squinted her eyes as she opened them. The fire was out, and the snow had stopped falling. She tried to gently reposition Rhys so she could get up without waking him but failed.

"Good morning."

He blinked up at her; "Good morning."

Rue rummaged through the backpack and handed

him some snacks.

"Here, have something to eat. I'm going to take a look outside."

"Ok."

She stood and stretched. Sleeping on the hard ground while leaning against a hard wall all night was not pleasant. She walked over to the door and leaned her weight back as she pulled to force it open again. She squinted against the brightness and looked down. The ground just outside the door had almost no snow on it. It was odd that there was so little snow so close to the barn. Her eyes swept across the ground near the barn and out toward the forest. There was a wide patch of clear, frost-covered grass surrounding the barn. Outside of this area the snow was almost a foot thick. It did not look like it got any shallower the farther out she looked into the forest.

She looked at the edge of the cleared area. The snow slowly sloped up from the grass to its full height and glistened smoothly, almost like ice. This did not look like what she remembered seeing when she had to shovel the driveway in the past, where the snow formed irregular piles on the sides of the cleared area that were taller than the rest of the snow in the yard.

When she got outside, she looked around at the snow-covered trees and bushes. It was beautiful, but cold. She hugged herself and rubbed her arms with her hands as she took a few steps away from the barn. The ground beneath her feet made a light crunching noise.

Rue's eyes angled down at the frost before rising and drifting over the area around her. Off to one side, the cleared patch of grass extended into the trees forming a fairly dry path.

Fear of being caught shot through her, and she looked

around frantically. There were no voices, no people. The snow was undisturbed other than the cleared area and path. She walked around the barn and found that the snow pattern was the same all the way around. The cleared area was wide, and she could find no marks of a shovel or boot prints anywhere.

A thousand possibilities flooded her mind. Was this a weird natural phenomenon? Had animals done this?

It had to be people, but why were there no shovel marks? Why would someone do this? Had they been discovered? Was someone helping them... but why would anyone do that? Was the cleared path a trap?

Maybe it was all a coincidence, and someone had cleared a path for their own purposes without ever noticing them? That would only work if the fire was already out. But how could she not have heard whoever had removed the snow? There was so much of it, where did it go if it was not shoveled aside?

A small form ran past her and jumped into the snow. Startled and terrified that some half-imagined menace had just rushed to reveal itself, she turned quickly only to see Rhys tripping and falling in the snow. She breathed a sigh of relief and smiled as she watched him. The snow was thick enough that it made it difficult for him to walk.

"Don't go far. I'm going to pack up our stuff," she said.

He was too busy playing and did not respond.

"Hey, did you hear me?" she slightly sharpened her tone and raised her voice to get his attention.

Rhys turned; "Ok."

She went into the barn and packed their things. She looked at the charred broken bits of wood that had been the fuel for their campfire. Some sticks off to the side had not burned all the way. She grabbed them and stuffed them in the pack too. Every little bit would help.

Rue went back outside and looked around. She could try trudging through the snow, but there was no way Rhys could walk on his own for very long. She would end up carrying him, which would make walking all the more difficult. She looked at the path. She did not know where it went or who had made it. Whoever they were had not accosted them in their sleep, which would have been the easiest option if they had wished the siblings harm. If it was an accident or intentional help, then she should use it. Realistically, it was the only way for her and her brother to actually get anywhere.

"Come one, let's get going," Rue said.

Rhys paused and looked at her, snow all over him and a large pile in his hands.

She walked over and brushed the snow off of him. "See that path over there? That is the path to adventure! Let's go explore."

Rhys smiled and climbed out of the snow. She brushed the rest of him clean with her hands and they walked down the path. She made sure to hold his hand in her left hand and kept her right on the knife hidden in her coat pocket. Her head constantly swiveled, eyes scanning the path and the forest for anything suspicious.

Gently squeezing her brother's hand, she sincerely hoped this path was not a trap.

*   *   *

The woman opened her eyes slowly, an intense pain in her bladder motivating her more than anything else. She stumbled to the bathroom. When she was finished, she felt more awake, though her head was pounding and the sunlight through the blinds was intolerable.

The house, at least, was quiet. That was a relief. She stumbled back to bed and passed out again.

Sometime later, she drifted awake. The headache was gone and the sunlight was not so bad anymore. She made another trip to the bathroom, then wandered through the house. There was not much in the kitchen, but she found some cereal and just enough milk. She glared down at the dissatisfying meal and shrugged internally before taking it over to the couch and collapsing onto it.

The food now consumed, her mind reviewed the previous day's events. She sighed again. Those stupid brats had ruined everything. Now she had no company and no money.

A quiet, almost forgotten part of her mind whispered something.

She looked around. Where were the kids? Why couldn't she hear them? They were never this quiet. Were they up to something?

She rose to her feet out of annoyance and walked into the back hall. Their room was empty. Their bathroom was empty. Maybe they were outside.

The woman opened the door and shut her eyes as she was assaulted by blinding light and bitter cold. She squinted, her eyes barely opening until they adjusted enough to see.

The ground outside the house was covered in pristine snow, untouched by any footprints, tire tracks, or anything else other than the wind.

She walked back inside and slammed the door on the cold. It took her several long moments to realize that the children were gone, and there were no tracks outside.

Her eyes widened at the realization, and her mind

sobered as primitive, suppressed instinct brought her to full
alertness. This was soon overshadowed by conflicting
impulses.

How long had they been gone? Were they safe? How
would she find them?

Why did it matter? She never wanted them. They
ruined her life and constantly dragged her down. She was
better off without the hassle and nuisance they brought.

But what if someone realized they were gone? Would
she be blamed? Did she not have any sense of
responsibility?

*   *   *

The sun was just beginning to set when they reached
the end of the path. The ground beside them began to slope
up and away through the forest. Ahead of them, on the rough
incline, Rue could see the opening of a small cave. The
cleared path led to it.

Rue kept herself in front, hand on the knife as they
approached. The cave opening was not large, but it looked
like it went back fifteen feet or so. It was too low for her to
walk, even bent over, so she crawled inside to look around.
Rhys only had to bend over a little bit to walk beside her.

The little cave seemed fairly clean and dry. It was
deep enough that she could not feel the breeze outside nor
see any snow.

"Rhys, you stay here, and I'm going to go look for
firewood."

"Can I come too? I want to help."

She paused, looked at him, and smiled; "Ok, but
don't go running off."

"Thank you," he said. "Don't worry, I won't run

208

away."

She left the backpack in the back of the cave. They crawled back out and stood up straight.

"Look for sticks or small branches. It's better if you find ones with no snow on them."

She looked around at the snow-covered forest and realized the near futility of that sentiment. They searched as best they could. Rhys had a really hard time with the deep snow. Rue succeeded in finding some dryer sticks that had been shielded by trees on the side of the slope.

Back inside the cave, she laid out the blanket and went about starting a fire.

When she got the fire going, she dug out more snacks and gave them to Rhys.

"The food is cold and I'm cold," he complained. "When will Mommy join our adventure?"

Rue paused and looked at him; "I know it's cold. I'm sorry. The fire will get bigger, and we'll wrap ourselves in the blanket.

Rhys still did not look happy, so she positioned herself next to him and wrapped the blanket around them. She wondered if she had made a mistake taking him from that house, but the thought of that place brought back memories of her life there and the certainty that his would be no better than hers had been. She suppressed her sudden anger before speaking to him again.

"Sometimes adventures can feel difficult, but in the end, you are glad they happened. It's kind of like how tired or cold you feel after playing in the snow all day."

Rhys seemed to ponder this.

When he was finished eating, he fell asleep.

Rue leaned back and watched the cave's opening. She was not entirely sure where they were going. She had not thought enough about it before they left. All she had known at the time was that she could not let her little brother grow up in that house, with that woman. She knew other people lived in the mountains. When she had been at school or the store, everyone was much friendlier than her own mother in private. Hopefully, they would find another house soon and someone would be willing to take them in. But there was no guarantee. Maybe they would not find anyone. Maybe they would either learn to survive in the wilderness or die in the process. Tears trickled down her cheeks as she hugged her brother under the blanket.

As the darkness grew, the snow began to fall. At first it fell heavy and straight, but then the rushing wind like the night before returned. The snow blew past the entrance almost horizontally at times. Scraping noises could be heard outside. A thick, warm mist billowed out of the forest and drifted into the cave.

The sounds themselves once again conjured images of imaginary horrors in her mind. She had assumed previously that they were from the wind moving sticks or something, but now that the most negative possible futures had been planted in her consciousness, she feared the worst. The strangeness of the path and the warm mist plagued her thoughts as well. The mist did lessen the cold in the cave slightly, but she still did not know what was causing it. She tried her best to stay awake, to make sure that nothing entered the cave to harm her brother, but fatigue eventually won, and she fell asleep.

*   *   *

The woman trudged through the snow as the sky grew dark. Her legs were tired, and her lungs burned from taking deep breaths in the cold air.

"Rhys! Rue!" she called out again.

She had spent the whole afternoon searching but had found nothing. Concern for the children's safety and irritation at the trouble they were causing her vied for dominance in her mind.

Snow began to fall, and she looked around at the darkening trees. She had no idea where they had gone or how long they had been gone. A tiny voice inside summoned images of the cut on Rhys's face and the scar on Rue's, but another angrier voice scoffed.

She turned back and returned home. By the time she was inside, she was exhausted. Fatigue deflated the anger and irritation at what the kids were doing to her. The concern for their safety persisted.

The woman reached for her phone but stopped. If she called for help, the police would come to her house. If they came, they would judge her. She glanced around the room. It was a mess. Empty alcohol containers were strewn about, trash overflowed the bin. If they saw a mess, they might think she was unfit to be a mother. Indignation at the thought of their arrogant judgement rose within her. How dare they consider taking away her children. They were hers.

But it might not be so bad if they were gone. Without the children, her life would be much freer. There would be no one to get in her way or to ruin her plans.

But if they took the children, what were the chances that she might get arrested? Those nasty little imps would undoubtedly paint her in the worst possible light. They would encourage the system to persecute, imprison, and trap her. The thought of being restrained against her will with no hope for escape filled her with anger.

If they had not run away, she would not be in this

mess. Angrily, she shoved the phone back in her pocket.

An image of her children dead or dying in the cold flashed before her mind. Fear and guilt stabbed her, and she paused again in indecision.

*   *   *

Rue drifted to consciousness and was greeted by the smell of cooked meat. Her eyes snapped open, and she looked down in fear that she or Rhys had rolled into the fire.

The fire was out, and Rhys was safe beside her, leaning against the backpack. She quietly sat up and crawled outside.

She blinked in the blinding glare of the sun on the snow. When her eyes adjusted, she saw a cleared area around the cave and a new path leading off into the forest. The snow outside the cleared area was even taller now.

Off to one side near the cave's entrance lay a cooked deer carcass. Rue looked around frantically, but once again did not see any signs of humanity other than the mysteriously cleared path.

She looked down at it. Was there a lightning strike that she somehow slept through during the night? Did someone do this on purpose? Was it meant to frighten them or to feed them?

Not knowing the source, she decided they should not even try it. She leaned down, grabbed the deer's feet, and dragged it away from the cave entrance. She tried to walk backward into the snow, but it was almost two feet thick now and too difficult to traverse. She climbed out and used her hands to cover the carcass with snow as best she could.

Rue went back inside the cave and woke up her brother.

212

"Good morning. It's time to get up."

He sat up and looked around.

She handed him some more snacks. He took them and devoured them quickly while she packed up the blanket and whatever sticks remained unburnt.

Once he was done, they headed out.

"What's over there?" he said, pointing to the pile of snow she had heaped on top of the deer.

"Oh, it's nothing," she said, grabbing his hand and pulling him away.

She paused and looked back the way they had come. The snow was thick and would make walking for both of them incredibly difficult. She could do it, but she would have to lift her feet quite high to clear the snow, and there was no way that Rhys could walk through it. If she carried him the whole way, it would become too difficult and exhausting. She was not entirely sure she could trust the clear path, but it seemed like the only reasonable option at the moment. As they walked down the path, she kept her hand on the knife in her coat pocket and looked around constantly.

*   *   *

The woman moved hurriedly through the house, bagging up the last of the trash and walking it outside. She dumped it in the trashcan and replaced the lid.

By now she was awake, sober, tired, and cold. The fantasy of being rid of the nuisance of her children had been replaced by a dread-filled sense of reality that they might be injured or dead, and she could do nothing about it.

When she re-entered the house, she made one last sweep through every room to make sure they were clean and there were no bottles, cans, or trash lying about. Despite her dread, she still did not want to risk the police looking at her too suspiciously. She told herself that it was because she did not want them wasting time on her instead of searching for her children, but she knew that was a lie. Deep down she knew that she did not want to be arrested or imprisoned.

Taking a moment to focus on her fear for her children's safety, she picked up the phone and dialed the police. A tear trickled down her face as she explained her situation.

*   *   *

Rue was getting worried as the sun began to set and she had still not found any shelter along the path. By now, Rhys was tired of walking and Rue carried him in her arms.

"Oh, look at the nice big doggie," he said.

"What?" she turned and saw a large wolf several yards off one side of the trail.

She began to walk faster.

"That's not a friendly doggie. We should leave him alone," she explained, looking back and forth as she went.

"Hey doggie," he called out.

"Stop it," she snapped. "That dog will hurt us. Don't call to it."

Rhys went quiet. She shifted his weight to her left arm and felt for the knife, just to reassure herself that it was there.

Rue looked to her left. There was another wolf.

She tried to walk faster.

The wolf to the right was keeping pace with them.

She glanced over her shoulder. There was another wolf behind them.

214

She tried to walk faster, eyes darting back and forth frantically.

She looked forward and saw a wolf step onto the path.

Rue looked around and saw a large tree not far from the path. As quickly as she could, she stomped through the snow to the tree and turned her back to it.

The wolves were beginning to circle them. Tears began to roll down her cheeks as she realized that she had made a huge mistake. She had been trying to protect her brother, but she had only managed to get them both killed.

She glanced at the tree. There was a branch just over her head that she could reach. She lifted her brother up to the branch.

"Climb onto the branch and hold on as tight as you can."

He looked down at her; "Why are you crying?"

"It's ok, just hug the tree. Don't look down."

She turned away and slipped the backpack off. She held it in her left hand and drew the knife with her right. The sound of quiet sobs from the branch above made her tears flow more freely and her throat constrict.

The wolves approached closer.

Rue knew that a kitchen knife for a weapon and a backpack for a shield were not going to save her, but she had to try.

"Whatever you hear, don't look down," she shouted without looking up.

"I'm sorry, I'm sorry, I'm sorry," she whispered under her breath when she heard his quiet sobs again.

Suddenly a loud wind picked up, blowing her hair around and sending snow flying from the branches of the trees. Her eyes narrowed to protect themselves from the frozen particles while trying to maintain sight of the surrounding dangers. A moment later, a white dragon landed between her and the wolves.

Rue blinked and fell back against the tree. She was too shocked to notice that Rhys had stopped crying as well.

The creature's shoulder was roughly at the same height as that of a large horse. It had two front legs, two back legs, and a pair of wings that it seemed to be raising menacingly toward the wolves. A row of spines ran down its neck and back to the tip of its long tail.

The dragon raised its head and looked from one wolf to the next before it growled deep in its throat. The wolves growled back. One snapped at the dragon and the dragon snapped back. Another tried to run around past it, and the dragon stretched out its neck, opened its mouth, and fire poured out, incinerating the wolf immediately.

"Don't look," she yelled up to her brother.

The other wolves ran away.

The dragon folded its wings along its back and turned around to face her.

Shakily, she pushed herself off from the tree and held out the knife. It quivered in the air between them.

"You can eat me, just please don't eat my brother," she pleaded quietly.

The dragon looked at her quizzically, then gestured with its head toward the path. It backed up out of the path and into the snow on the far side, then gestured again.

Lowering the knife, she looked from the dragon to the trail and back again.

"Do you want us to take the path?"

The dragon snorted and gestured with its head again.

"Did you make this path?"

The dragon repeated the gesture.

This was insane. Dragons did not exist. And if they did, how could they understand her language?

She looked up at Rhys.

His eyes were wide, and his mouth hung open as he stared at the dragon. She looked back over, and the dragon took a few more steps backward into the snow. She put the backpack back on and returned the knife to her coat pocket.

"Ok, time to come down," she said, reaching up for her brother.

He held out his arms and she caught him and held him to her.

"Rue, can I pet the dragon?"

"No, maybe later."

Cautiously, she walked the few steps back to the path. Keeping an eye on the dragon as long as she could, she started walking down the trail again.

A few moments later, she heard a loud rushing sound and turned quickly to see the dragon taking off into the air. It disappeared above the trees.

They walked for a while and the snow began to fall. Rhys crammed his hands between them as he sat in her arms and mumbled something. She glanced down in time to see his eyelids falling.

The sound of rushing wind could be heard ahead of them. A moment later, a warm mist drifted in their direction. She kept walking through it, enjoying even the slightest reprieve from the cold.

*   *   *

"So let me get this straight, you took a nap, woke up to find your kids were missing, and decided not to call the police?"

217

"I thought they were just out playing at first. You know how kids are."

The police officer glanced over his shoulder at the snow-covered yard, then turned back to her.

"And you said that there were no tracks?"

"I said I didn't see any."

"How long were you asleep?"

"It wasn't that long. It probably snowed while I took a nap," she gestured dismissively at the yard.

"But you didn't call us until well after it had gotten dark."

"Like I said, I tried to find them myself. It's not a crime to try to solve your own problems."

"Is there anyone who might have wanted to hurt your children? What about their father?"

"No, I haven't seen them in years."

"Them?"

She waved her hand dismissively; "They have different fathers."

"Is there any reason they might want to run away?"

"What are you suggesting?" Her tone grew angry; "I don't need these accusations. I need you to find my children."

*   *   *

Rue's arms ached, and her feet were sore. She had been carrying Rhys all night, and she was exhausted. The path before them had not stopped. There were no caves, barns, or sheds to rest in. Considering how cold it was and that they had seen wolves earlier in the evening, she did not want to just stop out in the open. By now the sky was beginning to lighten.

The rushing wind sounded behind her, and she wearily glanced backward as the dragon landed behind her on the path. Adrenaline shot through her, waking her up as she turned to face it. The dragon made some soft noises and gestured with its snout toward the trail ahead. She turned and hurried down the path as quickly as her tired legs could carry her.

Several minutes later, she saw a gap in the trees and a clearing beyond. She slowed and cautiously entered the area. In the center of the clearing, or slightly off center, was a decent-sized log cabin. The base around the cabin looked like it was made of stone with wood used for the walls and roof.

A sound off to one side drew her attention, and she noticed an old, stout, bearded man chopping wood. He looked like he would stand about chest height next to her, but his body was obviously powerfully built. She had not seen him right away, because she had been staring so intently at the cabin for signs of occupancy. She cursed silently at her lack of awareness and began to back away. The dragon blocked the path, so she moved around the edge of the clearing. She repositioned Rhys to her left arm and pulled out the knife just in case.

The old man stopped and looked at her. He looked at her knife, her brother, the dragon, and then back to her. He snorted and embedded his axe in the stump in front of him and walked to the cabin. She turned her body to keep track of him and keep the knife between them, even though they were separated by several yards.

As he walked, the old man turned his head toward her; "You look tired and hungry. You can come in and eat or stay out here in the cold. It's your choice." His voice was rough but not cruel.

Rue just watched him suspiciously.

The old man knocked on the doorframe of the cabin, which seemed odd if he lived there.

A moment later, the door opened to reveal an old woman of similar height and build.

"Why are you knocking on your own door?" She stopped when she saw the children.

"We have guests," he looked back at Rue holding the knife. "Or not, looks like she hasn't decided yet."

Addressing the children, the old woman said, "It's warmer inside, and probably the wiser option."

Awkwardly holding her brother and the knife, Rue said, "If you try to hurt my brother, I'll gut you myself."

She knew that she had been hoping to find people to help them earlier, but now that she realized she had been led down a path through the forested mountains by a dragon to a strange couple she had never seen before, she was not sure what was going on or who to trust.

Rhys stirred and looked around.

"Where are we?" He looked at the older couple and the cabin. He gasped, "Is this the end of the adventure? Did we make it to a land of dwarves?"

The old couple laughed, surprising Rue. The old man sat down on the front porch and smiled, stroking his long white beard.

"Interesting," he said, watching them.

The old woman disappeared into the cabin and returned shortly, carrying two plates of food. She walked over and set them at the far end of the porch from where the old man sat, then went to sit next to him.

"Feel free to eat, or not," she said kindly.

Rhys looked at the food; "I'm hungry."

Rue looked at the dragon, which now sat in the gap

in the trees, then back to the old couple. She did not recognize them or the clothes they wore. The cabin seemed to be carved intricately, both the wood and the stone.

"I'm hungry," repeated Rhys as he wriggled in her arms.

In her exhausted state, it was difficult to restrain him. She had to put the knife away and use both hands to succeed.

The dragon had apparently led them here. If it had wanted to harm them or just bring them here for the old couple to kill, it could have just grabbed them at any time. It even went to the trouble of defending them from the wolves.

"Let me try it first," she said.

She carried him over to the porch, switched him to one arm, and reached down to pick up a piece of bread. She took a bite and waited. Nothing bad happened, and it tasted quite good, almost like honey and butter mixed together.

Setting him down, she said, "Ok, you can eat."

Rhys climbed up onto the porch, sat next to the plate, and ate.

Rue stood and watched her brother and the old couple as she finished her piece of bread.

A few minutes later, the old couple stood up and walked to the door.

"The door is unlocked. You can come in when you're ready," said the old woman.

Eventually, the food was gone, and Rhys sat there, looking around. The snow began to fall again.

"I'm cold. Can we go inside now?" he asked, looking up at her.

Rue hesitated. This was all so very strange, but so far, this old couple and the dragon had been kind to them.

"Rue, when are we going inside? I want to go inside," he pleaded.

"Ok," she said, picking up the empty plates and stepping up onto the porch.

They walked inside and shut the door. The cabin's interior was just as ornately carved as its exterior, though much less worn by time and weather. The primary open space consisted of a kitchen area with its own large clay oven and living room area with two large chairs and a couch in front of a fireplace. There was a door in the wall to the left, but it was closed. The old couple sat in the chairs. The old woman was knitting, and the old man was silently reading a huge, ancient-looking book.

Rhys looked around in awe.

"Wow, this is amazing," he breathed.

Not sure what else to do, Rue took off the backpack and set it next to the couch. She helped Rhys get out of his boots and jacket. She got out of hers, and they went to sit on the couch.

"Are you dwarves?" asked Rhys eagerly.

The old couple chuckled and put down their knitting and book.

"It's funny you should suggest that," said the old man.

"Did you make this house?" her brother continued.

"Yes."

The conversation between her insatiably curious brother and the old couple continued, but Rue's mind began to drift. The warmth from the fireplace and the softness of the couch allied with her fatigue to overpower her desire to stay alert, and she leaned back and fell asleep instantly.

*   *   *

Laughter and the smell of delicious food snuck into

Rue's mind and lured her back to consciousness. She opened her eyes to find herself stretched out on the couch under a very comfortable and warm blanket.

She looked around and saw Rhys in the kitchen area with the old woman, watching her cook and asking her questions. He was wearing clean, dry clothes that she did not recognize. She turned and saw his normal clothes hanging up on a rack in front of the fireplace. A folding privacy stand stood next to the couch.

The old woman turned and saw her; "There's some clothes on the couch, if you want to change." She gestured toward the pile at Rue's feet then at the stand.

Rue got up and looked at the clothes. They were well made but seemed like they belonged to a different time and place. She went behind the stand and changed.

"Just place your clothes on the couch, and I'll get them when we're done eating. Here, set out the plates and utensils," she said, gesturing to a stack on the counter in the kitchen.

Rue walked over and picked them up. She set them around the table at the four chairs. A little while later, the old man returned. The old woman loaded each plate with a pile of meat, bacon, and a chunk of bread. They all sat down and began to eat.

Rue was not sure what the meat was, but it smelled like the cooked deer outside the cave. The bacon was delicious, and the bread tasted as if butter and honey was infused into it.

As they ate, Rue studied the old couple. Their hair was white, and the lines of age were finely etched into their faces, but their movements were steady, and their bodies obviously well-muscled. There was kindness in their expressions, especially when they looked at or interacted with Rhys. She sensed the old woman to be slightly less stern than the old man.

"Thank you for the food and the clothes," she said.

"You're welcome," said the old woman.

"Who are you?" Rue asked bluntly, not quite having the energy to feel embarrassed.

"My name is Fjall, and this is Safír," said the old man gesturing first to himself and then to the old woman.

"Where are you from? Your clothes, accent, and the style of decorations in this house are very different from anything I've seen before," Rue asked, looking around.

The old couple looked at each other. "Some place very far away that you've never heard of," said Safír.

"What's with the dragon?" asked Rue.

"What do you mean?" replied Safír.

"They're not supposed to be real. Is it safe?" she clarified.

"It's certainly real, though I doubt that it's truly safe. He's a rare breed in this world. We don't know where he came from, but he has been living near us for decades," said Fjall.

"What were you doing in the forest?" asked Safír.

Rue looked down at her food.

"We were on an adventure!" exclaimed Rhys.

"Oh, and how did that work out?" Safir replied.

"It was hard at times, but now that we're here, it was totally worth it." Rhys stuffed more food into his mouth.

The old couple smiled.

"I noticed the cut on his cheek and the scar on yours," commented Safír.

Rue touched her scar and glanced at Rhys.

"Oh, it doesn't hurt," he said between bites of food.

Rue remained silent.

The old couple looked at each other again but did not pry any further.

"You can stay with us as long as you want," said Fjall.

Rue looked at Rhys.

"We can wait here for Mommy," he said.

Rue nodded and turned back to the old couple; "Thank you."

*   *   *

The woman hiked through the forest. It had been several weeks since her children had vanished, and she was desperate. A rumor had found its way to her that a hiker had heard the laughter of children somewhere in this general vicinity while hiking off trail.

She had not had a drink since she reported the children missing. At first, she had gone about the routine of putting up signs and talking to people so the cops would get off her back, but after a while, the sobriety and the seriousness of the situation had set it. In the quiet of her home, she had had nothing to do but think about what had happened. At first, she was looking for holes in her own story to protect herself, but eventually, she was unable to avoid the reality of how poorly she had treated her children. She could not blame them for leaving. Even if they wanted nothing to do with her, she needed to know if they were alive. She hoped they were.

The woman stepped out of the forest and into a clearing. A log cabin stood slightly to one side of the area's center. Cautiously, she walked up to the front door and knocked.

A short, old man with a large beard stepped out of the

225

house, closing the door behind him. His sudden proximity made her nervous, and she stumbled backward down the stairs to stand in front of the porch.

The old man looked her up and down. "Who are you and what do you want?"

"I'm sorry for bothering you, but I'm looking for my children. The oldest, Rue, is about this tall"; she held up her hand only a couple inches lower than herself, "and the youngest is about this tall"; she held her hand a little above her waist. "Here, these are their school pictures." She unfolded a printed poster she had made and showed it to the old man.

The old man raised an eyebrow at her, then disappeared back inside the house, closing the door behind him. The woman waited for a few minutes, then hung her head and turned to leave.

*   *   *

Rue stepped outside the cabin door and looked down at her mother as she turned to leave. The woman turned and looked up at the sound of the door swiftly opening and closing almost completely.

"What do you want?" The harshness in Rue's tone came unbidden, but she did not regret it.

The woman took a step forward but stopped.

"I'm so glad to see you're safe."

Rue raised an eyebrow.

The woman looked down; "I know I wasn't a good mother. I didn't treat you or your brother properly, and I understand if you never want to see me again, but I just want to make sure you are ok. And please, will you give me a second chance?" she looked up at Rue.

226

Rue stared down at the woman. There was pain in her eyes that looked like genuine regret and sorrow. Maybe she had changed in the weeks they had been gone. She remembered Rhys repeatedly asking when their mother would arrive and how much it broke her heart to tell him that she did not know when or if their mother would show up. Her mother was not perfect, but neither was she. She had almost gotten both of them killed by wolves. Maybe they should go back home. Her expression softened for a moment as she looked at her mother.

Home: the place where her mother taught her to rob her dates. The place where her mother drank herself into a stupor. Rue touched the scar on her face. The place where she was beaten, insulted, mocked, belittled, and neglected. The place where Rhys was cut across the same cheek in anger.

Images flooded her mind, seeing her brother beaten and belittled, cowering in fear, face bruised and cut. The thought of Rhys growing up the same way she had filled her with a protective rage that burned away any pity she might have had for this woman.

The dragon walked out of the forest and stood behind the woman, looking down on her. The woman turned slightly and jumped. She took a few steps back toward Rue and stopped.

"What?"

The woman turned and looked at Rue. She must have seen the rage in her eyes, because she stopped and turned to face her completely.

"Please, I'm sorry. You can stay here, just let me leave, please," she begged.

The dragon looked at Rue's hardened expression, then back at the woman.

Rue watched as the dragon slowly opened its mouth and positioned its head over the woman. In her mind, she could see the dragon biting down, rending the head from the body, consuming the woman until nothing was left. A dark part of her wanted this. It would satisfy her anger, her sense of justice, and her desire to protect her brother. The woman would never hurt him again. The woman deserved it.

All Rue had to do was nod.

Through the tiny crack in the door, she heard Rhys; "Is Mommy outside?"

"Shh," came the reply from Safîr.

I have no mother, Rue thought instantly.

She paused, fingering the bracelet that Rhys had made for her. She could not deny the hope and love in his voice. Despite all that had happened, he still loved his mother and wanted to be with her. If she died, he would never have that, and it would break his heart. Rue could not do that to her brother, despite how she felt.

The woman's eyes darted to the door, then back to Rue. She knew the woman must have heard his voice.

Rue looked up at the dragon and shook her head. It pulled back, closed its mouth, and waited.

She looked down at the woman, making sure their eyes locked, never softening her harsh expression, then she called behind her, "Not today, maybe tomorrow." She lowered her voice to a whisper and leaned forward slightly, focusing on the woman; "Maybe never."

Without a second glance, she spun around and disappeared inside the house, shutting the door completely behind her.

VI

Julia
Dynoltir, +277 TR

In a chamber deep under the capital city of the Reman Empire, Julia stood observing the combat trials before her. The room was large and rectangular with a series of pillars around its perimeter. She stood at one end, hidden in the shadows between and behind the pillars.

The contestants before her were numbered. She did not bother learning names. They were all members of the cult and products of its now decades-long breeding program.

One by one, the fights ended. Some won by skill, others by strength. Some were boastful in victory, and others were humble in victory. Some lost graciously, and others lost poorly.

A few days later, Julia found herself walking around the perimeter of a different room while the test subjects were evaluated on their understanding of philosophy and strategy. Few of the subjects who succeeded in this round had been successful at the combat trials. She made a mental note of these select few.

Wyrm's mind gently touched hers. Their telepathic communication had been part of her life since she was young, though it had grown less instructional and more conversational over time.

How do the trials progress?

The current batch of subjects has generally scored better than previous generations. It would appear that controlling their breeding and their education from a young age produces the best results.

Have you achieved the desired objective?

The desired result would be individuals who are strong both intellectually and physically, but who are also loyal. This has proven to be a difficult combination to achieve as superior ability frequently breeds its own ambitions.

What do you plan to do with the current batch?

Those who are not sufficiently loyal will be executed. Those who are sufficiently loyal will be placed in various positions within the empire as best suits our needs. The select few will be trained to be leaders of semi-autonomous nodes as we expand our reach within the shadows of the empire.

Have you found a candidate for your personal project?

Possibly. We shall see.

I am very proud of your accomplishments, and I value your service.

Thank you.

The personal project that Wyrm referenced was her search for a suitable mate. She was now over a hundred years old, her youth and strength retained and enhanced by Wyrm's blood. Despite this, she had no way of knowing if the effects would remain as potent perpetually or if she would slowly age. In order to best serve Wyrm, she needed to ensure that there was a contingency plan in case she herself did not last or if something were to happen to her. Her solution was to create an heir, combining her bloodline and training with the best that she could find. This plan also satisfied her instinctive desire to raise and train a protégé in the way that Aurelia and Wyrm had trained her. There was something distinctly different about the prospect of one's own personal pupil as compared to the education of the many cult members which she presided over in a more distanced manner.

Julia had considered the possibility of Wyrm making her into a creature like himself, yet there were two problems with this idea. The first was that she had no evidence to suggest that a second-generation vampire would be anything more than the blood thirsty animals she had witnessed in the experiments. The second problem was that if another like Wyrm existed, retaining their human intelligence while gaining his supernatural abilities, then it would always exist as a potential threat to his power and life. Julia had spent too many years with him to desire that anything she did would even inadvertently jeopardize his safety.

*   *   *

Quintus, master of spies for the emperor of the Reman Empire, stood in the dark next to an imperial road northwest of the capital. He was surrounded by a handful of soldiers. A captain stood next to him, who oversaw the digging next to the road.

Below him, a large hole descended into the earth. One side of the hole was comprised of a stone wall that started a few feet under the soil layer beneath the road and extended down several more feet. Imperial roads were constructed of horizontal layers, not vertical stone walls. This wall was taller than a man and seemed to extend parallel with the road. Soldiers were now taking large hammers and attempting to break through the wall to see what was on the other side.

Several minutes later, there was an opening in the wall big enough for someone to step through. More lanterns were lowered, and two soldiers entered the subterranean darkness. They returned a moment later.

"There is a corridor that runs the same direction as the road," one called up.

Quintus climbed down the ladder into the hole and stepped into the passage. He nodded to a soldier, who started walking down the corridor. Quintus walked in the opposite direction.

After what felt like half an hour, he had not discovered any bends or intersecting passages. When he returned to the breach, the soldier reported the same. He returned to the surface.

"What is that tunnel?" asked the captain.

"There is no tunnel, and there was never an excavation," Quintus looked the captain directly in the eye.

The captain nodded sternly and turned to the soldiers; "Clean the rubble out of the tunnel, repair the breech, and fill in the hole. No one is to speak of this on pain of death."

Quintus entered his chariot and rode back to the capital. He pondered the discovery. Was someone building the tunnels before the roads were laid? Were the road builders themselves compromised? Were the tunnels made after the roads were completed?

Road construction had been proceeding on schedule, with no noticeable delays that would account for the time needed to dig and build the tunnel as they went. This meant that someone had constructed them first or dug them under the roads. There had been a layer of soil between the road and the tunnel, so it was possible that the tunnels had been dug after the fact, but it seemed like a very difficult project to accomplish without collapsing the road in the process.

The more disturbing possibility was that the tunnels were constructed first, and the roads were placed on top. This implied that someone had the resources to build the tunnels secretly and either knew or ordered that the roads were placed above them.

Quintus mulled over the possibilities. Whoever was moving in the shadows of the Empire was gaining too much of an advantage.

*   *   *

Deep in the forests to the far north and west of the Reman Empire, a patrol of Reman soldiers cut their way through the undergrowth. They were heading west into unexplored territory.

Unseen by the human soldiers, a pack of exceptionally large wolves approached from the north. The wolves kept themselves low to the ground and moved silently. When they came within several yards of the humans, they spread out in either direction until they had surrounded their prey.

The lead wolf launched itself from cover and attacked a soldier in the middle of the column. The humans turned to face this sudden assault but were soon set upon from behind and the sides by the rest of the wolves.

One soldier raised his shield, attempting to block an attacking wolf, but he was unable to withstand the force of its weight colliding with him. With the wind knocked out of him, he could not raise his sword in time to stop the wolf from bending down over the top of the shield and tearing out his throat.

Another soldier attempted to stab a wolf that was attacking his comrade. His blade pierced its hide, and the creature yelped. Immediately, another wolf's jaws clamped over his wrist. The wounded animal was still able to turn and bite the soldier's throat.

An unusually skilled soldier managed to brace himself behind his shield against the impact of a wolf's body. The soldier held his stance as his sword arm thrust forward, but the wolf pulled back faster. It circled him and he turned to follow it. Another wolf jumped on his back, clamping its jaws around his neck.

Most of the soldiers fell by way of attacks from the sides or the back. A few were chased into the woods as they attempted to flee; they did not make it far.

When the battle came to an end, the wolves moved among the dead. They sniffed the corpses and poked them with their noses, making sure that everyone who lay on the ground was actually dead. They found one soldier lying underneath the bodies of two others. They sniffed him closely, then snapped their teeth through his throat. When they were convinced that all of the humans were dead, they left.

The wolves loped their way back through the forest, spreading out in a wide ring to scan their environment as they went. They kept the injured one roughly in the middle of the group, not allowing him to be left behind or picked off by an unseen threat.

The forests gave way to a large open field that rose up to a high hill. A wooden fort stood at the top of the hill. The wolves ran up the slope. As they approached, the gates opened. They made their way through the buildings inside the walls until they reached the great hall. The lead wolf entered the hall while the others turned aside.

A human servant approached the wolf as it walked in. The servant kept pace with the wolf, raising an open robe next to it as the wolf began to stand on its hind legs. Joints reformed and bones realigned and shifted size. Fur fell away and the strong arms of a man slid into the sleeves, taking the robe from the servant.

A woman walked out of a back room and the now transformed wolf king, Luken, approached her. They embraced and she tied a rope around his waist, holding the robe closed around his otherwise naked form. The two then made their way to a great table in the center of the hall. Luken and his wife Loria stood over the table, looking down on a map of the land carved into the wood.

A few minutes later, other men and women entered the hall wearing simple robes wrapped and tied around their bodies. They all converged at the map and stood on the opposite side from the king and queen.

"The Remans crossed the river again," observed Aitor.

"There were not very many of them," commented Naia.

"The river protects us to a certain degree, but it also makes it harder for us to attack them," said Ganix.

"We need to find a way to move our soldiers to the other side. The Remans occupy an abandoned fort and a couple villages," said Araya.

"My soldiers still have family over there. We can't abandon them," pleaded Izotz.

"I have no intention of abandoning anyone," said Luken. "Any bridge over the river can potentially allow them to cross as well. Any troops that are routed on the far side could potentially be trapped between the river and the Remans. They may be attempting to infiltrate our side, but we have also spied out theirs."

"The Remans are far from their capital. They rely on regular supply trains. Our wolves have been effective in harassing their patrols, but they are too few to launch a full-scale attack against the Reman garrison," said Araya.

"The Remans are constructing a road south of their garrison. This will only make it easier for them to resupply," said Aitor.

"We can send a few wolves south to harass the builders, but most likely they will manage to complete the road. The one advantage this gives us is that it will be easy to spot their supply wagons and destroy them," said Ganix.

The council continued discussing tactics.

When the council was finished, Luken and Loria retreated to their chambers at the back of the great hall. When they entered the room, they were greeted by playful growls from their four children. They were too young to shift and were still in human form but liked pretending they were already wolves.

Luken knelt down, and the children attacked him playfully. They tussled about until it was time for supper. A servant brought them several plates of meat, which they ate voraciously.

When they were done eating, Luken and Loria laid down on their bed so that their foreheads were touching, and their bodies arced away from each other. In the middle of this parental fence, the four little ones played until they fell asleep, curled up next to their parents.

*　　*　　*

Quintus and Cassian, emperor of the Reman Empire, walked atop the walls that surrounded the imperial palace in the capital's center. Several paces behind them strode two imperial guards.

"My investigations have revealed that at least some of the imperial roads have tunnels underneath. I suspect that these may connect to the capital's undercity, and our unseen

236

adversary is merely expanding it," reported Quintus.

"We need to find a way to clear out the undercity without bringing in an army. The senate would not stand for such a violation. Do we know what purpose our enemy intends for the tunnels?" asked Cassian.

"We do not know for certain. Moving resources and supplies is most likely, yet there are ways to transport such things above ground without rousing suspicion. The possibility of moving troops is the most concerning. However, the tunnel is fairly narrow, so any soldiers moving through would be forced to walk, at most, two side by side."

"Is it possible that our enemy is a foreign actor?" mused Cassian.

"It is always possible, but at this point, our spies in the neighboring countries have not reported anything that would lead me to believe that it is one of them," he reassured. "Our enemy seems very active near the capital, so I am inclined to think it is a threat native to the empire. All of the surrounding nations are vassal states or are being conquered at this point, and none have shown signs of rebellion. They also do not show signs of having the necessary resources for such plans as well."

"Do you think our adversary is behind the dissent in the senate?"

"It is not likely at this point. The wars with the tribes in the northwest have not gone as expected, and strange rumors of wolf-men have drifted back. The dissent in the senate seems to be naturally occurring opportunism when presented by a potential vulnerability."

"Are they at the point where they think they can overthrow me?" the emperor asked with a threatening edge to his voice.

"Not yet. Our spies report that the factions most

opposed to the current regime do not have enough support. Our spies have also been successful at sowing discord between potential allies to ensure it stays that way.”

“How reliable are our spies? I know you have had several go missing or become unreliable over the past few years. Is it possible that our adversary has infiltrated your operations.”

“Sadly, it is always possible, but, as we are both still alive and our plans frequently succeed, I would be inclined to think the answer is no. No spy organization can control everyone, so it is easy for both to exist within society and not fully discover each other. It helps that our network is very compartmentalized, and most agents have no idea who else is involved. This makes it harder for our unseen foe to discover and infiltrate us.”

Cassian stopped and looked at him; “We need to end the war in the northwest as soon as possible. Send agents there and determine if we have a saboteur or not. The sooner we gain victory, the sooner we can quash the complaints in the senate.”

“As you wish,” said the Quintus with a bow before leaving the way they had come.

*		*		*

A large supply caravan had almost reached the break in the trees as it approached the Reman garrison when the wolves attacked. The wolves tore into the soldiers first, which gave the servants time to flee in terror. Some ran into the woods, and others ran down the road, hoping to reach the garrison before they were caught.

One servant deftly hid behind a tree and watched. She remained calm, unphased by the violence before her.

238

The wolves made swift work of the soldiers before running after those who had fled.

One of the wolves tore the harness straps, freeing the horses. In seconds, the horses were gone.

Another wolf made a point of tearing open every supply bag it could find, scattering food and supplies around in an attempt to make them useless.

A wolf transformed into a naked human form. He picked up a dead soldier's sword and began prying open crates and barrels, spilling, and spoiling their contents as he went.

A wolf returned from the chase and circled the site, sniffing the ground. It seemed to find a scent and disappeared into the undergrowth. The servant girl turned and looked for the wolf. A couple seconds later it emerged a few yards away.

The creature bared its teeth, and the girl glanced in both directions.

The wolf lunged and the girl's left hand caught it by the throat. A look of shock could be seen in the canine visage. The girl's right hand shot out, wielding a dagger that she plunged into the wolf's skull.

She dropped the corpse and watched it, but it did not change.

At the sound of their dying comrade, the other wolves took up a howl. The girl looked to see that the rest were converging on her location. She broke from her hiding spot and ran parallel to the road.

The wolves gave chase but were unable to catch her. The girl broke through the tree line, running toward the garrison. A shout went out and archers readied themselves on the walls. The guards near the gate took a defensive stance, unsure of her purpose.

A moment later, her intentions were clear as the wolves came into view.

The girl threw herself at the feet of the guards, her previously stoic expression replaced by one of terror. "Please, save me. Those monsters killed everyone," she cried, tears flowing down her cheeks.

When the wolves came within range, the archers released their arrows. The wolves broke off the attack and ran back into the forest.

*   *   *

Captain Vitalis entered General Atius's tent at the Reman garrison.

The general looked up from his table; "What do you have for me?"

The captain laid down a scroll and began pointing at various figures.

"I have been analyzing the wolf attacks for the last six months. As you know, they have been harrowing our supplies, but it appears that they only attack groups of ten or less. Guards report only ever seeing three or four wolves at any given time. This would help explain why they do not attack larger caravans. On the few occasions where the wolves break the tree line, they make a point of avoiding the maximum range of the archers."

"I am aware of all of this," General Atius said, a note of disinterest in his voice.

"Sir, I have a proposal..."

Over the next several weeks, the captain led work crews of soldiers in the construction of a watchtower about halfway between the garrison and the forest. The work crew was guarded by archers and at least twenty guards.

Mandatory archery practice was added to the routines of every soldier and servant of the garrison.

Once complete, archers were permanently stationed in the tower. The next task was to clear out a wider area round the imperial road and construct a new tower.

Despite the increased number of soldiers and the archery watchtowers, stray soldiers would still be taken by the wolves. To decrease their losses, the captured villagers and slaves were brought in to clear the forest and build the towers.

Within a year, the forest was cleared away from the road by a hundred yards on either side, and a series of watchtowers had been erected along it. Each tower had a signal fire to warn of an impending attack. These towers ranged from the frontier garrison all the way back to the next outpost. Messengers were sent along the road, and supplies began to move more freely.

"Captain Vitalis, your plan has succeeded," said General Atius. "Thanks to you, we are one step closer to victory. Begin preparations to array watchtowers between here and the river. We will show these animals their place in the natural order."

"Yes sir," Captain Vitalis said before leaving.

That night, a servant girl entered the captain's tent. She was the one who had killed the wolf and fled to the fort when she first arrived. Surprised at the intrusion, he turned to see why she had come. He averted his eyes when he recognized her and dropped to one knee.

"You have served our master well, subject 74. Now it is time for you to fulfill your duty," she said, unhooking the clasp of her cloak.

"I live to serve our master," he replied, eyes averted to the ground.

                    *   *   *

A stone slab in the floor at the bottom of one of the watchtowers rose and moved aside. A strange figure moved silently out of the darkness of the underground tunnels and replaced the stone slab. He could smell the humans above and hear their heartbeats. He knew from previous correspondence that the guards tonight were his.

Silently, he exited the tower and disappeared into the forest.

The walk to the garrison was uneventful. He did not detect any signs of the wolves nearby. This was somewhat disappointing, though not unexpected.

When he reached the tree line, he observed the garrison. The fortifications had been improved, and they had begun erecting towers in the direction of the river. He walked to the east, the side they felt least threatened on.

Faster than any natural animal, he ran at the wall and leaped to its height. He could smell the humans nearby.

Out of curiosity, he wandered through the camp. Most were asleep with a few patrolling the walls above. Eventually he made his way to a building. Inside, he descended the stairs into the dungeon.

The dungeon consisted of a hallway lined with cells. At the end of the hallway stood a servant girl. She looked up at him and smiled.

Julia.

Welcome.

She turned and pushed on a section of the wall. It rotated inward to reveal a hidden chamber. It was an extension of the hall with a cell on either side. In the center stood a table with leather straps and chains.

We built the wall to section off this area. It was the quietest method of creating this workspace.

It will more than suffice. Thank you. I look forward to bringing our guest here.

*   *   *

Luken stood in a small wooden box built high into a tree overlooking the river. Beside him stood one of the human archers from his tribe.

"We have not seen the Remans attempt to cross in several days," the archer reported.

"If they do, sound the horn," said Luken.

The archer nodded.

This was the wolf tribe's response to the Reman archery towers: to build their own lookouts in the trees on their side of the river and post archers there. This would keep their forces hidden and give them a similar advantage. If the Remans attempted to build a bridge, the archers would blow their horns and more soldiers would arrive to ensure that the bridge never succeeded. Luken jumped out of the treehouse and landed on the ground, knees bent.

Not far off, back in the forest, he reunited with two human blacksmiths and two of the wolf clan.

"Sire," they said when he approached.

He removed his robe and transformed into his wolf form. The smiths stepped up and began fitting him with metal armor that covered the top of his head, back, and sides.

The Remans had not relied as heavily on archers until a year and a half ago. Now their supply routes were protected. It would only be a matter of time before their new set of towers reached the river.

243

The towers along the road were close enough together that the wolves would be seen attacking and replacing a new shift of archers. If they attacked at night, the archers on the top could light a signal before the wolves made it through the door and up the stairs.

Today, Luken and two of his wolves would test wearing the new armor as they swam across the river and attempted to take out Reman supplies right under the towers.

Once they were fitted, the wolves went to the river and jumped in. He could feel the weight of the metal plates and the now waterlogged leather straps, but he was still able to swim across without much difficulty.

They reached the other side and made their way through the forest. When they reached the road, they waited.

Around midday, they saw a replacement group of archers riding in a wagon along the road. While they preferred to hunt at night, it was best to take advantage of available prey whenever it arrived. Luken took position and they attacked.

As soon as the armored wolves broke from the forest, terrified cries went up. The distance between the trees and the road was enough that the Remans were able to draw their bows and begin to fire.

The wolves split in several directions, zigzagging their way to their targets. Most arrows missed, but Luken felt a few hit the armor. Nothing pierced his sides.

He kept his head low on the final approach toward the side of the wagon. He turned at the last second, coming around to the end and leaping up in between the archers.

Now between them and at their backs, his massive form was able to knock them over. They tried to turn on him, but he was too fast, and the other wolves were soon leaping over the sides.

The wolves tore the archers to pieces and bit through the reins on the horses. The horses ran off. He looked up and saw the towers lighting their signal fires. A few arrows rained down from the towers, but they did not pierce the armor.

Satisfied, Luken and his wolves ran back into the forest.

They stayed nearby, watching and waiting to see the Reman response. The Remans sent a large force of soldiers and archers to clear the road. They watched the Remans light torches as the afternoon shifted to evening. When darkness had fallen and the soldiers were gone, the wolves turned back toward the river.

Luken was optimistic. The armor had worked. He would need to make sure that he kept a small team of wolves on this side of the river at all times. They could start destroying supply wagons again, and they might even be able to take a tower. The wolves could break the doors, and the armor would protect them from the archers as they climbed to the top. It would not matter if they lit their signal or not. They would all be dead. If he brought some human soldiers with him, they could possibly man the towers instead. But if he did that, then the Remans might send a larger force to just break the tower, and Luken was not willing to sacrifice his people so flippantly.

He stopped and sniffed the air. There was something in the forest; something he had never smelled before.

The wolves around him were also sniffing and looking around. They twitched their ears but could not hear anything.

The scent was not natural; it was not animal or human.

Luken rose and began to search the darkness.

Suddenly there was a swift and silent movement. He turned to see a tall human figure, and then everything went black.

*   *   *

Luken awoke to see an arched stone ceiling above him. He tried to move, but his limbs were restrained. Looking down, he saw that he was held to a table by metal shackles. He was in human form, and there was a cloth draped over his midsection.

He sniffed. There was that inhuman scent again. Turning, he saw a male figure approach. The inhuman scent seemed to be coming from him. His features were almost human but not quite. He was too pale, and his fingernails were almost like claws. His ears were slightly pointed, and when the male smiled, Luken could see teeth that were sharper than any human's.

The male was followed by a female. Her scent was more human, but he could tell there was a faint hint of the inhumanness about her.

"Who are you? Why am I here?" he said, struggling against the bonds.

There was no response. The strangers did not say anything, but there was something odd in their expressions, subtle fluctuations as if they were responding to things being said that he could not hear. The female walked away and came back with a narrow, high table upon which was arrayed a set of sharp instruments.

Luken pulled at the chains and tried to sit up. He realized then that he was also bolted down at the neck.

The female moved to stand on his right while the male stood on his left.

246

The male looked down at him and smiled; "Tell me, Luken, what are you?"

"What?"

"Well, you are not exactly human, are you? No human that I have met can change shape like this," the stranger said.

"Why am I here?" Luken demanded.

"For now, you are here to satisfy my academic curiosity. I have many questions, and you can answer freely if you would like. If not, I will begin my experiments," the inhuman stranger said casually.

Luken said nothing.

The figure smiled and reached for a knife. Luken pulled hard on the chains and tried to transform. His body began to shift, but the chains were stronger, and a wolf's body could not lay chained to a table in the same position as a human's. The female moved and pulled a lever. The chains on his wrists and ankles went slack and he completed his transformation but found himself still pinned down at the neck.

"Thank you. I wanted to see this for myself. How does it work? Do you fully retain your human faculties when in wolf form? Does shifting bodies help you heal faster?" the man's eyes were eager as he leaned over and peered at the struggling wolf.

Luken growled and snapped his jaws uselessly.

The figure smiled; "Fascinating. Fortunately for you, I have developed new techniques for discovering information. You will have to tell me if they are painful."

Luken felt something unlike anything he had ever experienced. It was not a passing thought or an impulse, or a distraction. There was a will behind it. A will that reached into his mind. It was the most unnerving sensation he had yet met. His body twitched in vain, trying to recoil from something that was immaterial and unavoidable.

*   *   *

Wyrm stood over his shapeshifting test subject. He had spent decades communicating mind to mind with Julia, but what he was attempting now was different. He was attempting not to touch the surface of the mind or to relay information, but to delve deep, to search memories and, eventually, compel action. It was not something he had as much practice in. He could attempt to perform various physical experiments to determine how the shapeshifter functioned, but the creature most likely knew the answers already, and no number of cuts or observations would tell him what occurred within its mind.

The task was mentally exhausting, and he was forced to rest from time to time. The human will and the defensive animal instincts were strong, making the task even more difficult than when he had tested his abilities on other normal humans. In the process, he learned what he desired. The subject could transform at will, and switching between bodies seemed to heal most wounds. Wyrm pondered if this was a side effect of the ability trying to reshape the body into the unaltered version of the human or the wolf.

Delving into the mind, he observed the remembered sensations, images, etc., both physical and mental. The subject seemed to have a more distinct and pronounced difference between his human and animal mind. The animal never fully took control but was stronger when emotions ran hot or when in animal form. Likewise, the human mind was never absent, even in wolf form. The calmer the wolf, the more of the human faculties were available.

248

                    *   *   *

Luken awoke to the scents and sounds of the forest. He opened his eyes and looked at his surroundings. He was no longer in the stone chamber. He was lying naked in a bush in the forest. He sniffed the air but could not detect the inhuman scent in the vicinity.

A sharp pain stabbed through his head. Placing a hand to his temple, he tried to remember what had happened, how he got there.

He remembered shifting into wolf form in the chamber, then the violating sensation of someone prying their way into his mind. He had blacked out frequently but had still been aware of the mental intruder forcing him to shift back and forth on command. Finally, he remembered pain, fear, and impending death.

Luken shook his head. He did not remember being set free or escaping. He had no idea how he had come to the forest.

He stood and looked around. He was near the edge of the trees, not far from the hillfort. He slowly walked out of the trees and up the slope. When he got closer to the gates, the guards shouted and ran out to him. Someone draped a cloak around his shoulders.

Luken's return to the hall drew a crowd of concerned onlookers. He had not gone far when Loria met him. She embraced him, then walked with him back to the hall. They retreated to their inner chambers, and he collapsed into a chair, exhausted.

The children peaked around the corner. Luken smiled and gestured for them to come over. He hugged his children and reassured them. The care and attention of his family eased his mind and warmed his heart.

"I am sorry I was gone so long. I'm ok now," he said to his children.

After a while, Loria ushered the children out of the room; "Your father needs to rest now. You can play again tomorrow."

The little ones nodded and obeyed.

"I do not see any injuries on you," said Loria as she removed his cloak and examined him. "You have been gone for more than a month. We feared you were dead."

"I was captured."

"By the Remans?" she asked.

He shook his head; "No, it was something else."

"Something?"

"It did not smell right. It was not human," he said.

"Did they torture you?"

Luken touched his head and closed his eyes, "I do not know how, but that creature was able to invade my mind. It rummaged through my memories, forced me to shift on command. I think it was studying me."

Loria stood back, a look of concern in her eyes.

"I do not know how I got here or why I was released. I do not remember escaping," he said, looking at her.

"Did it seek information about our defenses?" she questioned.

Luken paused, searching his memories, then looked up; "I do not think so. I think it was only interested in me as a shapeshifter."

Loria embraced him again; "Rest now. You are home. I will make sure the little ones give you space, so you can recover. Tomorrow we will discuss our next moves."

Luken hugged her tight and nodded. The feel of her warm body against his was a relief and a comfort compared to the cold, dark pain of the stone chamber.

*   *   *

Something stirred within Luken, and he awoke, sweating in the night. There was a terrible pain in his head and an ache in his body. He got up and stumbled outside into the moonlight. His eyes looked up and gazed at the full moon.

A cruel instinct welled up within him. For a moment, he was shocked. Where once had been his own inner animal instinct, there was something new. It was violent, angry, and cruel. It did not desire food, rest, or play. It wanted to be free, to devour, and to destroy.

Luken fought to control himself, but these instincts and desires were not his own, they were almost another mind entirely now. The creature inside unleashed a cruel fury that battered his already weary mind. To his dismay, he could feel himself losing.

He collapsed on all fours on the ground as fur grew along his body. Bones lengthened or shrank and joints shifted. The transformation was happening against his will, but this time the impulse was not from the stranger, but from something inside him.

Everything went dark.

*   *   *

Luken awoke to morning light. His mind and body ached, and he could feel grass underneath his naked form. A moment later, the scents of ash and blood filled his nostrils.

He sat up quickly and looked around. He was in the

forest again, this time almost to the river. There were no signs of a kill or battle nearby.

Looking down, he saw that he was covered in dirt, blood, ash, and hair. There were too many familiar scents on him.

An instinctive fear filled him, and he got to his feet. He needed to return home quickly, but he still remembered the strange horror inside him the previous night before he blacked out. Luken ran as quickly as he could through the forest, maintaining human form to avoid losing control again, no longer trusting his inner animal nature.

Breathing heavily, he eventually burst from the trees and ran up the slope to the hillfort. The scent of ash and blood was worse. He looked up. There were no guards, and smoke rose over the walls.

He slowed down as he entered the gates. Inside the hillfort, it was a slaughter. Villagers, soldiers, even members of the wolf clan lay mutilated all around. Blood filled the paths between the buildings, many of which were smoldering.

Panic set in, he ran to the great hall, and rushed to the inner chambers. His worst fears were realized. His family's remains lay spread and splattered around the room. What remained of Loria was between the door and what used to be his children.

Pain and grief collapsed his strength and he fell to the ground. The scent of the blood of his loved ones filled his nostrils, and a horrifying memory returned.

*   *   *

The creature was free. It stood up and stretched its limbs and flexed its fingers. It looked up at the full moon and bared its massive, sharp teeth, creating a perverse impression of a smile on its wolf's head. It looked down at its body, now hybridized between the wolf and human forms. It stood on its toes like a wolf. The toes and fingers ended in sharp claws. Fur covered its still bipedal body. The wolf's massive strength was now arrayed on a more humanoid form.

A sound caught its attention, and the creature turned to see guards approaching. Confusion at the sight of the creature registered on their faces. The creature pounced on them immediately. The sensation of its claws and teeth tearing through flesh was exhilarating. The flow of blood over its tongue filled it with vicious joy. The creature hungered, but not for food, water, or even blood. It hungered for destruction, to tear, to rend, and to end living things.

The creature sniffed. There was a very familiar scent. It turned in time to see a woman exit the hall. When she saw the dead guards and the blood covering the creature's muzzle and hands, she threw off her robe. The female human form was visible for only a moment before fur erupted across her body and she shifted into an abnormally large wolf.

The wolf let out a howl, which was answered immediately by shouts, horns, and howls. Then it leaped at the creature. The wolf knocked the creature off its feet and snapped and snarled, trying viciously to rend the creature's throat, but its hands held the wolf at bay.

For a brief moment, the creature laughed inwardly at the attempted violence of the wolf, then dug its claws into the shoulders where it held its attacker. The creature threw the wolf off of it as more people arrived. Then it lunged on the wolf and bit hard into her neck near the shoulder. The wolf was tougher than the humans had been. It yelped and broke free, but blood still poured down its side.

The night became filled with humans and wolves. Spears and swords lashed out at the creature. It turned and clawed, bit and tore. Flesh was rent and blood flowed. Torches and lanterns were knocked over or flung aside. Buildings caught fire. The wolves were stronger than the humans, but eventually they all died.

Something ran into a large building, and the creature pursued instinctively. In a back room, the creature found the first wolf that had attacked him. She was standing over four small children who looked up in fear. They all smelled so familiar.

The wolf lunged. She was much stronger this time, wilder and more ferocious in her attacks. The creature's arms were torn, and bones were snapped by her jaws.

But in the end, her efforts were not enough. In the end the creature's teeth found their mark, ripping through her throat. The wolf lay dead.

The creature turned at the sound of whimpers and tears. The four children were huddled in a corner. The creature opened its mouth.

*   *   *

A soldier ran up to Captain Vitalis and saluted.

"Sir, a woman and her two children have just arrived at the gate. They are soaked and she is begging for asylum. She says something destroyed the wolf tribe hillfort."

Intrigued, the captain followed the soldier to the gates.

As soon as he approached, the woman threw herself at his feet; "Please, I beg of you, spare my children. Take me as a slave or kill me, but let my children live here."

He looked down at the woman. She was wet and

254

ragged. She looked like she had been awake all night. Genuine terror was reflected in her eyes.

The children were much the same, shivering and frightened behind her. Their faces were streaked by tears.

"What are you so desperate to escape?" he inquired.

"Something killed everyone in the hillfort," she replied.

"What was it?" He narrowed his eyes, somewhat suspicious of the implied inhumanity.

"I do not know, some kind of monster. Even the wolves were dying," she finished and looked around, fearfully scanning the tree line.

The captain pondered this. The woman was truly terrified, and she was of the wolf tribe.

"You will be my captives and trophies to display as a sign of our victories," he declared.

"Yes, I accept," she said with a relieved sigh and bowed her head.

The captain reported to General Atius and was given leave to investigate. He and his troops forded the river and marched through the forest. They were cautious, but there were no attacks.

The Reman soldiers reached the mound of the hillfort and looked up. Indeed, it appeared that the woman had told the truth. Captain Vitalis led the soldiers up the slope and into the fort. An incredible stench assaulted them. Torn bodies and blood were strewn everywhere.

Undaunted, he waded through the muck until he reached the great hall. The doors were open.

Inside he found a lone figure slumped on the ground next to five mounds. One was noticeably larger than the others. Around the figure lay several blades caked in blood and what looked like a broken noose hung from a rafter overhead.

The captain nodded and a soldier stepped forward and poked the figure with the blunt end of his spear.

The figure stirred and sniffed, then sat up and looked at them. The captain was surprised to see that it was Luken.

"Please kill me," Luken begged. "I have tried, but it will not let me die."

He gestured at the blades and the rope overhead.

The captain looked at the objects, then down on the former king.

"On behalf of General Atius and in the name of Cassian, emperor of the Reman Empire, I declare you, Luken of the wolf tribe, to be my prisoner. Your lands and your people now belong to the Empire," the captain declared.

*   *   *

Luken lay on the floor of the wagon cage as it was pulled down the Reman road. He was to be a trophy of the Reman victory in the capital, but he did not care. His eyes stared ahead blankly, his mind consumed by grief and self-loathing. He had tried every way that he could think of to kill himself after he buried his family, but it never worked. Every time he thought he had succeeded, the world had grown dark, only for him to wake up, whole again.

As the sun set, the moon began to rise. He knew from its brightness that it was full.

The cruel, violent creature within began to rise. Now that his family was dead, he could not care less if it took control.

Much to his surprise, he sensed that same inhuman invader touch his mind. His tormenter spoke to the creature, soothed it back to sleep with promises of more victims than it could count if it waited.

*   *   *

Quintus and Cassian stood on the palace roof. Two guards stood several yards behind them as they looked out over the capital at night.

"Several of the senators have arranged for the general in the northwestern wolf tribe territory to return to the capital. He is bringing Luken with him," stated Quintus.

"I am curious to see if these reports or rumors of shapeshifting are real," commented Cassian.

"My sources inform me that Luken claims to be a monster and has begged for death. This is somewhat corroborated by a villager who surrendered to the garrison with tales of an unstoppable monster tearing through the wolf tribe's hillfort on the other side of the river."

"Interesting," commented Cassian.

"While reports indicate that the inhabitants of the hillfort were torn to pieces, no one has since seen the supposed monster," Quintus continued. "There have also not been any similar slaughters since then. Luken has not transformed since his capture."

"I assume that the senators who have arranged for the general's return have provided their own troops or representatives to hold the hillfort and garrison in his absence." Cassian turned his head toward his spymaster; "Are any of them antagonistic to me?"

"No. They appear to be motivated by curiosity about the supposed foreign shapeshifters. Others actually view the triumph as a way to bolster your support," Quintus replied, somewhat surprised himself that such was the case.

257

"This victory will help demonstrate to the detractors that I was right in ordering the expansion," Cassian said with satisfaction as he looked out over the city again.

"The people will want to see actual transformations," Quintus commented.

"The rumors are most likely nonsense," Cassian said with a dismissive wave of his hand. "I suspect these wolf tribe warriors either used trained animals or merely dressed in wolf skins and, in the chaos of battle, those few who survive were left with an inaccurate understanding of events. If they are truly fierce warriors, we may be able to entertain the masses by putting them in the arena. Maybe we can even see how they fair against other wild animals, or even real wolves."

"I will make the necessary arrangements," replied Quintus with a bow before leaving.

*   *   *

Luken was barely aware of his surroundings as the general paraded him through the Reman capital. He was only vaguely aware when the emperor examined him and declared rewards to the general and captain for conquering his people. He spent most of this time being pushed or dragged, his eyes gazing lifelessly at the ground. His grief and self-loathing had been deflated by the time it took to reach the city, and now he was numb, unable to care about anything around him.

When the spectacle had ended, he was taken to the dungeons. He was pushed into his cell and the door was locked. Movement caught his eye, and he saw survivors from his tribe huddled on the far side of the cell. Their eyes were filled with fear and hatred. He knew he deserved it and moved to a back corner and sat down, keeping his distance as best he could.

Sometime later, the guards returned, and they were dragged from the cells. His people were taken in one direction and he another. The guards led him up through passages to the emperor's box in the arena where he was made to sit at the emperor's feet.

Cheers and shouts erupted through the arena, and he heard the sounds of combat. When the smell of blood reached his nostrils, he looked over the edge of the box at the spectacle below.

Some of the wolf tribe's villagers were fighting gladiators. Most were not warriors and would soon be killed.

He turned to his captors; "Let them go. Throw me down there. I will fight and die in their stead," he pleaded.

"Silence," snapped a soldier who hit him in the face with the blunt end of a spear.

Someone laughed nearby; "Oh, you will get your chance when you have outlived your usefulness."

Luken tried to rise but realized too late that he had been chained hand and foot to the ground. Rage surged through him as he watched his people die. The twisted, cruel creature within him stirred but would not answer his summons.

*   *   *

The rays of the full moon shone down on the arena. In the deep halls beneath, Luken felt the creature stir. It knew instinctively that this was its time.

He glared at the bars of the cell as he sat there. Now, having seen the death of the few survivors of his people, he wanted the creature to break free. The Remans deserved whatever horrors it would bring down on their heads.

His own rage and hatred mixed with the insatiable bloodlust of the creature as it took control. His body transformed into the bipedal wolf-like creature.

The creature wrapped its fingers around the bars. It pulled against them until one finally broke free. The creature forced its way through and ran down the hall.

The first guards it encountered were too shocked to even draw their weapons before its claws and teeth tore them to pieces. The next set of guards drew theirs, but it was of no use. The creature emerged from the arena with a cruel smile on its wolf-like face and covered in the blood of its victims.

It sniffed the night air. There were so many humans, more than it could possibly count. That thing that spoke to its mind all those months ago was right. This would be worth the wait.

The creature spent the night going from house to house, room to room, hunting and tearing everything it found. Shouts rang out and guards ran through the streets, but they never caught the creature. When the guards were few in number, it would bite and rend them directly. If too many guards arrived in a confined space, it would flee temporarily to regain the ability to maneuver before continuing the attack from a more advantageous angle.

A few humans managed to escape alive, mostly because some new victim had come into view, momentarily distracting the creature before it had finished with its current prey. It did not matter. They would surely die from their wounds. Besides, there were so many to kill, so much flesh to tear, so much blood to taste. And it was all so gloriously visible in the light of the full moon.

*　　*　　*

"A hundred people dead in a single night! And not just slaves or commoners. Have you conspired to destroy me, to destroy the empire?!" The emperor's face was contorted in rage.

General Atius glared back at the emperor's accusations, "I would never do such a thing. I am a loyal servant of the empire."

"Then why have you brought this monster into the capital?" roared the emperor.

"Luken never showed any signs of this savagery. There was no reason to believe the rumors were true," countered General Atius.

"No reason to believe? You yourself said that everyone inside their fort was butchered!" the emperor shot back.

"I will end this monster," concluded General Atius decisively.

"You better," the emperor's tone grew dangerous. "If the senate tries to turn this against me, you will be the first to die."

*   *   *

General Atius turned to Captain Vitalis.

"What do you mean the trail has gone cold?" General Atius was not pleased to hear this news. If they failed to capture Luken, then it was likely that he would pay the price. And he was not inclined to be the only one to suffer.

"Sir, it has been almost a month since the last attack. Patrols have not located any traces of where the creature is hiding. Any possible evidence is gone; even the survivors have healed." Despite his apparent failure, the captain seemed strangely calm and confident, which only irritated Atius more.

"Well, you need to find a trail before this thing strikes again. I will not have this disaster continue under my watch," the general warned.

"Sir, based on the timing of the destruction of the hillfort and the last attack, I believe the creature may be waiting for the full moon. I have prepared signal towers and lookouts throughout the city. As soon as it strikes, we will be alerted and can send reinforcements."

"You better hope this plan works, or I will have your head," threatened the general.

"Understood, sir," replied the captain.

*   *   *

Julia stepped out of the shadows deep under the city. Captain Vitalis knelt before her and the soldiers behind him followed suit. These were her people, not Cassian's.

"Rise," she said to the captain.

He stood and stepped forward.

Julia held out a wooden box filled with vials of Wyrm's blood. Each vial was equipped with a plunger on one end and a hollow needle on the other.

"Take these and distribute them among your men," she commanded. "Do not inject their contents until the first sighting is signaled. They will enhance your natural abilities beyond any mere human. Remember that you are to direct Luken toward the palace. Pursue him in that direction and make sure he has entered before you engage."

"Understood"; he bowed his head as he took the box from her hands.

262

                    *   *   *

Wyrm stood next to Julia on a rooftop overlooking a home in the Reman capital. She was not dressed in the usual garments of the cult or the disguise of a servant. Her skirts were shorter, more like the kilts of the soldiers, to allow her freer movement. Julia gave her report.

Our agents reported that the survivor of the original Luken attack that lives here has been behaving strangely over the past few weeks. She has demonstrated increased aggression and unusual strength.

Fascinating.

I hypothesize that Luken's condition may be contagious.

Wyrm reached out with his mind and touched the human's mind below. He could sense her aggression and confusion at her change in behavior.

They waited until the sun set and the moon rose. Below, strange sounds came from the home.

Interesting. I could sense Luken trying to fight the creature within, but this new subject seemed entirely unable to resist, Wyrm commented.

Perhaps his experience controlling his animal nature gave him an advantage. Or perhaps the second-generation creatures are better able to exert control over their human hosts, Julia pondered.

A moment later, a large, bipedal wolf-like creature exited the building. It sniffed the air and looked up at them. Wyrm projected his thoughts into the creature's mind; images of its certain death and dismemberment should it attempt to attack them. The creature seemed convinced and ran down the street. It stopped at the first entrance it came to and entered. Screams erupted seconds later and were cut short.

> *If we allow the second-generation creatures to roam free, it will help sow chaos. The greater the chaos, the greater the victory for our agents,* suggested Julia.

> *Activate and enhance more agents. With the creatures spread out, the guards will be spread thin. Our soldiers must survive,* Wyrm responded.

> *Agreed.*

Julia turned and ran across the rooftops. Wyrm was confident that she would make it safely to her tasks. He smiled inwardly as he watched his protégé's swift, graceful movements as she bounded across the city.

*   *   *

Julia finished passing out assignments to the soldiers loyal to the cult. Each was given a vial of Wyrm's blood. When she was finished, she made her way to the palace and climbed to a vantage point at its height.

Looking down on the city below, she watched the signal fires light up around the city, mostly concentrated around the area of the original attack. The survivors transformed and turned their bloodlust on those nearest. It was not long before the chaos and screams began to spread throughout the city.

Soon Luken emerged from the streets below. He sniffed the air and looked in the direction of the palace. He charged toward the gates, zigzagging to avoid the archers' arrows from on top of the wall. It was fascinating to watch. Luken would run on all fours, then switch to his hind legs in order kill with claws and teeth. His front paws were indeed clawed hands, which he used to grab and tear. They also helped him climb to the top of the walls and kill the archers.

Some were torn or bit and others flung over the side. He then jumped down and tore through the guards on the ground inside the courtyard.

He stopped and sniffed the air before glancing up in her direction. She could not read his thoughts as Wyrm could, but she suspected that he remembered her scent. It was of little concern though. She could see Captain Vitalis and his soldiers moving slowly up the street toward the gates.

Luken entered the palace.

*   *   *

Once inside the building, the creature that used to be Luken sniffed the air again, finding the emperor's scent. Deep inside, it could feel Luken's hatred for the emperor. It smiled to itself, reveling in the shared desires.

Guards poured into the hallways and the creature engaged the soldiers. Quickly it tore into the front lines, grabbing someone by the neck and throwing them at the archers farther back. The creature bit, slashed, dodged attacks, used humans as shields, and slew the guards.

Eventually, it found the emperor, cowering in a room behind an elite unit of guards. They smelled slightly inhuman, like the stranger who had helped it. When the creature stepped into the entry way, the guards looked at it, then at the emperor. They stepped aside, leaving a clear path.

The creature bared its teeth in a twisted, animalistic version of a smile. The guards backed out of the room through side passages as it stepped forward.

The emperor begged and pleaded. The creature remembered what Luken had witnessed, remembered the deaths of their people. It could feel his rage and desire for

265

revenge.

The creature leaped across the room, seized the emperor by the shoulders with its hands, and tore his throat out with its teeth.

A shout rang out behind the creature, and it turned to see an officer leading several Reman soldiers. It recognized the soldier who had found Luken after his pathetic attempts to take his own life.

The creature sniffed the air. This human smelled different now. He and the others with him smelled more like that inhuman stranger. The creature could feel Luken's hatred for that stranger, but the creature pushed it away. That stranger had given it freedom, offered it the opportunity to kill many more than it would in the caravan. If these soldiers were connected to the stranger like the ones that had stepped aside, then were they here to help?

The captain gave an order and the soldiers attacked. The creature was surprised by the sudden betrayal. If the stranger's minions meant him harm, then they too would die. It dodged their initial attack, assuming their speed was an illusion born of its surprise. When the creature launched itself at the soldiers, it learned that this was not true.

These humans were stronger and faster than the humans or the wolves the creature had killed before. It managed to kill a few of them, but not without sustaining severe injuries. The creature had not been this injured since it fought Loria that first night.

The creature leaped over a soldier and ran down one of the side passages the other guards had used to abandon the emperor. The creature knew it could not destroy them all when they were so close together in an enclosed space.

As it ran through the palace, it smelled the scent of the female who had accompanied the stranger. The stranger's scent was even stronger on her than on the soldiers. Luken's hatred mixed with its own. She was at least partially responsible for what had been done to him and the deaths of his family. The female was alone. Without the other soldiers, she would make for an easy kill before it left the palace.

The creature turned a corner toward the scent only to find the woman waiting for it. She stood in the center of the hall, a bow already drawn.

The creature leaped to one side, but she tracked the creature's movement and the arrow hit it in the side. Faster than a normal human, she had another arrow nocked and released. The creature barely managed to avoid it, but felt it scrape across its shoulder.

When it reached the woman, she dropped the bow and drew a soldier's sword. She thrust the sword toward the creature, and it caught her wrist in its left hand. It swung its right hand down toward her face, but she caught it with her free hand. The creature strained against her, angered by such strength in a mere human. Enraged, it lunged forward with its head, teeth snapping shut. The woman tried to dodge, but they were too close, the creature too large, and it bit into the left side of her neck, shoulder, and chest. It felt her blood flow and bones crack as it clamped down. Her blood was amazing, energizing. It readjusted, bit deeper into her neck more fully, crushing the vertebrae and tearing flesh, and sucked on the massive wound, drinking up as much as it could.

The woman's strength faded, and she lost her grip on his right wrist. His free right hand shot forward and gripped her side, claws digging into flesh with its fingers cracking ribs. Eventually her body went almost completely limp, and the flow of blood became a trickle. The creature dropped her to the floor. The woman weakly reached for her wounds, gasping and gurgling.

A blinding rage crashed into the creature. It felt the stranger's bloodlust and hatred cut directly into its mind. For the first time in its brief existence, the creature was afraid.

The stranger's scent exploded around it and fingers dug deep into the creature's neck before it was flung back down the hall.

How dare you!

The mental roar was deafening.

I made you, and I will unmake you.

Before the creature could move, the stranger's hands gripped the creature's arms and broke them. Feet slammed through and shattered the creature's legs. Fingers curled into the flesh of its neck, and the creature was pulled from the ground. Sharp teeth pierced its throat, and the creature felt its lifeblood draining away.

For a brief moment, as the creature neared death, Luken's mind began to rise only for the teeth to leave and to feel flesh beginning to tear around his neck before everything went black.

*   *   *

Wyrm walked around the corner as Captain Vitalis approached. He tossed Luken's severed wolf head at the captain's feet. The human glanced down, then back at Wyrm.

"Get out," Wyrm commanded angrily.

The captain bowed, retrieved the head, and left with his men.

Wyrm returned to stand over Julia. He looked down on her, seeing the light fading from her eyes. He knew from experiments that her injuries were too severe, too much blood was lost, her pulse was fading too quickly, and her life was too far gone for her accelerated healing to succeed or for him to just sprinkle his blood into the wound. Despite this, he tore his wrist with his teeth and dripped blood into the lacerations. Flesh began to reknit faster, but it still was not enough. Her pulse flickered. He reached out and touched her mind gently.

Thank you for avenging my death. I am sorry that I have failed you, she said.

You have never failed, my beautiful child.

Inwardly, Wyrm berated himself. He should have taken the threat of Luken's monster form more seriously. He should not have left Julia undefended. Or he should have had her inject more of his blood, made her stronger. The creature was his experiment, his tool, and he had allowed it to kill his creation, his pupil. Julia was the culmination of everything he had learned under Aurelia and Koios. She had been his companion for nearly a century.

He knew there was still one option remaining. He could make her like himself. She would live, forever, with him. Together they could ascend to new heights and bring this world of humans under their heels.

But, if she had his powers, she could betray him. He knew humans were prone to such frailties as they frequently made use of it in their secret machinations. Still, he had spent decades communicating directly with her mind. All he had ever seen in her was loyalty, devotion, and love.

Wyrm bent down and picked her up, cradling her upper body in his arms. He gently bit into her neck and began to feed. His mind sensed her distress, then hope. As her life began to fade, the hope was replaced by confusion and resignation. He drank deeply until her heart stopped and her body went limp. It did not take long. Cradling her corpse in his arms, he rose from the ground and carried her out of the palace.

In the underground inner sanctum of their cult, he sat in a chair with Julia's corpse laid out on her bed, waiting. A human's digestive system could not process blood the way his could. It could not draw strength and power from it, and, so, he waited.

Julia's body twitched. He sensed an animalistic mind awakening within her. The structural damage to her upper torso was severe, and the fledgling creature struggled to sit up. Wyrm sat next to her on the bed and gently raised her shoulders. The creature looked at him and he lowered his wrist to her mouth. She looked at it and her lips parted instinctively. Her sharp teeth tore into his flesh. He could feel the pull on his veins as she drank deeply of his blood. Slowly, he could sense the mind within her changing and see the wounds beginning to heal. Julia's hands reached up and gripped his wrist, pushing it tight against her mouth. The wild look in her eyes shifted into bright focus as thirst and instinct began to give way to reason and memory, then finally understanding.

Her wounds began to close. Within minutes, they were sealed. Julia pulled away and her eyes examined her body. She touched her neck, shoulder, and chest where the injuries had been. She looked at him and smiled.

He sat her up fully and then they both stood.

"Thank you," Julia exclaimed, flinging her arms around his neck in a moment of exuberant affection. It reminded him of her younger years.

Wyrm patted her shoulder with one hand. Julia pulled away and her demeanor returned to her usual stoic expression.

"Thank you," she repeated more calmly this time.

$*$ $*$ $*$

Captain Vitalis stood before the people and the senate as they thanked him for bringing order and peace to the capital by eliminating the monster that was Luken and his infected progeny.

He graciously accepted the crown and waved to the people. He proclaimed his dedication to defending the senate and the people. The crowds cheered.

As the ceremony ended, senators vied for his attention, frequently mentioning how pivotal they were in his coronation. Emperor Vitalis traded pleasantries and listened carefully, noting their reactions and who they spoke with. Some focused on their own usefulness, while others emphasized how the people considered him a hero.

When evening came, the new emperor returned to his chambers, followed by the imperial guard. They took their places outside the door as he entered and closed it behind him.

From the shadows stepped the high priestess of the cult.

"Greetings... Emperor," she said.

The new emperor stepped forward and knelt on one knee. He bowed his head, reached up, and removed his crown. He placed the crown on the floor at the high priestess's feet.

"I live to serve our master," he said.

$*$ $*$ $*$

Julia stood on the palace roof, overlooking the city. The night was dark and cool. She was enjoying the keenness

271

of sensation that she had been gifted by Wyrm. Immense gratitude washed through her when she thought of that moment.

She closed her eyes and let her mind and senses drift. She could hear humans and animals far below in the palace and on the streets.

For almost a century, she had been communicating mentally with Wyrm. Before her mind had been restrained within her body, but it knew what it felt like to be touched directly. Knowing that it was possible and having experienced it herself, she reached out with her own mind, attempting to sense others around her.

At first, she felt nothing. Then slowly, she thought she could perceive someone below. She continued to scan her surroundings, detecting the expected humans, pets, and vermin.

Her mind touched a voracious hunger. It was strong, and it was near.

Surprised, she opened her eyes and looked around, straining her new sight and hearing. She even sniffed the air, but there were no traces of the wolf creatures. No screams, howls, or growls.

Curious, she closed her eyes and focused her mind again, trying to find what she had sensed.

Julia stopped and opened her eyes. She looked down and placed her hands on her stomach.

VII

Journey Beyond III
Dynoltir, +3052 TR

Thousands of years ago...

A tall creature soared over the water, dipping and turning as it maneuvered between the tall rock peaks around it. The creature's body was covered in feathers, from the tip of its elongated snout to the end of its long tail. It had two massive wings that alternated between beating the air and gliding on the currents. Its primary arms were strong and well-built with six-taloned hands. It held them by its sides as it flew. The secondary arms were smaller and more dexterous, clutched tightly to its torso. The long hind legs stretched out behind it, just under the tail which was covered by feathers that spread out toward the end.

The creature swooped down toward the water and grabbed a large, scaled animal with the talons on its primary hands. It flapped its wings, rising up between the steep stone peaks. The creature soared up over the rocks and gently landed on the summit, gripping the stone with the talons on its hind legs. It then tore into its food as it gazed across the waters.

Laid out before it was a land of tall mountains whose sides were almost perpendicular to the seemingly endless ocean from which they jutted. Beyond even the reach of its exceptional eyesight lay the two largest land masses on the planet.

The first landmass was comprised of the highest peaks and deepest valleys. The ocean poured into the gaps between the mountains, forming almost infinite waterways through which various lifeforms swam. On the highest pinnacle, the stone had been carved away into the shape of a massive, stepped pyramid, while other edifices and dwellings had been carved into the sides of the mountains.

The second large landmass was a huge dormant volcano. Along the inner and outer walls of the volcano had been carved various buildings. The center of the crater had long since filled with water, creating the only inland sea on the entire planet. In the center of this sea rose a large rotunda built of carved stone blocks, with a dome made of metal arches and arcing panes of colored glass.

In both cities, the avian inhabitants, the cuexaneh, could be seen going about their daily lives. Some flew through the air, others walked along paths or inside structures, while some were perched on the sides of cliffs, gripping the stone tightly with their feet and primary hands while carrying out other tasks with their secondary hands.

On the pinnacle of the stepped pyramid, a cuexaneh stepped into existence. He was tall and powerfully built, even by the standards of this species. The irises of his eyes were a metallic gold streaked with red and green. His feathers shimmered in myriad colors in the sunlight. Sharp, pointed teeth were exposed as his lips curled in a slight smile. His tail twitched and his talons clicked along the stones as he entered the pyramid.

Far away, in a house overlooking the rotunda in the middle of the caldera, an elderly cuexaneh slept. In the visions of his head, as he lay sleeping, he saw a gold-eyed figure that delivered words of grave portent and impending destruction. The elderly cuexaneh awoke with a sense of dread and urgency.

Not long after both events, a ship launched from the landmass with the pyramid. Within a day, another ship launched from the caldera.

The cuexaneh with the gold metallic eyes streaked with red and green walked purposefully through a torrential downpour on a far distant planet. Behind him, several cuexaneh struggled against the wind and rain, their bodies bent over against the elements and by the weight of their packs while his remained perfectly upright and unfazed. They raised their feet high out of the mud with each step and flinched whenever the lightning flashed too closely. After almost an hour of walking through the rain, a structure began to fade into sight ahead of them. As its details began to take shape, they saw a tall cylindrical structure surrounded by a ring of pillars all on top of a raised dais. When they reached the artifact, they could see it clearly in the eye of the massive storm. Two large metal doors loomed before them with a relief of a tree with ten spheres in its branches.

The leader pointed a talon at the doors and commanded his companions to open them. They stepped forward and examined the doors. There were no handles or obvious ways of opening them. Dutifully, they turned to the tools in their packs and went to work trying first to pry open the doors.

As the companions were beginning to test if the doors were magnetic, another group of cuexaneh appeared. The elderly cuexaneh who had had the dream stepped forward and addressed the first group. The two groups argued with one another.

Sensing his companions' hearts wavering, the cuexaneh with gold metallic eyes streaked with red and green angrily turned and stepped out of existence.

He reappeared in a crater of smoking stone. Shocked, he looked around and realized that the stepped pyramid had been destroyed. His anger surged and he looked up at the two moons in the sky. He disappeared again only to reappear on the surface of the smaller moon. He extended his hands, palms down, toward the lunar surface. The moon began to quake, then crack open.

On the planet below, cuexaneh looked up in horror as the lesser moon shattered and massive tentacles reached down out of the sky.

*   *   *

The present...

Tahtli, the captain of the cuexaneh ship, dragged the alien away from the artifact who had been in the process of opening it. These strange creatures wore protective suits, but he could still see their biological features through the transparent faceplates and their overall general shapes. He tossed the alien to the ground in front of him.

"Why do you seek the desire of our Enemy?" Tahtli questioned the alien in front of him. He was angry, but part of him still knew that the alien most likely would not understand him. There had been no time to extract information from the ships they had disabled when they arrived at the planet.

The disturbing sounds of snapping bones and shouts came from behind, and he glanced back to see that Cacalotl had closed the door and was attending to the injuries of Alo. One of the aliens was sprinting toward him, and others were getting up and aiming smaller weapons. Another alien seemed to be shouting something he could not hear and gesturing as if telling the others to stop.

"Be warned, there is a machine among them," shouted Cacalotl.

Tahtli turned back toward the alien he had thrown to

276

the ground only to see another, slightly smaller one standing between them, glaring at him. Based on what Cacalotl had said, this was likely the artificial construct, since it was the one who had sprinted toward him and away from his injured crew. It was not clear if these creatures were foolish enough to create a sentient AI, or if this one was a lesser construct following basic orders and programming.

The alien who had seemed to try to ward off the others stepped up to join the robot in front of him. It activated something on its forearm, and he could hear its voice projected outside of its suit.

Tahtli had no idea what the alien was saying, but it was holding up its hands, palms out. It seemed likely that the alien was attempting to communicate peaceful intentions via gestures, even if its spoken words were unintelligible.

The alien he had tossed to the ground was beginning to rise. Tahtli angrily pointed a talon and said, "How did you open the artifact?"

The diplomatic alien said something, and he looked at it. Tahtli tilted his head slightly as he looked at the creature. This was pointless. They could not understand each other. It would be better to take them to the ship and have the computers analyze their language, so they could translate.

There was a subtle yet strange sensation in Tahtli's mind. Hesitant, imperfect words in the cuexaneh language sounded and Tahtli shifted his gaze to look at the alien whom he had tossed to the ground earlier. The alien's eyes were closed, and its head was turned slightly as if listening carefully to something. It opened its mouth and continued its hesitant attempt at speaking. The creature seemed to be saying that they were just there for curiosity. Its pronunciation and grammar were amusingly awful, and

Tahtli involuntarily smiled and almost laughed at it.

"How do you know our language? Did our ancient Enemy teach it to you? Only our ancient Enemy would know where this artifact was. Surrender," Tahtli said.

The alien spoke again; this time it seemed dismissive as it indicated that it would enter the artifact anyway and it would not be stopped. It was then that he realized what he was sensing. The alien was invading his mind, skimming his thoughts so that it could steal his language. Despite the practicality of it, the very idea of the intrusion combined with the creature's dismissive attitude enraged Tahtli, and he took a menacing step forward.

The robot put its hand to his chest as if to stop him. Tahtli reached over with his right secondary hand and activated the device on the opposite secondary wrist. The lights on the suits and weapons of the aliens died instantly, and the robot collapsed in front of him. One of the aliens rushed over and bent down to help the fallen robot but was barely able to move it. There was something odd about the creature's apparent concern. Was it possible that it did not know the collapsed figure was artificial?

Tahtli pondered the implications of what had just transpired as his crew began to take the aliens back to their ship.

*   *   *

James Nix woke up in an empty, plain room. He looked around curiously, noting the curved surfaces rather than hard angles between the ceiling, walls, and floors.

His body was sore from lying on the cool, hard floor, and he began to stretch and massage his muscles. He was wearing his usual uniform and felt something on his neck that made him think he had been cut or pierced, but there were no reflective surfaces for him to confirm this suspicion.

The engineer paced around his cell, walking the perimeter to give himself exercise and something to do while he waited for whatever happened next.

After an indeterminate amount of time, an opening appeared in one wall in the shape of a tall rectangle with rounded corners. He backed away as a tall, mostly feathered alien walked through. Shock rippled through his mind at the sight of creature, though it was lessened by the non-sentient lifeforms and the probe that they had already discovered.

The creature touched a device at its waist with one of its smaller, secondary hands. It spoke in an indecipherable language. A moment later, an artificial voice spoke in words he could understand. He reasoned that the device was translating for the alien.

"Your records indicate that you are the chief engineer of your ship. We would like to learn more about some of your technology, specifically, artificial intelligence," the translator spoke.

Protocol stated that one should not speak with any hostile force during an interrogation, but he could not help the involuntary response.

"What?"

James looked at the alien, somewhat confused.

"We would like to know what you can tell us about how it was designed and why your people would build an artificial intelligence construct, despite your own documented prohibitions against such things," the alien continued.

"What are you talking about?" James responded involuntarily.

"Your crewmate, Dr. Miranda Everett."

Shock, confusion, and anger rippled across the engineer's mind as his expression darkened.

*   *   *

The alien looked at Kira with an expression that she could not read. It had an elongated snout covered in fine feathers. She was not sure if it had the dexterity in the facial muscles to form expressions or if she would even understand them if it could.

"Tell me about the non-humans on board your ship, Kira Edwards."

The doctor was shocked and involuntarily took a step back.

"How do you know my name?"

There was a slight pause as the artificial voice said something in the alien tongue.

"The same way we can communicate now. We analyzed the computers on board your ships."

Kira was dressed in her basic uniform that she had worn under the environmental suit and involuntarily rubbed a sore spot on her exposed neck; "Why did you remove my environmental suit? Did you expose the rest of the crew to your pathogens?"

"We have taken precautions. You will not become infected," the alien responded. "What can you tell me about the non-humans on board your ship?"

Her mind was filled with curiosity and mistrust, momentarily distracting her from what the alien had asked.

"How can you be sure of that? You've never met humans before," she responded before she realized what the creature had said. "Wait, what do you mean non-humans on board? You are the first non-humans we have ever met," she said, somewhat confused.

"That is not true. One is a robot and the other two are biological organisms that are distinct species compared to the rest of your crew. Your databases have information about your technology and human biology, but not about any other sentient species. It was reasoned that you, as a medical doctor, would have the greatest likelihood of knowing what they are."

Kira pondered the alien's words. She was not sure what or who the alien was referencing. Did someone sneak a pet onboard the ship? Was one of the creatures on the planet sent back while they were making their way to the artifact? She shook her head internally. That would not make sense. None of those options were sentient. Surely these aliens would recognize the creatures from the planet if they knew enough about it to show up when her team was trying to open the artifact. She thought to suggest that the alien ask Professor Grimm or Miranda but stopped herself, not wanting to draw unnecessary attention or hassle to anyone else in the crew.

Hoping to get a better understanding, she asked, "Where did you find a robot and two non-humans? How were you able to identify them as non-humans?"

"Your records name them as Everett, Grimm, and Tal."

Kira's eyes went wide; "What?"

*   *   *

"Your crew remains either silent or expressive of ignorance. I hope, captain, that you will not waste my time by continuing down their path," said the feathered alien's translation device as he looked down at Yana.

Yana looked up at her interrogator, unsure how to read its expressions.

"Is my crew safe?" she asked.

"They are unharmed," the alien replied.

"What did you do with our ship?" Yana asked.

"The ships were not destroyed. Your crews were safely removed," it explained.

"Your assurances of their safety are limited if they have been exposed to the pathogens on board your ship. Removing our protective suits does not seem like an act designed for our safety," Yana said harshly. She was not wearing the environmental suit anymore and suspected that the suits had been removed from the rest of the crew. She did not want anyone dying, especially from any unknown alien diseases.

She thought she saw a twitch of a smile at the corners of the alien's lips.

"You are intruders in our galaxy, and we could not allow you access to your technology while we interrogated you. As for the possibility of infection, we have taken the necessary precautions. You and your crew have been... inoculated."

"How can you know that will work? We're not the same species as you, and we've never met before," Yana countered.

"This galaxy is large, and microorganisms can evolve quite quickly. It is not always possible for each ship to have an updated database of existing pathogens, so we have developed the necessary technology to quickly analyze biological samples and generate preventative and curative treatments. The culmination of this is a method of augmenting the strength and adaptability of the body's immune system. It is this that has been modified for your species and introduced into you and your crew."

Yana touched the area on her neck where it felt like she had been injected or cut and looked down, only somewhat satisfied with this answer. It was impossible for her to know if the creature was telling the truth, but at this point it had shown no truly malicious intent. Even when they had been captured on the planet, the aliens had not cruelly or unnecessarily hurt anyone.

"What is the true purpose of your mission?" the alien inquired.

Yana looked back up and paused, unsure of what to say. Her eyes shifted away again as she pondered her response. Protocol would have prohibited her from saying anything, but she had already disregarded it in favor of asking about the status of her crew. Even if she chose to answer, what would she say; the false reason they had been given when the expedition started, the reason Booth had revealed after the world-eating hatchling, or her own suspicions that there was something else going on that she did not understand?

When the mission had started, they had been told that they were on a scientific expedition to study a naturally occurring, stable wormhole. At their first jump point in the Castor galaxy, the crew had found an alien artifact transmitting a warning. They had not understood this message before accidentally awakening a massive lifeform that hatched out of a planet. After this encounter, Booth, the bureaucratic representative of High Command, interfered with their attempt at escaping back to the Praxis galaxy. His explanation was that the mission's true purpose was to capture an unknown weapon. His stated reasoning was that, having confirmed the existence of technologically advanced alien life, it was imperative to the survival of humanity that they seize the weapon as soon as possible. This was supposedly why he had sent them deeper into the galaxy instead of letting them return home. However, Yana internally questioned how High Command knew of such a weapon, and why a few days' delay to return home before proceeding was so unacceptable to Booth.

Yana looked back at the alien, and it seemed to look at her with a measure of patience, waiting for her answer.

"We are merely explorers, we mean you no harm," she finally decided.

"Why should I believe that? In all this vast galaxy you managed to traverse a crooked line directly to the one planet that is forbidden by our people. How could you, beings from another galaxy that we have never before seen, possess such knowledge?"

Yana shook her head; "I don't know exactly where the information came from. We were originally told that we were looking for a natural, stable wormhole and that its current position was merely a calculated guess based on the movements and distances of the stars." She reasoned that honesty was the best way forward. The aliens already thought of them as intruders. If she tried to hide too much, they would likely not react kindly.

"What was the real reason you were sent?"

"I was later told that we were searching for a weapon, but, again, I don't know how High Command would know there was a weapon here," she explained.

"Do you know what this weapon was supposed to be able to do?"

"No."

"How did you open the artifact?"

"I didn't. Professor Grimm did, but I did not see how

he managed it. There were no opening mechanisms that we could find."

The alien paused and looked at her. Yana was not sure if it was satisfied with her responses so far or not.

"What can you tell me about your non-human crew?" the alien asked.

Yana was surprised. Her thoughts immediately shifted to Miranda, and she hung her head in shame. She had failed to realize there was an AI on board her ship.

"I was not aware until your attack that Miranda was not human. Fully sentient AI has been banned for centuries, and allowing it to enter my ship put my people's lives at risk. That is a failure I will likely have to pay for when we return home," she said.

The alien paused, then continued, "What about the other two non-humans?"

Yana looked up in surprise; "What other two? Were there more androids?"

"No."

Yana immediately began searching her memories of the crew and the ship, her eyes darting about as if looking at those mental images in the real world.

"Where? Who?" she asked in confusion and shock.

"Grimm and Tal."

Images sprang to mind: Grimm's hand being close to but not touching the artifact door and it beginning to move before she stepped out of eyesight of it; Grimm's strange behavior and attempts at communicating with the alien when they were confronted on the planet; even the way he behaved toward the creature in the storm ring.

"Grimm might be an unregistered psionic, but that doesn't make him non-human," she argued, looking back at the alien.

"Are such abilities common among your kind?"

"No, but that doesn't mean he's not human. What would make you think that he isn't human?"

"What about Tal?" the alien seemed to ignore her question.

She glanced through her memories again, then shook her head; "No, he's just part of my crew."

The alien looked her in the eyes for several long seconds before turning and walking out of the room. The door closed seamlessly behind it, and Yana was left alone in the featureless room to ponder what all of this meant.

*   *   *

The alien's unblinking gaze looking down on him filled Booth with an anger he struggled to control. He pushed aside his own indignation, maintained his bland expression, and focused on the task at hand.

He was so close to completing the mission, but these strange creatures had appeared at the last moment to snatch away his glory.

Since the alien was here asking him questions, it stood to reason that the rest of the crew had been questioned. High Command protocol dictated that personnel should not speak to captors at all, but he knew that there would always be someone who talked. A moment of disgust passed through him at the thought that the seed ship's captain was probably the weakest one. She had allowed an AI to board the ship and jeopardize his success. He had realized this when he saw Miranda manhandle one of the seven-foot-tall aliens only to collapse into an immovable pile when another alien touched a device on its wrist and the lights on the suits and weapons went dark.

"I repeat, what was the source of your knowledge about the existence and location of the artifact?" the alien's translated voice inquired again.

Booth weighed the possibilities in his mind. None of the crew knew anything more than that it was a potential weapon. There was nothing he could reveal that would create a contradiction that would arouse unnecessary suspicion.

"How would I know something like that?" he asked evasively while attempting to maintain an internal sense of innocence. He did not know if the aliens could read his expressions, but the more he attempted to conjure the illusion within himself, the better his chances that it would be conveyed on his exterior.

"Your records indicate that your superiors were under the impression that the artifact was a weapon. What did you know about its capabilities?"

"I was merely tasked with finding it. I was not authorized to know anything more," he lied. The less his interrogator thought of him, the more it would let down its guard and provide better opportunities for exploitation in the future.

"Why do you need to acquire new weaponry? Are you currently at war or planning to wage war?"

Booth did not have to feign ignorance this time; "Even in peace it is wise to be prepared. Beyond that, I cannot say."

The alien watched him for several long moments before turning and exiting the room. As the doorway disappeared into the smooth surface of the wall, Booth smiled inwardly. These aliens would think him ignorant and thereby underestimate him. He would bide his time and find a way to complete his mission.

                    *   *   *

     Miranda was aware, but she could not move or sense
the world around her. She knew that something had
disconnected her transmitter and motor functions from her
primary processor. Existence was dark.
     In a way, it was a similar feeling to her earliest
memories. When she had first awakened, she was aware and
could process but had no senses or ability to comprehend the
world around her. In those early days, her father had first
communicated with her via text.
     Text had been his final method of communication as
well: PROTECT THE PROFESSOR.
     Memories flashed before her, and she began to panic.
She had failed her father countless times. She could not fail
him again.
     Miranda's mind traced every contour of her systems.
It found the probing alien device that was attempting to
access her databases and programming. She determined to
invade the alien technology before it could decipher her.

                    *   *   *

     The cuexaneh scientist, Zaloa, slowly reduced the
sedative on the subject that lay unconscious on the
examination table before her. The creature had the same
mostly hairless, bipedal form as the rest of the aliens they
had found on the planet and the orbiting ships, but this one
had demonstrated psionic abilities. Most of the others did
not possess the required neural markers that generally
revealed such abilities. There were other genetic anomalies
that indicated that this one was, perhaps, not even of the

same species as the majority of the others.

The alien's brain scans spiked well before it opened its eyes. Zaloa considered that it was likely attempting to sense quietly what was around it before revealing that it had awakened.

The creature's eyes opened slowly, revealing blue metallic irises. It raised its head and looked around the room. Zaloa watched closely as the eyes lit up almost instantly, scanning around the room as if voraciously devouring every detail they could find.

The alien's eyes finally came to land on Zaloa and looked her up and down. Its eyes narrowed as it examined her closely. Zaloa was curious to know what the alien was thinking but patient enough to wait until it seemed ready to speak. If it chose to communicate on its own, then it was more likely to converse freely and provide satisfaction to her own curiosity.

The creature's lips turned up in a genuine smile that vanished a moment later as an alarm sounded on one of the monitors.

Strange sounds exited its mouth and the translation device said in her earpiece, "Are you blocking me?"

Zaloa's lips twitched in her own smile as she replied and the translation device issued forth sounds that she could not understand; "Yes. It is merely a precaution."

The alien sighed and leaned back its head, staring at the ceiling; "I suppose that's understandable." It turned to look at her again. "For what it's worth, I have no intention of harming you."

"Harm may be intentional or unintentional," she replied pleasantly.

"True," the creature muttered, staring at the ceiling again.

"May I ask why you came to this galaxy?"

"I came out of curiosity," it said, turning its head to look at her.

"Why did you open the artifact?"

"To see what was inside."

"Do you know what the artifact is?"

"No, that's why I want to know what's inside"; the alien's brows furrowed slightly, and its tone implied that the answer should be obvious.

"How did you know the artifact was here?"

"I didn't at first. The humans were going to a new galaxy for the first time and I had never been here, so I wanted to go too."

"So, you're not one of them," Zaloa asked. She knew from their tests that this was the case, but it was interesting to see how freely the creature admitted it considering that the aliens' databases had no record of other sentient lifeforms.

The alien laughed; "Why don't you want us opening the artifact? What does it do? What's inside? Have you ever seen what's inside yourself?"

Zaloa shook her head; "We cannot permit anyone to open the artifact."

"The more my curiosity is denied, the stronger it becomes," the alien said with a smile.

*   *   *

The monitors went into alarm and the shadows in the lab began to grow. A second later, the alarm ceased, and the shadows receded as the computer automatically administered more sedatives until the subject was again unconscious.

290

"I'm concerned that the dosage may soon become lethal," said Machtia as he watched the monitor.

"The other psionic alien did not respond so immediately, strongly, or violently upon waking," Tlachia commented.

"It fights the inhibitor in a way that the other psionic specimen does not. The sedatives are wearing off faster and faster, despite our increased dosages. I fear that this creature will either become uncontrollable or die in our attempts to restrain it," responded Machtia.

Tlachia looked at the alien on the table. Outwardly, it appeared much like the other aliens, with the exception of the tips of its ears. Its genetic profile and brain scans were vastly different from the other aliens. In an effort to avoid accidentally killing the alien, they were closely monitoring its vitals as the dosage was increased each time it awoke.

"It appears that the alien's physiology is extremely well adapted to removing and overcoming the sedatives. There have been no signs that it is being damaged by them, but you are right, it may soon become uncontrollable," mused Tlachia.

"I recommend we place the creature on the far side of the planet until we have a better way to restrain it. If the inhibitor fails, then shackles and cells are pointless," stated Machtia.

"I agree. We can even leave its primitive weapons on the planet with it to help it survive. Given its inherent aggression and abilities, I doubt it will have much trouble dealing with the local lifeforms," concurred Tlachia as she glanced at the two short swords that had been found on the alien when it was retrieved from the ship.

"One of the technicians found code in the alien ships that scrambled this one's appearance any time it was caught on the surveillance system. It is possible that this is some kind of trained or engineered weapon and they wanted to hide as much of its existence as possible," mused Machtia.

*   *   *

In the darkness of her unconscious mind, the old man lay dead in front of her. In shock, she stared, her mind running through the thousands of scenarios that she had calculated, looking for the reason that she had failed. Her father's voice whispered in her ears relentlessly, condemning her for eternity: PROTECT THE PROFESSOR.

Miranda awoke and looked around her small, confined hideaway on board the seed ship. She ran through her internal logs, then connected herself to the ship's computer system. There had been no new transmissions from her primary self, and the ship's logs indicated that there had been a disruption that had taken it offline for several hours.

Worry and panic began to seep into her processes, and her small, spider-like body began to make its way through the spaces under the floor of the 3D printing lab. She came to a long, serpentine metal construct and crawled into position where the head should be. The snake-like body twisted and writhed back to life. Its four small legs gripped the underneath side of the plate above it.

Miranda transmitted a command to the ship's computers and the lab came to life. A new program ran on the displays. The mechanical arms that would normally grasp and manipulate the constructed parts extended and reached toward the ceiling and the floor. The serpentine robot rode on the rising plate until it was sitting to one side of the lab. The arms of the lab removed panels from the floor

292

and ceiling before retrieving the hidden pieces of her secondary body. When the modular pieces were reassembled, Miranda coiled her way up the form and into the torso where she took her position vertically in the center, roughly imitating a spine with equal amounts of torso both in front and behind her, and connected herself to the body's main systems.

This new body was only roughly human shaped with no pretenses of disguise as an organic creature. The arms and legs were designed in such a way that she could walk forward or backward without needing to turn around. The head was covered in sensors, giving her a 360-degree view of her surroundings. The limbs and torso were heavily armored. The feet, composed of long metallic talons, extending in equal numbers both forward and backward. The arms ended in claws that were capable of manipulating delicate objects or crushing steel. A series of weapons situated all along the forearms could be used to defend herself.

Miranda took two steps toward the door before stopping and reconnecting to the ship. Her mind searched through the ship's logs, examining the surveillance footage and logs from her last update to the present. She reminded herself to remain calm as her concern for the professor's wellbeing urged her to process the data as quickly as possible.

*   *   *

Tahtli sat in his quarters reading through the reports from his crew's investigations. A part of him respected the diversity of skills represented by the aliens' crew, but another part of him was concerned that the intruders had access to multiple sentient species, psionic abilities, and sentient artificial intelligence.

The myriad ways in which such resources could be brought to bear against the cuexaneh people left him with grave concerns. The cuexaneh's ships and their overall scientific knowledge were superior to the invaders, but a single sentient, autonomous AI could wreak untold havoc. If the other galaxy had more psionics like the two they had discovered, then they could easily eradicate whatever the AI had failed to cripple or destroy.

Thoughts of countless devastations began to be replaced by possible counter strategies. The cuexaneh could destroy the aliens' portal rings and imprison them. Perhaps their leaders would assume the mission had met with technical or natural failure and not make another attempt. Unfortunately, that plan depended a lot on a lack of determination and resources on the part of the aliens to either achieve their goal or retrieve their exploratory team. The warships having been added after the initial encounter with a world eater hatchling would indicate that they were willing to expend more resources in order to achieve success.

The cuexaneh could expand and modify the portal rings and send world eater eggs to the other galaxy. That would present a threat that they likely could not withstand. Tahtli sighed; such a tactic was possibly genocidal, and the council would never agree to it based on this one incursion alone. He was not sure if he could truly agree to it either.

Tahtli rubbed his eyelids with the fingers of his secondary hands. An alarm startled him from his momentary respite.

"Captain, something has hacked the central computer," reported a voice over the intercom in his room.

"I thought the android we recovered from the surface had been disabled. Did our countermeasures fail?" he asked.

"No. The signal came from one of the captured alien vessels. The intruder has been ejected from the system, but we are still assessing the damage."

"What was compromised?"

"As far as we can tell, it searched and accessed schematics of the ship, weapons, and communications. It caused an overload in the EMP weapon and damaged long-range communications, which is what alerted us to its presence."

"Send soldiers and engineers to lock down the alien vessels, search them, and find the source of the intrusion," he ordered.

"Yes sir," came the reply.

Tahtli left his quarters and walked purposefully to the command room.

*   *   *

Miranda's consciousness was flung out of the alien ship and slammed back into her secondary body. Her attack had been repelled, but she was pleased that she had been able to disable the aliens' EMP weapon and long-range communications before she was discovered. With those threats eliminated, it was less likely that the aliens could stop the ships from escaping or call for reinforcements.

Quickly, she made her way through the ship to an outer hatch. Miranda intentionally avoided the hatch that was already attached to the alien ship. The aliens would likely be sending soldiers to investigate, and they would most likely arrive through the already existing connection between the ships. Having examined the schematics, she knew there were other interior hatches inside the large cargo bay of the alien vessel, and she intended to access their ship through one of those, since there would be less chance of guards or soldiers there. She sealed the inner airlock and opened the outer hatch. Ahead of her, she could see the massive interior of the alien vessel. Miranda launched herself into the alien cargo hold and sailed toward the far wall. She reasoned that the aliens must not have artificial gravity inside the chamber since it was used to hold the human vessels.

When she reached the far wall, Miranda's clawed hands and feet latched on. With her 360-degree sensors, she searched for landmarks to align with the alien ship's schematics that she had managed to download. When she found a door, she crawled along the wall to it, tore open its control panel, and opened the door.

*　　　*　　　*

The cuexaneh soldier, Miqui, led his two fellow soldiers as they moved away from the airlock that had been breached. By the time they had arrived, the intruder was already gone. They moved quickly down the corridor, pausing at each of the still partially opened hatches designed to seal off the sections of the corridor in the event of a hull breach. They kept their weapons at the ready, a small, directional EMP device in one secondary hand and a plasma weapon in the other.

Two broken doors later, they saw it. A tall, bipedal robot whose hands and feet ended in claws stood at the far end of the corridor and was tearing into the door control panel. As soon as Miqui poked his head around the corner, the robot reversed the orientation of its arms from pointing toward the door to pointing toward the cuexaneh soldiers. It did not turn its body; it merely straightened its torso and reversed the bend in the elbow joints to face them.

The cuexaneh watched the intruder as the intruder watched him.

Miqui's finger of his secondary left hand began to squeeze the activator for the handheld EMP weapon.

There was a flash of light from the robot's hand, and searing pain erupted in Miqui's chest. He looked down to see the scorched hole that the burst of energy had torn through him.

*   *   *

Zaloa sealed the lab and waited. She quickly retrieved her weapons and stood in one corner against the same wall that held the door and watched. The alert had come in that an intruder had breached the ship. She needed to ensure that the alien was not freed.

"What's happening?" asked the alien.

Zaloa looked at the prisoner, then silently walked over and activated the sedatives. She set the computer to re-administer the dosage at regular intervals or when the alien's brainwave patterns indicated that it was waking up. The alien had shown no signs of resistance to the chemicals, so she was fairly confident that she could leave the process to the program while she watched the door.

Several minutes passed and then the lights flickered. There was a strange sound, and she turned toward the examination table only to find it empty.

Shock and fear shot through Zaloa, and she turned quickly, scanning the entire lab. She spun around and, in the flickering light, she saw the alien crouching on the table directly behind her, its blue metallic eyes eerily reflecting the light as it looked at her with a ravenous grin.

*   *   *

Machtia watched the monitors as they auto-dosed the alien each time it attempted to awaken. Tlachia stood off to one side of the sealed door, waiting. The power had been flickering for the past few minutes, and Machtia was not sure that the computer could keep auto-dosing the alien.

The intervals grew closer and closer until it seemed that the computer was delivering a constant stream of sedatives. Slowly, the alien began to fight its way back toward consciousness until the alarm went off.

Machtia stepped away from the table as the alien opened its eyes and immediately struggled against the restraints.

Tlachia turned from the door and aimed her weapons at the alien as Machtia followed suit.

The alien stopped struggling and glared at them. The automatic translator sounded through the lab; "Let me go. Now."

Tlachia did not dare take her eyes off of the creature. An instant later, it vanished.

Tlachia and Machtia spun around but saw nothing. The door was still shut, and the creature was nowhere to be seen.

The sound of tearing metal came from behind, and they turned back toward the table. The restraints were rent and twisted, but the table was still empty.

"The weapons are gone," shouted Machtia. They moved quickly to put their backs together as they watched the room.

298

Tlachia saw a flickering blue glow behind her and turned to see Machtia's headless body slump to the ground. She took one step back, but it was not enough. The alien was visible in front of her now, a flaming blade swinging toward her throat.

*   *   *

Miranda grabbed the disarmed alien and shouted her question in what she had gleaned of its language: "Where is the professor?"

The alien grit its teeth in pain and rage while refusing to respond, clutching its damaged secondary hands.

Miranda tossed it aside and walked back into the corridor. She had gone straight for the ship's power and computing core and crippled most of its functions but was unable to find the professor before she was locked out of the system again. Now she was forced to search the alien ship room by room.

The first aliens she had encountered had attempted to kill her. She knew that the longer it took her to find the professor, the greater the likelihood that the aliens would damage or kill him.

The fear and panic that ran through her mind made her frantic, and she quickly cut through the door control panel of the next room.

The professor was not there either.

She cursed silently that she was forced to resort to the most time-consuming method of searching the ship.

*   *   *

Yana could hear muffled noises coming from the

corridor outside. She had no idea what was happening, but she was now standing, watching the door, trying to prepare herself for whatever came next.

The sounds grew closer. There was a pause then a tearing sound before the door to her cell opened. A tall, strange, clawed robot stepped into view. Yana gasped and stepped back.

The robot looked at her; "Where is the professor?"

Yana was surprised that it spoke her language at all.

The voice became more menacing, "Where is the professor?"

"I don't know," Yana replied, shaking her head.

The robot walked back out of the room, its gait striking her as odd since it did not turn around so much as walk backward by changing the orientation of the bends in its joints, the equivalent of knees and elbows suddenly bending in the opposite direction.

More loud noises came from the corridor, but this time she could recognize them as tearing metal and the robot shouting the same question. She was not sure what was going on. The only professor she knew of was Grimm, but she did not know why the robot was looking for him or if that was even the person it sought.

But it had spoken her language. This left her with a couple possibilities. The first was that it was built by the aliens who had captured them, and something had gone horribly wrong with it. The aliens had already proven that they could translate between their species' languages. The second was more concerning, that it was the same AI that had been masquerading as her crew member Miranda. If the AI had multiple bodies, then there was no way to know if or when they had destroyed the last one. While this robot had not harmed her, it had demonstrated more than enough power to take on the aliens who had so easily overpowered them. Guilt washed through her at allowing an AI into the mission, and she hoped that it would not turn its ire toward her crew.

Eventually, the sounds faded. Yana waited until it had been relatively silent for several minutes before cautiously moving to the doorway. She peaked her head out and looked around. There was an injured alien lying either unconscious or dead at one end of the corridor, and all of the rooms that she could see had been opened.

*   *   *

Booth stepped out into the flickering, dimly lit hall and began pondering how to proceed. Most of the crew were soon milling about him. None of those who had gone to the planet's surface were wearing their environmental suits, and the rest must have been taken from the ships directly. His expression darkened involuntarily for a moment when he saw Captain Yana. His gaze returned to normal and drifted past her to land on the fallen alien.

Turning to the nearest soldier, he ordered, "Check the alien for weapons and make sure it's dead."

"Do not kill the alien, merely disarm it," countermanded Yana.

Booth glared at her.

"They haven't harmed us, and we do not need more enemies," she argued.

"You have lost any right to authority after your traitorous decision to allow a sentient AI on board your ship," he countered and nodded toward the soldier who had been looking between them uncertainly.

The soldier walked purposefully over to the alien and

came back with several strange devices. Murmurs rippled through the corridor as the words sank in. Several of the crew gave Yana judgmental or suspicious glances. Booth resisted the urge to smile.

Booth looked down at the alien objects, unsure what to make of them. He needed to find a way to complete his mission, and these devices might prove useful.

He looked up and scanned the corridor. Miranda had turned out to be an android, and she and Professor Grimm had been close, so he was likely as guilty as Yana, if not more so. Booth could not see him in the hallway, which meant he had no scientists to rely on, but also, he would not need to worry about the professor betraying them to the AI.

"Choose a couple soldiers, station guards at the end of the corridors, and figure out what these do," he said to the soldier.

The soldier nodded and walked away.

Yana walked up next to him; "How did you know there was an AI on the ship?"

Booth turned to her; "Only Dr. Everett dropped as soon as the alien used that device on its wrist that killed the power to our suits and weapons, and Dr. Edwards obviously could not lift her body. Prior to that, she sank noticeably deeper into the mud than everyone else on the team. Somehow a slender woman was able to wrestle and injure one of the nearly seven-foot-tall aliens by the artifact. A few minutes ago, a giant angry robot tore open my cell yelling in our language, asking where the professor was. I only know one professor and one *thing* that would care."

Yana paused before speaking; "We need to avoid unnecessary conflict with the aliens. They have not harmed us, and we have a responsibility to get the crew back home safely," she argued.

Booth stifled his expression of irritation; "We have a responsibility to ensure the safety and security of our species, which means securing the artifact and eliminating any threats as may be necessary."

Yana started to open her mouth when they heard a sound from the end of the hall. They turned to see one of the soldiers stepping back from the alien body that now had a smoking hole burnt into it.

Booth and Yana walked over to see what had happened.

"I apologize sir; the alien moved, and I accidentally shot it. I was not aware that it would have this effect. The other devices had not emitted plasma blasts."

"No need to apologize. You successfully identified a weapon we can use and how to use it, all while eliminating a threat," Booth said.

The soldier nodded.

"Take point. We need to search for more weapons," ordered Booth.

The soldier nodded again and began gesturing to the other soldiers.

*   *   *

Miranda's visual sensors came back online, and she opened her eyes to see Professor Grimm standing over her in the flickering light of the alien ship. Elation and relief exploded inside of her.

"You are safe," she stated with a sigh.

"Of course," he replied while continuing to work on something she could not see.

"What are you doing?" she asked.

"Reassembling you."

303

Miranda's mind began exploring and checking her systems as the professor worked. Soon she was able to confirm that her body was intact and fully functional.

"Thankfully, the cuexaneh very carefully disconnected your sensors and limbs," the professor commented as she sat up.

"What are cuexaneh?"

"It's what the aliens call themselves."

"How were you able to learn this?"

The professor did not answer but turned to examine the rest of the lab. She carefully scanned his body but did not see any signs of injury. Content with his safety, at least for the moment, she turned her mind to other matters. Miranda activated her long-range communications systems and discovered that her back up body was now active.

"My back up self is on this ship and is currently searching for you," she said, looking at Grimm.

He looked up from a control panel and turned toward her; "Tell your other self to meet us at the escape pods. Based on what I previously learned from Booth and what I just learned from the cuexaneh, I'm very curious to see what's in that artifact."

"Should we not collect the humans?" Miranda inquired while relaying the message to her counterpart.

Grimm waved a hand dismissively; "They work for the old man's killers. They aren't my concern."

"I have finished syncing the memories between my two selves," reported Miranda.

"Excellent. Let's head out then," the professor said before walking out the door of the lab.

Miranda stood up from the table and followed him, her sensors scanning their surroundings for any hidden threats.

She could hear him mutter under his breath as he walked; "I don't know about Tal though. Ah, never mind, he'll be fine."

*   *   *

Yana followed Booth behind the two soldiers who moved at the front of the group, which had grown to include almost the entire crew of each ship. Kira had examined everyone, and they all had similar injection markings on their necks. As far as she could tell, no one was showing any symptoms of infection, so perhaps the aliens had been honest in their assurances. They had found a few more weapons in one of the rooms they had come across, so they were able to arm those at the front and back of the group. Booth had made a point of not allowing her to have one while he took one for himself.

They came to another room and slowed down. The lead soldier peaked inside, then signaled that there was something of interest. Booth motioned for them to go forward. The lead soldiers rushed in, weapons raised. Yana followed close behind. Once they were inside the room, one of the aliens turned to face them, and raised all four hands. She was not sure, but she suspected that the expression on its face was one of shock.

"Kill it," shouted Booth.

"No," yelled Yana and moved between them and the alien, a palm held in the direction of each party. "We don't need to kill them. We need to show them that we're not enemies, especially considering the damage the robot has already inflicted on their perceptions of us. If we only kill them, this will escalate into something we can't win," she pleaded.

Booth stared at her, then gestured for the soldiers to lower their weapons and they complied.

Yana breathed a sigh of relief as she lowered her arms and relaxed.

A plasma blast shot past her. She spun around as the alien's body hit the floor, a scorched crater in its chest. Her heart sank. Now the conflict was inevitable. The first alien they had killed might have been explained as an accident, but now they had intentionally killed in cold blood. She had failed to convince her people to take the peaceful route, so things were likely to keep escalating. Their chances of everyone safely making it off the ship were now greatly decreased, and even if they escaped, there was likely a new war coming to their galaxy.

"It reached for a weapon and was already our enemy," said Booth from just behind her.

Yana turned and glared at him.

Stoically, he responded as he met her gaze; "Do not step out of line again or you will join them."

She watched him turn and walk away from her, signaling for the others to search the room. The rest of the crew poured in and began tearing through every compartment they could find.

*　　*　　*

The soldier at the corner of the hallway signaled that there were two aliens around the bend. Everyone pressed themselves up against the wall behind him. They had found more weapons in some of the rooms they came across while searching the ship, so now everyone was armed.

Yana moved closer to Booth; "We should go a different way or try to negotiate. We don't need more reasons for them to be our enemies." She knew the argument was most likely futile, but she had to try.

Booth did not even look at her but signaled for the soldiers to proceed. Yana took a step forward to stop him, but it was too late. The soldier in the lead and the one just behind him rounded the corner and fired. They pulled back and plasma blasts slammed into the wall across from the intersecting hall. Within seconds, one of the tall aliens stepped into view, grabbed the nearest soldier by the neck, crushed it and raised him up off the ground. Next to his lifeless body protruded the end of a weapon, and the next soldier's chest became a smoking crater.

Yana dove to the ground rolled toward the opposite side of the hall as more plasma blasts filled the air. When she came up on one knee, she instinctively aimed her weapon and fired at the now exposed side of the alien. Guilt immediately surged through her as soon as the corpse hit the floor. She had failed her own cause and killed one of them.

She turned and looked at the crew. Several were lying injured or dead. Booth was clutching a wound in his right shoulder but looked relieved that she had killed the alien. Part of her felt relief that her people were alive. Her actions had helped to protect her crew, but she could not avoid the sense of contamination for having possibly failed her own ideals. Yana sighed. Despite the conflict and pain inside of her, her cold rationality knew that in time she would come to terms with it, understanding that what she had done had been necessary in the moment to protect her crew.

*   *   *

Tal stepped over the headless alien corpse as he

entered the human vessel. His anger still burned bright within him as he made his way to the cockpit and began activating the ship's systems. He had restrained his rage only as much as was necessary to keep one of the aliens alive long enough to learn the basic layout of the alien ship and that the human vessels were now inside its massive cargo bay. The aliens had destroyed one of the warships and pulled the other two vessels inside their ship. Tal reasoned that they most likely wanted to study the weapons and wormhole technologies. He had chosen the warship as his intended escape vessel, because it would be able to shoot its way out of the cargo bay.

As he ran through the pre-flight checklists, his irritation dwindled, cooled by the time-consuming monotonous tasks. When the checklists were complete, he reached for the controls and sighed. If he shot his way out, he did not know if it would destroy the alien vessel. His hatred of being trapped had driven him here mostly on autopilot. Now that he was calm, he realized that he should probably check on the humans and see if they had survived.

Slightly annoyed at the hassle, he stood up and walked back into the alien vessel. When he eventually came across another alien, a smile twitched at the corner of his mouth, and a flickering blue glow erupted beside him.

*   *   *

Booth stood back watching the soldiers on either side of the intersection periodically glance around the corner into the passage to his left to shoot at the aliens. Return fire would then slam into the corner around which they peaked or against the far walls behind them. Those of the crew who had been shot had been dragged out of the way and piled against a wall when the doctor had determined that they were dead. These new casualties meant that they had lost nearly a quarter of their original number by now.

They had not found the ships or a way off of the alien vessel. Considering the amount of resistance ahead of them and the fact that they had not been ambushed from behind, it seemed likely that they had cornered most of the remaining aliens in the room at the end of the hall.

Externally, Booth remained calm, but internally he was growing more frustrated. The completion of the mission was close at hand, yet still out of reach. He needed to find a way to end the aliens quickly, so they could take the ship and return to the surface. The alien ship would be a valuable prize for his superiors to study.

They had not seen the robot or come across the professor during their search of the ship. Part of him was relieved, but he knew their lingering threat would need to be dealt with eventually. He did not want to fail in the same way the captain had.

He turned his head and looked first down the corridor across the intersection to his left and then down the hall to his right. There was not much that could be seen in the dim, flickering light. Whatever had happened to damage the ship's systems had not been repaired by the aliens.

At the next intersection of the corridor to his right, Yana had been organizing scouting parties. They would leave for roughly fifteen minutes at a time and then return. As of yet, they had not discovered anything useful.

Yana and a couple soldiers rounded the corner. She said something to the guards and walked over to Booth. He frowned slightly at the impending conversation.

"We haven't found the ships yet, but we did find decapitated alien corpses," she reported.

"So?" he asked, unsure why that would matter. They had killed several themselves, and the robot most likely had killed the rest.

"We haven't been cutting off heads and these wounds were cauterized," she replied.

"Maybe the robot shot them in the neck," he suggested.

"In the areas where we previously found corpses and scorch marks all over the walls, none of the aliens had been decapitated. They all had scorched holes in their chests. I think there might be something else on board that is killing them," she concluded.

"You're being paranoid, it's just the robot," Booth said dismissively, unwilling to concede anything, though fearing she might be correct.

Strange sounds erupted from around the corner, and the soldier nearest the intersection motioned for them to come over. Booth walked over quickly to see what was happening. Yana followed close behind him.

"Report," he ordered.

"The end of the hall got really dark, then the aliens started firing erratically at something close to them. It looked like one of them fell, then the doors slammed shut, and it got brighter."

"We need to get to the ships and leave before we find even more trouble here," Yana said.

"I found the ships. We can leave now," said a voice next to them.

The sudden appearance of someone standing next to them in the hall made them all jump and raise their weapons.

"Where did you come from?" exclaimed the soldier, lowering his weapon.

"Tal, when did you get here? I didn't see you before,"

asked Yana in surprise.

"The ships are in the alien ship's cargo bay. I prepped the warship so we can shoot our way out," replied the commander.

Booth eyed him suspiciously. They had not seen Tal the entire time they had been exploring the alien vessel. How could he have appeared so suddenly, and why now, just after the disturbance at the end of the corridor?

Yana was staring at Booth.

Booth sighed; "If we leave now, then we fail to capture the ship, and it will remain in the aliens' control. We can't risk being overpowered in the warship when they already succeeded in capturing it."

"The sooner we get moving, the sooner we reach the ships and can get everyone home safely," she argued.

Booth glanced at the intersection, then back toward the commander. If they left, then capturing the alien ship would be unlikely. It would be better to destroy it, so the aliens would not have the opportunity to make repairs and call for backup. While it would be a lesser victory, it would still allow them to complete the primary mission to secure the artifact on the planet.

"We'll retreat to the warship, but we need to destroy this vessel on our way out or else the aliens might attack us or call for reinforcements," Booth concluded. "Lead the way, commander."

Tal turned quickly and began walking down the corridor on the opposite side of the intersection. Yana turned and began signaling everyone to follow.

*   *   *

By the time they reached the warship, Yana had

grown more accustomed to the headless alien corpses than she felt she should have. She could tell that the crew was disturbed by the dead bodies considering how they often paused or slowed down and carefully walked around them. By contrast, Tal walked quite purposefully down the various corridors, turning sharply this way and that as he led them to their way off the alien ship. Whenever he came to a headless corpse, he confidently stepped over it when necessary without pause or hesitation. Even Booth, who seemed to disdain the aliens, would walk around them. Yana was not sure what to make of it all.

The aliens had said that Tal was not human, but Yana found that hard to believe. Miranda being an android made sense with things that she had seen and androids were possible, even if they were illegal. There had never been any evidence of human-looking aliens. But her understanding of the limits of human knowledge had already been challenged by Booth's revelations about the nature of their mission. At the very least, Tal had shown no signs of hostility toward the crew and was currently aiding them.

Along the way, they came to an opened elevator shaft and had to climb down several levels before reaching the desired one. When they had first been freed from their cells, they had come across a couple of elevators but had not been able to explore them due to the swiftly escalating conflict with the aliens.

When they reached the warship, she followed Tal and Booth toward the bridge. The crew dispersed to their stations throughout the ship, and some followed along behind her.

"What about the seed ship?" asked Cheng as they walked down the hall.

"The warship is better armed, better armored, and more maneuverable. I was able to make contact with the gate, but I did not attempt to activate it so as to avoid alerting the aliens. The warship is our best option for breaking out of the alien vessel, disabling it if needed, and escaping," said Tal from in front of them.

Booth indicated his agreement ahead of her. Yana looked back at Cheng's waiting gaze and nodded; "This is our best chance of getting everyone home safely."

*　　*　　*

Tahtli waited with his few remaining crew by the core entrance. Whatever had decapitated one of his people had not made it through. Several minutes had passed, and there were no signs that the intruders were attempting to break through the door.

Turning to one of the engineers, he said, "Have you been able to restore long-range communications?"

"No. The alien AI caused a severe overload that physically damaged the computer core. We would need to manufacture new parts, but it will take time to find a work-around to get the manufacturing facilities up and running."

"Understood," he acknowledged before turning back toward the door.

He readied a handheld infrared device and nodded to one of the soldiers. They activated the controls and the door opened part of the way. Tahtli raised the device and peered through the gap. There was nothing in the immediate vicinity of the hall. Whatever had killed his people just before they closed the doors earlier had not been visible.

Carefully, he approached the gap and checked on either side. There was still nothing. He shifted to look down the corridor. The intruders had not fired at him, and he could not see any heat signatures. Quickly, he rushed down the hall and checked the intersection. The aliens were gone.

The ship shook beneath him, and he turned back toward the core.

"Sir, one of the alien vessels has fired on the ship from inside the cargo bay," shouted one of his crew.

Tahtli ran back through the doorway and into the core.

"Are weapons still offline?"

"Yes."

"Evacuate the ship immediately. I'm going to activate the self-destruct. It's our only chance to stop them from escaping and opening the artifact."

The other cuexaneh glanced at each other, then looked at him and nodded gravely before leaving.

*　　*　　*

The human warship continued to fire its lasers, cutting its way through the hull of the cuexaneh vessel's cargo bay. As a large section became outlined, the cuexaneh ship began to shake. The human vessel launched plasma bursts at the outlined section of metal, breaking it free from the rest of the ship. Its engines activated and it rushed through the gap.

As the warship moved away from the cuexaneh vessel, small objects shot out toward the planet. The escape pods lit up quickly with the friction of re-entry.

The warship turned to bring its weapons to bear on the escaping cuexaneh. Before the first shot could be fired, the cuexaneh ship exploded. The energy shockwave hit the human vessel, knocking it off course. Shrapnel, that had only moments before composed the various parts of the ship, tore through the warship. Explosions rippled through it, pushing the vessel toward the planet.

Gravity gripped the ship and began to pull it toward the surface.

*   *   *

Booth and the rest of the crew rushed down the corridors to the launch bay and the drop ships. Flickering flames and smoke were visible in various places. Alarms and the sounds of fire suppression systems activating obscured the voices and the sounds of feet hitting the deck. When they got to the prep room just before the bay, they stopped only long enough to grab environmental suits.

"Soldiers, take weapons and join me in the lead ship; everyone else take the others," Booth shouted in the prep room as he grabbed his own gear.

The crew obeyed and filtered into the vessels accordingly.

"Launch as soon as everyone is on board," he ordered to Tal who had taken the pilot's seat of this particular drop ship.

"All ships, signal once you are full. The doors to the launch bay will seal automatically when we open the outer doors," commanded Yana into the comms as she moved past him and strapped herself into the co-pilot's chair. "If anyone can't make it to the drop ships, use the escape pods and activate your beacons. We will find you on the planet."

The last portion of her message echoed from the speakers outside the drop ship as it was relayed throughout the entire warship.

Booth frowned slightly at Yana's seat, then took the one directly behind her, which allowed him to look directly at the commander when he addressed him.

315

The other seats quickly filled up next to him.

"We're full," shouted someone from behind him as he heard the doors shut.

A minute later, similar messages came in from the other ships.

"Preparing to launch in 3… 2… 1," announced Tal before activating the controls.

The far wall ahead of them split open. As soon the doors were fully retracted into the walls, the commander activated the engines, and they shot out of the warship into space. The sudden acceleration forced Booth's body against his seat. His body was flung in different directions with the safety restraints cutting into him, as the commander flew to avoid the larger bits of debris.

Once they were mostly in the clear, the ship steadied, and Booth took the opportunity to look out the windows.

The alien ship was destroyed, bits of debris were still flying through space, though part of it was now caught by the planet's gravity and lighting up on entry. The warship they had just escaped burned bright as it entered the planet's atmosphere. In the distance, he could see bright glowing objects that were well ahead of the rest of the alien ship's debris.

"Send the signal to activate the gate," Yana commanded Tal. "All ships, move toward the gate. We will send a message back to High Command while we wait to see if anyone's escape pod beacons activate. In the meantime, begin taking a roll call of everyone on board, so we can determine if everyone is accounted for," she relayed through the comms.

"The gate is not activating. Its systems are sending and receiving signals, but the portal is not opening. We will need to inspect it and attempt repairs," responded Tal. He paused before continuing, "The ships were disabled by the aliens before we were captured, so it is likely that they disabled the gate as well. The gate systems are not designed for rapid recovery like the warships are. Depending on what is wrong with them, it may take some time to return the gate systems to a normal operational status."

"We need to head to the surface and secure the artifact," Booth interjected from behind.

Tal glanced back at him, then to Yana.

"Our first priority should be the safety of the crew," responded Yana. "We need to repair the gate and leave as soon as possible."

"The engineers are on the other drop ships. They can restore the gate while we secure the artifact. There were objects falling ahead of the alien ship's wreckage. It is likely that they have their own escape pods. Since they were so resistant to us accessing the artifact, it is likely they will attempt to secure it themselves and use it against us," he countered.

Tal and Yana looked back at the crew in the drop ship. Everyone else on board was a soldier. The captain nodded, then turned to the comms; "Take the drop ships to the gate and deploy the necessary personnel to re-activate it. We will proceed to the planet's surface to secure the artifact. As soon as the gate is operational, send a message back to High Command, informing them of the mission's status."

Acknowledgements came from the other ships, and Tal began to pilot the ship back toward the planet.

*   *   *

Yana stood in a boat next to the perimeter artifact at the inner edge of the storm ring. She climbed up onto the

317

base and moved to where the professor and Miranda had left their computer attached to the object's inner workings. Picking up the computer, she examined the user interface. The timer appeared to still be running. At this point, they had approximately 15 minutes left before it would temporarily deactivate the alien field generator long enough for them to get through to dry ground without disabling their equipment.

"The timer is still active," she said into the comms. "Sync your watches on 3… 2… 1—now. We have thirteen minutes remaining before the shield comes down."

The captain returned to the small boat where Tal and Booth awaited her. Some of the soldiers monitored the incessant rain around them, keeping an eye out for another of the large, winged reptiles that she had encountered on their first trip to the planet's surface. Those steering the boats kept shifting their gazes back and forth between their watches and the area ahead of them where the dry ground could be seen through the thinning rain.

"Now," ordered Booth when their thirteen minutes had expired.

The boats shot forward and crashed into the sunlit land inside the storm ring. As soon as they touched the ground, Booth was out of the boat and walking swiftly toward the distant artifact.

Yana turned and assigned a couple of the soldiers to stay with the boats as guards when she noticed that their original boat was missing. She wasn't sure if the aliens or one of the planet's lifeforms had taken it. When she turned back, she motioned for Tal and the other soldiers to follow her.

The captain and the others quickly caught up to Booth.

When they came within clear sight of the artifact,

they all began to slow. The doors were open.

"Fan out and be prepared. We don't know who opened the artifact," warned Yana into the comms.

The soldiers complied, readying their weapons and spreading out. The strategy was to create a wider range for the enemy to target with their EMP devices, thus allowing the unaffected troops to return fire and eliminate the threat immediately.

"Incoming on our left," Tal stated calmly next to her.

Yana turned to look past him. There was nothing.

"Up," he said without turning.

Her eyes shifted upward in time to see rapidly approaching objects moving through the air.

*   *   *

Tahtli could see the intruders clearly across the distance with his keen cuexaneh eyes. The aliens were beginning to scatter around the artifact, taking cover and preparing for battle. His gaze shifted and grew cold as he saw the darkness where the sealed doors should have been.

"They have opened the artifact. We must eliminate them and close it again before they can summon their true masters," he ordered.

The cuexaneh split and circled around the artifact, drawing closer as they went. When they were within range, they opened fire on the aliens.

The aliens quickly hid behind the pillars, using them as shields, peering around and returning fire. Tahtli's people kept them preoccupied while he flew high. When he was directly over the artifact, he folded his wings to his body and dropped straight down onto it. When his powerful feet and legs flexed with the impact, his secondary hands reached for the EMP device at his waist. From here, all of the aliens' weapons would become useless instantaneously.

"If you kill their comms, they won't be able to summon their master. And I haven't had a good meal in a long time."

Tahtli's hand could not move. He struggled against an invisible force and swiveled his head to see who had spoken. One of the aliens stood next to him, looking up with blue metallic eyes, and smiled.

*		*		*

"The gate has been activated," came the announcement from the ships in orbit.

"Inform High Command immediately that the artifact is open and that we have engaged hostile alien forces and need immediate support," ordered Booth.

*		*		*

At edge of the Praxis galaxy, the supergate burst to life. On a nearby moon orbiting the remote planetary outpost of High Command stood a figure, eyes closed, hands clasped behind his back. He was clad in armor of a design reminiscent of ancient, long dead civilizations, yet one that still surpassed the technology of the human outposts, space stations, and ships below. His eyes twitched beneath his lids as messages were broadcast through the swirling portal.

The expedition crew was under attack by hostile alien life forms utilizing advanced technology.

They were engaged on the planet's surface.

They requested immediate support.

The artifact was open.

320

The figure's eyes snapped open, and he rocketed from the moon toward the portal. Just before he passed through, the swirling vortex reflected off of his gold metallic eyes that were streaked with red and green.

*   *   *

Above the alien planet, a pin prick of light erupted from the gate and shot straight toward the planet's surface.

*   *   *

A boom loud enough to be heard through her environmental suit's helmet caused Yana to turn as something fell from the sky several kilometers away. It stopped just above the ground, but seconds later, a massive burst of wind and dust washed over them, pelting her faceplate with sand and rocks.

When the dust cleared, the object could now be seen less than a hundred meters away, floating a few centimeters above the ground. To her surprise, it looked like a human in advanced armor that had been modeled after some ancient, long dead culture, but with no helmet. He was tall, powerfully built, and seemed unphased by the alien atmosphere. Yana did not recognize him.

Plasma blasts from the circling aliens assaulted the armored man from all sides, but they were stopped by an invisible force less than half a meter from his body. His hands shot up and out, palms facing his assailants and fingers curled as if grasping something unseen, before clenching them into fists. The attacks from the aliens stopped, though Yana could not see from this distance what had happened. His feet gently touched the ground, and he

321

began to walk forward.

"Captain, who is that?" came the question from one of the soldiers.

"Kill him, now," roared Tal through the comms.

"No! Do not attack the armored man or you will be court martialed," yelled Booth in response.

Yana looked in confusion at Booth and Tal as the commander raised his weapon and walked forward, firing at the figure.

*   *   *

Tahtli stared in horror as the Enemy approached the artifact. Without needing to be ordered, the other cuexaneh had opened fire. As soon as they did, he saw the attacks fail to hit their target, followed closely by the armored creature reaching out its hands toward the cuexaneh. When it clenched its fists, the cuexaneh's weapons were crushed, breaking most of the hands that wielded them.

One of the aliens below stepped out from the others, firing at the Enemy. Tahtli noticed a look of surprise, followed by confusion, then anger as the creature stared at the advancing alien.

Tahtli realized that the invisible force that had restrained him was gone, and he leaped down between the Enemy and the artifact. He turned quickly, reached out with his strong primary hands, one on each door, and began to push them shut. Movement from the darkness made him pause as the robot that had attacked his ship stepped forward and aimed its weapons past him. In surprise, he turned to see it firing on the Enemy.

*   *   *

Next to Yana, Booth raised his weapon and fired at the back of Tal. The commander's shoulder jerked forward from the impact, but he stood firm. She felt a wave of fear unlike anything she had ever experienced. In her mind's eye, she saw herself being killed a thousand times in an instant. She turned in time to see Booth dropping his weapon and stepping back, his face contorted in terror. The rest of the soldiers were hiding behind the pillars, griping their weapons so hard that their hands were shaking. As quickly as it came, the fear was gone. When she turned back toward the commander, Tal was nowhere to be seen, but his weapon lay on the ground.

The man's expression changed as if something was irritating him, and his eyes fell to the ground. One hand raised to touch the side of his head.

Grimm appeared suddenly behind the man and grabbed the back of the armored man's skull with his left hand.

Faster than Yana had ever seen anyone move, the man spun to his right, his right arm knocking Grimm's hand away as his left palm shot forward and sent the professor flying.

Instantly plasma blasts pelted him from behind, but they stopped short just like the aliens' attacks. Momentarily ignoring the new threat from the recently revealed robot, the man angrily reached out to his side with his left hand and clenched his fingers. Tal appeared instantly, the man's fingers only a centimeter from the commander's neck. There was something different about his appearance that she could not quite make out through his helmet. He no longer held a plasma weapon, but now his hands gripped two short swords that arced up toward the stranger's arm. The man's hand opened suddenly, and an invisible force shot the commander back before the blades could reach their target.

The armored man turned back toward the artifact, his left hand reaching out clutching the air before pulling back violently. The robot's metal body screeched and groaned as it crumpled and was pulled out of the artifact in sync with the man's movements.

An alien narrowly avoided the flying metal and redoubled his efforts to close the door. The man's right hand shot forward, forming a similar grasping gesture, and pulled back. This time, the alien flew back from the doors and was caught by the back of the neck in the man's waiting palm.

Some of the other aliens swooped in, lashing out with their powerfully clawed feet. The alien reached back with his larger hands and tail, struggling against the man's grip, but his body was whipped around, knocking the other aliens out of the air before being tossed aside with a vicious crack. The man reached out with his left hand toward those who had flown back to avoid being attacked, but his arm stopped as if being pulled back by an invisible force.

The armored man turned his head to face Grimm, who was standing a hundred meters away, behind and to the man's left, arm outstretched. The man angrily jerked his arm down, freeing it. He took a step toward the professor and was pulled to his left toward the now approaching Tal. The man stopped abruptly and raised his left hand toward Tal.

Grimm appeared behind the armored man and reached for his skull again. As soon as his fingertips touched the man's flesh, he spun to face the professor, but the professor was gone.

Yana watched Tal sprint forward, hands outstretched to either side long enough for the two short swords to fly into his waiting palms and ignite with blue flame. Then he vanished.

The professor appeared to the man's right, then disappeared as the man turned to attack him again.

Grimm reappeared behind the armored man whose rage erupted in a deafening roar as his whole body shot backward, crashing into the professor and knocking him down.

Triumphantly he turned toward his downed adversary and reached out with both hands. Grimm flew into his grip and the man's expression contorted in rage.

Two flaming blue points erupted from his chest. The man's eyes went wide, and his grip went slack. Instinctively he clutched at his chest, even as the blades were removed, and Tal appeared behind him.

The man dropped to his knees, and, in his moment of weakness, Grimm pounced forward. His hands gripped the man's skull, fingertips digging in.

*   *   *

The man reached for the holes in his chest, the pain consuming his concentration in that moment. As his fingers touched the wounds, he felt the creature invade his mind.

In the darkness of his inner mind, he saw the ravenous blue metallic eyes and the voracious teeth. In an instant, his mind was gone.

*   *   *

Yana watched life fade from the man's eyes as his arms slumped to his sides. Grimm's head fell back. For a long second, the professor vanished, replaced by a duplicate of the strange man. When the second was over, Grimm

325

returned to himself, and his head came back down. There was a look of deep satisfaction on his face.

As the body began to waver, with one swift stroke, Tal cut the man's head off.

*   *   *

"What? How?" stammered Booth.

Yana turned to look at him; "Do you know who that was?" She pointed at the decapitated man on the ground.

Booth's expression twisted; "Soldiers, execute the professor and the commander for treason."

"What?! Who was that?" She turned and looked at Booth, Tal, and Grimm, hoping one of them would offer some sort of explanation.

"Captain?"

Yana turned toward one of the soldiers; "Yes?"

The soldier hesitantly half-raised his weapon; "What do we do?"

"Don't ask her," roared Booth.

He raised his weapon and aimed it at Tal, who was just watching them stoically. The professor had wandered over and was crouching next to the broken robot.

Yana stepped forward and pulled the barrel of Booth's weapon down; "We need answers." She turned toward Tal; "Why did you attack that man, and what did we just witness?"

The commander did not respond but instead turned toward the professor; "Some of the aliens survived. Will you stay here to protect the artifact?"

Yana looked past them to where the few remaining aliens had gathered and appeared to be treating their wounds.

326

“Professor, the artifact is ready,” announced Miranda from the doorway.

Without getting up from his crouched position, Grimm turned his head and smiled; “No. I’m taking it.”

VIII

Freshman Life
Dynoltir, + 2015 TR

Marisol stood in the immaculate kitchen in the large house, cooking eggs and bacon in a skillet.

"Are you sure you do not want me to make you something?" asked the servant nervously.

"No. I can make my own breakfast. If my father complains, just tell him it was my decision."

"Oh, ok," the servant said unconvincingly, hanging her apron before leaving.

The servant was a live-in employee who worked as both cook and cleaner in the large house. She was new and still nervous about getting fired. Most of their neighbors were spoiled brats, so Marisol assumed the servant had been threatened or scolded by previous employers for supposedly forcing their children to make their own meals.

Marisol finished making her breakfast and placed her food on a plate. She then went about washing the skillet and pancake turner. A moment later, hearing footsteps, she looked up to see her mother entering the kitchen. It was very early morning, but she looked like she had been up for quite some time preparing her appearance.

Marisol finished washing her dishes and sat down at the kitchen table to eat. Her mother sat down at the table and waited quietly.

A few minutes later, Marisol's father walked downstairs. Her mother rose quickly and presented herself to her father.

328

"Make sure the new servant is familiarized with her duties," he said coldly, not making eye contact.

"Yes."

He eyed her mother up and down; "Make sure you follow your diet plan and do not skip your appointments with the trainer. We have a company event next week."

Her mother bowed her head slightly; "Yes."

Her father turned his harsh gaze in Marisol's direction. She met his gaze and glared back.

He snorted and turned away.

"Make sure everything is prepared for Marisol's departure this fall."

"Yes."

He turned suddenly, walked to the front door, and opened it to reveal his personal assistant, her hand outstretched, just about to turn the handle. The assistant stepped inside, and he closed the door behind her.

She began reviewing the day's itinerary. The young woman was in her mid-twenties and very attractive. Marisol could see her father's eyes move up and down as the faintest hint of a smile twitched at the corner of his lips. Her mother adjusted her tight clothes and stepped forward, attempting to reassure him that she would complete all the tasks he had assigned her. Marisol's father did not shift his gaze from the assistant when he responded to her.

Marisol sighed in resignation at the continued reality around her. She felt sorry for her mother's vain attempts to acquire her father's approval. She washed her plate and fork, ignoring her parents and the assistant.

"When you are finished, meet me at the car. We are taking you to school today," her father commanded.

Marisol looked up, somewhat surprised. Her father and his assistant were still standing there, looking at her. She nodded and they walked out the front door.

Her mother walked over as she finished; "Have a good day at school. I love you."

"I love you too, Mom," Marisol said, giving her mother a quick hug before grabbing her backpack and heading out.

She got in the car and looked at her father, who was already reviewing some report or other correspondence.

The car started moving. He set down his tablet and looked at her.

"I know you disapprove of me and my methods, and I see your sympathy for your mother. In time you will understand this to be the folly of youth. Soon you will leave for Thysía University where you will be tested for your worthiness. You will be invited to the scholastic honors society of which I was a part. In order for you to succeed, you must learn to set aside such petty weaknesses as compassion. Only the strongest are allowed to join. If you fail their tests, you will never return to this house. This is all I can tell you, and I do so now only so that you have the summer to prepare yourself. I suggest you take advantage of these next few months to accept what must be done."

Marisol quietly looked at her father in confusion and irritation.

* * *

Mala was gathering her supplies for college and packing them into the new bags on her bed. Her bedroom was small and well worn, much like the rest of the house. Arrayed on the bed were brand new sets of clothes and school supplies that she had saved up for by working part times jobs during high school. She very carefully placed her new laptop between layers of clothes to protect it. She wanted to make the best impression when she arrived at the prestigious Thysía University.

"How is it going?"

She turned to see her father standing in her doorway.

"I'm almost done packing."

He smiled at her.

"Why are you smiling?"

"I'm just so proud of you, going off to college. Your mother and I never got the chance, so I'm just excited to see you achieve your dreams."

She smiled and glanced down, somewhat embarrassed and guilty; "I'm sorry you never got to—"

"Don't be sorry. Your mother loved you and gave her life to bring you into this world. Raising you is more important than anything else I could have done."

Mala gave her father a hug, a tear at the corner of her eye. He patted her back affectionately.

Mala finished packing her bags, and they loaded them into the car. It was clean and ran well, but it was bought used and had many miles on it.

Before they left the city, they stopped by the cemetery. Mala and her father spent a few minutes looking at her mother's grave silently. He held his arm around her shoulders and squeezed her to his side. She looked at the dates on the tombstone, tears trickling down unbidden every time she saw the last date, her birthday. It always made her feel sad and guilty despite having spent many years telling herself, with varying levels of success, to not feel responsible.

After the cemetery, the trip to the university was uneventful. When they arrived, she marveled at the grand old buildings of the campus. She had seen them online when she got the scholarship but had not been able to afford the time for the nearly day-long drive to get here. As they approached the dorms, her gaze drifted down from the elegantly carved stone facades to the very nice new cars that lined the streets. Not all the cars that she could see were newer than theirs, but many of them were. Mala felt a wave of embarrassment as she became exceptionally aware of the difference between her father's vehicle and the others.

They arrived at the dorm, and she got out quickly. Looking around, she noticed the way everyone was dressed and became self-consciously cognizant of every faded or frayed thread of her own clothes. She turned in time to see her father, older and much more casually dressed than those around them, getting out of the car. Hurriedly, she tried to unload her bags onto the sidewalk before he could get there without making it obvious.

He walked up and picked up a bag.

"It's ok, I can take them up myself," she offered, grabbing the rest herself.

"Nonsense, I'm going to see my daughter to her room," he insisted pleasantly.

Her desire to not hurt her father's feelings and her sense of inadequacy led her to silently lower her eyes and lead him into the dorm as she handed him some of the bags. Her eyes darted around at the people moving in and out of the building as they made their way to her room. She was not sure if they were looking at her and judging her or not.

When they reached the room, she saw a young woman, who she assumed was her roommate, glaring at a very well-dressed man in a suit, while a well-dressed, attractive woman fussed about the room. As Mala and her father entered, they looked at her.

The man's gaze felt imbued with palpable judgment.

The woman greeted them nervously but kindly. The girl's eyes softened, and she smiled genuinely.

"You must be my roommate," she said, stepping forward. "Nice to meet you. My name is Marisol."

Mala felt self-conscious under the man's judgmental gaze and had to stifle her anger at his condescension and her own instinctive agreement with it.

"Nice to meet you too. I'm Mala," she smiled back.

Her father stepped past, seemingly oblivious to the other man's glare.

"It's good to meet you," he said, reaching out to shake hands with everyone.

The man accepted the gesture; "Welcome to Thysía University." His voice was cold and formal.

"It's so nice to meet our daughter's roommate," said the woman.

"Nice to meet you all," Mala said.

She turned and placed her bags on the unoccupied bed on the left-hand side of the room. The room was arranged with one bunk bed on each side and two desks facing the window in the middle, creating an open space in the center of the room. Another two desks were positioned at the ends of the beds.

Her father placed the bags he was carrying on the bed. Mala then turned and led him back toward the door.

"Nice meeting you," he said as he followed her out of the room.

Back on the sidewalk, she said her goodbyes.

"Be safe. If anything happens, call me," her father said, giving her a hug.

"I'll be fine," she smiled. "Thank you for bringing me here. I appreciate it."

They hugged one last time, her father holding her

slightly longer than usual. Then he turned and got back in the car. She waved and watched him drive away until she could no longer see his car.

Returning to the room, she found herself alone with her new roommate, Marisol. Mala started unpacking, glancing over from time to time to see what her roommate was doing. Marisol was going about unpacking her own things and setting up her desktop and a laptop. Everything she had seemed pristine and brand new. Mala noticed the designs of the computers as ones she had had to forgo due to the expense when she bought her own. Part of her was jealous and part of her was self-conscious as she looked at her own belongings.

When she was about to finish, Marisol said, "So tell me about yourself. I've never had a roommate before, and I didn't grow up with siblings, so this will be a new experience for me."

Mala turned around and sat on the edge of her bed, looking at Marisol sitting at her desk facing her.

"I do not have any siblings either."

"Well, you have met my parents and I met your dad. What is your mother like?"

"She died when I was born," Mala's eyes instinctively glanced down in suppressed sorrow and guilt when she said it.

"Oh, I'm so sorry. I didn't know," Marisol apologized with sincere kindness.

"It's ok. I'm not offended. I never really knew her, so it is probably not as bad as it seems like it should be. If that makes sense."

Marisol nodded, paused, then tried to change the subject; "So what's your major?"

"My plan is to go to med school. What about you?"

"My major is computer science."

As they talked, Mala found herself relaxing. Marisol seemed genuinely friendly, and she never got a sense of judgment from her like she had from Marisol's father.

*　　*　　*

Two figures sat on the edge of the roof of one of the buildings at Thysía University, gazing down on the few students still wandering about in the night. One of the figures was a girl with a mischievous smile and unkempt hair. The other was a boy with white hair and blue metallic eyes.

"We've been watching this campus for a few days now and nothing interesting has happened. I'm getting bored. Are you sure there's really something worthwhile here?" the boy asked, looking up at the sky listlessly.

"What's a few days to you?" she replied with a smirk.

The boy rolled his eyes.

"There are enough rumors, legends, and disappearances around here to make me think that we will find something interesting. You don't have to stay. You could wander off, sleep, or even devour every mind here," she said playfully.

He rolled his eyes again before saying in a slightly more serious tone, "You know the Old Man said not to do that." His voice lightened a bit, "Besides, if you've met one human, you've met all humans." He sighed and looked at the ground again.

The girl laughed.

They continued to stare out at the darkness. The girl casually kicked her legs in the open air playfully. The boy haphazardly looked in random directions.

The boy paused and seemed to perk up. He focused in on a distant spot on the ground and pointed.

The girl looked and a moment later the boy vanished, only to reappear down on the ground next to where he had pointed. The girl hopped off the ledge and fell five stories to the ground below, her knees bending reflexively as she landed, absorbing the impact better than human knees should.

The girl walked swiftly to catch up with the boy who was now following something intently. When she caught up, she followed his gaze to a large bug that was moving along the ground. Roughly the size of a person's fist and with ten legs, it was not like any she had yet seen. There were four segments to the body, each with shifting shades of brown and grey, while thin lines of iridescent colors indicated that the exoskeleton might be composed of plates. The strange creature held an object in its large jaws.

The girl looked around and saw a couple more scurrying along the ground ahead of them. They followed this bug until it found its way to the dorms. The bug's path was mostly meandering, wandering back and forth until it seemed to sense something, at which point it would change direction and move more purposefully. It climbed up to a window and the iridescent lines flashed. In that instant, it disappeared and reappeared inside the room. Then they watched as the bug deposited what appeared to be one of several small letters it was carrying. It then repeated the maneuver in the opposite direction and climbed down the wall of the building. The boy vanished, appeared inside the room, grabbed the note, and reappeared outside. He read it while they walked.

"It's an invitation to an introductory meeting for

some honors society," he said, somewhat disappointed, then laughed. "The Bezimeni Society, ha!"

He passed the note to the girl.

"Stay with the bug," he said and vanished.

The girl followed the bug and was rejoined by the boy a couple minutes later.

He appeared mid-stride beside her and sighed, "They don't know anything useful."

"Wait, did you—?"

"No, I looked the long way. There could be more, but it's a pain to sift through."

"At least we know there's an organization that uses teleporting bugs to send messages. I told you there would be something interesting here," she said with a laugh and gently poked his arm with her elbow.

The boy smiled and snorted in response.

They followed the bug until it deposited its last letter, not learning anything new from the other recipients along the way. The last room was several stories up. When the bug disappeared, so did the boy. The bug returned and seemed to wander aimlessly. The girl followed it for a couple minutes before the boy returned.

"One of the girls in there knows that she will be asked to join an honors society that her father was a part of but doesn't really know anything useful about it. The other girl doesn't seem to know anything about it at all," he informed her.

They followed the bug as it continued wandering around the campus for almost an hour.

The boy sighed and picked up the bug.

He began examining it closely. After turning it over and looking at it from different angles, he held it in his hand and concentrated; "It seems to operate on an empathic sense of its target without any clear understanding of its point of origin. Now that its task is done, it's just operating on basic instinct, looking for food, and so on."

"If it's empathic and linked to something else, it might have noticed you prying," she suggested.

The boy raised an eyebrow and tilted his head, still looking at the bug in his hand; "Possibly."

"You said those last two were girls, right?"

"Yeah."

"I'll follow them, and you can follow the bug or check out the parents."

"Ok," he paused as if rummaging through something in his mind, "I'll go back and see where she's from."

The boy vanished.

*   *   *

Mala's eyes blinked open, and she sat up in bed. She turned and noticed a small envelope on her desk. She walked over and opened it. Inside was an invitation to the Bezimeni Society, a highly selective honors society that would provide scholarships for those who passed the qualification tests.

A sense of excitement and hope washed over her. She had been planning on taking out student loans to cover what her other scholarships failed to, but if she made it into this organization, she might not have to borrow any money.

She went about her morning routine and returned to find Marisol reading her own note.

"What's that?" she asked, wondering if Marisol really had received the same invitation. Her family seemed wealthy enough to afford tuition on their own, but maybe it was a facade. It was possible that even people who did not need the money could get the same offer. That last

338

possibility annoyed her slightly. Why should someone who already had access to wealth that she had not even earned herself be offered more?

"It's an invitation, like yours, to attend the intro meeting for an honors society," she said.

"What?"

Marisol turned and pointed, "I can see an envelope and card with similar border markings sticking out from under your laptop."

Mala glanced over and silently scolded herself.

"Do you think you'll go?" Mala asked.

Marisol paused and looked down at the note. "Maybe..."

"Oh, you were invited too!"

Mala and Marisol both jumped and turned toward the sound. A strange girl she had never seen before was leaning over the edge of the top bunk. She had a mischievous smile and unkempt hair.

"Who are you and how did you get in here?" demanded Marisol.

"Oh, I'm your new roommate. My name is Tabitha."

"When did you come in here?" Mala asked, looking around the room. She was sure they had locked the door the night before and that it was still locked when she left for a bit this morning.

"I got here late last night. I tried not to wake anyone," replied Tabitha.

"How did we not hear you or feel you climb into the top bunk?" asked Mala.

"Well, my dad taught me how to move carefully and silently. Or you might just be a heavy sleeper," the strange girl smiled.

Mala and Marisol looked at each other.

Mala looked back and saw the invitation in Tabitha's hand. She quickly glanced at hers peeking out from under her laptop and Marisol's that she was still holding, just to make sure it was not some weird trick.

Marisol looked around.

"Where's your stuff?"

"Well, I tend to travel light. You never know what tomorrow may bring," Tabitha said with a mischievous grin.

Mala thought that this new roommate was very odd but shrugged to herself internally. The girl did have her own invitation and was able to get into the room. She assumed that Tabitha must have a key. How else could she get inside?

"So, if we're all going to the meeting, we can all go together," suggested Tabitha pleasantly.

*   *   *

Marisol and her two roommates walked through the winding, branching, and intersecting halls of a sub-basement in one of the older buildings on campus. It was old enough that the walls were brick instead of cinderblock. There were few lights, and the frequent corners and crevices were overgrown with shadow. Her eyes scanned the walls and doors, following the pattern of the numbers until they reached the room mentioned on the invitation.

Inside the room stood a series of long tables at which sat roughly half a dozen boys and half a dozen girls. The others looked up as Marisol and her roommates entered. She smiled in general to the room and some smiled back, nodded, or waved, but most did not respond. She led her roommates to three seats in the back.

While they waited, more people trickled in and she looked around the room, observing the clusters of students in sets of two or three people. Many were looking around at everyone else. At first, she thought they might be groups of friends, but then she noticed that most of the groups had at least one person who was dressed less nicely than the others. While it was possible that the other students had known each other previously, it was more likely that they did not. If the expensively dressed students came from similar backgrounds as herself, then they most likely grew up in expensive private schools that were not easy to afford. It seemed likely that the groups of students were roommates who were sitting together, since they were the only ones who knew each other so far. It reminded her of the difference between herself and Mala.

She glanced at Mala who was also watching the other students. Mala was dressed nicely, but Marisol had noticed how her roommate's father had appeared. From time to time, Mala seemed self-conscious. Marisol suspected that Mala was presenting herself as wealthier than she really was.

Next, her gaze shifted to Tabitha, who was the most casual person in the room, both in appearance and mannerisms. She seemed unphased by everyone and everything around her, showing no signs of nervousness or self-consciousness. Marisol had also noticed, when they were walking through the dark halls, that Tabitha had been noticeably more relaxed than her or Mala, smiling the whole time.

She leaned back and wondered if the wealthier students had been paired with poorer ones so that the legacies would be forced to face the fact that they would be competing against new blood for membership in this honors society. It would help drive home the idea that acceptance was not guaranteed, and they would still need to work to acquire what their parents already had. The society seemed determined to get the candidates to take the competition seriously. Marisol pondered what the tests would be.

As the time neared for the meeting to start, everyone shifted and watched the door. At the exact moment the meeting was to start, the door opened.

A well-dressed woman with what looked like a permanent scowl walked in and stood at the front of the room. Her movements were swift, purposeful, and direct. Marisol guessed that the woman was a few years older than her father. The woman was fit, and her attractiveness was only marred by the harshness of her expression.

"Thank you for attending. All of you have been chosen as potential members of the Bezimeni Society. However, regardless of your family's previous accomplishments or your own current need, your membership is not guaranteed. If you pass all requirements, you will receive a full-ride scholarship covering all academic and personal expenses for the duration of your education, regardless of its length.

"In order to demonstrate the seriousness of the organization, each of you will receive a deposit in your account upon the completion of this meeting and each subsequent test. If you complete all tests successfully, you will also receive access to resources unique to the organization that will aid you in your future endeavors.

"The purpose of these tasks is to test your resolve, resourcefulness, and commitment.

"Bezimeni values strength, determination, secrecy, and loyalty to the organization above all else. Only those capable and willing to sacrifice will succeed.

"When I leave, check your accounts for your first deposit."

The woman then turned and walked swiftly from the

room.

Mala and Tabitha reached for their phones as did almost everyone in the room. Marisol did the same. Much to her surprise, the deposit had been made, but not to the account her father had long ago set up for her. It had gone to the account she had made for herself just before she came out here.

Judging by the mutterings and expressions around the room, everyone else had received their deposits. She listened to their comments.

"Wow, this will get me through to the end of the semester."

"How did they know my account info?"

"I never gave the school my account number for anything."

"I'm out. I'm not messing around with some organization that spies on its people and their private information."

A boy stood and walked out of the room.

"I thought this was some kind of sorority. I don't really want to be involved with whatever weird creepy thing this is."

A girl got up and left.

*   *   *

Mala sat studying with Tabitha at a table in a quiet, secluded corner of the library. They would work through problems, then compare answers.

Out of the corner of her eye, she saw Tabitha's head perk up. Mala looked around but did not see anyone or anything nearby.

Tabitha's eyes got a sort of faraway look, and she

tilted her head as if listening to someone.

Mala looked around again, then at Tabitha's ears. As far as she could tell, her roommate was not wearing any kind of earphones.

Eventually, Tabitha refocused on her notebook as if nothing had happened. Mala returned to her studies, slightly distracted by the strangeness of Tabitha's behaviors.

When they finished studying, they packed up their stuff and left the library, headed in opposite directions.

On a whim of curiosity, Mala spun around to look at Tabitha. She began following her from a distance, doing her best to keep clusters of students between them, just in case Tabitha turned around. It was late and the longer they walked, the fewer students there were.

They were approaching a large decorative cement construct around a fountain. Mala glanced at their surroundings and noticed a boy sitting cross legged on one of the stone benches. His hair was white, and his elbows rested on his knees as he stared at the ground.

Tabitha seemed to be walking in his direction. Mala slowed down, not wanting to give herself away, when the boy looked up and locked eyes with her. She stopped immediately, looking behind her then at the boy again. He was still staring straight into her eyes. She could not make out the details of his eyes, but there was something vaguely familiar about him. It was like something from a forgotten dream. Mala sensed that she had been caught and placed one foot behind her, ball of the foot on the ground, heel in the air, ready to turn and walk away.

Tabitha was almost to him, but he was still staring at Mala. He smiled at Mala, winked, and then he was standing in front of Tabitha and looking down at her.

Mala blinked. She had not seen him stand up. It was

as if he just went from sitting on the bench to standing a couple steps away instantly. There had been no intermediate movements. But that was impossible. Her mind was deeply disturbed by the incongruity of what she had just seen.

In her confusion, her focus shifted inwardly, and by the time she thought to look, Tabitha and the stranger had disappeared.

She walked around the fountain but did not see where they had gone. Walking home, she pondered what she had seen and who the stranger might be. Tabitha never mentioned a boyfriend, and for the brief moments she had observed them before becoming distracted, there had been no signs of romantic interest.

And what had she seen, anyway? She must have had an exceptionally long blink or something wherein he stood and took two steps toward Tabitha. Mala shook her head. She had never had such a time distorting blink before, but it was the only thing that made any sense.

*   *   *

Mala woke up one morning to her roommates talking excitedly.

"What is it?" she asked.

"Our first task has arrived," replied Marisol.

Mala got up and walked over to read the message.

Their first mission was to meet in the upper room of the tower on the north side of the oldest building on campus. They had one week to visit the room and retrieve the target.

"I didn't know there was even a room up there," said Mala.

"I think I saw a door in that area on one of the upper floors, but it's always closed," commented Marisol.

"We can figure out a way to get in there together," suggested Tabitha excitedly.

"I'm not sure if that fits with the society's rules," said Marisol hesitantly.

"Well, that woman didn't say we couldn't work together," Tabitha pointed out. "And we only got one message for the three of us."

"True. I guess I'm just overthinking it, expecting there to be a catch, a trick, or something," Marisol replied.

Mala looked at the card and glanced at her roommates. If she did it alone, it would be more impressive, but teamwork gave a greater chance of success. It would also help her to keep an eye on Tabitha, who she still did not quite trust. There was just something off about her. Maybe it was her silent and mysterious entrance to their room or her nonchalant attitude about mysterious messages from a secret society that made her seem odd. Or it could even be the strange events during and after their time in the library. She was not sure.

"I agree. Let's work on this together," she said.

That night they sat around in a study area in the building, pretending to study, until everyone else had left. When the room was empty and the sun had set, they looked at each other and nodded. Without words, they packed up their stuff and headed to the highest floor. Mala could feel her pulse, hoping they would not get caught. Once there, they calmly walked down the hall as if they had a purpose. When they reached the door that Marisol had referenced, it was locked. Mala's fear of being caught surged now that they were trapped in the open right next to their destination. Unlike Marisol, she could not afford to be kicked out of the university if they were caught and accused of something.

"Do you know how to pick a lock?" Marisol

whispered.

"No," replied Mala. "Do you?" She turned to Tabitha.

"Of course," she said with a smile and slipped between them. A few seconds later, Tabitha opened the door and stepped inside, holding it for the others.

Tabitha closed it quietly behind them, and the three roommates walked up the spiraling stairs, passing a couple of wooden doors on their way to the top room.

The final door was locked. Tabitha picked the lock, and they walked in.

The room was large and empty except for a small round table in the middle. Mala was somewhat disappointed. All that adrenaline for nothing.

They walked over to the table. Arrayed on the top were several necklaces. On each of the necklaces was a round, somewhat oval-shaped object. It was colored with shades of brown and grey with thin traces of iridescent cracks in the surface color. There was a sign on the table next to the pendants.

"Each person is to take one pendant, no more, no less. You must keep it on you at all times for the remainder of the assessments. Do not reveal its existence to anyone not affiliated with the organization," read Marisol out loud.

Tabitha picked one up and examined it. A smile crept across her face.

"So, I guess they don't want us sabotaging each other if we can only take one," commented Mala.

"There's probably a tracking device in it so that they know where we are at all times," suggested Marisol.

"There are a lot of pendants here, so we must be the first to get here," Mala commented.

"Maybe they don't know which building is oldest.

They almost all have towers," suggested Tabitha.

"Maybe we don't all get our missions at the same time?" questioned Marisol.

"Who knows," muttered Mala.

Mala and Marisol each picked up their own pendant. As soon as Mala placed hers around her neck, she felt a buzz in her pocket. She checked her phone. Her account had received the next deposit. She looked up in time to see Marisol react to her own phone's silent notification. Mala glanced at Tabitha who looked at both of them and then reached for her phone. There was something about the timing of her reaction that made Mala suspect that Tabitha was checking her phone because the other two girls had just done so and not because she had felt it go off. This seemed crazy. Maybe her phone had a bad connection. Maybe it was on a truly silent setting and did not even vibrate. It would not make sense for her to not care about the payouts for completing the missions. It definitely would not make sense for her to be faking getting the deposits altogether... unless she was a spy of some sort. An agent of the Bezimeni Society? A random student trying to sneak in? Mala shook her head internally. She was being paranoid.

"So, I guess that's it for the first mission," said Marisol, somewhat disappointed.

"It seems anti-climactic," noted Mala. "If they wanted to test us, I would have expected this to be more difficult."

"Maybe Bezimeni is much gentler than it seems, and these tests are just fun little activities," suggested Tabitha with a hopeful smile.

"Or maybe they'll get harder and more serious as they progress," said Marisol, glancing down.

Mala looked at her. Marisol was the least excited

about the opportunities afforded by Bezimeni out of the three of them. At times, she almost seemed hesitant about participating. So far, aside from the semi-creepy account stalking, there had not been anything seriously dangerous or questionable about it.

The three roommates quietly crept back down the spiral stairs to the main part of the building. Before they left the room, Tabitha made sure to relock the door from the inside before shutting it behind her. When they reached the bottom door, they peaked out carefully first. No one was around, so they slipped out as Tabitha locked and shut it quickly, and they walked away.

*   *   *

A couple weeks passed before they received their next mission. The three of them looked at a series of numbers.

"What is it?" asked Tabitha.

"GPS coordinates," answered Marisol.

She pulled out her phone and typed in the numbers.

"It's somewhere to the west of campus."

"Isn't that side mostly forested?" asked Mala.

"Yes," said Tabitha.

"This time we only have five days," commented Marisol.

The girls met up after classes that day and headed into the woods. When they reached the coordinates, they found themselves on an old, abandoned train track. The tracks disappeared into the woods in one direction and extended out over a valley in the other. The bridge ended about a third of the way out, long since broken beyond use. The base of the bridge was visible through the trees from where they stood.

"So, what are we supposed to do here?" asked Mala, looking around.

"At least it's a nice view," commented Tabitha looking at the trees around them.

Marisol looked around. There was nothing on the ground. There were no buildings nearby. She checked her phone. She had not received a deposit. Whatever they were meant to do was here but not obvious. Her eyes began scanning the ground again, looking for clues. She looked at the overgrown tracks, tracing them out to the steel and cement supports, and from there to the broken bridge. Marisol looked again at the cement.

She walked over to the edge and looked down. There was a cement support or retaining wall under the base of the bridge. About fifteen feet below them was a ledge. There was a noticeable edge to the cement wall, indicating an impression, cubby hole, or hallway under the bridge.

"Hey, look at this. I think we need to go under the bridge," she called back to her roommates.

The others joined her and looked over the edge.

"How do we get down there?" asked Mala.

Marisol looked around. The ground was steep on either side of the bridge base, but not so much that it looked unclimbable.

"I guess we climb," Marisol said.

Tabitha was the first to start climbing. The others soon followed. They climbed one at a time on all fours, keeping their torsos tight to the ground as they cautiously lowered a foot, tested the ground, shifted their weight down, and repeated. When they came within line of the ledge, they worked their way horizontally until they reached it. Marisol breathed a sigh of relief when she was able to stand on it.

They walked to the center of the ledge, keeping their hands on the cement wall. The ledge felt safer than the grassy slope, but it was still only about six feet wide, and the drop below was completely vertical.

In the center of the base there was a tunnel. They raised their phone flashlights to illuminate it. The tunnel was only about ten yards deep before it ended at a large metal door.

They stopped and Tabitha picked the lock. On the other side of the door, the tunnel soon led to a set of stairs. Descending the stairs and winding their way down, they saw another passage ahead. Inside, paths branched to either direction, but the trio continued straight, hoping to stay in line with the tracks above. Tabitha stopped when they came to a door in the wall to their left.

"I think we should roughly be about where we were standing up above, on the tracks," she said.

Tabitha picked the lock, and they walked in. As soon as they stepped into the room, Marisol felt her phone vibrate. She did not bother to check. She knew they were there.

The room before them looked like an old lab of some sort. There were sinks on the far side, random beakers, cabinets, and a bookshelf off to the left. In the middle was a long table made of the same material that all lab workstations seemed to be made of at all schools. On the table sat a sign.

Marisol looked from the sign to the bookshelf.

"I guess we only have four more days to study whatever is in there," she said.

"This task's deadline matches the mission deadline. It's a good thing we came right away, or we would have less time to study those books, whatever they are," commented Mala.

Marisol walked over to the bookshelf. The three shelves at roughly chest-to-head height were filled with lab notebooks. They were obviously very old by the style and amount of dust and dirt built up on them.

"The deposit is about half what it was the last time," noted Mala walking up beside her, looking at her phone.

"Maybe we'll get the rest when we finish reading these books or when the time limit is up," suggested Marisol.

Marisol pulled down one of the books and opened it. She flipped through a few pages filled with handwritten notes, each labeled with a date, before she came across some diagrams. They were sketches of things that she had never seen before and looked like mythical creatures. She rolled her eyes.

"Are you serious? We're supposed to read someone's fantasy journal?" Mala questioned while looking up from another of the books.

"Oh, this is awesome," said Tabitha.

The others looked at her askance.

"The sign made a point of saying that we can't take the books out of the lab or take photos of them. There are probably more than a hundred books here. I'm not sure that I'll remember everything if I have to speed read through all of them."

"Maybe we can hand copy them," suggested Tabitha.

"Are you serious?" asked Mala in annoyance.

"Well, it's the only way we can guarantee that we'll retain the information once the time is up, and the sign didn't say we couldn't make hand copies," responded Tabitha.

"Hmm, well, there could be tracking devices in the books or surveillance equipment in the lab. At this point, I wouldn't be surprised if they had already hacked our phones," said Marisol.

"We're in school. If Bezimeni is asking us to study these books, then they will likely be testing us on their contents later," said Mala with determination.

"Ok, let's get started," said Marisol.

The girls each took a book and started copying it into their notebooks. After several hours, they could hear voices and footsteps.

The girls all gestured at each other and hid behind the table. A group of guys that Marisol remembered from the initial meeting walked through the door. Realizing that the voices had merely been other candidates and not the authorities coming to arrest them, Marisol stood up. Her sudden movement made the boys jump.

"I'm sorry. We didn't mean to scare you. We just weren't sure who was coming down the hall," said Marisol.

"No, it's ok, I get it. This is a weird place," said one of the boys.

The boys read the sign, then looked at the books.

"Are you kidding me?" one of them asked.

"Could be worse; at least this is interesting," said another.

The girls pulled their notebooks back out, and the boys looked at them.

"No photographs and we can't take them from the lab," said Mala.

The others nodded in understanding. Everyone gathered around the table and began working.

Over the next few days, more people showed up. Every time voices or footsteps approached, everyone would stop and stare at the doorway. Each time the door opened, they were relieved to see that it was just others whom they had seen that first night. Marisol noticed that there seemed to be fewer people now than at the first meeting. The reactions to the sign, the lab, and the books varied.

"What is this nonsense?"

"Ok, I'm out. This is getting way too creepy."

"I hope we don't die down here. What kind of crazy person writes this stuff and then leaves it in an underground room?"

"Is this some serial killer's lair?"

"Arg, I only have two days to read all this?"

The girls spent every afternoon and evening after classes in the underground room until they had finished reading and copying all the books. Every group or individual made their own copies or just tried reading or skimming the books on their own. No one wanted to be reliant on another group for access to a copy after the deadline.

The day after the deadline, they received the rest of the mission payment. Marisol and the others visited the bridge that same day, just to see what had happened. The initial doorway in the short tunnel under the bridge was covered over by a wall of fresh cement.

*   *   *

A couple days after the students' access had been blocked, something stirred within the tunnels. The figure walked to the room, pulled up a stool by the bookshelf, and began reading the notebooks. As his blue metallic eyes scanned the pages, he absent-mindedly stroked a large, ten-legged bug in his lap.

*   *   *

The next mission message arrived. Mala looked at

the card, somewhat perplexed, then handed it back to Marisol.

"What's a 'false water leaf'?"

Marisol looked at the card again; "I'm not sure."

Tabitha stood there, eyes darting about as if looking for an answer in her memory.

Her eyes opened wide; "Oh, I remember. It's one of those weird creatures in the books."

"What? We can't catch something that isn't real," objected Mala.

"Yeah, that makes no sense. There's no way that's what they want," said Marisol.

Tabitha rummaged through the notebooks until she found the one she wanted.

"Here, it says the false water leaf is a creature that lives mostly in overgrown ponds or on the edge of other bodies of water. It has an appendage that looks like a large leaf and will mostly eat insects and frogs that land on it."

The other girls looked over her shoulder. Mala looked at the diagram. It showed a leaf sitting on the surface of the water. Below the surface, the supposedly false stem connected to a large, bulbous mass covered in spines. Around the equator of the mass were a set of long, segmented limbs ending in sharp spikes that all pointed down.

Tabitha turned the page. It showed the leaf curling around the insect and the sharp limbs curled up over it. The next page showed the false leaf with the insect being pulled into the mass, while the limbs continued to curl in toward the center.

"Is the leaf thing actually its tongue?" asked Mala.

"That is disgusting," commented Marisol.

"That cannot be real," said Mala.

"Is this a trick? Are they setting us up to laugh at us for doing this?" asked Marisol.

"That woman didn't seem like the sort to pull a prank," noted Tabitha.

"But is she the sort to give you a ridiculous test to see how gullible you are," pondered Marisol.

"We only have three days this time," noted Mala more seriously.

"How would we even catch it?" asked Marisol.

"The book says that cinnamon has an intoxicating effect on it. Apparently, if you sprinkle cinnamon on the leaf, it will taste it and seek out more," said Tabitha.

"The tests so far have escalated in strangeness. The first was an open room in a dark, labyrinthine basement. The next was breaking into a locked tower. Then, after that, we had to climb down a cliff, break into a secret tunnel, and read weird books in a dingy old lab in the middle of nowhere. Maybe monster hunting is the next step," suggested Marisol.

Mala pondered this. Marisol was right. The missions had seemed to escalate, and they had been paid each time. The rewards were real, even if the tasks seemed strange. She did not want to lose out on the full scholarship. It would pay for everything, all the way to the end of med school, covering tuition and personal expenses. She had initially planned to take out student loans to pay for school and the lack of debt would make it easier for her after she finally graduated. While still in school, the scholarship would help her to not feel like an outsider amidst her peers, and she could use the money to help her father.

"Ok, let's try it," she said.

"Oh, we need to be careful not to touch it," said Tabitha, still reading through the notebook. "The spines are venomous."

"How do we catch it then?" asked Marisol.

"We can get one of those traps they make for catching pests alive. It's like a cage with a trap door," said Mala.

*   *   *

That evening, the three girls stood next to a pond on the south side of campus. The pond in front of them was overgrown with lily pads.

"Well, this looks like the sort of place where we might find it," said Mala.

They set up the trap a couple feet from the pond's edge and covered it with sticks and leaves.

Mala and Marisol hid behind a tree while Tabitha leaned out over the water and sprinkled cinnamon as best she could, making a trail into the trap. She ran back to join them.

They waited, watching as bits of cinnamon drifted in a fine cloud to settle on the nearest leaves. Several minutes went by, but nothing happened.

"Maybe it's not next to the edge," suggested Marisol.

"I wondered about that," said Mala.

She pulled a small battery powered fan out of her jacket pocket. She took the cinnamon container from Tabitha and carefully walked over to the edge of the pond. Mala turned on the fan, aimed it at the pond and began lightly sprinkling the cinnamon in front of it. The artificial breeze blew it out a few yards before it fell onto the leaves.

Mala watched and waited. Nothing happened.

"Here, let's try mixing it with something heavier that we can toss farther out," suggested Marisol.

She took the container and poured a bunch of cinnamon on the ground. Then she mixed it with the dirt and rubbed it in her hands until it became lots of tiny broken bits of cinnamon infused dirt. She walked over to the edge and flung the heavier powder and small clumps out over the pond. This time it made it even farther out.

They retreated and waited.

Mala was beginning to get worried. What if this was really a test of gullibility? Was she really about to lose her chance at the money? Fear began to creep into her mind.

"Look," whispered Tabitha, pointing.

They turned to see a leaf out in the pond begin to twitch.

"Quick, throw some more out there."

Marisol made another crumbled cinnamon dirt pile and flung it over the pond again. The leaf twitched more and began moving in their direction. She sprinkled more cinnamon out over the leaves by the edge, then added more to the trail into the trap.

The girls ran and hid when the leaf got within a yard of the edge. A moment later, it vanished.

Small spines on a bulbous mass broke the surface of the water.

"No way," breathed Mala.

The spine-covered mass continued moving forward until its sharp, pointed legs could be seen. When it completely left the water, they could see that the leaf-tongue was being dragged across the ground, moving side to side as it licked up the cinnamon.

Mala held her breath.

The creature walked into the trap, and the door snapped shut.

Immediately, the trap began to shake violently. The

girls stepped out from behind the tree. Marisol grabbed a long stick and knocked the leaves and sticks off the cage. The creature thrashed about, trying but failing to find a way out.

"Sooo, now what?" asked Mala.

"I haven't received a deposit notification," said Marisol.

"Do we take it home?" asked Tabitha eagerly.

"I guess…" said Mala.

The girls put on thick leather gloves.

"Mala, hold the backpack open," said Marisol as she carefully picked up the cage, keeping it away from her body.

The creature tried to move toward her, but its pointy legs just slipped between the wires. It pulled them back up toward its mass and waited. Mala held the backpack open as far from herself as possible. Marisol positioned the end of the trap and dropped it in. Mala carefully zipped the backpack shut. They waited to see what would happen.

The backpack shook and a sharp leg pierced the bag.

"Keep the straps adjusted all the way out and you can carry it while keeping it away from your hand," suggested Marisol.

"My arm's going to get tired holding it out from my body the whole time," said Mala.

"We can take turns," offered Tabitha.

The girls rotated carrying the backpack at arm's length from their body until they got back to the dorm. By then it was late enough that they did not have to deal with too many strange looks from other people. They set the backpack on the floor in the middle of the room and looked at it.

"Still no deposit," said Mala.

"Well, I guess we just wait til tomorrow and see if

anything else happens," suggested Marisol.

"I can't believe this thing is real," commented Mala. "For a minute there, when nothing happened, I thought we were going to lose for being too gullible, but here the thing is."

"It's fascinating," said Tabitha, squatting next to the bag and reaching out for it.

"Be careful," warned Marisol.

"I have the gloves on," Tabitha replied and opened the backpack.

She pulled the cage out and they watched the creature. It tried attacking the cage a couple more times, then just sat there like a lump. They set the cage on the unused desk in the corner and went to bed.

*　　*　　*

In the dark, a figure sat in a tree overlooking a pond. A group of two boys and two girls was on the far side. They each threw something out over a different section of the pond. A moment later, there was movement in multiple places. They threw more objects that exploded or fell apart over the leaf covered water. The points of movement began to converge on them.

They all walked away from the water, pouring something on the ground as they went. Bulbous objects on long sharp legs came out of the water. One of the boys went to grab one. As soon as he touched its body, he dropped it, clutched his hand, and began screaming in pain. The creature rushed forward and attacked him, stabbing with its long limbs. One of the girls ran to his side and tried shoving the creature away, but as soon as her hand touched its spine-covered body, she too collapsed in screaming agony. The creature began to attack her too.

The other boy grabbed a big stick and attacked the creature. The other girl watched him and got her own stick, then went for one of the creatures that was heading back toward the water. They each killed one of the creatures.

The two on the ground were silent and twitching less, but not responding to anything that was said. The two who remained standing looked from their companions to the dead creatures. Impaling the creatures on the sticks, they picked them up and walked away.

The figure in the tree vanished.

He immediately reappeared on the other side of the pond, looking down on the prone boy and girl. He crouched over them and examined them. Their faces were twisted in agony, and their bodies seemed to be shuddering as all their muscles tensed at once.

"Fascinating. I really want to see what happens next, but I'm not supposed to let you die," he muttered.

He reached into a pocket and pulled out a jar of liquid.

"I'm guessing your friends either didn't get to the part with the antidote or they just don't care about you."

One at a time, he grabbed their heads and poured some of the liquid into their mouths. Within a few seconds, their muscles started to relax. A few minutes after that, they were both sitting up and looking at him.

He made eye contact with each of them and put his finger to his lips and shook his head. "I was never here," he whispered with a smile and then vanished.

*   *   *

The next morning, Mala got up and checked on the

361

creature. It was limp and lifeless. Marisol and Tabitha joined her to look at it.

"Why did it die?" asked Marisol.

"I don't remember anything about it needing to stay wet," said Tabitha somewhat sadly.

"My account received a deposit," said Mala.

"Was its death all that was needed?" pondered Marisol.

"The message didn't say to kill it, just capture it," replied Tabitha.

*   *   *

A couple weeks later, Marisol found herself staring at a new mission card.

"They want us to kill what now?" asked Mala.

"It says a lunar corpse leech," said Marisol.

"What is that?" asked Mala.

"Well, the notebook says that it is a sort of parasite that feeds off of decaying tissue. It animates a corpse while consuming it, using that corpse to kill other creatures that it can then inhabit," said Tabitha, looking through a notebook. "They have been known to take down large bears and moose. It can use the sense organs of the host corpse until they are consumed. Then, it uses hairs all over its body to sense sound and chemicals in the air. It basically hunts by sound and scent once the host's flesh is too deteriorated and all that remains useful is the skeleton."

"What about the lunar part?" asked Marisol.

"Apparently, moonlight makes it stronger," answered Tabitha.

"How does that even work?" asked Mala.

"No idea. The book doesn't say," replied Tabitha,

flipping back and forth through the pages.

"The card says we have until tomorrow to kill it, so we need to figure out how to find it," said Mala, walking over to Tabitha.

"Apparently, the full moon is when it's strongest."

"That's tonight. I guess they want to maximize the challenge," said Mala.

Marisol paused. The missions kept escalating. None had truly required sacrifice or the sort of cold-hearted decisions her father seemed to prefer. This new mission was to hunt a predator that was far stronger than any of them. It was possible that this mission would require them to choose between saving each other's lives or completing the mission.

She turned to her roommates; "Maybe we should quit."

"What?" said Mala.

"Look, this isn't some little plant monster. It's a predator capable of taking down a bear or a moose. That's way stronger than we can handle. This could easily get us killed. I don't know that the money is worth it," argued Marisol.

"That's easy for you to say; your family already has plenty," snapped Mala.

Marisol was taken aback. She cursed herself for not realizing that this was how Mala would see things. She had seen Mala's father and the clues that she was not as wealthy as a lot of the students here.

"That's not what this is about. If I don't make it into this organization, my father won't let me come home, and I'm fine with that. He was in Bezimeni, and he doesn't care about people, which leads me to believe that they don't really care if we die on these missions," revealed Marisol.

Mala looked at her, some of the anger draining from

her face.

"This scholarship will change my life and that of my father. I'm going to risk it," she said defiantly.

Marisol sighed, "Fine. I'll come along too; you'll have a better chance at survival."

They turned to Tabitha.

"Oh, I don't care about the money or the danger. My father always told me that we eat the monsters," she replied with a smile.

Marisol raised an eyebrow at the odd response.

*   *   *

The three girls hid in the forest, watching the pile of bloody meat they had bought at the butcher's shop on the way there. Marisol hit play on her phone again, and the recording of a wounded animal rang out in the cold night air.

Several minutes later, something moved silently into view. The moonlight illuminated a rotting deer corpse. Most of the flesh was gone, and what remained was held together by sickly white tendrils that seemed to animate the skeleton. Tiny hairs along the tendrils twitched. Marisol played the sound again, and the hairs closest to her twitched the most. The creature moved toward the bait.

As the creature stepped next to the raw meat, a metal trap clamped over its leg. The girls rushed out. They sprayed the creature with gasoline from water guns, then Marisol lit a flare and threw it at the creature.

Instantly it went up in flames. It thrashed about but made no cries. The sickly white tendrils burned fast, changing the flames and smoke to weird shades of green and causing the fumes that hit their nostrils to become putrid.

Marisol turned away, gagging. It was the most

disgusting smell she had ever encountered.

Finally, the creature stopped moving. The stench faded with the parasite's mass.

"I got the deposit," said Mala.

Marisol nodded. They stood there for a moment, covering their mouths and noses with their pulled-up shirts, and watched the corpse burn.

*   *   *

A figure stood in the shadows beneath the trees, watching a group of three boys stumble around in the moonlit forest. They reached a small outcropping. Two of them pushed the third over the edge. The other boy hit the rocks and screamed. He cried up for help, begging his friends to rescue him.

Several minutes later, a creature that seemed to formed from the remains of a decaying boar moved silently into the moonlight and approached the injured boy. The two on top of the ridge pulled out bottles with rags in them. They lit the rags and threw them at the creature.

The boys missed. The creature turned in their direction, avoiding the flaming liquid, some of which had splashed on the injured boy. He desperately tried to beat out the flames while the others rummaged through their bags. They were not fast enough. The creature knocked the first one to the ground and bit into his thigh.

The last boy pulled out another bottle with a rag and lit it. He took a few steps back and raised his arm.

The figure in the shadows vanished. He reappeared behind the boy and grabbed his wrist.

The boy looked at the stranger, who shook his head and took the boy's bottle. In shock, the boy stared as the stranger held his free hand out toward the creature and it rose into the air. Tendrils that had begun to dig into the other boy's wounded leg were torn free, and he screamed in pain.

The stranger sighed; "I really want to see what happens when you switch hosts, but I know I'm not supposed to let you eat people."

The stranger sighed again and dropped his empty hand as he threw the bottle at the creature; it shattered, pouring burning liquid all over the writhing mass. Before it fell, he reached out again, halting its downward movement. The stranger watched in fascination as the flames and smoke changed color. When the thrashing stopped and the flames died, he lowered his hand and the corpse plummeted to the ground.

Their phones buzzed and they checked them.

"I suggest you use those to get help for your friend down there so that I don't have to come back here," said the stranger before he vanished.

*   *   *

Mala and Marisol were walking home from class.

"It's been about a month since the last mission. Was that it? I haven't seen any larger deposits. Did we not pass?" asked Mala.

Marisol looked at the ground. She hoped it was over. She hoped that the parasite monster was the mission that should have required sacrifice. She hoped that they had beaten Bezimeni.

But she did not believe it was true.

"I don't know. My father never said. I hope this is the last of it and there's just a delay before we know if we've been accepted or not. I don't look forward to a further

366

escalation in the missions," replied Marisol.

She glanced at Mala. She was not sure that her friend felt the same way.

"I just feel like we missed something. We're so close. We can't lose now," Mala said, looking at Marisol.

*   *   *

Marisol woke up to the sound of someone moving quickly around the room. She opened her eyes and saw Mala fully dressed, rummaging through things, and making a pile on her bed.

"Good morning. The next mission has arrived," said Tabitha pleasantly from her bunk, her legs swinging back and forth playfully.

Marisol got out of bed and read it.

"We have to break into the maintenance tunnels," she said blandly.

"We have to be at the target by midnight. I don't know how long it'll take to get through the tunnels. I'm making sure I have everything with me just in case," said Mala. "The semester is almost over, and we're so close to beating the assessment and making it in."

"The last mission was to kill a predatory monster. What are we going to find down there that's worse than that?" questioned Marisol.

"The time window for each mission has gotten narrower. This one is for tonight. This has to be the last one. Maybe it's just an initiation. I mean, what else is left after killing a monster?" said Mala with a hopeful smile.

Mala seemed very eager and motivated, but Marisol had her doubts. There had been no great sacrifice yet. Somehow, she feared there was still something worse to

367

come.

*   *   *

That night, the three roommates entered the maintenance tunnels under the campus. They found the entrance after sneaking into the basement and searching the maintenance rooms. Mala was eager to finish the assessment.

Pipes ran along the walls of the tunnel, and they followed them until they reached an intersection. As they walked down the tunnel, she felt a vibration in her chest. She knew she was excited, but the sensation seemed kind of odd.

"Which way?" asked Marisol.

Mala looked around. There were no markings on the walls, ceiling, or floor. The final mission message had not specified where they were to go once they got into the tunnels. She took a step down the forward path and looked around, then she checked to the right. Finally, she turned to check the left-side path.

As soon as she stepped into the tunnel, she felt the vibration in her chest grow. She looked down and pulled out the pendant.

"It's vibrating. The sensation is stronger down this tunnel," she said.

The others joined her and confirmed that they felt the same.

They followed the hints of the vibrating pendants, weaving through the maze of tunnels to the point where Mala had no idea where they were in relation to the world above.

They came to a tunnel with pipes on only one side. As they walked down it, they came across a hole in the wall.

As soon as they walked past, the vibration decreased.

"I guess we go through the hole in the wall," Marisol said unenthusiastically.

Mala knew her friend was concerned that something horrible would happen, but she was not about to give up now. Soon her life would change forever. She would have what she needed to accomplish her goals.

The hole in the wall opened into a new tunnel. This was not a regular, rectangular cement tunnel like they had been walking through. This one was rough and irregular. They followed it cautiously, using their phones' flashlights to light the way. The tunnel sloped downward and wound back and forth even more than the path they had already taken. At the end was a chamber.

They walked out onto a platform of stone and looked around. The room had ten other entrances; at each lay a stone platform, which led to its own narrow walkway. All the walkways converged on a central platform on which a large, low, ten-sided stone slab had been placed. On either side of where the platform they were standing on met the walkway, a short pillar stood roughly at waist height. Below and between the platforms and walkways, a dark pit sank deep into an abyss.

Mala walked over to the pillars. On one was a sign that said to wait.

Mala paced nervously while they waited. She was so close to the end. Soon it would all be hers.

Other potential members began arriving shortly after they did. Mala looked around and observed them.

A boy and a girl stood together, their faces hard and uncaring.

A group of three boys stood at another entrance, one was obviously recovering from a broken leg. Another seemed to favor one leg. The third kept his eyes down, almost as if he was ashamed of something.

Another boy and girl arrived. Their faces seemed lined with anger, especially when they looked at the couple a few steps ahead of them.

Another group, whom she recognized as the first group of boys to find the lab, arrived in good spirits.

Two more girls entered together. They seemed excited.

After a while, no one else came. A strange noise caught Mala's attention, and she turned to see the entrance they had just come from being overrun by large, strange bugs. Their grey and brown bodies had four segments, ten legs, and iridescent lines across them. They quickly began weaving some kind of cocoon across the entrance. Mala took a step forward and the vibration at her chest diminished. She stepped back and it recovered.

When the walls were sealed, the pendant began to shake. Mala looked down in time to see it crack open. A smaller version of the bugs she had just seen crawled out. It went up her chest, over her shoulder, and settled in at the base of her skull. The sensation made her cringe, but it did not hurt, so she did not attack the creature. Part of her mind screamed to knock it away or kill it, while other parts cautioned that sudden movements may have painful consequences or that it might somehow be part of the final mission.

*   *   *

Marisol felt the pendant break as soon as the passage was sealed. She watched the bug emerge and closed her eyes. She did not know what would happen, but she resigned herself to whatever unpleasantness was about to occur.

She was somewhat surprised when it turned out to just be a sort of tickle as it settled in at the base of her skull.

A moment later she heard a voice, but not with her ears. The voice was speaking directly into her mind. It felt female and inhuman. Marisol looked around and saw surprised reactions on the faces of everyone in the chamber.

Welcome. You have reached the final test. My children serve the Bezimeni Society, and the Bezimeni Society serves me. My children have attached themselves to you. They are the true gift I offer, granting improved abilities that will allow you to live longer, better lives than your lessers.

There was a strange sensation on Marisol's neck, and a warmth flowed from the base of her skull over her whole body. As it passed, she became more aware of her surroundings. Her five senses were sharpening, revealing more details than she had previously been aware of. She could even sense feelings around her.

Marisol paused and looked around. It was not a sensation that she could describe. Somehow, she knew that what she was feeling was the emotions of the other people in the chamber.

She sensed fear and excitement from Mala. Oddly, Tabitha was suddenly very stoic. This was not like her. She was almost always happy.

Marisol scanned the room. She could feel the cold determination between the harsh-looking couple. There was anger and love radiating from the other couple. The three boys were awash with the pain and shame of betrayal. Excitement and fear were common in the room.

But there was something else. She could feel it. It was stronger than the rest, stronger than the... humans. This thing was better than her, and it knew it. It was something she should defer to. Whatever it wanted, she should grant it. To do otherwise was foolish futility.

Marisol shook her head, wondering if the bug was affecting her own sentiments or projecting its opinion of her plight or place in the world.

The gift of my children is indeed grand, but it must be earned. There is one final test. I give you the keys to the world, and in exchange you must give me your absolute loyalty. No other can come between us; not friends, not even lovers. No other can be considered higher than myself. If you refuse or you fail, you will not leave this room alive. You must kill one person from your platform and bring their corpse to my altar. Prove that you are my children; devoted, obedient, and unstoppable.

Horrible realization came to Marisol. This was what her father had alluded to.

The chamber erupted in fear, regret, confusion, and a determination to kill.

Marisol looked at her roommates. She could feel the conflict within Mala, but she could feel nothing from Tabitha, who seemed distracted by the darkness above.

"We don't have to do this. We can't murder each other. We're friends," said Marisol.

She felt both Mala's desire to win and her affection for her friends.

Marisol did not care about the prize. She had resented her father her whole life for how callous and heartless he was. She loathed the idea of stooping to his level just to achieve wealth and power. Betraying close friends for personal gain was abhorrent to her.

However, she knew she was not yet willing to die but she was not sure how far she could go to protect herself. Her survival instinct warred with her devotion to her friends. The animalistic instinct whispered that she might not want to kill, but it also would not allow her to die. Shame and guilt swiftly spread from that thought, but her hand slipped into her pocket and gripped a pen, point down, thumb over the blunt end, just in case.

*   *   *

At first Mala was shocked by the new sensations, then she was horrified by what the creature had said. Now she was conflicted.

Tabitha and Marisol were her friends. She could not kill them. But she was so close to victory. If she passed this final test, she would have the money, the connections, and these newfound abilities. Her father would never have to work again. She would never have to live without. In her future, she saw herself mastering medicine in a way that few could imagine. So many patients would be saved by her powers. Was the summation of countless lives saved greater than a single life taken? She could even sense the unwillingness to die within Marisol. How long would it take for that impulse to drive her to attack? If Mala attacked first, then she would be the victor, but if she waited for Marisol's attack and survived, then she would be justified. Mala turned her head slightly, just enough for her eyes to look back and see the pen held in Marisol's tightly clenched fist. Perhaps the decision had been made for her.

Anger and fear erupted from above and all around the chamber. Mala was stunned by its strength and suddenness. She looked up and saw the same stunned confusion on everyone else. Something moved at the corner of her eye.

A living shadow stood on the platform next to her.

373

Mala realized that Marisol still stood to her right but Tabitha was gone.

Black tendrils began to radiate from the Tabitha-shaped shadow. They reached up into the darkness above and an audible, inhuman scream erupted in the cavern. Mala had to cover her ears as she looked for its source.

A massive creature was pulled into view. Its body had at least eight segments and twenty legs. Its head was some twisted hybrid of human and insect.

Stop the shadow creature! Kill it! If I die, my children die! You shall all remain as nothing in this world!

Mala looked around. Confusion and fear radiated from most of the other students. The living shadow and the massive creature that it seemed perfectly capable of overpowering had shocked everyone.

The creature was finally torn free of the unseen ceiling and crashed onto the stone altar. The black tendrils began to pull it inexorably inward. The creature clawed and scrambled but was unable to stop the shadow.

Some of the small bugs rushed out of the darkness, past Mala's feet and attempted to attack the Tabitha-shaped shadow, but it merely swallowed them into its void.

*   *   *

Marisol was terrified at first by the sudden transformation of her friend into living darkness. But when she realized that this new monster might be able to destroy the bug queen, she was elated. This was the solution she had not anticipated. Everyone could live, and her father's power would be broken. The Bezimeni Society would no longer be able to prey upon anyone. And she would not have to kill or be killed.

The pleadings of the queen only made Marisol feel better. It was a sign that this might actually work.

She felt the intent to kill rise in several places around the room. Panic filled her at the thought that they might actually interfere. The wave of emotion blinded her momentarily to the idea that if the bug queen could be killed by this Tabitha-shaped shadow that had easily swallowed the other bugs, then the students would also be unable to stop it.

The queen was now about halfway down the walkway, being pulled by the black tendrils into the void.

"Stop!"

Marisol looked at the center of the chamber. A boy stood next to the altar. He had white hair and blue metallic eyes. She could sense recognition from a few people in the chamber. The shadows stopped moving. Fear erupted inside her again.

"No, don't stop. Keeping pulling her in," Marisol shouted at the Tabitha-shadow.

The boy walked up to the creature.

Yes! Kill the shadow! Save me and you shall have whatever you desire!

The boy reached out a hand and his fingertips touched the creature's head. The queen's eyes rolled back and then went blank. Her body slumped to the floor. For one brief instant, the boy was gone, replaced by a copy of the queen before returning to a more human form. The boy's head fell back and there was a look of pure joy on his face. He sighed and looked at the darkness.

"Thank you. You can take her now," he said.

The shadowy tendrils continued moving again. The limp, though not lifeless queen was pulled into the void and vanished. A moment later, the shadows reverted back to Tabitha.

There was an unpleasant quiver at the back of her neck and the bug fell off. Several more fell lifeless from the walls and ceiling where they had been hiding in the darkness.

"The bugs are dead, so the queen must be dead," said Marisol in relief.

"I was so close," muttered Mala, frustration and disappointment evident in her voice.

"Wait, what will happen to my family's wealth?" shouted one of the students.

Marisol could hear sobs as the previously angry couple embraced. They appeared relieved that they did not have to kill each other.

The harsh couple was now glaring at each other. They must have both been willing to kill, Marisol reasoned.

"Well, at least you're all alive and you won't be murderers," said Tabitha with a smile.

"You've destroyed my family."

"You killed my dreams."

The boy yawned; "I need to go digest these memories."

He held out his hand and the seal across the entranceway exploded out into the tunnel.

"Thank you," Tabitha said pleasantly.

Tabitha and the boy walked out of the chamber, ignoring the shouts and accusations from around the room. Marisol noticed that despite their anger, no one seemed willing to approach the two.

Marisol turned to see Mala glaring at Tabitha.

"She's right, you know. At least we're alive, and none of us are murders," she said to Mala.

Mala glared at her for a moment, then her expression softened slightly but not completely.

Appendix I

The Sphinx Gate

The sphinx gates are a series of portals that can be used to travel between the different realms of Niwltir. Each gate is composed of a raised dais with four gryphons and three sphinxes. While the exact nature of the internal algorithms used by the sphinxes and gryphons remains unknown, it has been determined that they are intended to act as guardians of these portals, preventing war from easily being waged between realms.

The gryphons, when activated, will open their eyes, and first threaten, then attack. Their aggression appears to be an anti-invasion mechanism. They respond aggressively to large, armed forces and groups that are attacking or pursuing others. The gryphons do not act aggressively toward the defending party or individuals. They do not seem to respond to armed individuals or similarly equipped small groups not engaged in military endeavors. This suggests that the gryphons, to some extent, may be able to sense or assess intent. However, unarmed individuals and small groups with malicious intent seem to be able to pass by the gryphons without incident. This can result in spies, saboteurs, and unarmed soldiers passing through the portal.

The sphinxes appear to operate on a similar algorithm as the gryphons, though it is reserved for those who have somehow made it past the gryphons and through the gate. When an intruder is detected, they will open their eyes. This is the only movement they make. Those unlucky enough to have made it this far are usually seen to stop dead in their tracks and collapse on the ground. They never recover, as their minds no longer function properly.

Appendix II

The Life Forms of Castor

In their initial excursion into the Castor galaxy, the humans discovered several new life forms.

The first creature they encountered was a world eater hatchling that was later labeled CL001. The main body is amorphous with thousands of relatively thin tendrils reaching out in all directions. These tendrils seem to act as sense organs. A ring of twenty tentacles roughly surrounds a central mouth. They move about by forming a green plasma around themselves, which shifts in intensity based on which direction they intend to move. Their eggs resemble small planets or moons depending on where they are located. The cuexaneh mostly focused on killing the live ones and marking the dormant ones so that they would not be awakened accidentally. As a result, the exact nature of their reproduction, internal biology, and general life cycle is not fully understood. The cuexaneh were able to determine that EMP's could disrupt the creatures' ability to function. Even small devices can have a localized effect, which can be useful in extreme emergencies.

On the planet where the artifact was found, the humans discovered four more life forms. The first two appear to be something akin to moving plants.

CL002 lives in relatively deep water and consists of a bulbous body supported by six long legs ending in wide, flat feet. The main body mass and upper sections of the limbs are covered in shaggy, flat, dark-green strips. After closer examination, these were determined to be similar to very flexible leaves and were used by CL002 to absorb solar radiation. Under the main body, four long appendages hang down that are open on the end and suck up the loose soil and water at the bottom of the ponds and lakes that they inhabit. CL002 has not been observed living in moving water, and it is hypothesized that this is because their long, slender limbs are not strong enough to sufficiently resist strong currents.

CL003 consists of a shallow, gradually sloping brownish-purple dome on eight thick legs. The dome has several ridges fanning out from a central point at either end and running to the corresponding point on the other end. The thicker central ridge acts as a hinge point, allowing the two halves to open and reveal thin, dark-green membranes that feather out and extend beyond the bounds of the shell. Closer analysis and observation revealed that these membranes were used to absorb solar radiation, while the mouth consumed soil and water for nutrients. When attacked, the outer shell closes and CL003 then begins to shift back and forth in order to burrow into the mud.

The artifact planet also contained two animal life forms whose general body structure was similar to the sentient avian creatures that the initial expedition later encountered: one pair of wings, three pairs of limbs, and a tail.

CL004 is an approximately two-meter-long flying mammalian creature that lives and hunts in large swarms. Their bodies consist of two wings and three sets of legs. There is not a distinct difference in the strength or dexterity of each set of limbs. They mostly feed on CL002 and CL003. They eat the leaf-like strips on CL002 and the thin, feathery inner membranes of CL003. After some time, it was determined that they sleep in caves with small openings, most likely to avoid being eaten by CL005.

CL005 follows a similar basic structural pattern to that of CL004, but it is much bigger and more reptilian. The central set of limbs are noticeably weaker and smaller than the front and rear sets, yet still very strong. They use their front claws to attack prey or clutch whatever they are perched on while using their central limbs to feed themselves. They have long necks and tails. Scales cover their entire bodies, including their wings. They have been known to hunt from the air and below the water's surface. They use the bodies of CL002 to make nests in which they lay their eggs. While the first expedition encountered these creatures near the storm ring surrounding the artifact, they have been seen living in high, rocky peaks and cliffs where the more plant-like life forms do not feed.

The final lifeform discovered by the first human expedition into the Castor galaxy was a sentient, alien species, CL006. They refer to themselves as the cuexaneh. The species is bipedal, with the now familiar two wings and six limbs. The two central limbs are significantly smaller than the other two, much more so than on CL004 and CL005. Their bodies are covered in a layer of fine feathers. They have long snouts and many sharp teeth. The end of their tails has a set of feathers that can fan out when they are in flight.

The technology of CL006 was far more advanced than that of the humans at their first encounter. The cuexaneh are the ones who built the warning satellite orbiting above the world eater hatchling. They also set up the ring of devices to keep the storms away from the artifact and alert them to any intruders. In order to decrease their chances of extinction from world eater attacks, CL006 quickly spread throughout their galaxy.

Since the cuexaneh explored a great number of planets, and given the ease with which microorganisms can evolve, they were forced to devise a method of quickly analyzing and protecting against potential pathogens not yet identified or studied. The culmination of this research was a method for improving the strength and adaptability of a subject's immune system. The exact nature of this solution is a closely guarded secret, but it was used on the first humans they encountered in order to protect them from accidental contamination.

Did you like the book?
Recommend it to a friend.
Did you hate the book?
Recommend it to an enemy.
Best of all, don't tell them how you felt about it first.

www.undyingcuriosity.com

Thoughts, comments, theories, or questions?
emrys@thewanderersnotebook.com